# RETURN TO HOMECOMING RANCH

# ALSO BY JULIA LONDON

## HISTORICALS

*The Devil's Love*

*Wicked Angel*

### The Rogues of Regent Street

*The Dangerous Gentleman*

*The Ruthless Charmer*

*The Beautiful Stranger*

*The Secret Lover*

### Highland Lockhart Family

*Highlander Unbound*

*Highlander in Disguise*

*Highlander in Love*

### The Desperate Debutantes

*The Hazards of Hunting a Duke*

*The Perils of Pursuing a Prince*

*The Dangers of Deceiving a Viscount*

*The School for Heiresses* (Anthology): "The Merchant's Gift"

### The Scandalous Series

*The Book of Scandal*

*Highland Scandal*

*A Courtesan's Scandal*

*Snowy Night with a Stranger* (Anthology): "Snowy Night with a Highlander"

**The Secrets of Hadley Green**

*The Year of Living Scandalously*

*The Christmas Secret* (novella)

*The Revenge of Lord Eberlin*

*The Seduction of Lady X*

*The Last Debutante*

## CONTEMPORARY ROMANCE AND WOMEN'S FICTION

**Pine River**

*Homecoming Ranch*

**The Fancy Lives of the Lear Sisters**

*Material Girl*

*Beauty Queen*

*Miss Fortune*

**Over the Edge (previously available as Thrillseekers Anonymous series)**

*All I Need Is You* (previously available as *Wedding Survivor*)

*One More Night* (previously available as *Extreme Bachelor*)

*Fall Into Me* (previously available as *American Diva*)

**Cedar Springs**

*Summer of Two Wishes*

*One Season of Sunshine*

*A Light at Winter's End*

## SPECIAL PROJECTS

*Guiding Light: Jonathan's Story*, tie-in to *The Guiding Light*

## ANTHOLOGIES

*Talk of the Ton* (Anthology): "The Vicar's Widow"
*Hot Ticket* (Anthology): "Lucky Charm"

# RETURN TO HOMECOMING RANCH

JULIA LONDON

This is a work of fiction. Names, characters, organizations, places, events, and incidents are either products of the author's imagination or are used fictitiously.



Published by Montlake Romance, Seattle

www.apub.com



ISBN-13: 9781477823057
ISBN-10: 1477823050

Cover design by Laura Klynstra

Library of Congress Control Number: 2014900812

Printed in the United States of America

*Dedicated to anyone who has ever felt the urge to take a baseball bat to a car window.*

# ONE

When something goes down in Pine River, I know about it, because I have one of those faces that makes people want to tell me their life stories. You know, super handsome with movie star eyes. Plus, I'm in a chair, which makes people think I'm trustworthy. I'm not *that* trustworthy, because if I hear something good, I'm *definitely* going to pass it on. Anyway, I've heard a lot of amazing stuff about people in Pine River. Not amazing like *wow, amazing!* But more like, *who-does-that?* amazing.

You're probably wondering where I get my news, seeing as how I'm not exactly mobile. Here's the God's honest truth: I get a lot of my best information from the Methodists.

I know, *right?*

I know what you're thinking: Leo Kendrick, that's not nice. But, see, the Methodist's Women's Group get together to do good Christian works, like make quilts and give them to really old people. There are about fifteen church ladies in that group and they are *awesome.* Not only will they tell me things, but they take me out for walks and they bring stuff like the socks they knit and homemade apple pies. And now, they're batting around ideas for getting me a new van. I sort of planted the idea with them because I've got a date with the Denver Broncos and I need *wheels,* man. Besides, that's what I do, I think up genius ideas. Ask anyone.

Marisol doesn't have much use for the Methodists. She's the warden in the Kendrick monkey camp, the one who hoses me down and WD-40's my chair when it gets squeaky and talks to my brother Luke about his wedding stuff (seriously, Luke, get married already!), and helps Dad figure out the DVD player (come *on,* Dad, how can you still not get it after we've shown you like five hundred times?).

Yeah, Marisol gets testy about the Methodists. Just the other day she said, "What do you promise them? They come every day, those church ladies, and they *talk, talk, talk.*" She sounded like a chicken when she said that.

I said, "How do you think I found out Fred Heizer was caught in the park bathroom with some guy from the gym? I don't remember you asking me to pipe down when I told you that one."

But Marisol was not impressed, because she's been like super pregnant for about fourteen years and very cranky.

Anyway, Deb Trimble is the church lady who showed up on Elm Street with a big batch of bean soup one day and told me what Libby Tyler had done (side note: I didn't have the heart to tell Deb that the *last* thing anyone needs to give three guys in a tiny house is a big batch of bean soup, but Dad was like, "*Great!* I don't have to cook now," and then he pulverized it to put into my feedbag).

So Deb was *dying* to tell me, but she couldn't come over just to gossip, because Methodists don't think they do that, even though they are the *worst.* Between us turkeys, I think she dug that soup out of the back of her fridge, and trotted over (well, maybe she didn't trot. Deb's a little on the hefty side) and she said it in a big whisper, even though we were watching *Jeopardy*, and everyone knows the rule is no talking during *Jeop*. We *all* know that.

She said, "Did you hear about Libby Tyler?"

Listen, I've heard plenty about Libby Tyler. I've known Libby since we were six, and I'll be honest, I always had a thing for her hair. It's black, and super curly, and bouncy. And it goes great with her pale blue eyes. Hair aside, I've heard a lot about her recently, but I hadn't heard she'd taken a golf club to Ryan Spangler's truck and bashed out the windows, right there on Main Street in front of everyone.

Ryan was totally pissed off, and he got a restraining order, and now Libby can't go anywhere near him. Which kind of sucks when you think about it, because he has these two kids that Libby is really attached to. But I can see Ryan's point, because it is an awesome truck, an F-350, which is about as big and bad as you can get in a pickup.

Deb told me the story and she said, "What do think?"

And I was like, "What is crazy, Alex?" which of course Deb didn't get because she's not that into *Jeopardy*. I remember thinking that usually nothing surprises me—I mean, I've been through a lot and I also watch *Duck Dynasty*—but I was surprised. I did *not* expect that from Libby. Sure, I'd heard reports she was driving around Ryan's house and acting weird. But Ryan dumped her out of the blue, and you know, people do crazy things when they find out the guy they thought they were going to spend the rest of their life with was actually banging his ex-wife. Talk about salt on the wound.

Still, I never thought Libby Tyler would be one to pick up a golf club and go to town on Ryan's truck. She's got that really tight T-shirt that has a big flowery peace sign, and I thought she bought into that whole thing. Peace, I mean. And I *never* thought Libby would end up in the hospital. Not like *my* hospital, with a lot of IVs and catheters and nurses who are constantly sticking something into you, but a *quiet* hospital where they pipe in Yanni and you sit around and talk about your feelings and rest a lot.

She was only there a week, but in Pine River, any walk through the funny farm is Big News.

I've had time to think about this, and here's the truth: Libby Tyler is *not* crazy, no matter what you think you've heard. Sure, she's had some crazy moments, but you would, too, if you'd walked in Libby's shoes. Everyone has always loved Libby. Everyone. She joins everything, always wanting to help out, always wanting to do good. She's bubbly, she's always had this super positive outlook even when things were not looking so great to the rest of us, she's cute as hell, and she's got a great butt. Not that I've been ogling it or anything.

Libby went through some stuff is all I'm saying. Some people go through stuff and they bite down and shake it off, and then do something like make off with all your investments years later. Some people just reach that point where they can't take it anymore and they bash in a few windows with golf clubs, and then they're over it. That's Libby. I mean, would Sam Winters have a flaming torch for her if she was truly crazy? No way. So don't listen to the Methodists about Libby. Listen to me.

Oh, by the way, I'm Leo Kendrick. I have motor neuron disease, which makes me a genius, because the famous physicist Stephen Hawking has it, too, and I've never met anyone with MND who wasn't totally brilliant. I'm not bragging about it, I'm just letting you know that I'm right most of the time. It can be annoying to lesser mortals, but if you're a genius, you learn to live with a little disgruntled envy coming your way.

Anyway, there's a lot more about Libby and Homecoming Ranch you're going to want to know, so let's get this party started.

# TWO

*Two Years Ago*

On the last Sunday in June, the Pine River Colorado Church League held its final softball tournament. It had become such a major event in town that the officials had moved it from the municipal fields out to Pioneer Park on the old Aspen Highway. A cottage industry of junk food and bouncy castles had grown up along with the tournament, and even if a person wasn't terribly interested in church league softball, there was enough for a family to do on a Sunday afternoon.

Sam Winters, a deputy sheriff, had been back in town only a month after several months away. He hadn't been on vacation. He hadn't even been anywhere fun. He'd spent three months at a treatment facility in Denver for alcoholism, then another six months in a halfway house working construction while he tested the new, wobbly legs of his sobriety.

It was still difficult for Sam to say it, even at the AA meetings he attended each week: he was an alcoholic. A recovering alcoholic, thank God, but an alcoholic all the same. It had cost him everything—his job, his marriage, the best years of his life.

Sam had come back to Pine River and a new position at the sheriff's office. He'd once been on track to be the chief deputy with an eye toward running for sheriff one day. Not anymore. He was fortunate that the sheriff had let him back on the force in any position.

Since coming back, Sam didn't get out much. Sobriety was still something he was learning to live with, and he felt safest away from the temptation of life up at his house up in the mountains. It was a lonely place to be, but it was necessary. Women, friends—there were too many opportunities to drink, too many reasons to convince himself he could have just one. Sam couldn't have just one. He'd come back from the depths of his own personal hell and he never wanted to be there again.

Still, it was a beautiful afternoon, and Sam liked softball. A church tournament sounded innocuous, and he decided to venture out.

Sam dressed in jeans and a T-shirt. He pulled a ball cap down low over his eyes—an old habit that he used to believe kept people from noticing that he'd been drinking—and drove down to Pioneer Park.

He arrived about thirty minutes before the start of the championship game and took a seat at the end of the bleachers, a bottle of water dangling from his fingers, a bag of peanuts by his side. He saw a few people he knew, and although he waved and dipped his head in greeting to a couple of them, he made no move to walk over and talk to anyone. He still felt raw and unfinished, a loaf of half-baked bread. He hadn't found his sea legs quite yet.

He passed the time waiting for the game to start by watching Leo Kendrick—on crutches now—throwing a football to some little boys who had crowded around him. He was sad to see that

Leo's dexterity had eroded a lot in the time Sam had been gone, and his toss was a little wobbly. The boys didn't care; they were tumbling over each other, laughing as they wrestled for the ball, and then happily racing back to Leo, who had advice for the best way to tackle each other.

Once the game started, Sam felt more at ease.

The two teams vying for the annual crown were the Presbyterians and the Methodists, and it was a hard fought battle. Just as dusk began to creep in under the sun, the Presbyterians closed it out for the win, the second year in a row.

It had been a good game, a perfect diversion on that sunny afternoon.

Sam was ready to leave then, to head back up to his place and feed his horses, but the lady sitting next to him said that The Bricklayers, a local band, was going to play. Sam used to listen to the band when he hung out at the Rocky Creek Tavern. He liked them. It might be the only time he would ever have the opportunity to hear the band outside of a bar.

Sam kept his seat on the bleachers, nursing his bottle of water, waiting for the band to come onto the temporary stage. The scent of barbequed meat filled the air, making his stomach growl. People were milling about, claiming space with blankets and picnic baskets for the band's performance.

Down on the field, Sam spotted Libby Tyler. It took him a minute to realize it was her. She was wearing a ball cap over her curly locks and a summer dress with a sweater. Sam and Libby had worked at the sheriff's office together before he'd gone away. He'd always liked her. Libby was pretty, with silvery pale-blue eyes. More important, she was nice. She had never failed to have a smile for him, even during his darkest moments.

She'd hooked up with Ryan Spangler a couple of years ago, and right now, she was playing a game with Ryan's two little kids.

Alice and Max, Sam remembered—Libby used to bring them into the office sometimes. Cute kids. What were they now, five or six? Sam smiled as he watched her chase the children, then pretend to run from them, letting them catch her and tumble her to the ground. But then she would pop up and grab one, lift them in the air and swing them around.

They looked happy, the three of them, like they'd skipped right out of a holiday commercial. Sam didn't see where Ryan was, and guessed he was manning a barbeque pit somewhere. Libby and the children scampered off toward the bouncy castles, and Sam lost sight of them.

He didn't like to acknowledge it, but seeing a family like that made him feel a little sad. Sam had always imagined that sort of life for himself, but he'd lost sight of starting his own family in a bottle somewhere. The disappointment with himself, with what could have been, cut deep. It made him feel older than his thirty-two years.

A little later, the lights of the temporary stage came on, and Sam stretched his legs out long. The sun was beginning to sink behind the mountains. He was hungry, and figured he'd listen to a couple of songs then head home. A shadow or something caught his eye, and he turned toward it.

Libby Tyler was approaching him, carrying a plate laden with food. She was smiling warmly, as if she was actually glad to see him. When people around town said hello to him, they didn't smile at him like this.

Libby climbed up the few steps to where he was sitting. "Hey, Sam Winters!" she said cheerfully. "You're back, huh?"

"I'm back." He could feel a smile curving the corners of his mouth. "How are you, Libby Tyler?"

"I'm great," she said. "Couldn't be better. But the more important question is, how are *you*?"

"I'm good," Sam said, and was aware that for the first time in a long time, he meant it.

"I am so glad to hear it. I've thought about you, you know. I'd hoped things were working out for you."

"Thanks," he said. That word seemed inadequate for what that meant to him. Just to know that someone as pretty and warm as Libby was hoping for him made him feel like he had done something worthwhile.

"I brought you some food," she said, holding the plate out.

"For me?"

"Yes, for you." She grinned as he took the plate. "I saw you sitting over here by yourself, and you looked kind of hungry, so . . ." She shrugged playfully. "Seriously, you've been sitting up here all afternoon. You've got to be hungry. And this is excellent brisket."

Sam was as surprised as he was appreciative. Touched, too. He missed having someone in his life to care about him. "Can't say no to excellent brisket. Thank you." He took the plate and picked up the plastic fork, taking a generous bite of the potato salad.

"You look really good," she said, and took a seat on the bleacher below him. "*Really* good. Healthy, you know? That's good to see."

"Thanks. You look pretty good yourself." He hadn't meant it to come out quite like that, but she did look great. She looked fresh and wholesome, and untouched by the ugly side of life.

Libby blushed a little and self-consciously pushed a corkscrew curl from her face. Sam envisioned pushing that curl back himself. The image caused him to look at his plate. It had been a long time since he'd thought of touching a woman. He'd thought of sex, yes, of course. But nothing as simply intimate as brushing a woman's hair from her face. Thinking of it now made him feel strangely empty.

"Are you coming back to work?" she asked.

"Not to Corita City," he said, referring to the sheriff's county headquarters. "I'm going to be a rural area deputy, stationed here in Pine River."

"Really?" Her voice was full of delight. "That's great news! When do you start?"

"A couple of weeks," he said, and bit into some brisket. She was right—it was excellent. "I pulled a muscle in my back and I've been driving over to Montrose two days a week for treatment. Once the doc releases me, I'm good to go."

Libby pointed at him. "Yoga."

"Excuse me?"

"*Yoga*. You should come to yoga class." She suddenly stood up and bent over to touch her toes. "Yoga will stretch you out, especially your back."

Sam laughed.

"I'm serious!"

"Libby!"

Libby turned; Sam saw Ryan walking across the field, a wire clothes hanger in his hand. "Where are the marshmallows?" he called up. "Hey, Sam."

Sam lifted a hand, then looked at his plate. Ryan's appearance had ruined one of the nicest moments he'd had since coming out of treatment. He liked talking to Libby. He'd always liked talking to Libby. She'd always had a way of making him feel like he mattered, even when he knew better than anyone that he didn't.

"They're in the black bag in the back of the truck," Libby said. "Right next to the cooler."

"I looked there. I can't find them. Come on, the kids are getting antsy."

Libby smiled at Sam. "Trust me, they are in the black bag," she murmured.

"Libby—"

"I'm coming, Ryan," she called cheerfully. To Sam, she said, "Duty calls. But seriously, Sam, think about yoga." She began to step down the bleachers.

"Thanks, but to be honest, I am probably not going to think about yoga," Sam said after her. "Hey, thanks for the food."

Libby had reached the last step. She turned back, put her palms together, and put them to her chest. "You're welcome for the food. Just try the yoga. You can thank me later. Namaste." She bowed her head. With a laugh, she jumped off the last bleacher and ran to catch up with Ryan.

Ryan swung his arm around Libby's neck and kissed the top of her head.

Sam felt a weird tightness in his chest. It felt like loneliness. Yearning. A buried desire for what Libby and Ryan had.

He finished his brisket, listened to a couple of songs, then stood up and stretched his stiff back before heading home.

Yoga, huh?

Sam's life resumed its normal rhythm, and after a couple of days, he didn't think about his encounter with Libby Tyler. Not until a week later, when he walked into the room the Pinero County Sheriff's Office had rented from the Pine River Police Department for him. There, on his desk, was a rolled up yoga mat and a DVD. On the mat was a Post-it note:

*Hi, Sam. Now you have no excuse not to at least try it. Good luck! Libby Tyler.*

He chuckled to himself with delight and picked up the DVD to read the back.

# THREE

*Present Day*

Sam wished he'd picked up a jacket before heading up to Homecoming Ranch. The wind that bowed the tops of the Ponderosa pines and knocked a few thin clouds around carried on it the scent of change. It felt as if the temperature had dropped twenty degrees in the last hour.

Eight miles from Pine River, the road up to the ranch was a drive through the best scenery the Colorado mountain ranges had to offer. Green valleys, dark mountains with bald tops, trees glittering gold and green. He drove through stands of pine and spruce, and cottonwoods that stretched out to each other, creating a canopy over the road; past horses grazing a meadow of spindly daisies, the herd increased by two over the summer, which he hoped—probably wrong, but still, he hoped—was a sign that the old ranch was turning around.

Sam happened to live off this same long road up the canyon. His log house was a right turn onto a dirt road at the old abandoned fishing cabin, about a mile up. He loved it up here, but living high in the mountains wasn't for the faint of heart. Winters were hard, and civilization was a good drive away. Still, it was one of the most serene places on earth—Sam knew God's hand when he saw it.

Eventually, the road grew steeper, and the surface changed to caliche. Sam bumped along until he came to the iron gate between two thick wooden posts. For decades, an old, weathered, wooden sign had hung over this gate, but now a new sign swung overhead in the breeze. It was shiny and red, big enough that Sam thought passengers in planes passing overhead could see it.

It read "Welcome to Homecoming Ranch."

It was an awfully big sign to mark a ranch that very few people saw.

The gate was open, so Sam drove through, down past more cottonwoods and spruce trees, past a manicured meadow where a few cows grazed. The property was fenced by split rails, and on the far side of the meadow were a dozen concrete tent pads. Two one-room cabins had been built, but the other pads remained empty, almost as if they'd given up. Through a stand of alder trees, one could see the ranch house, set back against the mountain and the pines.

Sam parked in the drive in front of the house with the pitched roof and funky gables. Libby's little red car was parked in front of the garage, but there were no other vehicles. He got out and looked around for the dogs. Four of them lived up here, usually lounging under the porch. He was a little disappointed that none of them was around this evening, because he really liked those mutts.

He jogged up the porch steps. They'd been recently repaired. He was glad for it, because the last time he'd been out here, he'd almost put a boot through one step. Been out to see Libby a couple of times in the last month. The girl had had a rough summer.

Sam rang the doorbell. He heard the sound of someone running, and then it sounded as if that person slid across the floor and was stopped by the door. It flew open, and Libby's wild, curly black hair filled the space behind the screen door. She was smiling—

Until she saw it was him, and her face instantly fell. "Oh. Hi, Sam." She peered past him, as if she were looking for someone or something else.

He would not take that personally. Much. "Nice to see you, too," he said. "Expecting someone?"

"Umm . . . no." She suddenly gasped and whirled around, disappearing from view. Sam waited a moment, listening, expecting her to come back. When she did not he called out, "Libby?"

She didn't answer him. He heard some banging that he guessed was coming from the kitchen. He knew what was going on here. Libby didn't intend to come back to the door. She was hoping he'd go away. Sam sighed, pushed the screen door open, stuck his head in, and shouted, "I'm not going away, Libby! You're going to have to talk to me if you don't want trouble."

"Trouble! What are you talking about, Sam Winters? I think you have the wrong person!" she shouted from the back of the house.

"I'm coming in," he warned her. He knocked the dirt off his boots and walked into the house.

His footfall on the worn pine floors echoed down the hallway. He followed the sound of the banging and the scent of fresh-baked bread through the living room, where a fire was glowing in the hearth and a chenille throw was draped over the couch, as if someone had been napping. He stepped into the adjoining kitchen, ducking his head to go through the door.

He liked this old house; it was homey. The kitchen looked straight out of the 1950s, with chintz curtains, an old stove, Formica countertops, and floral wallpaper. Each room had four walls—none of the big open spaces so popular now. But it was a charming, cozy house.

Libby had donned an apron and was pulling out pots and pans on the other side of the breakfast bar, pretending to be busy. Sam glanced around—papers were stacked haphazardly on the small breakfast table. Through French doors that led into the dining room, he saw candles and Mason jars and some strange bow-looking things strewn around the room. It looked like a massive craft project underway.

But the kitchen was spotless, not a thing out of place. And that smell—Sam wouldn't have minded in the least sampling some fresh bread, but he was fairly certain he would not be offered any. He took off his hat, put it on the breakfast bar, and dragged his fingers through his hair, which, he absently noticed, had gotten so long it touched his collar. He needed to do something about that.

At the moment, however, he had to deal with Libby. Again. He watched her moving around the kitchen, her wild hair twisted into thick strands to keep it from her face. "You can stop banging around, Libby, because it's not going to work. I'm not leaving until we've talked."

Libby slapped a frying pan down on the stove and whirled around to face him, her blue eyes turning wintery in the fluorescent light, her smile looking a little forced. "I'm always happy to talk to you, Sam!" she said with a cheeriness he didn't believe for a moment. "It's just that I have a lot of work to do. We're having a big event here in a couple of weeks, a *big* event, and Madeline should be here any minute." She glanced at her watch, then put her hands on her waist. "So! What did you need?"

As if he'd come all this way to ask a favor, or merely to shoot the breeze. He gave her the patient look he usually reserved for mouthy teens. "I'm a professional, remember? I've seen it all, heard it all, and you are not fooling me."

Libby muttered something under her breath.

"Pardon?"

"Nothing."

"Mind if I sit?"

"Can I stop you?" she asked lightheartedly, then waved to the stool. "Have a seat, Sam. Would you like something? Water?"

He smiled, and Libby's dark lashes fluttered, as if he'd shined a light on her. He slid onto a stool on the opposite side of the bar from her. "Nothing for me, thanks. You know why I'm here, right?"

"No. Why? To tell me our cows got out? To borrow a hammer?"

"A hammer?" he echoed with a chuckle.

"A tool," she clarified.

"I've got all the tools I need. You know why I'm here, Libby."

She sighed heavenward. "Well you don't have to sound like I'm one swan dive away from a straitjacket."

Sam almost laughed. Sometimes he thought she *was* one swan dive away from a straitjacket, but honestly, he kind of liked that about her. Libby was never boring or predictable, that was certain. He knew all about her stay at Mountain View Behavioral Health Center. He knew a lot about Libby, and sometimes, he felt as if he knew her in that cosmic way people have of knowing each other from time to time. He got her; he understood her. She was fun, and generous, and eager to be part of life. And she was sexy, all five feet five of her, seemed to get sexier with each year, with wild curly hair and those blue eyes, and lips that made his mouth water.

In a purely hypothetical way, of course, because Sam made it a point not to lust after women who violated restraining orders. Which Libby had done today.

It was a shame that Libby had been dealt such a bad hand.

"I know you're here because of Gwen," she said. "But she's kind of paranoid, don't you think?" Libby winced a little as if it pained her to make that observation. "Because really, it was just a stupid thing, Sam. And you didn't have to drive all the way out here to tell me that it was stupid. I mean, thanks and all that, but totally unnecessary. So you can go back to work now," she said, making a gesture to the door. She smiled as if that was that, and turned around to go back to whatever she'd been doing.

Nothing, as it turned out, other than moving things around on the counter, giving Sam a moment to admire her most excellent backside. Which, again, in his professional capacity as deputy sheriff, he ought not to be doing. But a man couldn't help but admire the soft, kick-ass curves on this woman. "If you didn't want me to drive all the way out here, you probably shouldn't have gone into town this afternoon, do you think?"

Libby laughed and glanced at him over her shoulder. "You're funny. I'm not prohibited from going to town, Sam. Actually, I can go wherever I want, because FYI, this is a free country."

He cocked a brow. "You're not prohibited from going to town, but you *are* prohibited from being within three hundred yards of your ex."

"Correct. But I wasn't within three hundred yards of my ex. I was near my ex's girlfriend. Or his ex-wife, or whatever we are calling her this week," she said with a dismissive flick of her wrist.

"Libby . . ." He sighed. "You know, I've never said this to you, but I think what happened to you was unfair," he said.

Something flickered in her eyes, as if the words had nicked her. She drew her bottom lip between her teeth a moment. "Which part? You mean when Ryan kicked me out for no reason one day? Out of the blue? Or because he didn't have the courage to tell me that the reason wasn't really *me,* as he wanted me to believe, but that he was having an affair with Gwen?"

"All of it," Sam said. "Unfair, every bit."

"Yeah, well, unfair doesn't begin to describe it, if you want to know the truth."

"It sucks, Libby. Nevertheless, you *have* to stay away from the man and his family."

She drew a deep breath and then released it in one long sigh. "I know, Sam. I *know*," she said, giving in, "but I didn't go to town to find him, I swear I didn't. I went to get some bowls for candles."

Sam wasn't sure why candles needed bowls, which Libby seemed to anticipate.

"You know, you float candles in the bowls. Floating candles. But they have to be wide and flat glass bowls," she said, sketching them out with her hands. "Crystal is better."

"Okay," he said uncertainly.

"I went to Walmart, but they didn't have what I wanted, so I went into Pine River because I thought Tag's Outfitters might have them, although I don't know why I thought *that*, and *Tag*, Jesus, that old coot! He was *no* help, but then I remembered there was that little gift shop near the cemetery. So I drove over there, and you know you can't go there without going by the park, and there they were. The kids were on the soccer field practicing, and I saw Max . . ." Her voice trailed off a moment, and she shook her head. "I saw Max," she said, her voice softer, and shrugged. "So I stopped."

Sam felt for her. How could he not feel for her? It was one hazard of his job, feeling bad for people who were doing things they ought not to do. "You should have driven on," he said.

"Well, I *know* that. But they were playing, and I thought, where's the harm? It's not like I ran out on the field to hug Max or called Alice over. It's not like I went looking for anyone."

"Gwen said you walked up to the sidelines. And then you wouldn't leave when she asked you to, and on top of that, you got pretty mouthy about it."

Libby studied him with those pale blue eyes, as if debating that. "Okay, I'm not going to deny that," she finally admitted, holding up a finger. "But in my defense, I'm a grown woman. I don't need someone telling me what I'm supposed to be doing. Especially the woman who was sleeping with my significant other behind my back. The same woman who basically checked out of her kids' lives and left me to raise them while she went to dental school, and suddenly, I'm the bad guy. She was the one telling me to leave, and I couldn't help it. I got . . . I got—"

"Mouthy?" he offered helpfully.

"That's not the word I was going to use, but okay, yeah, I got mouthy. It just made me *so mad.*" She curled her hands into her fists and tapped against her thighs. "I've been with those two kids every day for more than four years. They *love* me and I love them. And you know what?" she continued, beginning to pace now, "while their father was cheating on me with their mother—which sounds totally bizarre, doesn't it? But that's what he was doing, he was cheating on *me*—and all that time, I was taking them to school," she said, folding one finger down, "and making their lunches," she said, folding another finger down, "and picking them up and making sure they got to soccer and dance class and tae-kwon-do on time, and kissing their boo-boos and, yeah, okay, I stopped when I saw them today. *So?*"

"So, again, you aren't supposed to be anywhere near Ryan or his family since you took that golf club to his truck."

Libby groaned to the ceiling. "Geez, you have *one* confrontation with somebody, and suddenly, you're a threat to all the little children and senior citizens."

Sam smiled. "The only person who thinks you're any sort of threat is Ryan. And Gwen, apparently."

"Don't be so sure of that," Libby said, and walked to the fridge, pulling out a head of lettuce. "Sally Rushton saw me coming the other day and crossed the street so she wouldn't have to say hi." She marched back to the kitchen sink, threw the lettuce into it, and turned on the faucet.

Sam watched her wash that head of lettuce like an angry sous chef. He couldn't really blame her for feeling the way she did. First of all, everyone in town knew she'd been head over heels for Ryan Spangler. Second, everyone in town knew that Ryan Spangler was a player. Poor Libby found that out the hard way.

For reasons that completely eluded Sam, Ryan was one of those guys who could charm the pants off women. Way back when, Ryan had married Gwen, had two cute kids, got a good job at the propane shop, and had a nice little house on the edge of Pine River. Most men would be happy that they'd done something right, that they had a pretty wife and two great kids to come home to every day after work. Sam didn't know what went wrong between Ryan and Gwen, but something did. Gwen seemed solid; she didn't strike him as the type to walk out on a marriage. But that she did, walking all the way to Colorado Springs to get her dental hygiene license because there wasn't much work in Pine River. She had to leave her babies at home with their grandmas and their schools and their dad in order to get that marketable skill. Sam figured that was a tough thing for Gwen to do, no matter what Libby thought of it. The way he saw it, Gwen had done what she had to do to provide for her kids.

That was when Ryan met Libby.

Sam actually remembered it—Libby had been working as a clerk at the sheriff's office in Pine River at the time. Sam had worked there, too, before his life had spiraled out of control and he'd had to leave. He remembered Libby's fresh face, and how she'd bring cookies to the office. He remembered how she'd appear at his side with a cup of coffee when he showed up to work hungover. "Get some *sleep,* Sam," she'd whisper. She organized the office parties, too, and was the one person who could get grown men to do a Secret Santa gift exchange. Sam remembered that holiday season—after everyone had agreed, which had taken some doing, they'd drawn names. But the names were unfamiliar to them. It turned out that Libby had given them the names of the kids at the children's home in Corita City. She explained that she'd feared if she'd asked them to give a gift to the home, the deputies gladly would have done it, but would have handed off the task to their wives. She'd wanted them to connect to the kids, so she'd devised the Secret Santa.

The holiday party that year, with the kids from the home, was one of the best holiday parties Sam had ever attended. And there hadn't been a drop of booze . . . except in the flask in his patrol car.

Sam also remembered the starry look Libby had when she'd met Ryan. She'd been completely smitten by him, and had really taken to his two little kids. Danielle Boxer, who owned the Grizzly Lodge and Café, had once told Sam that Libby threw herself body and soul into Ryan's life and taking care of his children.

"She'd bring them down to Main Street on Saturday mornings, and they'd come into the café. Oh, she dressed those kids, Alice with a big bow in her hair, Max with his little high-tops. She'd take them down to the library for story hour, or over to the park to the new playscape they have over there. I'll tell you, Sam, she loved those kids as if she'd birthed them herself."

No one could ever fault Libby Tyler for effort.

Sam hadn't seen much of Libby around that time—he'd had his problems at home and a daily cat and mouse game of keeping his addiction a secret.

Gwen came back to town about the same time as Sam, with a new hairdo and a new figure and a new job that paid pretty well, and apparently, Ryan got the idea things would be better with Gwen. But Ryan wasn't the kind of man who could own up to his sorry truth; he kept his affair with Gwen under wraps, and told Libby it wasn't going to work out. Sam didn't know what Ryan had eventually said to Libby, exactly, but Dani said it was a cold-hearted rejection, a shove right out the door without explanation. As far as Libby knew, everything was golden between her and Ryan. She thought she was going to be stepmom to those kids until they had their own families. She thought she and Ryan would be adding to the brood. She thought Ryan truly loved her.

After that, Sam would see Libby around town with a yoga mat on her back, or having lunch with her mother at the local tea shop. She seemed the same bubbly young woman, still volunteering her time to help others, but Sam had noticed something different about her. The light was not the same in her blue eyes.

The sad thing was, Libby didn't know what everyone else knew—that Ryan had been having an affair with Gwen. When Libby found out about it a few weeks ago—months after their split, after trying to make sense of things—she'd lost it and picked up the golf club.

At the present moment, Libby was practically scrubbing that head of lettuce, then ripping the leaves and throwing them like grenades into the salad spinner.

"I told the Pine River cop that I'd handle today's incident," he said. "I asked Gwen not to make a bigger deal out of it. But Libby, you can't violate a restraining order and expect that you won't end up in jail."

Libby stopped ripping leaves from the head of lettuce and looked out the window over the kitchen sink.

"Look, I know it's been hard," he continued. "But if you want to see those kids, you're going to have to make nice. People don't want women who bash truck windows coming around their little ones, you know?"

Libby snorted. "So I hear."

Sam pushed a hand through his hair, tried to think of the best way to frame his thoughts. "You can't let your emotions get the best of you. This restraining order is temporary. You don't want to give Ryan any reason to make it permanent, do you?"

Libby didn't respond.

The headlights from a car swept through the kitchen as some-one pulled into the drive.

"So . . . you're going to obey the order, right?"

"Right," Libby said, and wiped her hands on her apron. She turned around and walked to the bar, standing beside the seat he had taken, and picked up his hat, clearly meaning to show him out. "Thanks for coming by, always great to see you, etc. But don't call me, Sam, I'll call you."

She grinned as if she were teasing him, but Sam knew she wasn't. Still, he smiled at her. He stood up, and stood so close to her that he could smell her perfume. It teased his nose and his thoughts, stirring something deep inside him as he took his hat from her. "That's Deputy Winters to you. And no one is hoping more than me that we can stop meeting like this." He meant that sincerely as he sat his hat on his head.

Libby's smile softened. "Really? Because I was beginning to think you kind of liked it." She gave him a friendly shove toward the door.

"I'll see you around town, Libby."

"Good-bye Deputy Winters!" she said in a singsong voice, and wiggled her fingers at him in a little wave.

"Good-bye, Libby."

Sam emerged from the house just as Madeline Pruett, one of Libby's half sisters, was coming up the steps. Four dogs were shad-owing her, their snouts on the grocery bags she was carrying. She paused, her eyes widening when she saw him. "Oh no," she said. "What's happened?"

"How are you, Madeline? Nothing has happened. Just check-ing in." He jogged down the steps, pausing to pet the dogs. "Have a good evening," he said, and walked on to his patrol car, aware that Madeline was staring at his back.

Libby Tyler, he thought as he turned the ignition. A little nutty, a lot cute, and a truckload of trouble. Wasn't this the way it always went? He was always drawn to the best-looking ones who caused the most trouble.

# FOUR

Libby could hear Madeline banging through the front door and kicking it shut with her foot. The dogs raced into the kitchen before her, crowding Libby, sniffing her, looking for a treat.

"*Hey,* you mutts!" Madeline shouted after them. All four dogs reversed course and scrambled out of the kitchen, presumably to where Libby could hear Madeline putting things down in the hallway. That was a remarkable turnaround from five months ago, when Madeline had first come to Homecoming Ranch. She'd been petrified of dogs and of sisters she'd never met. Honestly, Madeline had been petrified of *life*.

When Libby's father had died and left this run-down ranch to her and her sisters—meaning Madeline, whom she had never heard of until his death, and Emma, whom she definitely knew, but did not consider much of a sister if you got right down to it—Libby had been excited. After what she'd gone through with Ryan, and then her father's death, she'd had hope that somehow she'd spin right into a new reality, one with sisters and meaningful relationships. She'd even said as much to her mother.

Libby should know by now not to say hopeful things to her mother, because her mother, God bless her, thought it was her purpose in life to make sure that Libby was, at all times, completely grounded.

"I don't like to see you get your hopes up, honey," her mother had said one day as she treated Libby to lunch at the Silver Leaf Teashop. "They may be sisters by blood, but these are grown women with their own lives. You can't just throw three grown women together and expect that it will all be perfect and rosy."

"Thanks for the encouragement," Libby had said. "Who says a sisterly bond is only formed at the beginning of life?"

Her mother had shrugged as she'd nibbled on a carrot. "You lived with Emma, what, two years? What kind of bond did you form with her?"

"I was seven or eight then, Mom. I'm twenty-six now."

"It's just that you always have such high expectations, and when those expectations aren't met, you are so disappointed. I don't want to see you disappointed, Libby. I tried to warn you about Ryan, but you—"

"Okay, all right," Libby had said curtly, not wanting to hear the *I Told You So* chorus again.

But her mom was right, Libby had carried high expectations for her new family. *Too* high. When it fell apart, disappearing like the smoke and mirrors trick it apparently was, the emergence of sisters felt like a gift from God, tied up in a bow and given to Libby after losing her job and her family. She'd believed she deserved some happiness. Only Madeline and Emma hadn't been as excited by the prospect of instant family and a run-down ranch as Libby had been.

But Libby, reeling from the loss of Ryan and Alice and Max, had desperately needed something to *work*. So she'd doggedly insisted that they go ahead with staging the ranch for a big family reunion—their father had rented the ranch out for that purpose before he'd died—and Madeline had grudgingly stayed to help.

And then, as if to add salt to Libby's open wound, Madeline fell in love with Luke Kendrick. Big, gooey, hands-all-over-him love. Pretty Madeline with her long, dark hair and thick bangs, and big, rock-star handsome, rugged Luke, had fallen into the sort of love that burned a person up. Libby would see Madeline and Luke share a private joke and know they had a good thing, the real thing.

They had the sort of thing Libby had believed she'd had with Ryan.

That it had all been a lie had begun to weigh on Libby. It rooted into her thoughts, knitted into her days, sank into her heart. She couldn't sleep, couldn't eat. She had stopped living her life, had let things begin to slip and slither away.

It was Sam who had taken the golf club from Libby's hand the afternoon she bashed the windows of Ryan's truck, but it was Madeline who had called Libby's mother.

Her mother, in turn, had taken Libby to the Mountain View Behavioral Health Center. "What you need is rest, honey," she'd said as they drove to the facility on the edge of an industrial park near Colorado Springs. "The not eating or sleeping, the moping about, and now *this.*" She shook her head. "I am worried about you."

Libby had been too exhausted, too far past the point of caring to argue with her mother.

Now, a little more than a month since she'd come home, Libby still wasn't certain if she was grateful for Madeline's intervention or terribly resentful. But then again, everything still felt a little gray and fuzzy to Libby these days. Sometimes, she felt as if there was something between her and the entire world, and if she just tried hard enough, it would all come together. Now, five months since Ryan first asked her to move out, Libby still couldn't wrap her mind around it.

And then again, judging by what Ryan had said recently, maybe it hadn't been a lie so much as a huge mistake on his part—

*Can't think about that now,* not with Madeline in the living room.

Libby closed her eyes and took a series of deep breaths, a coping mechanism Dr. Huber had taught her at Mountain View. She reminded herself there were much more important things to think about, such as what they would do with this ranch they'd inherited from their dad.

Libby, Emma, and Madeline still hadn't decided what they would do with the ranch in the long run. Sell it, keep it, abandon it—who knew? For now, they were focused on what would be the third event at Homecoming Ranch in the six months they'd owned it. The first had been a family reunion. The second a wedding. The third event, scheduled to occur in two weeks, would be a civil union between Austin and Gary.

Gary—or more precisely, Gary's mother, Martha—had some very specific ideas for the ceremony, and that is what Libby made herself think about now. The event was tangible and imminent. Flowers, candles, wind chimes, a string quartet—if Libby concentrated on those things, she didn't think about things that made her so blessedly angry.

Madeline clomped into the kitchen, carrying groceries and eyeing Libby warily, as if she expected Libby to do something crazy, like pick up a knife and start stabbing the faded curtains over the kitchen sink. "Hey," she said, depositing her groceries on the counter. "Sam Winters was here again?"

"Yep," Libby said, sliding immediately into Friendly, Upbeat Libby. "I'm going to make some enchiladas. I love enchiladas, don't you? Cheese especially."

"What'd he want?" Madeline asked as she began to take items out of the paper bag. Bananas, coffee, paper towels.

"Just to chat. Hey, did you happen to get tortillas?"

Madeline slid a package of them across the kitchen counter to Libby. "So what did he want to chat about?"

It was obvious that Madeline spent her days waiting for the next thing that would send Libby back to Mountain View. She walked on tiptoes and then pretended she wasn't doing exactly that. It was annoying. The one time Libby had tried to explain, as best she could, why she'd lost herself that day, why depression had steamrolled over her, flattening her into a pancake with tunnel-vision anger, she'd come away thinking that Madeline didn't really understand what betrayal could do to a person.

To be perfectly honest, Libby didn't understand it either. She never once had any inkling that she was a person to resort to violence, not until the day she'd tried to speak to Ryan about seeing Alice and Max, and he'd exploded, telling her that she'd been too lenient with his kids and had turned them into little entitled monsters, and that it was best if she didn't come around them anymore, and didn't she get it, he and Gwen had been seeing each other behind her back for months?

That announcement had caught Libby completely off guard and sent her into a flaming tailspin. It was one thing to lose Ryan. It was an entirely different matter to lose Max and Alice. But it was another stratosphere of anger altogether when she realized that when Ryan had suddenly ended things, it was because he'd been cheating on her, and Libby *hadn't figured that out.*

She'd been overcome with a rage so intense that she really could not stop herself. Libby couldn't even describe that moment to Dr. Huber. She remembered feeling like the world around her had fallen away. She didn't know she was shaking until she tried to stop her purse from sliding off her shoulder and couldn't grab it. She remembered picking up the club from the bed of Ryan's truck, and how Ryan was almost frozen with shock. She remembered the squishy feel of the club's grip, and how she had been pleased she could get such a good grip on it.

Libby could remember taking the first whack and realizing she needed more muscle. She took another whack and the glass shattered, and she had felt adrenaline-fueled elation. Pure elation, like she'd just jumped from the top of a building and landed on her feet.

She could not remember how she kept Ryan at bay. She just remembered that when Sam took the club from her hand, Ryan had been standing there, his whole body quivering with fury. Libby hadn't cared, obviously, and soon after that, she'd been on her way to Mountain View. Days later, with some medicine to calm her down and some sleep to rest her mind, Libby understood that Ryan had a right to be angry, but the resulting restraining order was a huge blow—Ryan knew how much Alice and Max meant to her, and how much she meant to them. He knew the kids called Libby, still wanted to tell her about dance, about soccer, about the movie they watched that morning. They wanted just to talk to *her*, to the woman who had cared for them for the last four years.

"Libby, what did he want?" Madeline asked again, shaking Libby back to the present.

She blinked. "Not much. He was just checking on things. Gary and Austin's ceremony." Libby didn't even wince at that lie, which, on some level, was alarming to her. But the guilt would have to get in line behind a mess of other feelings that had been swirling around her since running into Gwen today.

Madeline frowned into her grocery bag. "What about it?" she asked, and put a jar of spaghetti sauce on the counter.

"He'd heard about it in town." *God, shut up, Libby.* She was not going to tell Madeline the true reason for his call. How could she? Madeline would flip out—restraining orders in general flipped her out. Madeline liked order and everything in its place, and everyone obeying the rules, and she did not like it when Libby did not obey the rules.

Libby could feel Madeline's eyes on her. She took some chicken breasts out of the fridge, some tomatoes and peppers. "Are you hungry?" she asked. "I'll make a big batch."

"Aah . . . well, Luke and I are going into town for dinner tonight. Want to come with us?"

The only thing worse than having Sam Winters remind Libby she was violating a restraining order was being the third wheel on a date with the lovebirds. "Thanks, but I've got a lot of work to do," Libby said. "Did you get the glass bowls?"

"They're in my trunk," Madeline said. "I'll get them." She started out of the kitchen, but she hesitated, brushed her bangs from her eyes and said, "Libby? You know you can talk to me if something is wrong, right?"

Madeline probably believed that. But there was so much wrong in Libby's life right now and Madeline Pruett felt like the last person Libby could talk to about it. If Libby told her half of what she was thinking, she guessed Madeline would hyperventilate herself right into a coma. "Thanks, Madeline," she said. "But nothing is wrong. I'm just . . . I am worried about the ranch, that's all." She tossed a smile over her shoulder that hopefully was reassuring.

"Yeah," Madeline said, nodding as if she was worried, too. "I've been thinking a lot about it."

Libby did not like it when Madeline had been thinking. Usually it meant she was thinking about why things wouldn't work, as opposed to how to make them work. "I think we should get a loan," Libby blurted before Madeline could suggest something she did not want to hear.

"Huh?" Madeline said, startled.

The thought sort of startled Libby, too. "A loan. You know, to spruce things up and tide us over until we can get some events booked."

Madeline was already shaking her head. "I don't think that's a good idea. You have to have a way to pay them back—"

"We could get a business loan," Libby said quickly. She knew that's what Leslie Brown had done when she opened up her salon in town. If Leslie could do it, so could they.

But Madeline looked shocked by the suggestion.

"I'm just saying we should at least talk to the bank, Madeline. We can't make any gains without a little risk. Or without fixing the place up. Or without marketing ourselves, right?"

"But we're leaking money, Libby. It seems to me the last thing we want to do is leak *more* money. How would we pay it back? And Emma would never sign off—"

"Don't worry about Emma," Libby said. She did enough worrying about Emma for the both of them, and besides, that was a bridge she would cross when she came to it.

"Okay, sure, we won't worry about Emma," Madeline said, calling her bluff. "She owns as much of this ranch as we do, but we won't worry about that because she's *sooo* predictable."

That was true—Emma was a loose cannon, a chess piece that had fallen off the board. "Look, all I'm saying is that if we had some money to advertise our place, and to make it so people will *want* to come here, we might get enough business so that we aren't leaking money. I figure we need at least six events a year just to break even."

"I don't know," Madeline said with a shake of her head. "We have no tangible reason to borrow."

"Right now, we're just talking about it."

Madeline bit her lower lip. "Okay," she said. "As long as we're just talking about it. I'm going to go get the bowls." She walked out of the kitchen, ending the conversation.

Madeline didn't say more about it. She came back to the kitchen with the bowls and talked about what she'd done in town that day, glossing over the conversation about the ranch. In Libby's mind, Madeline was always glossing over things. She wondered if Madeline truly feared setting her off into some manic explosion.

To be fair, Libby sometimes feared it, too. She still couldn't wrap her head around what she'd done. It was so unlike her, so unlike how she'd ever been. The little green pills she took each day were supposed to keep her calm and even-tempered, and Libby supposed they did. She felt fine. Almost normal. Her explosion of anger at Ryan's truck and, according to Dr. Huber, her very loud and very vile shouting, had come after several days of not sleeping or eating, of trying to sort things out in her head. That afternoon, after it happened, Libby had felt as if she were standing at the end of a very long tunnel. She could hear voices of people around her, but the voices had not seemed real. In fact, to this day, Libby still wasn't sure if they'd been real.

Maybe Madeline remembered more of that afternoon than Libby did. Maybe that's why she tried so hard not to upset Libby. Someday, maybe Libby would ask Madeline—when she thought she could bear to hear all the details.

When Madeline left a half hour later, Libby walked into the living room and stepped around four dogs, who were arranged in various poses of canine rest. She watched the taillights of Madeline's SUV bump down the drive.

When the lights disappeared, Libby stared out into the early evening, picturing Gwen in the kitchen of the house where Libby had lived with Ryan and the kids. She could imagine Gwen using the old, red Dutch oven to make dinner—six-year-old Max loved lasagna, and eight-year-old Alice loved pizza—while she told Ryan about her run-in with his ex-girlfriend.

She wondered how Ryan looked as he heard about it. Did he squirm just a little? Did he think back to his own encounter with Libby earlier this week in the parking lot of the grocery store? It had been an awkward moment—Libby hadn't seen him, not until she happened to look up, and there he was, walking toward her, his head down, too. They'd both stopped. "Hey," he'd said. "How are you, Libby?"

What was she supposed to say to that? *Miserable. Crazy. But of course you know that.* "Fine," she'd said.

And then she had realized she was standing too close to him, that she was in violation of her restraining order. She'd started to walk away, but Ryan had said, "I'm sorry, Libby."

That had stopped her in her tracks. "Huh?"

"I'm sorry," he'd said again, and damn it if he hadn't looked sorry. "About what happened between us."

Libby had been so surprised that she couldn't quite grasp what he was apologizing *for.* "I have to go," she'd said, as if that weren't obvious, and she'd hurried away, that damn restraining order on her mind.

But since then, she'd wondered what he meant. Was he saying he'd made a mistake? Or did he tell Gwen about it that night, the two of them laughing at how she'd fled?

Libby was reminded of one snowy night early last winter, when she'd been in the kitchen where Gwen was now. She was making cinnamon rolls, and Alice was twirling around in her little dance shoes, telling some convoluted story of a princess. Libby remembered the way Ryan had looked at his daughter, and then at Libby. He'd said, "You are so good with them. God, I love you, Libby."

That was a year ago. One lousy *year*.

Sometimes, when Libby thought of Ryan, she had that same, disembodied, numb feeling she'd had the afternoon she'd taken a golf club to his truck. Sometimes, she feared that she was sinking into anger again, losing her objectivity.

The sound of her phone ringing startled her. She hurried back into the kitchen where she'd left it, vaulting over a dog, and grabbed it up from the counter. She smiled when she saw the display and answered it. "Hi, Alice. What are you doing?" she asked, and with the phone to her ear, began to tidy up while Alice talked about dance class.

# FIVE

A couple of sun-drenched days later, Libby drove into Pine River. Thankfully, she'd been very busy since the day she'd stopped at the soccer fields and hadn't had time to dwell on it. She'd mowed the lawn at the ranch with an ancient mower. She'd painted the gazebo, a much bigger job than she'd realized. But that had kept her mind on tasks that had to be done for the civil union ceremony of Austin and Gary, and today, she had things to do and people to see, not to mention lunch with her mother.

She had every intention of driving past the back entrance road into the subdivision where Ryan and Gwen lived. *Every* intention. But as she neared that road, she couldn't stop herself from turning in, from driving by Ryan's house. She never knew what she was looking for—some signal that there was trouble in paradise? That it wasn't perfect? Or was she looking for signs of perfection, of a happy family that didn't include her? Why did she even do that to herself?

That was a problem of late—she could never seem to stop herself from doing it.

Libby turned in and cruised around the winding streets up the hill to where the Spangler house sat, a sentry over the other, similar-looking Craftsman houses. When Libby lived here, she'd thought the house looked cozy and homey, but today, it didn't look so special. It was in need of paint, which Libby had mentioned to Ryan more than once. Max's Razor scooter was in the yard, just asking to be stolen. There was a bench beside the front door, shoes in various sizes piled next to it.

*Sloppy.*

The house had a big backyard that was perfect for the dog she'd let the kids get. It had a front porch and a bed of roses just below the porch railing. Two chimneys, one in the living room and one in the playroom, faced each other from either end of the house.

Libby had once loved this house.

She hated it now. It almost sickened her to look at it, the place where she'd once belonged, where she'd once put all her hope for a bright future with a big family. It was like looking at the worst car wreck—she couldn't turn away.

She rolled to a stop across the street from the house. Gwen's Subaru was in the drive, next to Ryan's truck. What was he doing home from work at ten in the morning? Sex? A shudder of revulsion ran down her spine. Ryan was always so horny in the morning. Gwen had probably strutted around in some shorty shorts and a cute, tight T-shirt with a funny saying, knowing that Ryan would pull her back into bed.

He used to do that to Libby. There was a time he couldn't keep his hands off of her, when he would tell her she was beautiful and he loved her. When had he stopped doing that?

She stared at the house.

She wouldn't be here now if he hadn't talked to her in the parking lot of Safeway. Libby debated going up to the door. But that would be truly crazy of her.

Or would it?

Maybe Ryan meant what he'd said, that he'd made a mistake. Maybe he wished he could take it all back. Maybe he needed an opportunity to grovel as he asked her to forgive him, which, of course, Libby would not do. At least she didn't think she would.

Better still, maybe Alice would come to the door.

Before she could decide, however, the garage door began to slide up. "*Shit*," she whispered, and tried to start her car, but as usual, the junker wouldn't turn over on the first attempt. As Ryan walked out onto the drive, she got it to catch and hit the gas. The damn thing puttered and spit before picking up enough speed for her to pull away from the curb. She sped down the quiet residential street with her heart pounding, ignoring the old woman walking her dog who shouted at her to slow down.

She turned recklessly onto the main road and headed into Pine River. She relaxed a little, but then happened to look in her rearview mirror. Ryan's truck had just turned onto the road and he was barreling after her.

With a squeal, Libby careened into the parking lot of a convenience store. She slid down in the seat as far as she could go hoping that Ryan would drive by. But the sound of his truck rumbled in behind her, and she winced. She grabbed her wallet, her mind whirling around what she'd say, how she'd explain sitting out front of his house.

She saw him in the side view mirror, walking up to her car. Her view was of his midsection, and she had the wild thought that he looked like he'd gained a little weight. Reconciliation with Gwen had given handsome Ryan Spangler a gut.

He tapped on her window and motioned impatiently for her to roll it down. Libby didn't roll the window down—she climbed over the console and popped out the passenger side, putting her little car between them—just in case—and looked at her ex-lover across the hood of her car. *Damn it*, why did she feel that old fluttering in her belly? It was infuriating—Ryan Spangler did not deserve even the slightest bit of fluttering.

He was frowning at her, his dark brown eyes full of irritation. He had a small scar across one brow, the result of a couch jump he didn't execute well when he was twelve, that turned red when he was angry. How many times had she touched that scar?

Ryan sighed. "What the hell was that, Libby?" he demanded. "Are you *stalking* me now?"

"What? *No!*" she said, as if that were preposterous instead of perhaps a bit true. "Get over yourself, Ryan."

"What if Gwen had seen you? Or the kids?" He groaned, removed his hat, and ran his palm over the crown of his blond hair. "Look, I'm really trying to do this right."

"Do *what* right?"

He looked at her, his gaze sliding over her like it used to. "Libby, I'm sorry," he said, and put his hand to his chest. "I am really *sorry*."

Her heart skipped; it was the grocery store parking lot all over again. It was an apology, a wistful look. But the first time, she'd run from it, concerned about the restraining order, afraid that it was really more rejection wrapped up in a pretty apology.

But there was something about Ryan's expression that made her step around the back of the car and move toward him, her eyes locked on his. She heard a car drive up behind her, but ignored it. "What are you trying to say, Ryan?" *Say it. Say you are a sleaze and you wronged me and I deserve* so *much better than you.*

"What am I saying? That I am sorry about everything." His gaze drifted to a point over her shoulder. "Glad you're here, Sam."

Libby's heart plummeted. She risked a look behind her; Sam was standing there, the door to his patrol truck still open. He arched a brow, silently questioning her.

Libby despised him in that moment—his timing was awful.

"Ryan?" Sam said, and his gaze shifted to Ryan. "Is everything okay here?" He asked it casually, strolling up to them as if they had all met here to have a drink. But he had one hand on the gun he wore on his belt. His hat, Libby noticed, was turned around, so that the bill was in back, and his hair was brushed back beneath it. He was wearing a departmental polo shirt tucked into jeans, the sun glinting off the badge he'd clipped to his pocket.

Ryan sighed wearily. "She's stalking my house," he said. He didn't sound particularly angry, just matter of fact. His eyes were soft, almost sad, and Libby realized the breath she was holding was actually a sigh of longing. There was something about his eyes that had always gotten to her. Good God, what was *wrong* with her? He, of all people, didn't deserve the slightest bit of longing from her. What he deserved was a good kick in the ass.

"That true, Libby?" Sam asked.

"No! I wasn't stalking you, Ryan," she said, unwilling to look at Sam, honestly uncertain if what she had done constituted stalking. Was driving by his house stalking? Or did stalking begin the moment she pulled over? At that moment, however, her heart was beating too fast for her to think clearly. "I was passing through. It's a shortcut, you know that."

Ryan gave her a look that said he knew the opposite was true.

Sam shifted to stand before her, which forced her to look at him. His hazel eyes, she noticed, did not look happy.

"You're supposed to stay three hundred yards away from me, Libby. We just had this reminder two days ago," Ryan said.

"I wasn't within three hundred yards of you two days ago," she pointed out. "And I can drive on any road I want to."

"But can she stop and stare at my house?" Ryan asked Sam.

"Ryan, for heaven's sake!" Libby protested. "I was driving by. Cutting through!"

His brown eyes narrowed. "I don't believe you."

She wasn't going to win, and Libby was on the verge of admitting it, her thoughts whirling around why she had driven by his house—surmising that wanting to see Ryan grovel would probably not fly with anyone here—when Sam said, "I think this time, it's true."

What did he just say? Libby jerked her gaze to Sam.

"She'd agreed to meet me here and she was probably running late."

"Meet you?" Ryan asked. "Why?"

Libby also wanted to hear that answer.

"Because she's helping me out with some less fortunate folk." Sam stared down at Libby, his gaze full of warning not to contradict him. "You know how she is, always willing to help others." He gave Ryan a pointed look.

Ryan looked a little flustered by that. "Well," he said uncertainly. He studied Libby a moment. And then, for the first time in months, he smiled at her. He propped his arms on the hood of her car and said, "Listen, Lib. I know this has been really hard for you. I get that, I do. Honest to God," he said, clamping a hand over his heart. "I wish things hadn't happened like they did. I'm sorry."

He said it again! Libby glanced at Sam to see if he'd heard it, too. She wanted to ask him why the sudden change of heart, if he'd told *Gwen* he was sorry for having left her.

"I mean, you were—you *are*—really special. I wish things had turned out differently, but, you know, I'm kind of stuck with the consequences now, aren't I?"

*Stuck?* What did he mean, stuck? Did he mean he was *stuck* with Gwen now? Was he really, truly *sorry*? And what exactly was she supposed to do with that? *No*—this wouldn't do. She wanted a grander apology. A marching band, balloons, expensive jewelry! *Prove it. Prove you're sorry.*

"So I'm asking you to please ease up for now. I don't like that we have this restraining order—"

"Me either!" she said with a gush of relief.

"But I need you to ease up."

"Ease up," she repeated, looking for clarification, and unthinkingly she started toward him again, but Sam clamped his hand around her wrist and held her where she was.

"All I'm saying is . . . let things settle," Ryan said. "These little run-ins we keep having are pretty hard on Gwen. And . . . and probably you, too. And me, to be honest. As a personal favor, I'm asking that you let things ride for a while. Will you do that for me?"

A personal favor? As if they were big buddies or something? Libby's pulse was racing so hard it was fluttering in her ears.

"Let's just take a step back, let the dust settle. Can you do that for me, Lib? Please?"

What possible answer could she give? *No, she would never let the dust settle? She would never ease up?* She wanted to punch him, to put her fist right in the middle of his flapping gums. But she said, "I guess."

His smile went deeper. "Great. *Thank* you. You don't know how much I appreciate it." He straightened up, gave the top of her car a couple of pats before he stepped away. "And, remember to pump the gas once or twice before you try and start the car," he reminded her, as if the last five months had never happened, as if he were aware of the trouble she'd been having with it. "Thanks, Sam. Again."

Sam didn't say anything. He just kept a firm grip on Libby's wrist.

Libby watched Ryan walk back to his truck, hitching up his Wranglers before he climbed in. He put the truck in gear and drove past her, giving her a wave out of his window before pulling onto the road.

Libby was too stunned to move. *I wish things hadn't happened like they did. I'm sorry.* Was he really apologizing for all of it? Of course he was; what else could he mean? *You are really special.* Did he still love her, is that what he was trying to say? *Let's just take a step back and let the dust settle.*

Let the dust settle! Into what? Where could that dust possibly settle?

Libby's thoughts were racing. Dr. Huber said that Libby's fantasy of Ryan telling her he'd made a horrible mistake, and that he loved her and wanted her back was only a fantasy, and perhaps an unrealistic one to hope for. That may very well be true, but Libby held on to that fantasy in the most private reaches of her heart. She just wanted Ryan to realize how stupid he'd been, how he'd lost the best thing that had ever happened to him. That was it, some acknowledgment that he was wrong. Beyond that, she only wanted to see the kids.

Ryan had treated her so badly. But she had loved him so, more than anything, and more importantly, she had loved Alice and Max with all her heart.

Could a man like Ryan truly recognize a mistake? Could he ever make it up to her? Could she ever forgive him, at least forget what he'd done, for the sake of Max and Alice? She didn't know, but she didn't mind his lame apology one bit. A small smile of vindication began to curve at the corners of her mouth.

She turned around, and collided with the hard wall of Sam. She'd completely forgotten him in the last few moments. She hadn't even noticed he was still holding her wrist.

He let go of it now, folded his arms, and stared down at her. "You want to tell me what that was all about?"

"Umm . . . no," she answered honestly. She didn't think it was a good idea to tell Sam anything about Ryan. But damn it, she couldn't keep the smile from her face. "No, I don't believe I do.

But thanks for . . . stopping by." She gave him a friendly pat on the upper arm, stepped around him, and walked into the store.

"Good morning!" she called to the woman behind the counter.

"Well good morning," the woman said, surprised by her cheerfulness.

Libby marched to the freezer section at the back of the store. She heard the tingle of a bell as the door opened again, but she continued to peruse the frozen cases, debating the idea of consuming ice cream before ten in the morning, particularly given her recent bit of weight gain from such practices.

But it was an extraordinary morning, and Libby picked up a pint of Rocky Road. And a pint of Neapolitan. And one of Caramel Crunch for a well-balanced breakfast. With the pints stuffed into the crook of her elbow, she stepped back and let the freezer door shut—and stared into the eyes of Sam Winters again.

"Let's try this again," he said congenially. "What were you doing up at Ryan's house?" He leaned his shoulder against the freezer door, as if he thought they were going to be here awhile, chatting it up like neighbors. He looked a little odd in such a casual pose—Sam was an imposing man with big shoulders and bigger arms. He probably intimidated a lot of people.

But he did not intimidate Libby. "Sam," she said, smiling, "I hope this doesn't come across as rude, but it's really none of your business. And yet, I'm going to tell you, because I know you will insist. I was using a shortcut to go to town. So . . ." She shrugged. "I guess I'll see you around." She started to move past him, then paused, stepped back, and said, "By the way, thanks for . . . you know, helping me," she said, referring to his telling Ryan that she was meeting him and running late. "See you." She walked on.

At the counter, she put her ice cream down and dug out a ten from her wallet. Her money situation was not great. She'd gotten a little bit of severance when she was given the "opportunity" to leave her job at the sheriff's office, which was a nice way of saying she was fired. She was lucky to have free room and board out at the ranch, and hoped that she might make enough off the events they held out there to live. So far, nothing could be further from the truth. It was bad enough that Madeline was paying for the utilities, but half the time, Libby didn't have money for groceries.

Lately, she'd been thinking she might have to sell her shitty car if things didn't turn around, and buying three pints of ice cream was definitely not high on her priority list.

"Caramel Crunch!" the woman said. "That's my favorite. Must be that time of the month," she said with a wink.

"Do you have a spoon?" Libby asked.

The woman's brows waggled up to her hairline. "Girl needs a fix. Over there, sweetie, next to the pickles and hot dogs."

Libby swept by the condiment stand, grabbed a handful of spoons, and walked outside. And who should be perched against the hood of her car, his ankles crossed, his arms still folded? Sam Winters. This guy was like a Whac-a-Mole game—he kept popping up.

"We're going to have this conversation if you like it or not," he said before she could speak. "So don't try and brush me off again. And be nice when you answer me. What were you doing in the Vista Ridge subdivision this morning?"

"You're tenacious, I'll give you that," she said. "But did I miss a constitutional amendment memo? It's still a free country, right?"

"I said be nice. Didn't we review the concept of *free* for you just a couple of days ago?" he asked, making a little swirling motion in her direction.

"Yes." Libby sat down on the curb, reached for the first ice cream in her bag in preparation for The Talk. Rocky Road—that would do. She pulled the top off the carton and stuck her spoon into it.

"Why were you driving by Ryan's place after we had chat number . . . what was it, three, four?"

"Four," she said. If there was one thing that could be said for ol' Buttinsky, it was that he possessed a pair of gorgeous hazel eyes. They seemed to pierce holes in Libby every time he looked at her. She always had an uncomfortable squirmy feeling that he was seeing more than she intended to show. "And in answer to your question, *yes,* I was driving by his house," she said, and stuck a spoonful of ice cream into her mouth.

Sam sighed. He looked up at the sky a moment, as if he was carefully considering his response. Or trying to keep from blowing his cool. "Girl, you're just begging for trouble, aren't you?"

"No. No, I am not begging for trouble," she said thoughtfully through a mouthful of ice cream. She swallowed. "I don't expect you to understand this, but some things are beyond my ability to control." She glanced up. "I don't mean in a baseball bat kind of way. I mean, in general."

"What, driving by Ryan Spangler's house when there is a restraining order against you is beyond your ability to control? Because that's a fast-lane ticket to jail."

"No, not that," she said, shaking her head a little, then pausing to push unruly curls back from her face with the back of her hand. "I could control that if I wanted to. But I *don't* want to. I want to drive by and see what's going on, and *that's* the thing I can't control." Anger management issues, her mother had said. Dr. Huber was a little more sophisticated in her diagnosis. She'd said Libby had suffered from Brief Reactive Psychosis, and it was nothing a little psychotherapy, antidepressants, and the development of coping mechanisms wouldn't cure. So far, eating was the only coping mechanism Libby had managed to ace. She wasn't in therapy—that cost money, and that was something she didn't have a lot of. But her mother had paid for the medicine, and she was taking that religiously.

In spite of the meds she was taking, Libby was not feeling zen, she was feeling strangely giddy in that moment, her mind swimming with Ryan's apology. That meant she had *not* manufactured their relationship or their love. After beating herself up for so long for being so stupid, that realization alone made her want to do cartwheels.

She wondered if she could still do cartwheels and stuffed another big helping of ice cream into her mouth. Sam was studying her, almost as if he was waiting for her to say more.

When she didn't, Sam pushed away from her car, stepped off the curb, and sat beside her. There was a lot of warmth in his eyes. Libby had noticed that before, on the day she'd gone off on Ryan's truck. Sam had not looked afraid of her, like Sarah Drew, who clutched her purse to her breast, staring in horror. Sam had looked as if he understood. She could remember feeling comforted somehow that it was him who took the club, as if he was one person in the midst of the chaos who was there to help her, not hurt her. She remembered feeling grateful to him—for stopping her, for being there, for protecting her.

He smiled a little now, and his eyes crinkled in the corners. Libby felt a tiny little wave of electricity go through her that she found both disturbing and exciting.

She handed him a spoon and her bag of ice cream.

Sam looked into the shopping bag. He took out the Caramel Crunch. "We can talk about your lack of control a little more while we take a drive," he remarked as he popped the lid off the container.

That brought Libby's head up. "Take what drive?"

"The drive I told Ryan we were going to take," he said, digging his spoon into the ice cream. "You know, to help out the less fortunate."

Libby laughed. "Good one."

Sam did not laugh. He turned those eyes on her again, and Libby felt the heat behind them sidle down through her spine. "I just lied to keep you out of trouble. So we're going to turn it into a half lie, you and me. And by the way, don't expect me to ever lie for you again."

"No. No, no," she said contritely. She glanced at her watch. She had two hours before she had to be anywhere. "I've got some things I have to do today," she pointed out.

"Like what? Drive by Ryan's house again? What about his work? Maybe you should drive by there, too. Go in and say hi. Oh, and while you're at it, maybe stop in at the school and see what the kids are up to."

"Not funny," she said.

"I didn't intend it to be."

Libby groaned, took another generous bite of ice cream. "I am not driving by his *work,* Sam. It's not like I'm a professional stalker here."

"You sure about that?"

"Yes!" Libby was not going to let him drag her down. She was feeling buoyant for the first time in weeks. "What is the purpose of this drive, again? So you can explain the concept of freedom to me again?"

"I will if you need it. But if you will promise not to get mouthy or go where you're not supposed to go, I promise not to bring up the R.O."

Oh, how Libby hated that term. It sounded so . . . *criminal.* "How kind of you, officer." She spooned more ice cream. "Where are we going?"

"Like I said—to see about some less fortunate people. It might do you some good to see that there are others out there with bigger problems than you."

Libby snorted. "I know. I volunteered at every charity in town, remember?"

"Yes, I do. Why don't you start volunteering again? It might help you keep your mind off those things that are beyond your control. Why'd you quit Meals On Wheels?" he asked.

She suddenly remembered one cold afternoon more than a year ago when Sam had brought a truckload of potatoes to the Meals On Wheels kitchen. He'd gone down to Gunnison to get them from a farmer there. Libby just happened to be working that afternoon and had been happy to see him, because the two old men sorting through the food donations were as humorless as that gray afternoon.

Sam had teased Libby as he'd tossed the potatoes to her, scoring her efforts to get them into storage boxes before he tossed another. It had been a really nice afternoon.

Libby looked down at her ice cream, embarrassed. "Gas," she said. "I'm a little low on funds."

"Well, come on. We're going to go see an old acquaintance."

"Who?"

He winked. "You'll see. And the other one is a mechanic," Sam said. "I bet he could help you with your car."

That certainly caught her interest. Libby looked at her junk car—she needed more than help, she needed a new car and the money to buy it. "Is he cheap?"

"I'd bet so. He could use the work, too."

Libby shifted her gaze to Sam, prepared to give him a vague answer. He wasn't smiling, exactly, but looking at her in a way that made her stomach do that strange little fluttery-buttery flip again. Before she could figure out what the look was, Sam stood up.

"Come on, it will be good for you," he said. "You can take some notes about how law-abiding citizens live."

"Can I bring my ice cream?" she asked, and extended her hand for him to help her up.

Sam pulled her up, and she landed so close that she could see how clean-shaven he was, and how square his chin was, and how his hair was not really brown, but more coffee-colored. When she stood this close, she didn't see the badge at all.

His gaze slipped to her mouth for a splintered moment, but long enough for her to feel that woozy electric charge run through her again. He said, "You can bring anything but a golf club."

A corner of her mouth turned up in a half smile. "You're just a laugh riot today, Deputy Dog. Give me back my Caramel Crunch."

Sam smiled and handed her the container, then opened the door to his Dodge Ram patrol truck for her.

# SIX

On the way out of town, they drove past the old county coliseum where the Rotary Club held the annual Halloween Carnival. About a year ago, Sam had ended up working the carnival, filling in for his old friend Dirk, a fellow deputy. Dirk was the only one of Sam's acquaintances prior to rehab with whom he'd kept in touch. Sam was embarrassed by what had happened for one thing—the upward trajectory of his career at the sheriff's office had ended in flames—and besides, he'd always made sure to buddy up to the guys who drank too much. Dirk wasn't much of a drinker, and as far as Sam knew, he didn't judge Sam for being a recovering alcoholic.

Dirk had signed on to work off-duty at the carnival to make a little extra money, but the afternoon of Halloween, his sister had gone in for an emergency appendectomy in Montrose.

Sam had been happy to step in for Dirk. He'd had nothing better to do, and he liked seeing the little kids in their Halloween costumes. All he had to do was keep watch, make sure no one got out of hand, and if they did, play bouncer.

For kids who lived up in the mountains, who didn't have subdivisions to trick or treat in, the carnival was the best candy haul around. And because that was true for the children, the carnival had evolved—now it offered something for everyone: games and candy for children, petting zoos, and a best-costume contest. For the adults, there was beer, dancing, and carnival food.

For most of the evening, Sam had stood around watching children in store-bought and homemade costumes fill buckets shaped like pumpkins with candy. He could remember watching families and thinking how he'd always imagined taking his own kids trick or treating. He'd always wanted a big, close family—the opposite of what he'd had growing up. He and his sister had lived with his mother after his parents' divorce. He rarely saw his father, and what he remembered of him was that he always had a drink in his hand.

Sam had lived like most middle-class kids. He'd had his own Batman costume. He'd played sports, as many as he could. He'd turned into an adolescent, when every waking moment had been filled with thoughts of girls. He'd gone to college, gotten married, let alcohol get the best of him . . .

But one of Sam's fondest childhood memories was his friendship with Brian Campinelli. Brian had four brothers and two sisters. The Campinelli house was always loud, always a mess, and always fun. Brian's mother was always hugging and kissing her children, even if they didn't want it. She would even wrap Sam in her thick arms and hug him tight. He felt wanted in that house.

Sam had envied the chaos and the affection in the Campinelli house. It made him want that very thing for himself when he grew up—a big, rambunctious family, and every member assured of how much they were loved. But given that he was practically starting over with his life, he didn't think that was in the cards any longer.

Libby leaned over to check the speedometer. "You drive like a grandpa."

"I drive safely. You could use some tips in that department."

Libby snorted. "You know where your driving tips are on my list of things to care about? Way down here," she said, fluttering her fingers down to the floor. She smiled at her joke and began to scrape the sides of the Rocky Road container of ice cream.

"Are you going to polish off the other two pints?" he asked, amused.

"Maybe." She paused, her spoon filled with melting ice cream. "Do you know how much weight I've gained in the last five months? Ten pounds. *Ten* pounds! And five of those since Mountain View! I thought nervous breakdowns meant you didn't eat. Well, it's quite the opposite," she said, waving her plastic spoon around. She filled her mouth with the last bite of Rocky Road ice cream. "I have to stop."

Sam didn't think she needed to stop anything. He thought she looked good with a few curves on her.

He remembered the way she'd looked the night at the carnival, dressed as a scarecrow. She'd painted her face, big black rings around her eyes, a red dot on her nose, pink cheeks. She had straw coming out of the waist of her baggy pants, and sticking out her arms and legs, and from beneath the brim of her wide hat. Naturally, she'd had Alice and Max in tow—Sam rarely saw her without those two. Max was dressed as Buzz Lightyear, and little Alice was a ballerina.

He'd first spotted them at the kid's spinning wheel. Alice spun the wheel, and it landed on an image of a piece of candy in a wrapper. Libby leapt into the air with a cheer. Little Max, his face tipped up to Libby's, mimicked her.

They'd spun the wheel a couple more times, Libby celebrating with each draw. When the kids had their candy, she pointed to the petting zoo and started the children in that direction. As they walked past Sam, Libby said, “Great costume, Deputy Dog. You must have worked on that for days.”

He glanced down at his street clothes. “Hey, it takes a lot of creative talent to pull off the off-duty deputy look.”

Libby had tossed her head back with a gay laugh. “Then you should be proud, because that is *exactly* what you look like.” He recalled how she’d given him a fluttering finger wave as she led the kids away. Same as she’d given him a couple of nights ago out at the ranch when she’d wanted him to leave.

“I think Rocky Road is my favorite,” she announced now, peering into the empty container. “What’s yours?”

“I guess I’m a plain-chocolate kind of guy.”

Libby snorted. “Why does that not surprise me?” She tossed the empty Rocky Road container into the bag.

Sam wondered if she remembered that night at the carnival. If she remembered Jim Burton, or what she’d done. He would never forget it. He’d been watching an old couple two-step around the room, their steps so familiar to one another that they looked in opposite directions, seemingly lost in the rhythm of a lifetime together. He was so entranced by them that he didn’t notice Jim Burton or the beers he was holding until he was standing right next to him. “Hey, Sam, you call this working?” he’d asked jovially. “How about a beer?”

“Better not,” he’d said. Looking back on it, Sam didn’t think he’d felt that panic he’d felt fresh out of rehab when someone offered him a drink. He just remembered feeling uncomfortable. Annoyed.

“These Rotary boys won’t care if you have a beer. It’s a party, man!” Jim had held out the beer to Sam, swaying a little as he did.

Sam had put his hand on Jim’s shoulder, looked him in the eye. “No thanks, Jim. I’m good.”

"Good! You can't be good if you're dry. Come on, what's one beer?"

One beer was the difference between life and death to Sam. That was a hard thing to explain to most people, much less a drunk one.

"Don't be a wet rag," Jim had persisted, and he pressed the beer against Sam's chest.

Libby had come to his rescue. She'd suddenly appeared from behind Jim, and with her arms raised, she'd shouted, "*Boo!*"

Jim had jumped. "Shit, Libby, I didn't see you," he'd said, holding a beer over his heart now.

She'd smiled and handed Sam a bottle of water. The bottle wasn't completely full. "Here you go, Sam. Sorry it took me so long."

He hadn't asked her for a bottle of water. He'd guessed it was hers and she was intervening between him and Jim's beers.

"How are you, Jim?" she asked, shifting, so that she was standing a little in front of Sam.

"Hey, Libby." Jim shifted his gaze to the dance floor and drank from one of the beers.

"Are you dancing?" she'd asked brightly, and did a funny little swing of her hips. "Let's go dance the 'Monster Mash.' It's a graveyard smash." Sam remembered the sound of her laugh, light and easy.

"Ah, no thanks. I'm not much of a dancer."

"Really? What about you, Sam?"

"I'm working," he'd said.

"You can have a little fun, can't you?"

"That's what *I* was saying," Jim had said, clearly disgruntled, judging by the sour look he'd given Sam.

Another, very clear memory rushed back at him, and Sam glanced out the truck window. The only fun he'd been able to think about at the time was off limits—because it had involved Libby, and she was Ryan Spangler's girlfriend.

"Can't you dance?" Libby had asked.

He'd given her an apologetic smile and said, "I have two left feet."

"Great. That makes two of us. Do you mind if I drag him to the dance floor, Jim?"

"Better him than me," Jim had said, and took a good long swig of his beer.

Libby had grabbed Sam's hand and had tugged him out to the dance floor just as "Monster Mash" came to an end. Another tune, a bluesy song, was next up on the disc jockey's playlist. Sam had recognized the classic "Ghost Song," from The Doors. It was one he could handle, and he'd taken Libby's hand and swung her around, then twirled her back into him.

If he asked her now, would she remember him asking if she'd really wanted to dance, or if she'd been saving him from Jim and his beers? Would she remember the way they'd sort of twirled around, and how she'd swayed her hips and dipped down, her eyes sparkling through the black scarecrow circles?

Would she remember how, toward the end of the song, he swung her out a little too hard, and she'd stumbled, twirling back into him, right into his chest with an *oof,* and had said, "What finesse we have!"

Would she remember the spark between them at that moment? Or had he imagined it? Had her eyes really glittered with something more than laughter, or had he just wished it was so?

He had gazed down at her, and Libby's radiant smile had begun to fade, and she'd said, "Sam, I—"

He would never know what she meant to say, because that was the moment Ryan appeared.

"Hey, there you are," he'd said.

"Hey!" she'd said to Ryan, and did a little dip.

Sam had let go of her hand. The radiance had returned to her smile now that she was looking at Ryan. Everyone in the damn coliseum could see it.

"Here you go," Sam had said, and had handed her off to Ryan.

"Thanks for dancing with me, Sam!" Libby had called after him, just before Ryan swung her around and away.

Sam had walked off the dance floor that night, back into the shadows. He'd watched Ryan and Libby dance, watched Ryan dip her, then kiss her. Libby had had to grab her scarecrow hat to keep it from falling. They had looked like they were in love.

Which was why he couldn't grasp what Ryan was doing with the other woman when he saw him later. A woman whose face Sam could not see because she was standing so close to Ryan. But he could see Ryan's hand, and it was on the woman's hip.

He didn't get how someone could look so adoringly at Libby, then grope another woman in the shadows.

"Where'd you go?" Libby asked curiously, drawing him back to the present. "You're too quiet."

Sam shifted his gaze to her. She looked the same as she had that night. But nothing was the same for her. "I was thinking that you need to stop doing drive-bys of Ryan's house. That's what I expect of sixteen-year-old girls, not grown women."

Her cheeks pinkened a little at that admonishment. "Actually, me too," she admitted. "But come on, Sam. Have you never been curious to know what someone was up to and maybe happened to drive by their house?"

"No," he said flatly.

"It's called seeking closure."

"In your case, it's called seeking a night in jail."

"Spoilsport," she muttered.

He decided to change the subject—he didn't want every conversation with her to be about Spangler, even if it was his job. Just the man's name aggravated him for reasons Sam was unwilling to examine at that moment. If ever.

"So . . . what's going on up at Homecoming Ranch?" he asked. "Got some events lined up?"

"A wedding," she said. "Well, technically, a civil union. But with wind chimes and candles and dogs, so in my book, it's a wedding."

"Dogs?"

"Yep. The groom and the groom wanted to include their yappy little dogs in the ceremony." She gave him a playful roll of her eyes. "I don't even think it was their idea. I think it was one of the grooms' mother's idea. We convinced them that little dogs could be carried off by hawks." She laughed, and the sound of it surprised Sam a little. He hadn't heard it in a while. He liked it a lot—it was pleasant and light. Girlish. Happy. He missed it.

"You should meet Martha," she said. "Gary wanted to have the ceremony up in a clearing near the waterfall. You know the Sapphire Waterfall?"

Sam knew it. It was about a quarter of a mile from the house on Homecoming Ranch, and a pretty steep walk up an old logging road and some hiking trails. "That doesn't seem very convenient."

"Exactly!" Libby exclaimed, casting her hand and the spoon she held wide. "I told him that the weather is a little unpredictable this time of year, and what if it snowed or rained? It would ruin the whole waterfall experience. Not to mention, how do you get a bunch of women in four-inch heels up a trail?"

Sam had no idea, but he wouldn't mind seeing that. "So what's your idea?" he asked.

"The barn," she said confidently. "Madeline and I are going to open both ends and hang lanterns inside and make it look very rustic and chic." She ate another spoonful of the Caramel Crunch. "We looked it up. It's kind of a thing right now," she said, making invisible quotes with one hand. "We saw pictures in a magazine."

Sam wasn't a wedding kind of guy, and he had a hard time picturing it. "I've never seen a chic barn."

Libby laughed. "Neither have we, except in a magazine. Gary's mother isn't convinced either, so wish us luck."

She flashed a knock-your-socks-off sparkly smile, and Sam had to force himself to look at the road. But he could still feel it lighting up the interior of his truck and trickling through him.

"So what comes after the chic barn wedding?"

"That is a good question. We're going to have to drum up some business." She peered into her ice cream container and scraped the side of it with her spoon. "Actually, I have an appointment with the bank today. I'm going to talk to them about the possibility of a loan."

Sam thought that was encouraging news. Maybe she was thinking forward at last, looking ahead from her split with Ryan. "Good to hear you're thinking long-term," he said.

She snorted. "What I'm thinking is that we need money *now*."

"So are you borrowing against the ranch? Or do you have a way to pay it back?"

"The only way we can pay it back is with some business. But I have some ideas. I'm going to do some advertising around town and online with ads on wedding sites."

"Do you think you'll get a lot of events from people in Pine River?" He tried to imagine how many rustic weddings were going to happen in a town of roughly twenty thousand.

"That's the plan, so I hope so!" Libby said laughingly.

"And if you can't book more events? Then what?"

Libby shook her head. "I haven't gotten that far. But I am going to make it work. I'm determined."

Sam hoped for her sake that she could make it work. He thought about saying more, but it wasn't his place to guide her. He was a deputy sheriff, for God's sake, not a career counselor. Still, it seemed to him that Homecoming Ranch was too far out, too remote to ever become a profitable wedding venue. Who would go all the way out there?

His silence apparently made Libby anxious. "What?" she asked him.

Sam drummed his fingers against the steering wheel.

"*What?*" she said again.

He glanced at her, sizing her up. "You want the truth?"

"Like you'd tell me anything less?" She laughed. "Go ahead, I can take it." His hesitation made her brows sink into a frown. "Don't tell me you are worried I *can't* take it. Let me put your mind at ease—this is very different from finding out how your perfect little world came tumbling down. Trust me, I am not going to overreact."

"I didn't say anything," he protested.

Libby rolled her eyes. "You don't have to say anything. No one in this town has to say anything, because everyone looks at me the same way since my meltdown. Come on, tell me what your problem is," she prodded him.

She was right, he was making assumptions. He said, "I think the event destination thing is going to be a hard sale."

"I know. You're not telling me anything I haven't thought to death already. But it's all I have, Sam. And honestly? I'm a little desperate these days. I've got a car that's about to tank and no money for another one. The ranch is pretty self-sufficient but there are bills. Do you have any idea how much it costs to fill a propane tank?"

"Yes, I do. Have you thought about getting a job?"

She laughed. "Of *course* I have. But I want to make Homecoming Ranch work. It was handed to me on a silver platter. I *need* it to work."

Sam thought he understood her. He certainly understood how sometimes, the only thing a person needed was for something just to *work.* "All I'm suggesting is to keep gainful employment in mind," he said.

"Duly noted. And by the way, you suggest a *lot,*" she said, and closed up her pint of ice cream and returned it to the sack. "I'm curious, are you like this with your girlfriend? Or do you reserve all your suggestions for scofflaws?"

"Exclusively for the scofflaws."

Her brows rose and she laughed with surprise. "How do you have so much time to drive around and poke your nose in other people's business anyway?"

"That's my job, remember?" he responded congenially as he pulled off the main road onto a bumpy dirt road.

"That's debatable, and you're avoiding the issue. How old are you, like forty?"

"Hey!" he said with a startled laugh. "I'm thirty-four."

"Okay, thirty-four. Most men your age are looking for someone to do their laundry."

"Wow," he said, smiling curiously at her. "That's an *awfully* jaded viewpoint."

"Do you blame me?" she asked with a slight shrug.

"You're not going to use the I-was-hurt-and-therefore-I-am-down-on-guys excuse, are you?"

"No. But that's a good one," she said, nodding thoughtfully. "Maybe I'll use it from now on. So?" she asked, settling back into her seat. "Girlfriend?"

"And you're nosy, to boot," he said. "I'm not exactly living in a hotbed of dating activity up here, you know."

"The lack of a good dating scene didn't stop Arnie Schmidt. He just ordered a bride right out of Russia. You should ask for the catalogue. If you want, I'll help you pick."

Sam laughed roundly at that. "Thanks . . . but you'd be the last person I would ask for an assist."

"I am an excellent judge of potential wives!" she protested. "Ask Luke Kendrick!" She was now filled with the sort of enthusiasm he used to see in her, all shiny and bright-eyed with a man-appealing twinkle.

"You didn't put Luke and Madeline together," he said, calling her on that. From what he knew, they'd been adversaries—Luke wanting the time to buy back his family's ranch, which his father had sold, and Madeline eager to sell it as quickly as possible.

"That is a matter of interpretation," Libby said smartly. "If I hadn't been so focused on the ranch and putting my fist through Ryan's face, they wouldn't have had so much time together."

That wasn't entirely true, but it was true that Libby had put all her energy into the ranch. Sam knew what it was like to be in Libby's shoes. He knew what it was to seek that thing that would keep you from corroding from the inside out. He also understood how hard it was to look in the faces of people he'd known for many years, knowing that they understood how far he'd fallen.

They crossed a cattle guard, and the truck bounced up the pitted road until they reached Millie Bagley's run-down bit of metal and stone house. The roof had been repaired so many times it looked like a patchwork quilt. The house sat unevenly, too, and looked as if it was sinking on the right. As they drove up, a dozen or more rail-thin cats, lounging on the porch and under the porch steps, scattered.

"Ohmigod!" Libby said, sitting up to peer out as a number of cats scurried away. "What is this, a meth lab?"

"Do you really think I'd take you out for a leisurely drive to a meth lab? This is Millie Bagley's place. You remember her."

"Millie Bagley!" Libby squinted out the front window. "Boy, do I ever remember her. She was on my route when I did Meals On Wheels. I didn't know she'd moved out here. Probably better for all involved, because that woman is as mean as a snake."

Sam couldn't help but laugh, because that was absolutely right. "I figured you hadn't forgotten her. And believe me, time has not mellowed her, so don't take anything personally," he advised, and opened the door.

"Wait!" Libby said, but Sam had already exited the truck.

Millie Bagley had lived in and around Pine River all of her life. She'd buried her parents, her brother, and, a couple of years ago, her husband. She had a daughter, too, somewhere—Sam thought Salt Lake City, but he wasn't certain. She'd moved out here a few months ago to her family's old homestead. It had probably been a fairly decent ranch at one point, but now it was nothing more than the old house on rocky ground, a shotgun, and an army of cats that looked to have grown by a dozen more every time he came around.

Millie viewed everyone as suspect. When a census taker had appeared last spring, she'd fired a warning shot in the air through her window, convinced the poor man was a government agent come to take her house away from her.

Sam noticed the shotgun propped up against a sagging porch railing and stopped short of the steps. Sam didn't much like checking on her, but he had a conscience, and he was painfully aware that Millie Bagley didn't have anyone to look after her. Neither did Tony D'Angelo, the Afghanistan-war veteran who lived in the old Baker house down in Elk Valley.

"Ms. Bagley, are you in there? It's Deputy Winters."

He heard some banging around inside the small house, and a moment later, Millie emerged in a filthy housecoat and tennis shoes. Her gray hair was clipped up behind her head in one of those plastic claws Sam saw on young women, and her skin had a greenish cast to it. A few of the cats hopped up on the porch and began to wind around her legs, meowing for food.

"Morning, Ms. Bagley."

"Who is *that?*" she said, eyeing Libby, who reluctantly had come out of the truck.

"It's me, Ms. Bagley—Libby Tyler. Remember me?"

"Libby Tyler!" she said. "Why'd you bring her up here?" she asked of Sam as she took Libby in from the top of her curls to the canvas sneakers she was wearing.

"She's helping me today. I brought you a few things."

Millie's gaze shifted back to Sam. "I don't need nothing, I told you I don't. I told you to stay off my property. What'd you bring?"

He hadn't brought much: canned beans, bread, and the like. "I thought maybe you and the cats were hungry, so I brought out a few groceries. I'm going to get it out of the truck. And while I'm getting the things, I want you to promise me you're not going anywhere near that shotgun."

"I got a right to bear arms," she said defensively.

"But you don't have a right to wave it at a law enforcement officer." Libby, he noticed, had inched much closer to him. He could have reached out and put his arm around her.

Millie flicked her wrist at him. "*Ack,* you're always talking. And I don't need your goddamn charity."

"Well, I'm going to leave a few things all the same. If you don't want them, you can pass them on. Libby, will you help me?" He turned to look at Libby, but she was already scurrying for the back of the truck.

"You ain't nothing but a two-bit sheriff's officer out here in the middle of nowhere cuz no one else will take you!" Millie snapped.

Whether Millie knew that for a fact or had somehow managed to blindly hit a nerve, the truth in her accusation stung Sam. Because he'd once been more than a two-bit deputy. And now, the only post he could get was this one.

He opened the gate of his truck and handed a bag of cat food to Libby.

"Told you. Mean as a snake," Libby whispered.

He picked up the box of canned goods and walked around the truck, Libby just behind him.

"I didn't ask you to bring me *nothing,*" Millie continued to complain, her gaze locked on the food.

Sam put the box down on the bottom porch step, and Libby put the bag of cat food beside it. A few of the cats rose up, stretching long before wandering over to sniff the bag.

"And don't think you can bring that crazy bitch girlfriend of yours around me," Millie added for good measure, gesturing to Libby.

Libby gasped. "I'm *not* his girlfriend. And I'm not crazy!"

"Then what the hell are you doing up here with him?"

"I told you, Ms. Bagley, she's a friend," Sam said calmly. "Now look, you know winter's coming. If you like, I could come out and chop some wood for you and make sure you don't have any cracks that will let the wind in," he suggested.

"Maybe *you're* the crazy one," Libby whispered.

"I don't want you coming out here! Next time you come, I'll just shoot you and your tramp. How many times do I got to tell you, you ain't welcome on my property?"

The cats were beginning to circle around Sam and Libby, their tails high, rubbing against his leg. Sam had seen a lot in his time, but if there was one thing that gave him the creeps, it was these cats. "I was just offering," he said. "Have a good day, Ms. Bagley. I'll be back to check on you in a couple of weeks."

"Don't come back!" She reached down to pick up a cat. "You come out here again and, by God, I *will* shoot you! I do all right on my own!"

Sam put his hand to Libby's waist, nudging her toward his truck.

"Good-bye, Ms. Bagley," Libby said.

"Oh for shit's sake, girl, just go on," Millie said disdainfully, and dropped her cat, bending over to pick up the box of canned goods. "I don't want your type anywhere near me. They should have kept you locked up if you ask me. No telling when you'll go off again."

Libby halted and turned back to Millie Bagley.

"Come on, Libby," Sam said. "Don't give her the satisfaction."

But Libby didn't move.

"What?" Millie demanded. "You got something to say, Libby? I always knew you was a loon. I'm just glad they got you before you did any more harm. You keep taking your medicine now."

"I'm curious, Ms. Bagley. Did you think I was a loon before or after I delivered your meals twice a week? Because I don't remember you thinking there was anything wrong with me then."

"Come on," Sam said, and took her by the elbow, forcing her to walk as Millie cursed at her from the porch.

He opened the door of his truck and helped her inside, then walked around to the front, giving Ms. Bagley a cold look as he did. Not that it mattered—she had her food and was cooing to one of her cats now.

Libby was already buckled in before Sam could get into the truck. He turned the ignition and headed down the pitted drive.

When they had cleared the house and were on the paved road again, he pulled over and looked at Libby. "I'm sorry about that," he said. "I had no idea she knew about you other than from Meals On Wheels."

Libby responded with a flick of her wrist. "Don't worry about it."

"Libby, I—"

"No, really," she said. "Do you think I don't know what people say about me, Sam? I have lived in Pine River all my life. I know all these people, and I know how they talk. I know what they think of people who have nervous breakdowns, and it's not good. Half the people in that town think there's no burden you shouldn't be able to bear, that what doesn't kill you should make you stronger, and that God never ever hands us more than we can handle. They have no use for people like me, and I know it. The only difference between everyone else and Ms. Bagley is that she has the guts to say it to my face. So . . . it's okay."

Sam was in no position to argue with Libby, because she was right. Like her, he knew how talk circulated in this town. How someone could smile and ask about you, and offer to help in some way, but then sit at the bar an hour later repeating what they'd heard, how you looked, inventing signs of trouble.

Libby smiled a little. "But she really *is* one crazy old bat."

Sam chuckled. "I won't argue with that. But she's had her share of problems. Sometimes, life has a way of making people hard."

Which is what he feared would happen to Libby if she didn't get some ballast into her life.

"Are you taking me back to my car now?" Libby asked. "I've done my penance, haven't I?"

"Nope. Got one more while we're out this way," he said. "Tony's a little more laid back than Millie." Then again, entire militant nations were more laid back than Millie. The truth was that Tony was a walking, ticking time bomb of self-destruction. But Sam still held out hope for him.

"Hopefully someone who is just a little more receptive to me, if you please. Is it just me, or is something else going on here today?" Libby asked. "I have this funny feeling that you're trying to tell me something."

There *was* something else going on here, but Sam couldn't say what it was as he took in the spill of curls framing her face, the eyes intent on him, her very lush, pursed mouth. If he said it, he'd have to face it, and it was best just to let some things lie deep and still. "When did you get so paranoid?" he asked casually. "I'm just trying to keep you out of trouble, one day at a time."

"Hmm," Libby said, her gaze still zeroed in on him. "I don't trust you, Sam Winters. Not one bit."

He laughed and said with a wink, "The feeling is entirely mutual, Libby Tyler."

# SEVEN

Libby wouldn't admit it to Sam, but she'd forgotten just how mean Millie Bagley could be. Libby had been shocked by Millie's in-your-face reminder of her collapse.

But not as shocked as Sam, judging by his appalled expression.

She looked curiously at Sam as he pulled the truck out onto the main road and headed in the opposite direction of Pine River. Why did he care so much, anyway? About Millie, about this Tony guy, and most of all, about her? He didn't have to care, he didn't have to do anything but enforce the law. So why didn't he do just that instead of driving around with a bunch of groceries in his car?

Even though she had been called a Good Samaritan from time to time, she was suspicious of them. At least she knew why *she* did it. It made her feel like her life had meaning. Is that why Sam did it? She couldn't imagine going to see Millie Bagley on a regular basis, much less taking groceries to that old bag of bones. She *could* imagine being doubly sure to never drive down Millie's road, and if she did, to do it in an armored vehicle.

Sam was squinting at the road ahead of them beneath his Ray-Bans. He didn't have classic good looks, no, but he was handsome in a rugged way. He was a big man, but trim, with a lot of muscles everywhere. He looked rugged, like someone you would easily believe lived by himself on the side of a mountain and drove a big truck over bigger rocks, just like in the truck commercials. She remembered the first time she'd met him, back when they both worked out of Corita City. He came to work with an infectious smile and always seemed eager to get to work. She never would have guessed at the trouble brewing inside him. Looks were deceiving that way—they masked the history in everyone. No one knew what trouble had been lurking inside her, either.

Least of all, her.

If there was one thing about Sam that Libby would have found knee-bendingly attractive, it was his eyes. She had never seen eyes like that on a man, the color of them reminiscent of an Irish sea. Or, at least what she imagined an Irish sea to look like. They were knowing eyes, too—Sam had a way of looking at her that made her feel he could see *in* her, knew what she was on the inside, knew the thoughts that went through her mind.

He must have felt her looking at him, because he glanced at her as he propped his fist against the wheel. "Something wrong?"

"You're a nice guy. A do-gooder."

He looked surprised and smiled a little. "Is there something wrong with that?"

"No," she said. "Someone has to be the good guy. Is it really part of your job to go and see Millie Bagley?"

He shrugged. "I guess it depends on your interpretation. I like to think it falls within the guidelines for community policing. I'm just trying to head off a problem before it happens."

Too late for that, Libby thought. "So . . . how many people do you check on?"

"Ah . . . just a few," he said vaguely, shifting his gaze out the window. "We're going to see Tony next."

A few miles up, he turned off the main road onto a little two-lane county road, which Libby knew led into Elk Valley. She saw Tony's place on the side of the hill long before they reached it—it was a double-wide trailer perched up on a narrow patch of land. A clutter of car parts, lawn chairs, and a grill filled the small lawn below the decking attached to the house.

As they drove up the drive, a slight man emerged from the trailer and walked unevenly out onto the deck. He lazily lifted one hand as Sam pulled the truck into the trip of leveling before the house. Sam opened his truck door, and it knocked against one of the decking posts. "Watch your step getting out," he said to Libby.

When she opened her door, she saw the reason for his caution—she had about a foot of caliche-covered drive before a drop-off into steep terrain. She walked carefully around the back of the truck and smiled hesitantly at the man on the porch decking. He was young, probably no older than Libby's twenty-six years, but somehow, he also managed to look twice as old as she was. He had pale blue eyes that he fixed on Libby. His eyes looked sad. Deeply sad.

He nodded to her and moved toward them in an uneven gait. When he reached the steps, Libby saw why—he had a prosthetic limb from the knee down, visible because he had cut the leg from his camouflage cargo pants. At the end of his prosthesis was a clunky black shoe. His other foot was bare.

"Hey, Tony," Sam said congenially. "I'd like you to meet a friend of mine, Libby Tyler."

"Hi," Tony responded.

"How are things?" Sam asked.

"Okay, I guess." Tony scratched his cheek. "Been flying solo."

"Oh yeah?" Sam said. "Tess hasn't been out?"

"Nah, man," Tony said. "We had a big fight and she took off.

Somebody down at the Rocky Creek Tavern told her they'd seen me in there with that chick Diane from Pine River."

"You mean Dana?"

"Yeah, Dana," Tony said, and reached into his pocket for a pack of cigarettes. "You know me, Sam." He tapped one out. "I don't get out. I ain't seen Diana, Dana, in over a year. But Tess, man, she blew up."

"Sorry to hear that," Sam said, but he didn't sound the least bit sorry about it.

"Don't be," Tony said, pausing to light his cigarette. "She likes to create drama. You know how that is."

"Yes, I know all about that," Sam agreed.

Libby glanced curiously at Sam. How did he know all about that? It occurred to her that she didn't really know when or how his marriage had ended.

"This your woman?" Tony asked, startling Libby back to the here and now.

"Woman!" Libby sputtered, surprised he would ask that question in that manner. "*No*," she said quickly. She could feel Sam's gaze shift to her, and she felt a little contrite for speaking so quickly and firmly. It was out of the realm of possibility, yes, but not because of anything to do with Sam.

Nevertheless, Sam shot her a look.

"Libby's just helping me out today," he said, focusing on Tony again. "And I was hoping maybe you could help her."

Tony took a long draw off his cigarette, then exhaled skyward. "Don't know how I'd do that."

"Libby's got a car that needs some work," Sam said. "You know cars. I thought maybe you could help."

"What's wrong with it?"

The two men looked at Libby for an answer. She blinked. How the hell should she know? It was a car, and it wasn't working properly—what more was there to be said? "I don't know," she said. "It doesn't run sometimes."

"Do you feel it jump sometimes? Maybe feel it trying to give out while you're driving?"

"I don't . . . I don't know," she stammered.

"See anything out the exhaust pipes? Smell anything?"

"I don't think so."

Tony's gaze narrowed suspiciously, as if he suspected Libby of withholding valuable information. "All right. I'll take a look."

"I don't have much money," Libby quickly added.

Tony shrugged. "Neither do I."

"And . . . and I'm not sure I could get all the way out here in my car. I live north of Pine River."

Tony took another long drag from his cigarette as he studied Libby. "That's a problem," he agreed. "I'm not exactly driving these days."

"I could give you a ride," Sam said. "How about Thursday?"

*Thursday*. A tic of panic erupted in Libby. Thursdays, Alice had dance classes. Libby wasn't sure why that mattered—it wasn't as if she was going to *go* to Alice's dance class, because that would be idiotic in light of the restraining order.

Libby could feel Sam staring at her, waiting. So was Tony, but his gaze was more of dispassionate curiosity. Sam's gaze, on the other hand, was burning a hole through the side of her skull, almost as if he could see her thoughts. "Sure," she said quickly. "Thursday would be great."

Tony nodded, dropped his cigarette, and casually ground it out with the heel of his prosthesis.

"Great," Sam said, and Libby had the mental image of him checking off a box. *Get the vet a job. Check.*

Sam and Tony chatted about some things for a moment, but Libby didn't pay much attention to their conversation—her mind was whirling in that frenetic way it did when she thought of Alice and Max, of the reason she couldn't schedule a mechanic around a dance class that she couldn't attend. And really, what *had* happened with Ryan today?

She was staring at her feet, lost in thought, when Sam touched her elbow. "Are you ready?"

She was ready, all right, ready for Ryan to really, truly apologize so she could finally put this ordeal behind her. "I am." She smiled at the vet. "Thanks, Tony. I appreciate all the help I can get."

"Not all," Sam muttered.

"I said *help*," she muttered back. "Not interference."

Tony touched two fingers to his forehead in a sort of semi-salute. Libby responded with a wave before getting back into Sam's truck.

On the way back to town, Sam chatted about the end-of-summer music festival in Pine River, his gaze wandering over to her, watching her. Libby responded to the many questions he put to her, but her thoughts were jumbled.

When they pulled into the little grocery parking lot, Sam parked his truck, got out, and came around to open the door for her.

Libby picked up her bag of melted ice creams and slid off the passenger seat onto the pavement. Sam was standing before her, one arm propped on the open door. She was aware of him physically, of how big he was, of how his body dwarfed hers. She risked a look at his eyes.

He gave her a charming, lopsided bit of a smile.

She smiled, too. "Thanks for showing me everyone in Pinero County who is down on their luck," she said.

"You're welcome. And thanks for the ice cream."

Libby felt a little fluttery-buttery again, standing so close to him. "Sure. Okay, well . . . I gotta go," she said, and moved to step around him.

But Sam stopped her with a hand to her arm, and Libby felt that touch wave through her like a tsunami. She looked down at the big, rough hand, and the sudden image of it on her breast flashed through her mind's eye. Wait, *what*? It went deep, and Libby was suddenly reminded of another time she'd felt that sensation, another time with Sam. They were dancing on a Halloween night, and she'd felt something wave through her, just like this.

"Do me a favor?" Sam asked. "Stay away from Ryan. No driving through Vista Ridge. No showing up at the soccer fields."

The fluttery feeling began to dissipate. "I *am* staying away from him," Libby said, and stepped back, so that his hand fell from her arm. *Stay away from Ryan.* What did Sam think that she would do after hearing him apologize? She wasn't going to *do* anything. Except maybe seek clarification on her role with Alice and Max. And only because she believed that Ryan had opened a door.

But as usual, Sam seemed to be reading her thoughts. His eyes narrowed and he leaned forward, so that she could see the flecks of brown and green in his eyes. "I mean it, Libby. Because I will put you in jail if I have to."

"Sam—you don't have to worry!"

He didn't look as if he believed her. He actually looked a little worried. But he started back to the driver's side of his truck.

As Libby watched him walk away, a shadow that had been lurking on the edge of her thoughts suddenly emerged, leaping into focus. "Hey!" she said.

He turned partially toward her.

"Who else do you check on?"

"What?"

"You said you had one or two more people you had to check on. Millie, Tony, and who else?"

Sam said nothing.

"Who else, Sam?" she demanded, her pulse beginning to ratchet up. She moved closer to him, wanting to see his face when he said it. "What other crazy do you need to check on?"

"First of all, no one is crazy—"

"*Who?*" she persisted.

He frowned. "You know who."

That was it, the thing that was bothering her—the idea that Sam might really believe she was nuts, just one hop and a skip away from a straitjacket. Did he believe that? *Really* believe that? In spite of their admittedly oppositional relationship, she *liked* him, she'd always liked him, and she wanted him to like her. She had assumed he was a friend. Not her keeper.

And yet, he apparently viewed her as someone who was as much in need of being checked on as Millie Bagley and Tony D'Angelo. The realization stung much deeper than Libby would have guessed and she felt oddly betrayed by him. "You don't need to check on me. I had a bad experience. I reacted badly, and I'm dealing with it. But that doesn't mean I need supervision, or whatever it is you are doing."

"I know," he said in a patient tone that sounded dangerously close to Dr. Huber's.

Libby's heart began to race with anger. She hated being in this position, of somehow having fallen into a category of citizens who needed to be checked on from time to time. "Okay, Sam," she said, a little breathlessly. She rubbed her palms on her skirt. "I'll be honest. It may be possible that Ryan and I will agree to some happy medium—"

"A what?"

"For the sake of the kids," she added hastily, and threw up a hand to stop him before he began his lecture. "That's all. But I need you to know that I am dealing with my issues as best I can and I am moving on. So . . . so don't lump me in with everyone else you think needs to be looked after."

Sam stilled. His expression turned as dark as she'd ever seen it. It was thunderous, the kind of look that could make a person quiver. Come to think of it, Libby had never seen Sam Winters angry. Frustrated maybe, but this . . . *this* was angry.

She didn't like the way he was looking at her, or the way he started to move toward her, one deliberate step at a time. She scrambled backward and instantly bumped into her car.

"Libby, *listen* to me. I am going to say this once. After that, you can do whatever you want, but I am going to try and get through to you one last time. You and Ryan are never getting back together. *Ever*. It's just not going to happen, do you understand?"

His adamancy was surprising. "I didn't say I was getting back with him! And anyway, how do *you* know?" she demanded.

"Because I know," he snapped. He leaned forward, bracing himself against her car with one arm, locking her in between him, the vehicle, and his rebuke. "He let you go. Dumb as that is, he did. He's moved on. He's moved on so much that he got a *restraining order* against you."

"Because he was mad—"

"Because he is *done*," Sam angrily interrupted her. "Don't create some fantasy in your head. Leave him alone. Don't make me have to arrest you."

She didn't like what he was implying. Ryan had apologized—it wasn't as if she was fantasizing about it. She was almost certain she wasn't. "He just said it this morning!" she insisted. "You *heard* him. He said he wished things hadn't happened like they did, and that he was sorry, and to let the dust settle. What does that mean? It means he is sorry!"

"Jesus *Christ*," Sam muttered incredulously.

Libby dipped under his arm and put some distance between herself and those piercing hazel eyes. "Don't come and check on me. I don't need you to hold my hand and tell me what to do. I *know* what I'm doing."

Okay, maybe she didn't know exactly, but this was her problem. Not his.

Sam pressed his lips together, as if he was working hard to bite back a few choice words. "Okay," he said tersely, and abruptly turned around and walked back to his truck.

Libby watched him get in, back up, and drive on. She watched his truck disappear around the corner.

Her breath was still coming in angry gulps.

Sam was wrong. He had to be wrong. Because it wasn't impossible that Libby and Ryan could patch things up, at least enough that she might see Alice and Max. And besides, it wasn't Sam's business. This was her life, not his. Sam didn't know what had gone on between Libby and Ryan. No one knew but her and Ryan. And Libby knew Ryan well enough to know that it took a lot for him to say that he wished things hadn't ended.

She would be the first to admit that she couldn't be sure what had been real between her and Ryan after all that had happened. But what she did know was that it couldn't *all* have been a lie. *I'm crazy about you, baby, crazy in love. I can't live without you and I never will.*

That's what Ryan had said the night he asked her to move in with him and the kids.

How did love like that suddenly disappear?

It didn't.

People made mistakes. Ryan had admitted as much to her twice this week. Alice was calling her every afternoon. It wasn't ridiculous to imagine some level of reconciliation could happen, if only for the sake of Alice and Max. Because no matter what had happened between her and Ryan, her relationship and her love for those two kids was as real and as deep as anything she had ever felt in her life. She wasn't going to walk away from that. Alice and Max meant more to her than anything else in the world.

Sam may not get that, but he didn't have to get it. This was Libby's life.

She got into her car and drove to town, pulling into a spot on Main Street, just outside Tag's Outfitters. She was still brooding over Sam's anger, and as she looked up at the door of Tag's, she was suddenly reminded of a sunny afternoon in early May. It was the first time she'd come to town since Ryan had sat her down at the kitchen bar, had even filled her wineglass for her, and had told her that she had to leave. That he was through, that he didn't love her anymore and hadn't for a long time.

"Through?" Libby had said. "How can you be through? What are you talking about?" She'd been so confused. Of course she knew that things were a little strained between them, but she never would have guessed that he was thinking to end it, that she was headed out the door.

"Afraid so," he'd said. "It's just not working for me. I think it's best if you leave."

"*Leave?*" she'd all but shouted. "There's no discussion? No talking? You just announce you're done and I have to leave? Just when did you think I was going to do that?"

She would never forget the look he'd given her. It was indifferent, uncaring. "Well . . . now," he'd said with a shrug.

Everything had blurred after that. Wine had spilled along with her tears. There had been a lot of shouting, a lot of accusations, but Ryan had insisted there was no one else, there was nothing but Libby and a love he didn't possess anymore.

And then Alice and Max had come home.

Libby closed her eyes, unwilling to think of the moment Alice and Max had understood what Ryan had done.

Libby shoved angrily against her car door to open it, and stepped onto the sidewalk.

She remembered something more, as she hitched her purse over her shoulder. Libby had nowhere to go and had moved in with her mother. After two weeks of stumbling around blindly, painfully, her mother had insisted she get out and get on with her life. As if Libby hadn't spent the last four years creating a family that was now gone. As if Libby were wasting time. Libby had tried to move on.

She remembered walking down this street, on her way to yoga. Yoga would center her, yoga would ease her, she'd reasoned. It was right here that she'd run into Sam. Literally. She'd been darting around tourists and had even clipped a mailbox in her haste, her mind racing, her thoughts in another place altogether. She'd had her yoga mat strung across her back.

She didn't notice Sam until he spoke to her. "Libby, hello," he'd said, and he had smiled so warmly that she'd had to fight the urge to burst into a sudden torrent of tears. That happened quite a lot to her in the beginning.

"Oh, hey Sam." She'd slowed down, even taking a step backward to keep from passing him. She'd smiled, too, or at least she thought she had. But Sam had instantly dipped down to have a closer look at her with those knowing eyes.

"Are you okay?"

"Me? Sure!" she'd said. Because after a couple of weeks back home, Libby had learned to say everything was okay so her mother would not hover and harp. "How about you? I heard about you rescuing that couple on the Divisidaro Trail last week. Dani Boxer is singing your praises. She said they were scared to death. They were staying at the Lodge and told her all about it."

Sam had chuckled, and Libby had realized then that, judging by his casual manner, he hadn't heard about her. He was just being nice when he'd asked how she was. "Dani is quick to sing praises," he'd said. "They weren't very lost. They hadn't strayed from the trail nearly as far as they thought they had. But then again, they had a special glow about them from all the weed they'd been smoking."

"Aha," Libby said with a grin. "The rolling papers should come with instructions, shouldn't they? Please do not hike while stoned."

Sam grinned. "Going to yoga?"

"Yes. Are you coming?" she'd asked and, grateful for the few normal moments, had playfully poked him in the shoulder. "The offer still stands, you know. You never took me up on it. Where is that yoga mat, anyway?"

"In my office. Right between my desk and the wall. I'm still mulling it over."

"Liar," she'd said. "You told me that last time I saw you. It's been over a year now."

"I like to mull things to death."

She'd actually laughed a little, because so did she. "So how is that back of yours, anyway?"

"Stiff as a board," he'd admitted.

"*Knew* it," she'd said. "I better get going or I'll be late. Have a good day, Sam." She'd moved to pass him, and had accidently brushed against him when she did. Sam had surprised her by impulsively catching her hand in his, and she remembered thinking her hand felt so small in his. As small as she felt inside.

"Hey . . . are you sure you're okay?" he'd asked, peering closely at her.

Libby could remember the swell of gratitude that he cared enough to ask, to even notice. In those weeks after Ryan told her he didn't love her anymore, she had needed that reassurance. "I'm sure," she'd said. She wasn't too convincing, because he'd arched a dubious brow. Libby had sighed. "I've just got a lot on my mind.

My dad is really ill, and . . . and . . . you know, that puts a strain on things at home." It wasn't a lie. She'd even asked Ryan if her preoccupation with her father's slow death had caused him to change his mind about her. Ryan had said no, but as nothing else made sense, Libby wasn't sure she believed him. But to Sam, she'd shrugged helplessly and said, "It's no big deal. Just life beating down the door, as my grandmother used to say."

"I'm sorry to hear that," Sam said, and he had looked sincere. "I hope everything works out."

"Oh, it will," Libby had said, because that's what she did best, she assured everyone that everything was okay. "It's just a bump in the road." That bump had suddenly felt insurmountable. Libby had pulled her hand free of Sam's and had started to walk, but had paused and looked over her shoulder.

He'd been watching her, and Libby had felt a rivulet of something sweet run through her. "Sure you don't want to come and do some down dogs with me?"

"I'm sure," he'd said with a wink.

"Suit yourself, Stiffneck." She'd moved on, falling back into melancholy.

Turns out, she didn't go to yoga that day, either. She just kept walking, past the studio, down to the park, where she had sat on a bench and cried some more.

No more of that. She hadn't cried over Ryan Spangler for a very long time now.

# EIGHT

Sam was up before dawn and stumbled into his kitchen, grimaced at the dishes still in the sink from last night's attempt at chili, and dragged his fingers through his hair. He grabbed a cup from the shelf and stuck it under his new single-cup coffeemaker. Coffee was the one vice Sam allowed himself, and he had fallen in love with this machine. It was probably the most expensive thing he'd bought for himself in a year.

Hell, it was probably the *only* thing he'd bought for himself in a year.

He turned it on, scratched his chin, felt the stubble of a beard there. He'd been off-duty yesterday, and when one lived alone, one tended not to groom one's face quite as often as one ought. He picked out a coffee—wild mountain blueberry—and jammed it into the cup holder. As the coffee brewed, he padded back across his little house, into his bedroom.

Admittedly, he wasn't the neatest guy in the world. He had clothes strewn around, draped over the back of a worn-out armchair he'd rescued from an eviction a few years ago. He sorted through that stack of clothing, found some jeans, and pulled them on. He stuffed his feet into his house shoes, pulled on a jacket with sheepskin lining, and retraced his steps. With his morning cup of joe liberally doctored with cream and sugar, Sam stepped outside onto the deck in the back of his house. He paused like he did most mornings, standing as still as he could to breathe in the quiet, crisp, cold mountain air.

His place was set back in the woods, a little two-bedroom log house with a big open kitchen and living space, a huge expanse of deck under the firs out back, a garden, and the work shed he'd built from logs and stones at one end of the deck.

A mountain stream cut across the back of his property, home to a family of river trout that had been there about as long as he had. He had a fenced meadow beside the house that was full of late summer wildflowers, and a small barn for the horses he kept for those rare occasions he had to go deep into the mountains to rescue a stranded hiker.

As a rural area deputy, Sam was assigned to the backwater, remote parts of Pinero County that could not be easily reached by main street emergency responders. When Mr. Gomez had had a heart attack two years ago, it had taken an ambulance forty-five minutes to reach him. Mr. Gomez didn't make it. Now, Sam had a defibrillator in his truck. He was a one-man show, the first line of defense. The man with the star who showed up to keep a lid on things until the cavalry could arrive.

He had an office and a small holding cell rented from the Pine River police department, which he used only rarely. Most of his work involved crimes like cattle rustling, poaching, and the occasional lost hiker. His workload was pretty simple now, very different than it had been back in the days he was patrolling the more populated part of the county. People who lived this far out tended to be pretty self-sufficient, taking care of trouble on their own.

The job suited the man Sam believed he'd become. He wasn't especially close to his family. His mother, in Dallas, had remarried after the bitter divorce from his father. His sister, Jan, was a financial advisor in Pittsburgh with a family. Sam heard from his father occasionally, but his dad had married a woman from Mexico and spent most of his time there.

For Sam, this little house in the mountains of Colorado near Pine River was as good a place as any to be.

It was certainly the easiest place to be.

Sam walked to the work shed and stepped inside. He flipped a switch and light erupted from a pair of single bulbs swinging overhead. He sipped from his coffee and looked around at the birdhouses stacked on the shelves. There were dozens of them, in various colors, shapes, and sizes. This was his hobby, the thing that kept him busy and his mind occupied on long winter nights. His birdhouses were elaborate, too: castles, multi-level houses with pitched roofs and steeples, condominiums. He made them in shapes of recreational vehicles, boats, airplanes, and spaceships. He'd made one that looked like a hamburger, only because it amused him.

He was pretty good at making birdhouses, but most of his creations stayed here. He had no desire to sell them. He just kept making them, kept stacking them around his work shed and hanging them in the trees around his house.

Once, his pal Dirk had said, "People would pay good money for these," as he'd admired one that was fashioned after a vintage Cadillac. "Especially rich people in Aspen."

Maybe Dirk was right, but to Sam, it felt almost like an invasion of his privacy and his solitude to let anyone know that his birdhouses existed, much less *sell* them. He'd given a couple away. One to Millie, hoping that would soften her up. It hadn't. One to Leo Kendrick, who spent a lot of time looking out windows. But other than that, this was something he preferred to keep to himself. It was his thing, his quiet pastime, his testament to his life up on the mountain: simple and solitary. *Safe.*

Sam put aside his coffee and selected a piece of tin to fashion into a birdhouse roof. He glanced at the little building plan he'd made and tacked to the wall, and began to hammer the tin into shape.

But the tin didn't have the same appeal to him as it normally did. His mind was elsewhere, his thoughts jumbled. He hadn't been able to erase the image of Libby's hopeful face as she'd stood outside his truck. He could even hear her voice.

*It may be possible that Ryan and I will agree to some happy medium.*

That statement had made Sam profoundly and irrationally angry.

That he cared enough for it to make him angry made him angrier still. He didn't care what Libby Tyler did with her life. It was not up to him to set her on the right course. Then why the hell didn't he just let it go? Let her do whatever she wanted, let the chips fall where they may! What difference could it possibly make to him?

There it was again, that feeling of something old and battered trying to dig out from underneath his rubble. He didn't like the feeling at all, and suddenly lost interest in the birdhouses. He put down his hammer, swiped up his coffee cup, and stalked out of his work shed.

The sun was coming up, and with it rose the chatter of the magpies and blue jays greeting their day. Sam stood very still, his eyes closed, taking in the morning.

Sometimes, when there was something going on up at Homecoming Ranch, and the mornings were this still, he could hear a little bit of laughter or voices drifting down to him. He was always glad to hear it, too—the place had been so silent and forlorn after

Mrs. Kendrick had died from cancer. Sam had been sorry when Mr. Kendrick and Leo abandoned the ranch for Pine River and sold the place to Grant Tyler.

He worried about Homecoming Ranch. Libby's intentions were good, but her ideas were such a gamble. Sam's thinking had been confirmed one day when he'd run into Jackson Crane, who had been Grant Tyler's financial guy. Jackson mentioned that the sisters would have to book a wedding every weekend to make it a go, and Sam was pretty sure that wasn't anywhere close to happening.

Still, Libby was pretty goddamn tenacious, and had as good a shot as anyone at turning the ranch around. She'd always been a go-getter, the first one in line to volunteer for whatever needed doing. A few years ago when the wildfires had come close to Pine River, he remembered Libby with a stain of ash on her face, tirelessly working to bundle up food, shoes, and water for evacuees. She was at the annual road race for bikers at the start of the summer, manning the rest stops. She'd been active in her church, had worked with the Chamber of Commerce, and had lobbied the city council for funding for pedestrian-friendly walkways and had won.

She was tenacious all right, so much so that he was pissed off all over again.

He opened his eyes and gazed out at the valley. *Forget it. She's not your problem.*

He lifted his coffee cup to his lips—and sloshed it down his bare chest when the ring of the telephone jarred him. Cursing under his breath and wiping away the spill, he walked inside, picked up his phone and looked at the display.

Terri. His ex-wife. Sam put the phone down and walked away from it. The last time she'd called, she'd been looking for money. He'd told her not to call him again. He couldn't bear the idea of her piercing the armor he'd erected around his heart and his memories again.

The phone stopped ringing, and a moment later, it started again. Terri again.

Sam turned off his ringer. He felt a swell of bitterness rise up in him, the sort he used to tamp down with drink. Four years ago, he would have opened a bottle. Today, he would take a shower and hope to God it erased the tension he felt.

He'd met Terri in a college government class all those years ago. She'd been the girl with straight red hair and dancing blue eyes. She was full of purpose and the desire to make a difference in the world. Sam had been caught up in the swirl of her energy, had fallen madly in love with her. *Let's join the peace corps,* she'd said. *Let's go* help *people.*

He had never wanted to help people so much in his life.

But even then, as young and idealistic as they were, there had been warning signs. Terri loved to party, for one, and Sam had been easy to pull along. She also had a volatile temper that was made worse with a couple of drinks.

Whether Sam had been too naïve to understand what was happening to her and to him, or too blinded by love, he didn't know. But he'd ignored those signs, every last one.

Sam and Terri married in a little church in Taos, New Mexico, the summer after he graduated. Terri, a year behind him, dropped out of school. *They're part of the establishment. They don't get it,* she'd said. That was the reason, she claimed, that her grades were falling. *Them, they,* the unseen faces of injustice that seemed to shadow her everywhere she went.

Sam and Terri moved around for a couple of years. They lived in Santa Monica in a rent house with a bunch of hippies who talked a lot about bringing peace to the world but did little more than surf. They made their way to Portland when Terri had the idea to own a coffee shop. *We'll have poetry readings,* she'd said brightly. They'd lasted three months.

Eventually, the need for money had driven them to Colorado Springs. Terri had big plans to take a job with the Forest Department, but took a job working for an insurance agent—still helping people, as she saw it. Sam joined the police force. After a couple of years, the opportunity to work for the Pinero County Sheriff's Office had cropped up. It had been a good couple of years for Sam—he'd done well, rising quickly through the ranks. The sheriff had liked him, and had taken Sam under his wing. Sam was the guy everyone assumed would run for office when the sheriff retired.

Many times, Sam had tried to pinpoint when it had all begun to get out of hand. When it was, exactly, that Terri had gone from a vivacious college girl to a woman who got into verbal altercations with people around town about ridiculous things and drank straight from a vodka bottle. When it was that everything had unraveled into frayed ends, when the shadows had begun to close in around Terri, when he found the answer to all his troubles in the same vodka bottle Terri favored. When had they become this couple?

It bothered Sam when he saw shadows around Libby, too. Libby's shadows were vastly different than Terri's had been, but still. He didn't think Libby was crazy, like he heard Mrs. Miller say at the Grizzly Café one morning. Or that she had some heretofore undiagnosed mental health issue that had suddenly manifested itself. He thought it was probably true what she'd said—she'd had a breakdown. He didn't believe she was gripped by anything more than a need to belong—to someone, to something. And in rapid succession, she had lost all her places to belong, and all the people who had mattered to her. That was enough to send anyone down the path Libby had traveled.

He knew what that felt like, that wanting to belong to someone. Sometimes, Sam could feel it slipping around in his marrow, tugging at his conscious thoughts. He could feel the ache of wanting children settling into the crevasses of his heart.

As for Libby . . .

He couldn't even define what it was that he felt about her. Frustration. Sympathy. More. Whatever *more* was, he didn't want to look too close. No good could come of his worry or his growing infatuation for her. The last thing he needed was to complicate his life with a woman like her. It was best for him stay up on the mountain with his birdhouses and devote himself to helping those who were in a spot he'd once been in. Like Tony D'Angelo. If he could keep Tony from falling off the wagon, if that was the only thing Sam did with his life, he'd be happy.

That's what he told himself.

# NINE

It was one of those early fall days when the sun began to sit lower in the sky and cast a gold light over the earth. It was perfectly still, not a breath of a breeze, and all across the meadow that stretched in front of the house, Libby could see dragonflies flitting across the empty tent pads, the sun glinting off their transparent wings.

She was sitting on the porch steps Luke had repaired. She had dressed in a cotton skirt and canvas shoes, and a long-sleeved Henley shirt. She'd pulled her unruly hair into a pair of low tails behind her ears. Below her, under the steps, the four dogs were lounging, waiting and watching for a sign that something would happen.

Maybe today something *would* happen. Maybe today, Ryan would find a way to properly apologize to her. Maybe they would agree to start thinking about how to get on with life in the new reality. Libby was aware that meant forgiving his affair with Gwen, and all the lying. And while she wasn't quite ready to forgive Ryan for anything, she was acutely aware that it meant having Alice and Max back in her life. It meant having a family again. That Ryan had apologized for anything was a positive step, and it had put

Libby in a very good mood. She felt buoyant and hopeful for the first time in weeks. She relished the beauty of the day, the dogs lying beneath her, the dragonflies, the sun—*everything*.

Her host of problems didn't seem to loom quite as large today.

And yet, nothing had changed. Her plans for Homecoming Ranch were looking impossible. She'd met Michelle Catucci, a banker, and had explained the obstacles she'd encountered in getting Homecoming Ranch Events off the ground.

"Okay," Michelle said. "What sort of business plan do you have?"

"That's it," Libby said. "Making it an event destination."

"No, I mean a business plan," Michelle had said. "With goals and benchmarks and some cost estimates we could look at. We can't loan money without some sort of idea of what you'll be bringing in."

"It's kind of a catch-22, isn't it?" Libby had pointed out to Michelle. "I mean, I can't pay back the loan until I get some business. But I can't get business without a loan." She'd laughed a little, as if the conundrums of a business like hers were shared by all businesses.

"Come back with a business plan," Michelle had said as she'd put her Chanel-clad arm around Libby's shoulders and shown her out. "And your bank records. Get all that together, and we'll talk about this again. I want to help you, Libby, but the plan has to be truly feasible."

Libby had been too embarrassed to admit to Michelle that she really didn't know exactly what went into a business plan. But not nearly as embarrassed as she would have been if Michelle had seen her bank records.

"Hey, Libs."

She glanced over her shoulder as Luke sauntered out onto the porch, dressed in jeans and a plain white T-shirt.

Luke smiled at her, his teeth awfully white against the dark beard he was growing along with his hair, which he was wearing in a little tail tied at his nape. "What's up?"

"Not much."

He walked down the steps and leaned down, tugging on the dog ear of her hair. "You okay?"

Luke and Madeline were always asking her that since she'd come back from Mountain View. "I'm okay," she said. "Isn't it a gorgeous day? What are you two up to?"

"Pottery," he said with a roll of his eyes. "Don't ask."

"Hey!"

Madeline had emerged from the house in hiking pants, a halter-top, and a floppy sun hat, under which her sleek black hair hung down her back in a ponytail. At the sound of her voice, the beasts below the stairs began to rouse, coming out from their shade, stretching long, and yawning. Madeline was their favorite now, probably because she took long walks with them up the trails behind the house. Libby used to do that, but, well . . . things hadn't been the same lately.

"I'm waiting on a guy to come and fix my car," Libby said.

"Oh, good." Madeline maneuvered her way between Libby and Luke, placing a hand on the top of Libby's head to balance as she passed. "Luke, did you tell her about Sunday?"

"Right. Dad has invited some people to dinner on Sunday. The Broncos are playing their first regular season game, and in the Kendrick household, that's what's known as a Big Deal."

Madeline paused in her progress down the steps and looked back at Libby. "You'll come, won't you? I think you should get out," she said, before Libby could answer. "Don't you think you should get out more? I worry about you sitting up here, night after night."

"But I—"

"Sam's coming."

Libby was so startled that she couldn't speak for a moment. "Okay," she said slowly. "And why are you telling me that? Is he going to do something special? Whip out a guitar and sing a few tunes?"

"I just thought you'd want to know," Madeline said with a shrug. "I thought you were friends." She looked pointedly at Libby.

"Maddie," Luke said, tangling his fingers with Madeline's. "Leave her alone."

"Okay," Madeline said. "But will you come, Libby?"

There was hardly anything Libby wanted to do less, but she knew if she declined, Madeline and Luke would stop everything, sit on the step with her, and look at her gravely while they asked if she was *really* okay. "Yes," Libby said. "Wouldn't miss it. Is there anything I can bring?"

"No," Luke said. "Dad's going to grill, I think. Aunt Patti has the rest of it covered."

"I can make a cake," Libby offered. "Leo loves cake."

"For Leo, cake batter is better," Luke said. "The swallowing thing isn't going so well," he said, gesturing to his throat as he cast his eyes to the ground. "I'm sure Leo would love to drink cake batter through a straw, but I don't think Marisol will allow it."

Luke rarely talked about Leo's condition, but everyone in Pine River knew that Leo was a ticking clock, every second counting down on what was left of his young life.

The sound of a vehicle on the road caused them all to look up. Sam's patrol truck appeared and barreled up the dirt road.

"Oh no," Madeline said, and looked back at Libby. "Did something happen?"

"God, Madeline. One minute you're trying to hook us up, and the next you're worried he's coming to arrest me. Nothing happened," Libby said, and stood up. "He found a guy to work on my car, that's all."

"Oh yeah?" Luke said, sounding interested. "Nothing like getting under a hood on a day like this." He walked down to the drive as Sam's patrol truck rolled to a stop.

But Madeline was still looking at Libby with very intent dark-blue eyes. Dad's eyes, Libby thought, although she would never say that to Madeline. Madeline had never known their dad, and what she did know, she didn't like. "That was nice of Sam," she said. "So . . . you guys are kind of chummy, huh?"

"Because he is helping me out?"

"Well? Luke knows everyone in town. He could have found someone to work on your car a month ago. How does Sam even know your car needs work?"

Libby looked at Sam, who was shaking Luke's hand at that moment. She stepped past her sister. "There is nothing going on between us, Madeline, trust me. He knows a guy who is a vet and who needs some work. And he knows my car is crap because I told him. Nothing more to it than that."

Madeline nodded, but she was still studying Libby. She had a bad habit of doing that, of looking Libby up and down as if she was scoping for clues to some big mystery. "Good, then. I am glad you're getting your car fixed. By the way, Gary's mother called. She and the happy couple are coming early next week to check out the barn."

"Great!" Libby said. "We'll be ready." She had learned in the last few weeks that if she just kept smiling, and smiled long and hard enough, everyone calmed down and didn't stand around, waiting for her to break down again.

"Will we?" Madeline asked, wincing a little. "Because it really stinks in there."

"It does now, but we'll move the horses out of there. Not to worry."

"I hope not, because we have no backup plan," Madeline said, as if Libby needed reminding.

"You worry too much, Madeline," Libby said.

Madeline sighed. "I know I do. I try not to, but old habits die hard."

"Don't worry about this. We're in good shape," Libby said. "I better go see about my car." She continued down the steps before Madeline could voice any other concerns about the wedding, walking onto the drive where Luke, Sam, and Tony were standing.

"Hi," she said.

"Hey," Tony said when he saw her. "Where's the clunker?"

"It's in the garage with the other clunker," she responded, referring to Luke's late mother's Buick. She glanced at Sam, but he was squatting down, his attention on the dogs.

"I'll show you where it is," she said.

"Yep. Got some tools in the back of the truck," Tony said, and walked lopsidedly to the back of Sam's truck.

Sam stood up, his gaze barely meeting Libby's. "Hello, Libby," he said, and then he shifted his gaze to the back of the truck and called out, "Okay, Tony, I'll pick you up in a couple of hours!"

Libby waited for him to say more than hi. But he turned to Luke and said, "What kind of engine do you have in the Bronco?"

"Hemi," Luke said proudly. "Come take a look." The two of them walked away from her.

Libby blinked with surprise at Sam's broad back. All right, he didn't believe that she and Ryan could find a way to get along, but he didn't have to be rude about it. She found his aloofness unsettling—she was used to the Lone Ranger hovering around her.

"Okay, see you, Libby!" Madeline called out to her, throwing a tote bag over her shoulder and then lifting a hand. She walked up to where Luke was standing and slipped in under his arm.

A swell of jealousy and hope filled Libby. She wanted that sort of affection and love in her life and always had. She wanted to be wanted and needed. Funny how she kept ending up with people who didn't want her or need her.

"So . . . which way to the car?" Tony asked, having hoisted a rusted toolbox from the bed of Sam's truck.

"This way," Libby said, and turned her back on the happy couple and Sam.

Her car was parked next to Mrs. Kendrick's old Buick, which they kept around for emergency transportation when one of their cars was in the shop, as Libby's had been frequently the last few months. But lately, Libby had not been able to get that one to start, either.

Tony squinted at her car. He put down his toolbox, took a smoke from his pocket. "It's a Dodge," he announced.

"Does that make a difference?"

"Just saying." He wandered over to the car, and with a cigarette dangling from the corner of his mouth, he popped the hood and propped it open. "Oh yeah," he said, nodding.

"Oh yeah? Oh yeah what?" Libby asked, moving in beside him to have a look. Only she had no idea what she was looking at. A lot of greasy things were all she could see.

"It needs work." He leaned down, started sorting through his toolbox.

Libby heard the sound of two vehicles start up and drive away. She leaned to her right and through the open garage door she watched Sam's truck move down the road ahead of Luke's Bronco.

He hadn't even said good-bye, hadn't told her to stay out of trouble. It stung—ignoring him was *her* thing, and honestly, she'd started to come around to his showing up with basketsful of unsolicited advice.

She settled against the Buick as Tony began to dismantle parts of her engine. She watched him a few minutes and asked, "Did you learn to do this in the Army?"

"Marines. And no, my old man taught me about cars." He paused to take a drag from the cigarette he'd perched on the edge of her car, and then adjusted the dirty bandana he'd tied around his head.

"May I ask what happened?"

Tony squinted at her from the corner of his eye. "I'm guessing you aren't talking about what happened when my old man taught me about cars. I was in the Helmand province of Afghanistan. Heard of it?"

"Yeah, of course."

"Meanest place on earth, I'll tell you that. Ran into an IED." He glanced at Libby again. "Improvised explosive device. That's what the locals make to blow up big nation armies."

"I'm sorry," she said.

"Me too. Sure has put a crimp in my style." He leaned over the car again, tapping on something. His pants, Libby noticed, were stained, as if they hadn't been washed in some time. His shirt was torn at the hem. "If you know about cars, maybe you could get a job at Wilson's in Pine River," Libby suggested, referring to the oldest auto shop in town.

"Got no way to get there," he said. "No license, no wheels. Not to mention hard to drive without a leg." He grinned at her as if he found that amusing.

Libby wondered why Tony lived so far out if he couldn't drive. Once, her dad said that the people who came to live in the mountains around Pine River were usually running from something. At the time, she'd thought Grant was referring to himself, because if ever there was ever a man who ran from responsibility, it was him.

"Maybe Sam could take you," she suggested, absently studying her cuticle.

"Sam? He drives me around a lot, that's for sure. To the store, to the clinic. To my meetings. Not fair to ask him to come and get me every day and take me into work."

"What meetings?" she asked curiously.

"AA," he said, squinting at her again through a tail of smoke. "Twice a week. Sam, that dude has a sweet tooth. He likes the cookies."

The Stuffed Shirt formerly known as Sam didn't seem the sort of man who would drop someone off at a meeting and run in to get a cookie or two. "You mean you bring him cookies from your meeting," she clarified for her own benefit.

But Tony shook his head. "It's not my meeting, it's our meeting. We go twice a week, and everyone gets a cookie. I mean, you sit for an hour or so. People get hungry, so they put out cookies."

While Tony explained the reasoning behind providing cookies at meetings, a bell was clanging in Libby's head. "Wait—Sam goes, too?"

"Sure," Tony said, his focus on the engine of her car. "I thought you knew that."

She probably would have if she'd thought about it. It occurred to Libby that Sam seemed to know an awful lot about her, but she really didn't know much about him. He suddenly seemed mysterious to her—there was a life standing behind that badge and the warnings to obey the rules, and she knew only bits and pieces of it.

"Yeah, this is going to have to come out," Tony said.

"What?" Libby asked, alarmed. "Listen, I don't have a lot of money. As in none. I can't afford parts."

"Parts!" He scoffed. "I don't do parts. I rebuild." He wiped his hands on his pants, and Libby thought that the man definitely needed a clean pair. "It's going to take some time. Maybe a couple of days."

"A couple of *days*?"

He looked down at her car. "Well, if you want to rely on it, it needs to run. Agreed?"

"Agreed," she said carefully. "But I don't have the money to pay you for that kind of work."

"Don't get all bent out of shape—we'll work something out," he said.

Libby didn't know how they were going to work anything out, but he was already under the hood with his wrench, turning something.

At half-past six, he was still working, and she was a little frantic.

Libby was in the kitchen, baking banana nut bread she'd made from the fruit Luke had bought and then not eaten. She had gone down to the garage twice to offer Tony something to eat, and both times he'd informed her matter-of-factly that he only ate one meal a day, and never while he was working. She wanted to go down there again and beg him to stop, that there was no way she could ever pay him.

Libby saw the swerve of headlights turn onto the road as she checked the loaf, and recognized Sam's truck. The shoulder from the local meat market had arrived, and Libby decided to stay inside, because she didn't care to feel the icy blast from him again. She heard the truck stop, heard the low hum of the engine idle and a door slam. Apparently, he was in as much of a hurry to get out of here tonight as he had been earlier today.

Moments later, she heard voices, truck doors shutting, and then the unmistakable sound of Sam's boots on the porch stairs.

He knocked on the door.

The dogs, sprawled in every doorway between her and the front door, lifted their heads, their ears rotating toward the door. Roscoe began to growl. Libby put her hands on her hips, debating.

He knocked again.

"Okay," she said to the dogs. "I'm going to answer, see what he wants, and not engage. Got that?"

Roscoe responded with a thump of his tail.

Libby walked to the front door, wiping her cheek with the back of her hand before opening the door.

Sam was standing with his hands in his pockets. He'd shaved, and his hair was combed. And he was dressed in a suit and tie. "Evening," he said.

It took Libby a moment to respond, because she wasn't used to seeing him without a badge or a gun. Or looking so *hot.* He didn't look official or intimidating, he just looked . . . *hot.* Jesus, had he always been this handsome?

One of his brows arched above the other as she let her gaze slide down his body and up again. "Is there something wrong?"

"Yes! I've never seen you in a suit."

"Well now you have," he said. "If you've got a minute, there is something I need to speak to you about."

"Why? I haven't been to town."

Sam could not suppress a small smile. "Believe it or not, for once, this is not about you. It's about your car."

"Oh, great," she said, steeling herself. "Go ahead, give me the bad news."

"Tony thinks he has a way for you to pay him. Do you want me to freeze to death out here, or will you let me in a minute?"

She glanced down at the dogs, all of them standing between her and the door. "Where's Tony?"

"He's in the truck, wolfing down a burger I brought him. This will only take a minute," he said, glancing at his watch. "I'm running late as it is."

Libby leaned over the dogs and pushed the screen door open. All four of them quickly darted out and around Sam, running down the steps as if someone had called them.

Sam stepped in and stood just inside the door.

"You know . . . you look *nice*," Libby said, nodding approvingly. He looked more than nice, he looked completely delectable.

"Don't look so surprised."

"Going somewhere fun?" she asked, peering closely at him. "Dinner and a movie, maybe? Or, wait, a concert? Are there any concerts in Pine River tonight?"

"I don't know—maybe you should Google it. So listen, Tony took a look at your car. And the Buick, for that matter. He says they both need some major work, nothing he can do in a day. It might take him a few days to get both up and running smoothly."

"I *knew* this would happen," Libby groaned. "I'm low on cash, Sam." As in completely tapped out, save the bottom-of-the-barrel living expenses.

"That's okay. Because what Tony wants is a place to stay for a few nights and food. That's all."

"How could he not want to be paid?" Libby asked, surprised.

"Sometimes, there are things more valuable than money. I was thinking that maybe he could bunk with Ernest."

Sam was referring to the ranch hand who had been at Homecoming Ranch for more than twenty years. Ernest Delgado had lived in the bunkhouse forever, never marrying, never leaving except once a month, to see his mother in Albuquerque.

As for the bunkhouse, there wasn't much bunking to it—from what Libby had understood from Luke, Ernest had been the only one to ever have bunked there.

"I can't drive Tony back and forth every day," Sam said, sensing her hesitation. "And apparently, neither can you. All he wants is to get out of that run-down house for a while."

"Here?" she asked, and rose up on her toes to peek over Sam's shoulder at Tony.

Sam leaned closer to her so that he could shut the door behind him, presumably so that Libby wouldn't stare at Tony. "Here, while he works. It's a bunkhouse, Libby. I don't think Ernest would mind the company for a couple of days. Is that a problem?"

What was that she smelled, cologne? It was *nice* cologne, too. He *did* have a date!

He glanced at his watch again.

"Are you going on a date?"

Sam slowly lifted his gaze from his watch. "Was there an answer to my question in there somewhere?"

"No, I changed the subject. It's not a problem, there's your answer. So why don't you want me to know you're going on a date?"

He cocked his head to one side and looked curiously at her. "Why are you so interested?"

"Who says I'm interested?"

"Oh, I don't know, because of the way you keep staring at me and firing questions."

"I'm not *staring*," Libby retorted. "I'm making conversation. You told me to be nice. I'm being nice."

"You're not being nice," he said, his gaze dipping to her mouth. "You're being nosy. There is a fundamental difference between nice and nosy."

Libby gasped with indignation. "Pot and kettle!" she said, poking him in the chest. "You're *always* nosy, asking me where I've been and if I have a golf club in my car, et cetera and so forth."

"That's because I am a law enforcement officer, and you are a law violator. I have the right to do that."

"I don't get the big deal," she said. "If you have a date, why don't you just say so?"

Sam sighed. He folded his arms across his chest. "Okay, I have a date. Satisfied?"

"*No!*" she cried with disbelief. "You said you didn't have a girlfriend!"

"I didn't say anything," he corrected her, and rubbed his thumb across her cheek.

Libby swayed backward. "What?" she demanded, touching her fingers to tingling skin. "What was that?"

He tucked his thumb in his mouth. "Cake, I think."

She tried to rub away the shiver his touch had put in her cheek. "So I guess I know why you totally ignored me today," she said pertly.

He smiled a little. "Did I ignore you?"

"Totally *ignored* me."

"Why would a date make me ignore you? That makes no sense."

"Then why *did* you ignore me?" she demanded, propping her hands on her waist.

"I didn't. But I realized I don't have anything more to say to you. I've warned you, I've tried to counsel you, but you are clearly determined to do things your way. So, enough said. Life goes on. *I* go on. I've done my job."

Libby was rendered temporarily speechless. There was something about him stepping back and away from her that made her feel unsteady. It made her feel awful, really—she had never meant to push him away. "Just because I don't agree with everything you say doesn't mean that I don't want to be friends."

"Friends," he repeated, as if he found the suggestion ridiculous.

She suddenly reached around him for the door. "But go ahead, go on your date." She opened the door a little too hastily, and it hit Sam in the back.

His gaze darkened, and he caught her wrist. "I swear to God, you are the most stubborn, intractable, infuriating woman I have ever known. One day you want me to leave you alone, and the next you are upset because you think I ignored you."

"I am *not* upset—"

"Don't lie to *me,* Libby Tyler. You've got irate female written all over you." He pushed back against the door and in doing so, yanked her closer to him. She was suddenly staring into his eyes, which were silently, and effectively, daring her to deny it.

Libby couldn't deny it. She wasn't certain she could even speak, because suddenly, everything in her felt crooked. She was in that small space of teetering between righting herself and falling, her thoughts flailing about, looking for balance. Her gaze slipped to Sam's mouth. His very *lush* mouth. A mouth she had never noticed until this very moment. "So?" she said. "It's a free country."

He pressed his magnificent lips together, pulled her even closer, and lowered his head, dipping down so that he was eye level with her. In a voice dangerously low, he said, "If I hear that free country shit from you one more time . . ."

Her pulse notched up. "You'll *what*?"

He responded by kissing her so abruptly that Libby didn't have time to even draw a breath.

His chest was hard, but his mouth, oh, God, his mouth was *not.* It was soft and wet, and his tongue was in her mouth, swirling around, stirring up all sorts of feelings and emotions and flames. He put his hand on her face, cupping her chin, holding her firmly in place while he kissed her so thoroughly her knees began to give way. It was a bolt of lightning shocking through every vein, every muscle, every tissue. Sparks were swirling around scattered thoughts that she shouldn't be doing this, but she liked it, all of it mixing into one hot, wet mess. She could feel herself sinking beneath the haze of arousal, curving into him, pressing against his chest and legs, wanting *in.*

Libby grabbed his tie and held on, mildly disturbed that she had not even a whimper of protest in her, and worse, the fleeting thought that she would like to take off her clothes, right now, at the front door. All her female senses and desires were uniting in solidarity, making her willingly pliable so that his mouth and his tongue could do whatever they wanted to do to her. She hadn't felt a physical response like this in so long that it seemed almost magical to her. She was reminded that she was still a living, breathing, red-blooded woman, a sexual being who missed sex.

His hand slipped around her back and down. He grabbed her hip, kneading it, and pressing it against his erection, which was possibly the most tantalizing thing she'd ever felt. She forgot everything else but the feel of Sam Winters. She forgot dogs, and Tony, and the last five months. She forgot that she had found her lowest point in a sterile room in a place called Mountain View Behavioral Health Center. She forgot that she was broke and had no idea what a business plan was, what she should do, or where she even fit any longer.

She forgot Ryan.

She forgot everything but how amazing it felt with Sam's arms around her, with his body pressing against hers, his lips sliding across hers.

And just as abruptly as he'd started, Sam lifted his head. He did not let her go. He still held her face in one hand. His lips were wet, and his eyes, good Lord, his eyes had turned deep water–green. "*Libby*," he said roughly, his gaze sliding down to her mouth, to her chest, "something is burning."

She was burning all right, burning to a crisp—

"The banana bread!" she cried.

He dropped his arms from hers, grabbed the door and opened it. "Try not to burn the place down," he said, and opened the door. "By the way, I don't have a date. I'm giving a speech at a graduation ceremony." He smiled, stepped out through the screen door and let it slam behind him, stepping over a sea of dogs and down the steps of the porch while Libby stood there trying to catch her breath, her body still on fire.

She stood there after the taillights of his truck had disappeared, and kept standing until she began to smell a little smoke with that burnt banana bread.

# TEN

Here's the good thing about the Methodists: if they come up with a good idea, they're like dogs after dropped barbeque. But here's the bad thing about Methodists: they don't get good ideas that often.

Which is where I, Leo Kendrick, certified genius, come in. I am the oar in their little boat, guiding them down the stream.

Okay, so like I mentioned, I seriously need a new van. The van we have is possibly the uncoolest van in the history of all vans. It was a bread delivery truck before it was ours, and you can still see the outline of the words *fresh baked* on the side. I don't think I have to tell you that those words are not conducive to the life and moves of a chick magnet, which I happen to be.

So yesterday, the Methodists came to see me like they do every Wednesday. Deb Trimble always comes, and her friend Barbara Perkins does, too. You won't believe it, but this time, they brought Gwen Spangler! Gwen is a *Methodist,* can you believe it? I know Gwen, we were in school together, and I tried to kiss her under the bleachers once. She wasn't having it, probably because she was intimidated by my masculine physique, because I mean, look at the pictures, I was a *stud.* Gwen was cool, though, and I haven't seen her since she came back and shook up the Libby-Ryan apple tree. So I was *super* happy to see her, because I figured by now she was regretting her reluctance under the bleachers and I knew she was going to help me.

I asked Marisol if she could get some tea or something for the ladies, and Marisol said she wasn't the hired help, which technically, she is, but I guess she meant she wasn't the kind of hired help that got tea for anyone but me, and she hauled her enormously pregnant body off the couch and stomped off.

It was Dad who came back with the tea, and by that I mean he showed up with the Rubbermaid pitcher in one hand, and some stacked plastic cups in the other hand. Maybe it's just me, but is it too much to ask that we show some decent hosting skills from time to time?

Anyway, I was right in the middle of telling the Methodists that I really need a new van, because my *bread delivery truck* breaks down a lot and I can't rely on it to get me to my *important doctor appointments* when Dad came in and he was like, "*Whaaaat?* What are you talking about Leo, you've never missed a doctor's appointment because of that van." And I said, "Dad, don't help me," but he was on a roll, and he said, "That van has two hundred and fifty thousand miles on it, and she'll go another fifty, sixty thousand before we run into any big repairs. Hell, you can take that van down to Old Mexico and they'll get another fifty thousand miles after *that.* They don't make 'em like that anymore."

And then he sort of chuckled, like *try and top that one,* like he was super proud of the van for having that kind of mileage, and I ask you, in what other instance would a man be proud his old girl had that many miles on her? Which I pointed out to him not too long ago, along with the suggestion he sell the van for parts, and of course Dad got offended. "She's managed to cart *your* tush around, hasn't she?"

I'll tell you right now, I don't care if he gets all new insides for that van, I am not arriving at Mile High Stadium in *that.* I need wheels, and I need them bad, and I swear if I could use my hands, I would have given Dad the Vulcan death grip then and there.

Of course after his speech, no one said anything. Debbie and Barbara looked at each other like they were trying to figure out what to do, but then Gwen said, "That's a lot of miles, Mr. Kendrick. Maybe if Leo got a new van, you could keep that one around for backup."

I didn't know if she meant that she was worried another one of us might get MND, or if she thought a new van would break down a lot, but I didn't care. I wanted to kiss her. I wanted to kiss her *before* she said anything, but then when she said that, I wanted to kiss her times ten.

"That's what *I* was thinking," I said, which is not what I was thinking at all, I was thinking about sex, and I said, "Do you have any *ideas* how to get one?"

Sometimes, you have to lead the horse to water.

Gwen got this little wrinkle between her brows like she was thinking super hard, and she looked really cute, and I could see why Ryan would want her back, although Libby is no slouch in the looks department, but you know how it is, one man's gorgeous is another man's *meh*. Gwen said, "Well, I think a fundraiser. Because those vans are expensive . . . aren't they?"

You don't want to know how expensive they are. The problem is the kind of van I need isn't your average minivan. It's got to have a lift, so me and my chair can slide right into the back like a rodeo bull into a chute, and then there has to be a way to secure the chair.

I said, "Yeah, they're a little more than you'd think," because I didn't want to shock them, but maybe I should have said something a little more informative, because Deb said, "We could have a bake sale!"

We're talking at *least* fifty grand, and that is going to require a *lot* of muffins. But Gwen got it, because she said, "or maybe a series of bake sales and some other fundraisers."

"What about a fall festival event?" I asked them, because the wheels were already turning. "We could do one of those dunk tanks." I laughed at this.

But Barbara gasped like she was going to have a heart attack. "*Leo!* We can't put you in a *dunk tank*!"

I think it would be totally awesome to be able to sit on that little metal seat and then fall into the water, especially since I haven't actually been in a bath or a pool in like, forever. But I know none of the Dudley Do-Rights in this room are going to let me, probably because I couldn't bring myself back to the surface and there would be a lot of concern about liability and drowning, and *blah blah blah*. "No, I agree," I said. "But we can put Dad in the dunk tank."

They all laughed, but I was totally serious.

Anyway, we hammered out some *great* ideas, most of them mine, because that's what I do: I think. And when the Methodists left, we'd agreed to form a fundraising committee, and I was feeling pretty good, even if we didn't know who would be on the committee.

But when Marisol was hosing me down later, she said, "You use these Methodists, Leonard. They want to do good, and you use them."

First, my name is Leo, not Leonard, but Marisol refuses to acknowledge that when she's mad. Second, of *course* I am using them. It's not like I can go out and get a job and buy my own van, is it? People, I have to rely on my superior cunning and exceptional good looks to get through my own little hell on earth, and that's what I told Marisol.

So anyway, I am lying in bed with my legs stretched out as far as they'll go so they don't freeze in a crooked position, and I hear Luke come in. Even though I was watching *Shark Tank* and was totally into this one guy's innovative sippy cups (I have some similar ideas that will probably require a patent), I couldn't help noticing the voices in the living room. Sounded to me like Luke, Dad, and Marisol were having a "conversation" which is *never* a good sign.

Sure enough, Luke popped his head into my room, but I was ready for him.

He said, "What are you watching?"

Like it wasn't totally obvious. "*Shark Tank*."

"Oh, is it Shark Week already?" he asked, because Luke can be totally clueless sometimes. I mean, really, how can one person be so ignorant of important pop culture trends?

"Different shows, different networks," I told him, and honest to God, I tried not to sound condescending about it. "Let's just jump to the finish line here. What do you want?"

Luke looked kind of taken aback, and he said, "Geez, Leo, I just want to talk."

And he proceeds to talk about how I don't really need wheels, and that if I want to embark on some big fundraiser, what I *really* need is a new chair, especially if I am going to talk the Fed Ex guy into helping me out on the sidewalk like I did the other day so I could zip down to the ice stand at the end of Poplar Street and sweet-talk my way into a snow cone. Cherry limeade, my favorite. I even got the cute teenage girl to hold it up for me so I could eat it until Marisol came bouncing down the street like a beach ball and cussing at me in Spanish because I didn't "tell her" that I was "going out."

Anyway, Luke reminded me that the *bread delivery van* gets me to Montrose and the doctors, and he said it like that's high on my list, like he doesn't know they're total downers in Montrose, always talking about new seizure meds and feeding tubes and heart monitors and breathing machines.

I just let Luke do his big-brother, I-am-here-to-fix-everything talk, and then I said, "Luke, it's like this. The Methodists figured out how to get me *into* the Broncos game, which is super cool, but they can't figure out how to get me *to* the game. I *have* to go to the game, Luke. If I don't have that game to think about, I end up thinking about other less fun things, you know? Do you know how hard I've had to work to make it happen? And I did it. I did it from a goddamn chair. But I can't roll up at Mile High Stadium in a *bread delivery van.* That's not cool, Luke, *so* not cool. I have to have wheels! The Broncos are playing the *Patriots!* If I miss that game, go ahead and yank the tubes out of me, because I'm done."

At first Luke looked freaked out, like he thought I was really going to yank the tubes, which, you know, to get my point across, I would consider. Hell, I *have* considered it. But then Luke figured out I was more interested in seeing the Broncos play than offing myself, which, at this point in time, would be an accurate assessment, and he said, "But that's a lot of money for the folks of Pine River to come up with."

And I said, "Well yeah, but I will figure it out."

Luke looked at me like he'd never heard that before, but finally he reached over and he rubbed my gnarly, twisted foot, and he said, "Yeah, I remember. If anyone can figure it out, it's you."

Like, *hello*. Everyone knows that.

"Maybe you can put that ginormous brain of yours to the ranch," he said, because he was trying to change the subject. "We've only got one wedding lined up. If we don't get some business in the next couple of months, we're going to have to rethink things."

After all that mess with Dad practically giving away the ranch to Grant Tyler, who then up and died and left it to his three daughters, who didn't know each other, and Luke quitting his job in Denver to come home and figure it all out, and deciding okay, maybe the ranch should be this event thing, and now he tells me they have one little wedding on the books?

I told him that I couldn't solve all of his problems, and he said, no one asked me to solve *his* problems, and I said, get your hand off my foot, dude, or I will take it off for you, and some other stuff that brothers will say to each other when they're annoyed, and I was annoyed.

But I got over it. Which is why I told Dad to fire up the grill, we're going to have a party for family and close friends and chat about how they need to be on my new committee and raise enough money to get me that goddamn van. And while I'm at it, I'll talk to the Libster about Homecoming Ranch.

I ask you, what are these clowns going to do without me when I'm gone? I'm going to have to write a manual or something because I don't trust them to step up when I'm not around to tell them what to do. If I could hold a pointer, I'd give them a presentation they would never forget, and assign all the tasks. But I can't hold a pointer, which you probably already knew, so I'll just have to talk my way through it, and thankfully for them and for you, I am a brilliant speaker. It's one of my best talents.

# ELEVEN

Libby awoke several times wondering if she'd dreamed that kiss with Sam, only to open her eyes and realize she hadn't dreamt it at all. And then she would lie there recalling every single moment of it. *Every single one.*

She thought morning would never come. But it did come, sliding in cool and cloudy under the night sky.

In the gloomy light of a new day, Libby couldn't recall exactly how she had ended up attached to Sam's very scrumptious lips. What was said that managed to throw them together?

There was another thing: she hadn't thought about good, old-fashioned rolling-in-the-hay sex in a very long time. Several months, actually. Not that she kept count, for if she actually knew how long it had been, she might murder an innocent bunny or kick a helpless old woman.

*Thanks, Sam.*

She cleaned the kitchen after breakfast and tried to imagine wild sex with Sam. And in spite of the warm glow that gave her, she couldn't picture it. Sex just didn't compute with the deputy sheriff and his no-nonsense lectures. Sex computed with the guy in the suit and tie and the body made of hard planes and ironclad grip, yes. But that guy was *not* the same guy who showed up with his badge and his hat sitting backward to tell her to stay out of trouble.

Libby was going to have to confront Sam and that kiss. They had a professional relationship—sort of—as he had pointed out, and she couldn't be walking around thinking of kissing him. If she was thinking about kissing him, how could she possibly take him seriously when he was admonishing her? She had to try and fix this before it could get complicated.

She was fully prepared to do it that morning when Sam dropped off Tony, but the dropping-off job fell to the woman with bleached-blond hair and a tattoo of a rose on her chest. Even from Libby's vantage point at the window, she could see that rose.

Libby walked out onto the porch to greet Tony and realized that he and the woman were engaged in an argument, seeing as how she was calling him names. Libby thought maybe she ought to intervene before the woman yanked Tony's prosthesis off of him, but the moment she started down the steps, the woman slid into her little Pontiac and roared down the drive, bouncing over the pits and rocks.

Libby walked down to where Tony was standing, his weight on his hip, watching the woman drive away. "She's not going to come back with a sawed-off shotgun, is she?"

Tony bent down and picked up his duffel, and slung it over his shoulder. "I sure hope not."

"Come on," Libby said, her eye still on the road out of the ranch. "I'll show you the bunkhouse."

At the bunkhouse, she introduced Tony to Ernest, who was wearing thigh-high waders and a fishing jacket. Libby had mentioned Tony yesterday, and Ernest had seemed unfazed by it, but this morning, he eyed Tony suspiciously, his gaze sliding down to Tony's leg.

"How you doing, man?" Tony said, extending his hand. "I won't take up much space."

Ernest took his hand. "Vet?" he asked.

"Yep. Afghanistan," Tony said.

Ernest nodded. "Come in. I'll show you a room."

Libby left the guys to do whatever it was guys did in circumstances like this, and walked back to the house. She paused at the barn to glance inside. Homecoming Ranch kept three horses for working cattle. The horses spent most of the summer outside, grazing in the meadow around the tent pads they'd had poured after the reunion in June, but this morning, they were in the barn, munching contentedly from their feeders.

The horses were the biggest problem Libby had for the ceremony. She had to get them out so she could clean the barn and rid it of the smell of manure. Ideally, she would like to have that done before Austin and Gary showed up to check out the setting. Libby was convinced the barn setting would work very well, but she guessed that Austin and Gary would not be persuaded of that if they could smell manure.

This event was a lot of work. A *lot* of work. A lot of work she had not anticipated when she had put a cost to it.

She walked on, thankful to have something to think about other than that kiss. Or sex. In fact, the more she thought about Homecoming Ranch and all that had to be done, the more her senses were dulled into a throb of mild panic.

Madeline was up and puttering around the kitchen when Libby came in. She smiled sleepily and stretched her arms high overhead. She was wearing one of Luke's T-shirts that came to mid-thigh.

"How are things?" she asked, yawning.

"Good," Libby said. "Tony is going to stick around for a couple of days to get the cars going. He's bunking with Ernest."

"Oh, that's nice," Madeline said absently. She poured herself a cup of coffee and walked into the living room, a magazine tucked under her arm.

Libby was sorting laundry when her phone rang. She picked it up, looked at the display, and smiled. "Hello, sweetie," she answered.

"Hi, Libby, it's Alice!"

"I know! Why aren't you at school?" she asked curiously, looking at the clock. When Alice had begun calling her a couple of weeks ago, Libby had been suspicious, but Alice had told her twice that her father had given her permission. Libby hadn't understood why Ryan would do that, but now, it all made sense. He was allowing Alice to rekindle the relationship she'd lost with Libby, because he intended to apologize and allow Libby to see the kids.

"It's Teacher Day. Daddy's taking us to the movies when he comes home."

"Oh yeah? What are you doing now?" Libby asked, wondering where Gwen was.

"Watching cartoons. So is Max. We're watching *SpongeBob SquarePants*."

"I love SpongeBob," Libby said wistfully. "I *miss* you, Alice. I hope we get to see each other soon," she said as she wandered into the dining room.

"I told Daddy I want to go to your house and he said okay."

"He did?"

"He said maybe in a few days."

Libby frowned a little. "Alice? You know you should always tell the truth, right?"

"I am!" Alice insisted.

That confused Libby. Had the man who had said she was too lenient, was turning his kids into monsters, really had such a change of heart? While Libby couldn't wait to see Alice and Max, everything seemed so sudden. It made her feel uncomfortable. "Well, I can't wait," she said to Alice, her mind racing.

"I'm taking dance lessons!" Alice said suddenly.

"I know! Do you like your teacher?"

"Yes. Her name's Miss Janie, and I'm going to be a butterfly in the recycle!"

"Recital," Libby laughingly corrected her. "A butterfly! How cool is that? Are you going to have a costume?"

"Mommy said she was going to try and make me one. But she doesn't really know how."

Libby could imagine that was true. Gwen had never struck her as the crafty type. "Maybe I could make one for you," she suggested, realizing, even as she spoke, that it was the wrong thing to say. "I mean, if your mom agrees," she quickly added. "Anyway, I bet you'll be the best butterfly in the recital."

"You can make my costume!" Alice eagerly agreed. "You just have to get the wings."

Libby laughed. "Where do I get wings?"

"At the store. I want to be a purple butterfly."

"A purple butterfly, how pretty," Libby said. She sat down in a chair that was up against a wall and fixed her gaze on the wallpaper in front of her, on the corner that had begun to peel away from the wall. "Is Max there? May I speak to him?"

"Sure," Alice said. She put down the phone on her end, but Libby heard her yell at her brother and tell him to come to the phone. Then she heard Alice say, "It's Libby."

"Hi," Max said. At six years old, he was not the least bit garrulous, particularly on the phone.

"Hi, Max!" Libby said. "What are you doing?"

"Watching TV. We're not supposed to. We're supposed to be cleaning our rooms."

"Oh . . . where's your mommy?" Libby asked curiously.

"I dunno. Here's Alice," he said, and then he was gone.

"Libby, did you go to the hospital?" Alice said. "Daddy said you went to a hospital."

The question startled Libby; she'd not thought of what she'd tell the kids, and in a moment of decisiveness, opted for honesty. "Yes, I did. But that was a few weeks ago, and I'm okay now."

"What was wrong with you?"

"Well . . . I was really, really tired."

"Is that why you can't come to my house? Because you hit Daddy's truck with a golf club?"

Libby winced. "That's part of it. Hey, are you practicing your dance every day like the teacher said?"

"Yes. Are you going to come see the recycle?"

"I'll try my best, Alice," Libby said sincerely. "I really miss you, and I love you. And I can't wait to see you."

"Okay. I love you, too. I have to go. Bye!" Alice said cheerfully, and the phone went dead.

Libby clicked her phone off and sank back in the chair, her head resting against the wall, her gaze fixed on the peeling wallpaper. She could almost smell Alice's hair, could almost see the smudges of dirt on Max's face. That Ryan was allowing her to call—

"Libby?"

Libby sat up with a start; she hadn't heard Madeline come into the dining room. "Hey," she said with a nervous laugh. "I didn't hear you."

Madeline stepped down into the dining room, still holding a cup of coffee. She was staring at Libby as if she couldn't quite make her out, as if she had seen her somewhere and couldn't place her. "Who was that on the phone?"

Libby could feel the stain of guilt spreading across her cheeks. "Alice."

"Oh no," Madeline said weakly, and sat down on the step so heavily, it almost appeared she'd fallen onto it. "Libby, what are you doing?" she asked in a near whisper. "Are you *trying* to get thrown in jail?"

"What? No!" Libby said, surprised. "Of course not. It's not what you think, Madeline. She's been calling me—"

"Oh my God, *how*?" Madeline exclaimed.

"Calm down. You know Alice and I have a very strong bond."

Madeline closed her eyes. "Libby . . . he has a restraining order against you," she said, opening them again. "He doesn't want you anywhere near him or his family. People don't get restraining orders for the hell of it."

"Well I *know* that," Libby said. "But people also change their minds."

Madeline's eyes widened. "What do you mean, changed his mind? About the restraining order?"

Madeline's questions were making Libby question herself. She felt guilty. And wrong. She stood up. "He has apologized to me. He says he wishes things hadn't happened like they did." She stepped around her sister and went into the kitchen, desperate for an activity, anything so that she wouldn't have to listen to Madeline.

But her sister was right behind her. "Okay, you have to explain this to me," Madeline demanded, and put down her coffee cup. "Are you saying that Ryan has apologized for dumping you for his ex-wife, and lying to you, and then saying horrible things to you, and then slapping you with a restraining order? And you're *okay* with that?"

"No, I am not *okay* with that," Libby said firmly. "I was only explaining to you why Alice is calling."

"Because if he *has* changed his mind," Madeline said, sounding like she didn't believe Libby, "that doesn't make what he did to you any less horrible. In fact, it makes him even scuzzier."

"Madeline!" Libby said sternly, whirling around to her. "Is he not allowed to apologize? To regret what he did? Don't you believe that people can change?"

"Of course I believe it. People do change," Madeline said. "But some people are just really good at playing both ends against the middle, you know? Because I promise you, if he's told you he's sorry, he wants something."

"Jesus, you should have been a lawyer," Libby said. "I understand your concern. I don't want . . ." She paused, tried to gather her thoughts. "I miss Alice and Max, Madeline. I miss them *so much,*" she said, pressing both hands against her heart. "I miss having a family and I can't say good-bye to them. And what about them? I was the one who took care of them. They love me, too, you know. What about what *they* want? You don't know Ryan, you don't know what went on between us. You can't make judgments about it."

"You're right," Madeline said, still nodding, her hands on her hips now. "I don't know him or what it was like between the two of you. I'm only going by the fact that he basically used you to babysit his kids while he was running around for everyone to see with his ex-wife."

"For everyone to see?" Libby repeated. "No they didn't!"

"Yes, they did, Libby. Ask anyone," Madeline said, casting her arm wide. "Everyone in Pine River knew what was going on but you. He made you look like a fool," she said, her voice softer. "And if he is telling you anything other than he deserves to go to hell for what he did, he's lying."

Libby's mind was racing again, trying to sort through what was truth and what was her, trying to justify her feelings.

Libby's heart felt as if it would leap right out of her chest. She was angry and hurt, and felt a little breathless. She was second-guessing everything she thought she knew about the last four years. *Again.*

Madeline groaned. She covered her face with both hands for a moment, as if she was trying to regain her composure. "I'm sorry," she said, and dropped her hands. "I don't mean to . . . to butt in. But I really care about you, Libby. I don't want to see you hurt again, or . . . or—"

"Institutionalized?" Libby finished for her.

"Or that," Madeline admitted, and pressed her lips together.

"For heaven's sake," Libby said wearily. That Madeline worried she was fragile didn't hurt as much as it had right after Libby had come home. Now it was just a dull ache. "One week at Mountain View and I guess I'll spend the rest of my life proving that I'm not crazy to everyone around me. I had an emotional breakdown, Madeline. It's not going to happen again. But if there's a chance that I can have Alice and Max in my life—"

"Here we go," Madeline muttered.

"That was my family!" Libby cried angrily. "Don't you *get* that? They were my family and of *course* I want them back! Do you know how I ache for Alice and Max every single day?" she shouted, pressing her fist against her heart. "How much I miss hearing the details of their lives, or helping them brush their teeth, or watching them play? That was all yanked out from beneath me without warning, so *yes,* I *do* want them back. And if I have to take Ryan as part of the deal, I might just have to suck it up."

"But here's the thing, Libby," Madeline said quietly. "It wasn't really your family. It was Gwen's."

The truth detonated painfully inside Libby, exploding into painful little shards. "I can't talk about this anymore," she said, her voice shaking. She turned around and walked out the door, onto the porch. She stood there, trying to suck in deep breaths, trying to calm her racing heart.

It wasn't working.

She jumped off the porch and began to stride up one of the trails into the forest behind the house, her fists clenched tightly and her head aching from the many confusing, competing thoughts.

What was the truth? Or was she trying to create a new truth, one that suited her emotions, her sense of having been wronged? Libby truly didn't know anymore.

# TWELVE

Dani was behind the cash register when Sam stopped into the Grizzly Café for a coffee. "Good to see you, Sam," she said cheerfully. "The usual?"

"Please," he said. He glanced at the tables at the window—that's where he always sat when he came in for a cup of coffee—but his usual table was occupied.

It reminded him of another time it had been occupied. He'd been passing by, and had seen Libby through the window, sitting at his usual table. She was hunched over a mug with both hands wrapped around it, staring at the tabletop. Sam couldn't say how he knew, but she didn't look right to him. Something was off. Maybe Sam should have walked on. Maybe he should have not let his emotions guide him. For whatever reason, he'd changed direction and had come in.

She'd been on his mind a lot the last couple of days, obviously, after that damn impetuous kiss. He couldn't help thinking back to that day only a few weeks ago, and how she'd looked up when he'd entered, smiling a little and giving him a halfhearted wave. Her hair was always a mess of curls, but that day it looked as if she hadn't attempted to comb it. She'd rolled a bandana and tied it around her head to keep it from her face.

Dani had told him that she'd been like that for an hour, sitting and staring. Sam had gone over to check on her.

Libby had tried to perk up. "Hey, Sam," she'd said. "Sit down . . . did you come for coffee?"

"Yeah. Are you sure you don't mind if I join you?"

"Not at all. I could use the company." She'd laughed, but it had sounded hollow.

Up close, Sam had noticed that her complexion was sallow, and there were dark circles under her eyes. It had alarmed him—he'd never seen Libby look anything but healthy. "Are you okay, Libby?" he'd asked.

She'd laughed and looked away from his direct gaze. "Why does everyone keep asking me that? I really must look bad. But I'm fine. Really. I've just been battling a bout of insomnia, that's all. My mom gets it, too."

That had sounded to Sam like a practiced response.

"Sam?"

Dani tapped him on the shoulder, and Sam turned around. "I'll have your coffee right out," she said. Sam nodded. He sat down at a table near his usual one, his thoughts returning to the past. Libby had been so much on his mind recently that he couldn't help his thoughts wandering back to that day.

He remembered Libby asking him what was up, and his casual shrug.

She'd said, "Hey, guess who I ran into last week? Don Chadwick—remember him?"

Sam had remembered him—Don Chadwick had retired from the sheriff's office about a year before Sam's demise. "Sure. He was a nice guy."

"He always helped me with the holiday parties," Libby said. "He asked how you were doing. I told him you're doing great, that you're the county's rural area deputy now. And he said he was very glad to know that you'd landed on your feet."

Sam remembered thinking that it was nice of her to say something kind about him. He'd gotten past the shame of what had happened to him, but he still didn't mind a good word now and then. He'd told her that it was nice of her to say so.

"But it's true. You look great, Sam. You look happy." And then she'd suddenly leaned forward, looked at him with dull blue eyes. "*Are* you happy?"

It had seemed an oddly earnest question to him at the time, but in hindsight, he could see why. "I'm as happy as I can be, I guess," he'd said. "Are you?"

"Me?" She'd eased back, as if leaning away from that question. "Truth is, I've been better." She'd shrugged. "But I'm okay. Really."

"Are you trying to convince me? Or yourself?"

With a soft sigh, Libby had looked down and rubbed her eyes. "Maybe trying to convince myself. Do you ever wonder what might have happened if you'd gone one way instead of the other? Like, what if you hadn't gotten the job in the sheriff's office? Where would you be now?"

Sam thought then what he thought now—that he'd probably be drunk in an alley somewhere. "I don't know," he'd said.

"I wonder . . . what if I hadn't been in the office the day Ryan came in? I never would have known him. Poof, just like that, I would have had a different life. Maybe I would have moved. Maybe I'd have married someone. Maybe I'd be someone else right now, like a novelist or a singer."

"Do you like to sing?" he'd asked.

"No," she'd said with a funny little laugh. "I'm just saying, that but for one moment in time, your life could go down a completely different path."

He could see where she was going. He'd gone there, too, in the last couple of years. But he'd had the benefit of looking at it from a long lens. "True," he'd agreed with her. "But you can make yourself crazy imagining all the things you might have missed or avoided. There's no point to it. Personally, I think it's useless to look back."

"What do you mean? You never look back?"

"I used to," Sam had admitted. "I don't anymore. There's just too much water under too many bridges, and I can't change anything that happened."

"I hear you," she'd said, but Sam had been fairly certain she hadn't heard him at all. She'd looked at her wristwatch. "I've got to go." She'd gathered her things. "Sorry to sip and run." Her coffee looked untouched.

As she stood up, Sam had impulsively grabbed her hand and had said, sincerely, "Libby . . . take care of yourself."

"You and my mother," she'd said teasingly. "I will, Sam. I promised Mom I'd go to the doc and see if I can't get something for the insomnia. I just need to sleep, that's all. Then I'll be right as rain." She'd smiled as she'd pulled her hand free, but again, that smile seemed off to him. "I hope you have a stupendous day, Lone Ranger."

"I hope the same for you."

He'd sat at the table after she'd gone, thinking about what she'd said. When he heard the commotion outside, he hadn't at first registered what it was, not until he heard the sound of breaking glass.

By the time he rushed outside, everyone was shouting, Gwen was shrieking, and Libby was swinging the golf club. He'd run across the street and pulled Ryan back before he could launch himself at Libby, then put himself between Ryan and Libby.

"Libby!" he'd shouted.

He would never forget the way she'd looked at him, wild-eyed. Not all there.

Sam had lifted his hand, palm up. "Think about what you're doing. Put the club down."

Her grip on the club tightened, and she looked at the truck. She had bashed in all the windows except the window vent on the driver's side.

"This isn't solving anything," Sam had said quickly. "This is just adding to the problems you're having and making them worse. Give me the club, and let's talk about it. I'll help you, Libby. I'll help you any way I can."

Libby had lifted her arms, club in hand, as if she intended to have a whack at the last window. But then she had suddenly dropped her arms.

Sam had grabbed the golf club from her hand, and Libby had sagged against him. "I am so tired," she'd said hoarsely.

"Yeah, I know," he'd said, and put his arm around her.

That had only been a few weeks ago. Libby had a long way to go. And still, he'd kissed her.

Worse, he'd kissed her like a teenager in heat. But damn it, she'd been standing there with her blue eyes glittering up at him, and her hair in funny little ponytails. When she opened her mouth, his composure had cracked, and his mouth was on hers, and he was kissing her. He hadn't even realized it was in his mind. And now, all he could think of was all the other places of her body he'd like to touch.

This was the worst kind of trouble for a guy like him. First of all, Libby had some ghosts following her around, and Sam did not do well with women and their ghosts; he had a tendency to think he could fix things, to remove the ghosts, and he'd learned the hard way that he was no superman.

Second, Libby was violating her restraining order half the time, and he was enforcing it half the time, which made it more than just a bit of a conflict for him to walk around kissing her. Every cop knew not to fraternize with the people who break the laws they were charged to enforce.

There was nothing good that could possibly come from any desire for her, so Sam had studiously avoided her. Out of sight, out of mind, as the saying went. But the saying was not entirely accurate, Sam discovered, because he really couldn't avoid her in his thoughts. She kept popping into his head with those sparkling eyes and a charming smile, usually jabbering nonsense. He would push her out of his mind. But she would pop up again. And again.

There was no explaining the laws of attraction, but there was something about that woman that had crept under his skin.

He was startled by the sudden appearance of Dani, with his coffee and a creamer. "Sorry that took so long, I had to brew a fresh pot. So, are you going to be at the Kendricks' Sunday night?" she asked, sliding into a seat across from him.

Sam clearly didn't answer quickly enough because Dani slapped her hand down on the table. "Sam Winters, you'd better say yes! You hide away up there in those mountains and you don't come down. It's not good for a person to be so alone."

Sam chuckled and began to doctor his coffee. "What makes you think I'm so alone, Dani? For all you know, I've got a harem up there."

Her eyes narrowed. "I'm not as dumb as I look, Sam. And I'll tell you this—if I don't see you at the Kendricks' Sunday, I am liable to drive up there and fetch you." She suddenly smiled and stood up. "You want a cinnamon roll with that? I just made some fresh this morning."

"You bet. Thank you," Sam said. He wasn't as dumb as he looked, either.

# THIRTEEN

Dani's warning notwithstanding, Sam did not want to attend the Kendricks' dinner party. Sam wasn't a big party guy anymore, obviously. In addition to being an alcoholic, it reminded him too painfully of his life with Terri. He was no good at small talk, and he was even less good at watching people drink. That part of his life never got any easier. And frankly, he preferred to watch the football game in his living room without a lot of chatter.

Dani was right. He was alone.

Still, Sam might have been able to say no to Dani. But he couldn't say no to Leo. Not that he hadn't tried, but Leo had talked him to death. Sam had to give in to the man or lose his mind.

But moreover, Sam wasn't feeling himself. It alarmed him that in the last couple of days, he'd felt a creeping desire to drink unlike anything he'd felt in a very long time.

He knew himself well enough to know that the desire for booze was usually a good indicator of his stress level. Only Sam wasn't stressed. Why would he be stressed? Work was good, everything was good.

Everything but this thing with Libby.

There'd be no avoiding her tonight, so Sam had to have a stern talk with himself. He resolved to treat her like he treated his sobriety. He would see her, think of her as an alcoholic beverage, and walk away. He would keep his hands in his pockets. *Never touch drinks or women.*

He dressed in a collared blue shirt he'd picked up recently at Tag's Outfitters and jeans that were actually clean, and his cowboy boots. He combed his hair and tucked it behind his ears—reminding himself that he needed that haircut—and skipped the shave, leaving a shadow of a beard on his face. He fed his horses and headed into town.

The little green house on Elm Street where the Kendrick men had taken up residence was lit up, even though the sun was still hanging over the horizon. It was unusually warm for this time of year—old-timers would tell you that meant an early snow was coming—but on Elm Street, the only thing coming that night was light and music drifting out from open windows.

The house was set back from the street in a big square yard. A few months ago, a church group had built a ramp up to the front door for Leo. Since then, Luke had built a deck that wrapped around the house. Little pots of flowers graced the corners of the railings, and there were two lawn chairs around a small table on the corner of the deck, beneath the boughs of the old elm tree that draped over the house and lawn.

Luke had removed the old front door and installed a wider one so that they could get Leo in and out of the house easily. Luke had also added a third bedroom and bath. The house was still awfully small, but at least it was more suitable to house three grown men. And it still needed work—the kitchen in particular. But the place was starting to look like a home.

Sam walked through the gate of the chain-link fence, past the empty dog igloo, and waved at Jackson Crane, smiling a little at Jackson's pencil-thin slacks, rolled up over his bare ankles and leather loafers.

Jackson was probably in his early thirties. He was always wearing something that made it seem as if he'd just stepped out of an ad for private jets and fast cars, and it never failed to put a smile on Sam's face. In that getup, Jackson looked ridiculous playing washers with Luke's uncle, Greg Compton, who was wearing a sagging pair of Dockers and a T-shirt that had the Coors logo sprawled across the chest. "Hey chief," Greg called out to him, lifting a beefy hand in greeting.

On the deck, Greg's wife, Patti, was arranging chips and hot sauce on the little table. She was the de facto woman of the house from what Sam understood, the one who oversaw all family gatherings. Leo said she cooked for them once or twice a week so, as Leo put it, they wouldn't all succumb to salmonella poisoning.

"Sam! It's great that you could come," she said cheerfully. She was a round woman, and looked just like the late Mrs. Kendrick, her sister. She had big, heavy breasts, and Sam could imagine that more than one kid had been smothered in them in the course of a motherly hug. "Dani says you don't get down off that mountain much, so I'm really glad you did for us. Come in, come in!"

Sam resisted a groan. He asked, "Is that Norah Jones I'm hearing?" referring to the music that was piping out of the open windows.

"It sure is," she said, her smile beaming. "Are you a fan?"

"I am."

"Sam Winters, I always knew you were a man of discerning taste," she said. "You'd think I put on church music the way the

Kendrick boys reacted. Go in and get yourself a beer. We've got every kind you can think of because God forbid anyone should watch a football game without it. We're going to eat a little early so everyone can settle in for the game. Luke's rigged up a TV outside." That she said with a voice full of awe, as if it were a feat of modern engineering.

Bob Kendrick, Luke and Leo's father, was standing at the door when Sam stepped through. He reached out to shake Sam's hand. "Good to see you, Sam. You know Marisol Fuentes, right? And her husband, Javier?"

Sam smiled at the fiery Marisol. She was rubbing her hand over her distended belly. "How are you, Marisol?"

"Ready for this baby to come out," she said. "It kicks me, night and day. You want beer, there's beer in the fridge and coolers on the patio," she said, and began a laborious shift down onto one of two twin recliners in the room. Both recliners faced a blank wall where normally an impressive flat screen TV hung. Sam guessed it was outside.

In between the recliners was a large space where Leo usually wheeled in to watch his shows and play his video games. *Hounds of Hell* was his current favorite. Sam knew this, because when he'd stopped by last week, he'd had to listen to a detailed explanation of how Leo had made it to level fourteen.

"Sam, come with me," Bob said. "I'll show you where the drinks are."

As they walked into the tiny kitchen, Sam heard Leo shout, "Hey, is that Sam? Sam, get out here!" Sam bent down and squinted out the little square window of the backdoor. Leo was on the deck, holding court like a fraternity brother. There was a picture in the house that Sam had once seen. It was of Leo, before his disease had manifested itself. He'd been a football player, a big tackle with a scholarship to the Colorado School of Mines. The picture of him had been taken on a river's edge, and Leo stood a head taller than his companion, his arm looped around the guy's shoulders, holding up a string of trout and grinning irrepressibly. It was the same grin Leo usually sported, but now it was made crooked by the betrayal of his muscles.

Bob opened an old white fridge and pulled out a bottle of water. "Leo's in fine form tonight," he said. "When he gets like this, he's usually cooking something up. Be prepared." He smiled as he handed the bottle to Sam.

"Thanks," he said, and with the bottle of water in hand, he walked out onto the back deck. He noticed that a brace had been added to the headrest of Leo's chair to keep his head from flopping to one side. It kept his head upright, but Sam realized Leo was even less mobile—now he couldn't seem to turn his head at all.

"Sam!" Leo said, looking genuinely pleased to see him as he maneuvered his chair around to get a better look at him. "Hey, have you met Dr. Levitt? He's my in-town doctor. Not to be confused with my Montrose doctors. So get this," Leo continued as Sam extended his hand to Dr. Levitt. "Mark here doesn't know who was the first quarterback to catch a pass in a Super Bowl. Can you *believe* that?"

Dr. Levitt smiled apologetically at Sam as he extended his hand. "Leo is very disappointed in me."

"Then I guess he's going to be disappointed in me, too," Sam said, shaking the doctor's hand. "I have no clue."

"No clue about what?" Madeline Pruett materialized at Sam's elbow. Luke was right behind her, clapping his hand on Sam's shoulder in greeting, and speaking to Dr. Levitt.

"Wow, Madeline, you look *gorgeous*," Leo said. "Hubba hubba, if I weren't in this chair . . ."

"If you weren't in that chair, you'd be down at the Rocky Creek Tavern, buying cheap wine for cheap broads and you know it,"

Madeline teased him, and leaned over to kiss his cheek. "What is it that Sam has no clue about?" she asked, looking around at the men.

"Who was the first quarterback to catch a pass in a Super Bowl," Sam said with a chuckle.

"Oh," Madeline said with a flick of her wrist. "As if the answer isn't obvious to everyone here." She snorted. "Give him a tough one, Leo."

Sam looked from her to Leo.

"Come on, Sam!" Madeline said, nudging him playfully with her elbow. "It's John Elway, 1989!"

"There's nothing that turns me on more than a woman who knows her football," Leo said gleefully, "but it was 1988."

"Was it?" Madeline said, and frowned a little as she tapped her finger to her lip. "You're right, Leo. 1988."

Sam and Dr. Levitt exchanged a look of surprise at Madeline's knowledge of useless football facts. Madeline tried for at least a minute to seem very nonchalant about it, but then Luke sighed, and she burst into laughter.

"Hey, I can't help it!" she said to Sam's confused look. "This week is John Elway week at the Kendrick house, and it's mandatory participation. Now that you've had your fun, Leo, I'm going to go say hello to Dani," she said, and excused herself, walking past the men and down the deck steps onto the lawn, where Dani Boxer was chatting it up with Sherry Stancliff, who ran the Tuff Tots daycare.

Leo whipped his chair around to watch Madeline. His hands curled like claws, but he could maneuver that chair like a champ. "Dad's making his famous shoe-leather brisket tonight," Leo announced. "Dad! Sam wants chips and dip!"

"No, I—"

"Just go with it," Leo advised, wheeling past Sam to the ramp. "We were giving Dad the business about his culinary skills, and I think his feelings got hurt. Excuse me, gentlemen, but I see ladies," he said, and sailed down the ramp at what seemed like a breakneck speed to Sam.

"My feelings did not get hurt," Bob Kendrick said, appearing at the kitchen door with a big red bowl full of chips. "All I said was that I would shove that dip down his throat with my fist if he didn't knock off the food talk." He handed Sam the big red bowl. "The kid's got a mouth on him."

"As if that is news to anyone in Pine River," Luke added cheerfully. "Hey, Dr. Levitt, could I talk to you a minute?" he asked the doctor. "I've got a couple of questions." He and Dr. Levitt moved to one side, leaving Sam standing alone on the deck with a big red bowl of chips in one hand, a bottle of water in the other.

He looked down at the lawn and the people gathered there, wondering what to do with it.

"Is that your own personal chip stash, or are you sharing?"

The sound of Libby's voice slipped through Sam like a soft whisper and swirled around in the pit of him. He glanced over his shoulder; she was standing just outside the kitchen door in skin-tight black pants and a pair of leopard-print high heels. She wore a loose white pullover that swung around her hips, and had piled her wild curls into a loose bun on top of her head. A charge ran through him—Libby looked sexy as hell.

"Want some?" he asked, extending the bowl.

She shook her head as she walked across the deck to him. As she neared him, Sam could see that she was wearing makeup. He'd always liked the natural look Libby generally sported, but tonight, the dark, smoky lining around her lids had the effect of making her pale-blue eyes seem to leap off her face. She settled her weight on one curvy hip, holding a glass of white wine in one hand.

Sam's blood rippled through his veins. She looked spectacular, and that did not help Sam's muddied thinking. He did not want to think of Libby as "spectacular" or "attractive." He didn't want to think of touching her or kissing her. He didn't want to think of her at all. He'd spent the last two days working very hard *not* to think of her.

Her gaze fell to the tub of chips he was holding. "You sure?" he asked, shaking the bowl a little before putting them aside on a table. Libby casually sipped her wine as she eyed him over the rim of her glass.

"You look nice," he said, and instantly regretted it, because her eyes sparked with pleasure.

She glanced down at herself. "Thanks. I've been cleaning out the barn for the last two days and I couldn't take it any longer. I had to put on something that didn't smell like horses or could be worn to ride or groom horses. And, you know, it's my first party since Mountain View, so I wanted to make a big splash." She winked.

Sam told himself to look elsewhere. He dropped his gaze to the water bottle and twisted the top off of it. "How's Tony?"

"Tony? Tony D'Angelo? The guy you deposited at the ranch and then never came back to see? Tony is good. Tony is rebuilding my car, one screw at a time."

"I told you he was good."

"I was hoping he might speed things along. I need a car so I can go to town."

Sam didn't want to care why she needed to go to town. But he did. "Town, huh?" he asked, and casually drank his water.

"Yes, town, Lone Ranger," Libby said. "In spite of what you are clearly thinking, I learned a funny thing while clearing out the barn—I need one of those big shop brooms."

"Walmart," Dani Boxer said as she sailed by in her signature Guayabera shirt and some chunky turquoise jewelry.

"See?" Libby said to Sam, gesturing to Dani's back as she stepped inside. "I need to go to Walmart. So?"

"So . . . ?" he asked, confused.

"*Sooo*, are you going to come check on Tony, or are you going to leave him at the ranch forever?"

Sam had checked on Tony. Not a day went by that he didn't check on Tony. He'd given him a disposable phone before he'd sent him up there, and had been diligent about calling. But he smiled at Libby now and asked, "Are you advocating checking on Tony? Because I was under the impression that you are adamantly opposed to checking."

"I am opposed to people checking on *me*. I didn't realize that meant you'd never return to Homecoming Ranch."

"I've been busy," Sam said.

Libby gave him a withering look. "Really? That's your answer? I find it very curious that you are suddenly so busy, Sam Winters. Just a few days ago, you'd hardly let me go to the bathroom without coming around to issue some sort of warning. And then . . ." She stopped talking and arched a feathery brow.

Sam waited for her to say it.

Libby didn't say it. Her brows sank into a *V*. "*You* know."

Yes. He knew. But he was unwilling to talk about it.

"Okay, why the big no-show all of a sudden?" she demanded.

"I told you, I've been busy. I also told you that I've given you all the advice I have to give. It's your life, Libby. You can do whatever the hell you want. You want to ignore a restraining order? Go ahead."

"Wow," Libby said, clearly startled by his tone.

So was Sam. "Excuse me," he said, and turned around and walked into the house, looking for a place to dispose of his water bottle.

Everyone else, however, was moving outside, apparently ushered by Patti. Sam stepped around Greg and into the kitchen to grab another bottle of water, and stepped aside when Marisol and Javier came through. "She's like a ship," Javier said, which earned him some strongly worded Spanish as Javier helped to maneuver his wife around the scarred kitchen bar and out the door.

On the deck, a few people gathered around Marisol. Sherry's hand went to Marisol's belly. Someone—Bob, he thought—said something that prompted everyone to lift their beers and wineglasses and clink together. They were toasting the baby. Sam thought he should go out there, join the party, but instead, he slipped through the door into the small living area and leaned up against the wall, breathing in a moment, trying to erase a pair of eyes dancing around his mind's eye.

He heard someone come into the kitchen, heard something being placed on the little kitchen bar. A moment later, Libby's head suddenly appeared through the doorway. She stepped into the living room. "There you are." She looked around. "What are you doing?"

*Trying to stay away from you.* "Taking a break," he said.

"From what?" she asked curiously as she moved a little closer and peered up at him. "You're acting weird, Sam."

He shrugged. "Free country."

Libby gasped indignantly at his use of her favorite rejoinder. "You know what I think?" she demanded, her hands finding her hips. "I think you're standing in here so you don't have to talk to *me*."

"You're right," he agreed. "I'm off-duty."

She gasped again. And then she took another step toward him. "Oh, *I* see what's going on here," she said, gesturing between the two of them. "You want to avoid the big elephant in the room."

"Mention any elephant you want," he said, but he really wished she wouldn't. He could already feel himself responding, that silent drumbeat of want sending out a call to arms in all body parts. "What do you want, an apology?"

"*No!*" she exclaimed. "I just . . . maybe we should acknowledge that it happened, and agree it shouldn't have happened, no harm no foul, and promise that it's not going to happen again, right? Because, you know . . . there can't *be* anything between us, right?"

Well if that wasn't rich, Crazy Pants telling him that she couldn't be with *him.* "Whoa," he said, throwing up a hand. "Did I say anything to give you the impression I thought there was something between us?"

"Well . . . no," she said, looking confused now. "But generally, a guy doesn't kiss a girl if—"

"Listen," he said before she could launch into any ridiculous theories about why men kissed women. They kissed women because sex was always on the forefront of their mind. That was it, no ulterior motive. "It happened. And it shouldn't have. And it definitely *will not* happen again."

"You don't have to be *that* adamant about it."

"Yes, I do. I have learned that with you, the clearer and more adamant I am, the better chance I have that maybe you will listen. So let me reiterate—we've acknowledged it. We've agreed it won't happen again. And now, you may go back to stalking people, and I can go back to law enforcement."

"Hey!"

"Sam? Libby? Are you guys in here? It's time to eat!" Patti sang through the back door.

"Coming!" Libby shouted back, a little too loudly, and with a glare for Sam—a decidedly hostile feminine glare—she marched out of the living room.

Sam pushed his fingers through his hair, then reluctantly followed her out.

He tried not to look at her bum as she marched down the steps to the table, but it was impossible to ignore it in those pants. He definitely tried to avoid watching her bend over Leo, or Leo struggle to lift a useless hand, which he still managed to slide over Libby's waist and down her hip, that horny bastard.

Sam pretended not to notice when Libby sat between Leo and Jackson and began to talk with great animation, her hands punctuating the air with the gestures she used to tell whatever she was spinning out for them.

Sam tried so hard not to notice all those things that he definitely didn't notice Madeline had taken a seat beside him until she nudged him and said, "Who are you eyeing? Michelle Catucci?" she asked, referring to one of the local bankers. "Don't bother. She's dating Ed Friedman." She winked at him, but her gaze traveled to Libby before she turned back to him and said, "Can I ask you something?"

"Of course."

"We need a favor," she said, and began to talk, something to do with Homecoming Ranch. Sam tried to listen, he really did, but his thoughts were in an infuriating tailspin around Libby Tyler.

"So?" Madeline said after a moment. "You haven't said much. What do you think about the horses?"

*Horses.* He really had no idea what she was talking about. But Sam hadn't been out of the marriage game so long that he'd forgotten to feign listening to a woman when he actually hadn't heard a word. He said, "Great."

Madeline smiled with delight. "Oh Sam, thank you! That's *such* a great help. I can't wait to tell Luke. He said it was a dumb idea to have a wedding in a barn, because what he knows about weddings is nothing."

"Yep," Sam said. God, what had he agreed to?

"I'm going to grab a drink. Can I get you anything?"

What Sam wanted was a bottle of vodka. He wanted to drink vodka so it would numb the desire to put his hands and his mouth on one very nutty woman. Yes, Sam wanted a drink to wash away the wanting of all the things he could not have, such as a wife and children and a life that didn't include walking a tightrope. He wanted to drink to fill up the holes in him that all that want had left behind.

But to Madeline he said, "No thanks," and held up a bottle of water.

# FOURTEEN

Libby had to admire the way Patti could take the Kendrick kitchen and turn it into something not only useful, but pleasing to the eye. She had dragged two picnic tables together, had dressed them with a red-checkered paper tablecloth, and heavy-weight paper plates, and had served tea in Mason jars. The best part was the sunflowers she'd put in old Coke bottles to dress the table up.

Maybe she ought to inquire if Patti had ever been to a barn wedding, see if she had a few pointers.

Libby was seated next to Leo at the head of the table. While Leo was flirting with Michelle, Libby chatted with Jackson Crane about the ranch. She had no desire to talk about Homecoming Ranch at the moment, but if she didn't talk, her fury with Sam would get the best of her.

Libby liked Jackson. She'd known him since almost the day he'd shown up in Pine River more than a year ago. She knew there was a lot of speculation about him—he'd told people he got tired of big business lawyering and had come to the mountains to chill out. But the truth was that Jackson was gone a lot, and he kept to himself. He didn't really date anyone in town, although Libby knew there were a few women in town who would definitely be interested. Sherry Stancliff, for one, judging by the way she kept trying to catch his eye.

Jackson had been Libby's father's last financial manager—Grant tended to fire them when they advised against outrageous and foolhardy investments. Jackson had come in at the last possible moment, a few months before her father had died. He couldn't stop the financial damage her father had begun—meaning, losing everything he'd ever had—but Jackson had managed to save Homecoming Ranch for Libby and her sisters.

Now that her father was gone, and the ranch had been probated, Libby didn't understand what Jackson *did.* He wasn't being paid by the estate any longer, but he still tried to help her and Madeline manage it. Tonight, he was grilling her on the specifics of the Gary and Austin wedding, shaking his head as she described what they'd planned and what Gary and Austin had agreed to pay.

"Where's the profit? There's no profit in that, Libby," he scolded her.

"There is *some* profit," Libby argued. "I thought it would be better to get the business so we could say we've had the experience rather than make a lot of money at first."

"That's not going to work," Jackson argued. "Yes, you need the experience, but you also have to cover your operating costs. If you really want to turn Homecoming Ranch into an event destination, you're going to have to figure out how to turn a profit. You need help, kid."

"I am painfully aware," Libby snorted. "I could use a *lot* of help."

"What about Emma?" Jackson asked. "She's an event planner, right?"

What about Emma? Most of the time, Libby couldn't get her

on the phone, and when she did, Emma was elusive or, worse, bored. "Honestly, I don't know what she does," Libby said. "But she's made it very clear, she's not coming to Colorado. Not to help, not to visit."

Jackson nodded and looked thoughtfully at his plate. "Look, I'll ask around, find someone we can talk to," he said. He put his hand over hers and squeezed it. "Don't worry, Libby," he said kindly. "I know how much you need Homecoming Ranch. We'll figure out something."

With that, he turned to talk to Greg on his left.

Libby stared at his back. What did he mean, she *needed* Homecoming Ranch? She inadvertently glanced across the table, to where Sam was deep in conversation with Michelle.

She instantly looked away and leaned back. She'd actually been a little excited when she saw Sam tonight, and more than a little curious as to what that kiss had meant to him. She hadn't expected that perhaps it didn't mean anything to him. He'd certainly made *that* abundantly clear.

*Free country.* Libby rolled her eyes.

And then again, what did she care? She had her hands full with the ranch and making nice with Ryan so that she could see Alice and Max. She didn't need Sam's kiss hanging over her head.

She glanced at Sam, at his square jaw, and the way one dark strand of hair curved over his temple. A fluttery feeling shot through her, and she looked away . . . right into Leo's eyes, who had shifted his chair around to face her. He smiled crookedly. "What are *you* thinking about, Libster?"

"I'm thinking I'm really full."

"Liar. You know MND is like going blind, right? You can't do as much stuff, but your powers of perception get like, *super* strong. Which means I am also very perceptive."

"You forgot modest."

He grinned. "I don't have enough time left to be modest. So what's up with the ranch?"

"What do you mean?" she asked. "We're meeting with Austin and Gary and Gary's mom next week."

"Not that. I'm talking about the *ranch.* Everyone's in a tizzy thinking that it's going up in flames because you don't have any anniversaries or retirement parties or bar mitzvahs lined up."

"Bar mitzvahs?" Libby said, trying to follow.

"Just raising the possibility," Leo said congenially. "What I mean is you've got folks worried that you don't have anything lined up, and ergo, Homecoming Ranch is going into the toilet. That would not be good. Not good at all."

"I agree," she said. "But right now, we have a lot on our plate in staging this civil ceremony. After it's done, I'm going to develop a business plan. I've already talked to Michelle."

"Hmm," Leo said, and frowned thoughtfully as much as he was able. "Sounds like something you'd say to cover up the fact that you don't have any ideas, Libs. Oh! I can see by your expression that I am *right.* Again! It's amazing, isn't it?"

Libby gave Leo a dark look. "You know, I am getting tired of everyone thinking that I am the one who came up with the idea to turn Homecoming Ranch into a destination resort, because I am not that person. My father and *your* father had that idea, Leo. I'm just trying to keep it together. It's not like I've ever done this before. I'm doing the best I know how to do and learning as I go."

"Point well taken," he cheerfully agreed. "Hey, did you see that season of *The Bachelor* where the dude was down to the last two girls, and he picked the super cute girl, but then, at the 'After the Final Rose' ceremony, he said he made a mistake and went with the not-so-cute one?"

Libby blinked. "*What?*" she asked, and shook her head. "What has that got to do with anything?"

"Are you kidding? I am constantly amazed at the lack of intuition around me!" he called up to a pinkening sky. "Okay, check it out, Libby-rachi, the dude had two perfectly acceptable girls. I mean *all* girls are acceptable, but you know, some more than others, right? He liked them both, but he thought he was supposed to go with the pretty, shiny one, but then, once he'd hung out with her a couple of weeks, he realized he'd chosen the wrong chick, so he said, oops, and he retraced his steps and he chose the *right* chick. *And* they have a baby now."

"That makes absolutely no sense, Leo," she said. "And it has nothing to do with the ranch."

"It has everything to do with the ranch. Just think about it. In the meantime, watch a pro at work," he said, and suddenly backed up, then twisted around so quickly that he bumped into the table and glasses knocked together, startling everyone. Libby was certain he'd done it on purpose.

"Oh hey, sorry. But now that I have your attention," Leo said, as all eyes turned toward him, "I have an announcement to make."

"Leo—"

"Dad, just let me get this out before you present the opposing viewpoint, okay?"

"Are you really going to do this here, before the game?" Mr. Kendrick demanded gruffly from the other end of the table.

"I can't think of a better time, Pops. By the way, for those of you not following, Dad is unhappy because he takes great pride in old bread delivery trucks. But then again, he's retired. What else is he going to do but work on old bread delivery trucks?"

Libby could hear Mr. Kendrick muttering under his breath, and it didn't sound very polite.

"Okay, so here's the deal. I have tickets to the Broncos-Patriots game on Christmas Eve, and I need a way to get there."

Several of the guests looked a few feet away, where Leo's van was parked.

"No, no, don't look at that!" he said quickly. "I *know* it looks like a van, but trust me, it's a bread delivery truck, and there's a bunch of issues with it. I won't bore you with the details, but it's like, *so* not going to make a trip all the way to Denver. And we Kendricks don't have the money to buy a *new* van, so I asked the Methodists if they could help us out."

"Oh," Sherry Stancliff said, sitting up a little, as if the Methodists somehow legitimized whatever it was Leo was about to say.

"And the Methodists were like, 'Oh, we don't know if we can raise money to buy you a *van* to take you to a *football game,*' like a football game is the mouth of hell or something, so I had to improvise a little and remind them that the van is also going to get me to really important doctor appointments. Right, Dr. Levitt?"

Dr. Levitt looked startled. He glanced around uncertainly. "Well, you need to go to your doctor appointments, yes."

"There, you see? So me and the Methodists, we came up with the great idea to form a committee to raise funds for my new van."

"Oh, what a great idea!" said Sherry. "Count me in."

"Me too!" Libby said enthusiastically. That sounded like something right up her alley, and she would love something other than Ryan, or the ranch, or deputies with bad attitudes, to think about.

Leo acted as if he hadn't heard her, which was impossible, because she was sitting right next to him. He launched into an explanation of what sort of van he wanted.

Predictably, he wanted something that sounded a bit over the top. Apparently Luke thought so, too, because he began to slowly reel in his brother, proclaiming the van did *not* need leather bucket seats or a DVD player, and it damn sure didn't need flame details on the side. By the time he'd managed to get Leo down to a van that sounded reasonable, it was time for the pre-game show.

"Be thinking of fundraisers, people!" Leo called to everyone as they stood up from the table.

Luke instructed them to take their plastic lawn chairs and move to the deck, where he and his dad had set up the big flat screen.

As Libby stood from the table, she said, "I really would love to help, Leo. I'm really good at that sort of thing."

Leo wheeled about in his chair so that he was facing her. He looked up at her with eyes that were just like Luke's—warm and blue and shining. "I know you are, Libby-rachi. You're the best. Hey, you're staying for the game, right?"

"A little while," she said. "I have a lot of work to do tomorrow."

"Work," Leo said as he began to wheel himself toward the deck's ramp. "Highly overrated!"

Libby followed him up to the deck, carrying her chair, which she set next to the others. There were still a few minutes before the game. The other guests had brought the chairs to the deck and then left them spread haphazardly about. Libby took it upon herself to organize them so Patti wouldn't have to.

But as she neared the back of the deck with the last few chairs, a conversation from the lawn caught her attention. Someone—Sherry, she thought—mentioned Gwen.

"Gwen will be a great chair," she said.

"But I don't think she knows about Gwen."

That sounded like Michelle. Who was *she*? And Gwen would be the chair of what? Libby glanced around to the lawn. The women's backs were to her.

"What do you think she'll do when she finds out? You don't think she'd go off and, you know . . . do something?"

They were talking about her. Libby started toward them, but a hand to her arm stopped her. It was Sam. He took a firm hold of

Libby's elbow and wheeled her about. "That was good brisket, wasn't it?" he said as he started to move her along.

"Hey! I was going to talk to Sherry and Michelle."

"Now is not a good time," Sam said.

"But they said—"

"I heard them."

"Wait," Libby said, and put her hand on his arm. "Sam, *wait.*"

He paused and looked down at her, his eyes swimming with . . . with what—What was that, *pity*? Did he *pity* her? Libby's heart lurched painfully. That was the last thing she wanted, the very last thing. She jerked her elbow from his grasp. "Please don't look at me like you think I'm going to lose it. Just tell me, is Gwen heading up Leo's committee?"

"So I hear," Sam said tightly.

"From who?"

He hesitated. "Leo."

A barrage of emotions began to cascade through Libby. She'd known Leo since they were children. He was like family; his brother was marrying her sister. *Gwen* would head his committee? Gwen Spangler, the cheater, the home wrecker? "That's great," she said, trying to be nonchalant in spite of the swell of anger she felt in her, the nebulous, indefinable rage at everything and everyone. "So I guess everyone thinks if I join the committee, I'll come in with golf clubs blazing, huh?"

Sam glanced to where everyone was making their way onto the deck to find their seats for the game. "I don't know what they think."

He said it so gently that Libby blanched. "Like hell you don't."

His gaze roamed over her face, as if he were debating what he would say. "I think it's fair to say that people are a little apprehensive around you."

Libby knew people whispered behind her back, that her breakdown had been the talk of the town. But what had happened had been directed at Ryan—it had never occurred to her that other people would be *afraid* of her. She suddenly whirled around and walked away from him and into the house.

Patti and Marisol were in the kitchen, tidying things up. "Game's starting!" Patti said cheerfully.

"Yep. I just need to, ah . . ." To *hit* something. A brick wall, a face, a truck. She gestured down the hall.

"Bathroom on the right," Marisol said, absently gesturing in that direction.

Yes, a bathroom, with lots of tile to kick for someone who was about to unravel. Libby walked down the narrow hallway to the bathroom, seething. She had lived in this town most of her life, had been a part of it, making herself join activities just so that she *could* be part of it. She had always been optimistic and hopeful, ready to start again, to help again. What everyone had known of her was overshadowed by the events of this awful summer and a brief stay at Mountain View. It wasn't fair. She could not be the only person in Pine River to have lost her composure.

"Libby, for heaven's sake. Couldn't you have just called him a few names and been done with it? People don't forget things like this," her mother had said on the drive up to Mountain View. "I don't know what's come over you. You've always been so easy to get along with, but now, all of a sudden, you act like everything is about you, a personal affront to you."

Libby hadn't been capable of a protracted discussion with her mom at that moment, but she recalled marveling at how her mother could possibly think that Ryan's cheating on her could be anything *but* a personal affront to her.

And once again, her mother had been right—people did not forget golf-club incidents.

Libby walked inside the bathroom, shut the door behind her and locked it, and turned around, barely registering the towels hanging neatly on the towel bar, the toothbrush holder, the two razors on the sink, or the fact that someone had put out some pretty little soaps, as if that would mask the fact that this was a bathroom men shared.

She leaned against the door and slowly slid down, onto her haunches, and wrapped her arms around her legs, pressed her forehead to her knees.

Her emotions were balling up and tripping over each other. Overhearing Michelle and Sherry is what Dr. Huber would call a trigger, something that unexpectedly set off the tiny pilot flame of rage that existed in her, causing it to flare out of control. When these moments happened, Libby was to breathe deeply and set her mind's eye on something pleasant, like a tropical beach.

When she'd been at Mountain View, she hadn't put much stock in that sort of thinking. In a sterile room, staring out a window onto a parking lot, all Libby had wanted was to sleep. To think of tropical beaches had seemed so far removed from helpful as to be ridiculous. But this evening, she had no choice. With her head down, her eyes closed, Libby drew a long breath, counting to ten, then slowly released it. Another breath, count to ten, slow release. And again.

She'd been stung, and now she had the task of convincing herself that it didn't matter what anyone thought of her. No one but she knew how hard she'd worked to put a family together, or how important she'd become to Alice and Max, and they to her. Or how Ryan had walked all over that as if it had all meant nothing, as if the energy and love she had poured into that family was worthless to him.

Outside, she could hear the voices rise to a crescendo at the opening kickoff. She lifted her head, breathed out once more. Dr. Huber was right—deep breathing did help. Libby pitched forward onto her hands and knees, then pushed herself up, down dog style, to standing. She looked at herself in the mirror. There was no sign that she was on the verge of exploding with disappointment and frustration. She sighed, tucked in a stray curl or two, smoothed her top, and with one last deep breath, reached for the bathroom door, unlocking it and pulling it open.

She let out a little squeal of surprise to see Sam standing there, leaning against the wall opposite the door. "What are you doing here?" she demanded.

"Everything okay?"

"Yes. Why?" she asked defensively.

Sam cocked a brow.

"I'm *fine*," she said adamantly.

"Okay," he said, and pushed away from the wall.

"But wait—I need to know something. Do *you* think I would do something to torpedo Leo's fundraising just because Gwen is involved?" she blurted, because it suddenly seemed of the utmost importance that Sam not think that, of all people.

"*No*," he said firmly. "Don't let it get to you, Libby. You know how it is out in the world today—people are more cautious than they used to be."

"So basically, what you're saying is all of Pine River is worried that I will be the one to pick up a gun and start firing."

He smiled sympathetically. "I wouldn't say *all*."

Libby blinked.

"I'm teasing you."

"Yeah," she said. "You should look into stand-up comedy."

"Maybe I will," he said, and moved forward. Only inches separated them now. "Are you ready to come watch some football?"

Libby sighed, and before she knew what she was doing, she dropped her forehead to Sam's shoulder. "I don't think I can."

"Sure you can," he murmured.

They stood awkwardly a moment—Libby leaning into Sam, her face in his shirt, her arms at her side. Sam standing stiff and still. But then Libby felt him lift one hand. He put it on the small of her back.

"Don't cry," he said.

She snorted. "I'm not crying. I'm too mad to cry."

Another hand came up and landed on her back. He gave her a strange, but friendly little pat, as if he didn't know what to do with her precisely.

Libby lifted her head. In that close hallway, Sam's eyes looked dark. "Sam—"

"No," he said quickly, cutting her off. "I meant what I said, Libby. No more hand-holding."

"I know. I heard you the first five times you said it." His eyes were the color of turbulent, churning seas.

"Great," he said as his gaze drifted to her mouth. "Then you understand that your problem is not mine."

"Good!" she said, studying his bottom lip, full and wet. A shiver of memory raced down her spine. "You're too bossy, anyway."

"God, don't talk anymore," he said, and lowered his head, his mouth hungrily finding hers.

Desire shot through her, and Libby sank into him. He pulled her closer, and she ran her hands up his arms, curved them around his neck, opened her mouth beneath his.

Sam met her, his tongue tangling with hers, his grip tightening. And suddenly they were moving. Sam had her firmly anchored with one arm around her waist. He was pushing her back, through the open bathroom door, and up against the sink. With his boot, he kicked the door shut. One hand slid down her back, to her hip, and his fingers sank into her flesh, kneading it, sparking a fire that flamed through all of her.

He lifted Libby up and sat her on the edge of the sink, slipping in between her legs. She wrapped a leg around him as he pressed his erection against her. He slid his hand up under her sweater, over her bare skin, to her breast, filling his hand with it.

Sam's touch renewed Libby, made her feel as if she'd been dragged out from behind the weeds, made to stand in the sun again. She felt desirable, felt all of the senses she thought dulled come alive. His kiss was demanding, but at the same time soft and reverent. He cupped her chin, ran his hand over her hair. He drew her lip in between his teeth, swept his tongue in her mouth.

Libby wanted more, wanted to feel him inside her.

*Feel him inside her?*

*Sam Winters?*

What was she thinking? What about . . . what about everything else? Everything else began to fade away, disappearing beneath the sensations she was experiencing in Sam's arms.

Sam cupped her face in both hands, brushed his thumb across her bottom lip. He didn't speak, just gazed into her face and eyes as if he was trying to work something out.

He dropped his gaze to the V of her sweater. He dipped down, kissed the hollow of her throat, and traced a wet path to the top of her breasts, then in the valley between them.

Libby was completely drawn in, her body supple and wet. Sam suddenly moved up, kissed her again, kissed her forehead, and then dropped his hands to the sink on either side of her, bracing himself there, putting himself at eye level with her.

"That's twice now," he said.

"Twice that you've kissed me?"

"Twice that *you've* kissed *me.*"

She smiled.

"It's not going to happen again, Libby."

She looked at his lips. The desire was swirling around in her, a confusing mix of not wanting and wanting him at the same time. "I know," she said breathlessly, and trailed her fingers down his Adam's apple, to the open collar of his shirt. "I was just about to tell you the same thing. Stop kissing me."

"Then we're on the same page." He kissed her again, and Libby slid her arms around his neck.

When she lifted her head, she said, "It's like the worst thing that could happen, you and me."

"Tell me about it," he said, and ran his knuckles across her collarbone before nuzzling her ear as his hand reached for her breast again. "So go on, get out of here."

"Oh, I'm going," she said, and slid her hands over his shoulder, down his chest, to his waist. "I'm getting the hell out of here."

Sam put a hand to her waist and pulled her off the sink. But he was still blocking her way to the door, and his hand was still on her breast. Libby kissed the skin beneath his open collar, felt his pulse beneath her lips, the warmth of his skin, and then pushed him aside. She walked to the bathroom door and glanced at him over her shoulder. He was leaning with one hip against the sink, his head lowered, his gaze devouring her.

She took him in, every delicious inch of him. "I must be truly crazy," she said with a small shake of her head.

"And it must be contagious."

Libby grinned. "See you around, Lone Ranger," she said, and straightened her sweater, opened the door, and walked out of that room, her body still thrumming with desire.

# FIFTEEN

In the few days that followed the Kendrick party, Libby busied herself getting the ranch ready for the final inspection by Gary, Austin and Gary's mother, Martha. Tony had not yet finished Libby's car—he'd had to send off for a part, but was vague about which one, or how much it cost, or where it was coming from. "I know a guy out by Durango," was all he would say.

That meant Libby hadn't been to town except once, and that was in the backseat of Madeline's SUV, while Madeline and Luke rode up front, giggling like a pair of teenagers, their hands on each other's legs.

Sometimes, Libby felt as if the whole world was a couple, spinning around her and laughing in couple-speak while she worked.

The feel of Sam's hands was still tingling on her skin and in her memory.

It all made for a very confusing mix of emotions. Libby didn't want to be intrigued by the physical response Sam had aroused in her, but she was. She kept reliving those moments in the bathroom, and in the hall here at the ranch, and imagining more intimate moments with Sam.

But on the other hand, she had loved Ryan, and she still desperately loved the children. Their faces kept coming back to her, their smiles flying through her thoughts.

She couldn't simply carve them out of her heart and pretend they had never been there. They were ever-present, always in her thoughts.

She had not imagined the good times the four of them had had. She thought of Ryan with his arms around her in the kitchen, nuzzling her neck while she made pasta sauce. Or the bitterly cold night they'd roasted marshmallows over the fire. She thought about reading the same book every night to Max when he'd been a toddler. It was a book of truck pictures, and he could name every one of them. She thought about how she would braid Alice's red hair in the mornings while Alice fired questions at her. *Why do I have to brush my teeth? Why do I have to take a bath? Why are faeries tiny? Why does Daddy have boots?*

It had been a good life, and Libby knew she wasn't imagining it. What was she supposed to do now? Give up hope of Alice and Max? Was that even possible?

Her thinking was further muddied by the fact that Sam hadn't come out to the ranch. Not that Libby was expecting him, exactly, as they had agreed there would be no more of that truly wonderful, sexy thing between them. She wasn't expecting him, but she was disappointed all the same. She wondered if he'd been out to see Millie Bagley. Or if he was having lunch at the Grizzly.

She wondered if he thought about her.

In the meantime, every afternoon around four, Alice called her, and Libby was thrilled to hear her voice. It was the brightest moment of her day. Alice talked about dance class, about her teacher, and about Tatiana, her new friend. She reported that Max wouldn't eat his peas or pick up his toys and had been in time-out a *lot.* Sometimes, Max would agree to let Libby speak to him on the phone, responding with a functional yes or no before dropping the phone to run off and play.

Libby asked Alice where Mommy and Daddy were, and Alice told her that her mother was at work, or that Kaylee, their teenage babysitter, was over. Libby said, "Alice, I don't want you to be in trouble. You need to ask Daddy if it's okay to call me."

"I did!" Alice insisted. "Daddy said."

*Daddy said.*

The very next day, Alice announced plans for a trip to Disney World. "Daddy said we could go."

"Said who could go?" Libby had asked, distracted by the task of counting place cards.

"All of us. Me and Max and Daddy. And you!"

Libby had looked up from her work. "Not me, sweetie."

"Uh-huh," Alice said. "They have princesses there. You can dress like a princess, too. Tatiana went and she told me."

This was getting out of hand. Libby needed to see Ryan, to talk to him about what was going on with the kids. Alice was not an untruthful child, but this made no sense. As much as Libby hoped it was Ryan's buildup to crawling back and begging for forgiveness—something she would very much like to see . . . in a public venue, preferably . . . with everyone in Pine River in attendance—she didn't believe it.

What she needed was to sort this out. She thought of calling him, but decided against it. The last thing she needed was for Gwen to see her number pop up on his phone. And besides, this conversation was one that needed to be held in person.

Thursday morning, on the day that Gary and Austin would come to inspect the grounds, Libby went out to the garage to check on Tony's progress with her car. Surprisingly, the hood of her car was closed, and her car had been washed and buffed. "Looking for these?" Tony asked, and held out her keys.

Libby gasped with delight. She took the keys, got into the car and started it up. The thing purred like new. Like *new.*

"Happy?" Tony asked when she stepped out of the car.

"Ecstatic," she said, smiling. "Really, thank you, Tony. I don't know how I'll ever pay you. What do I owe you?"

He glanced down at the bolt or screw or whatever it was he was polishing. "I could do with a few groceries," he said. "Still got this old Buick to fix up. Might take some time." He peeked up at her. "Ernest doesn't seem to mind."

Libby glanced around the garage.

"I do more than cars," Tony said. "And I can build just about anything."

Libby inadvertently and unthinkingly glanced at his prosthetic leg.

"Don't worry about that," Tony said instantly. "I get by. Look, I can stay out at the place Sam found for me, sure. It's nice enough, got everything a man could want."

Libby didn't think that place had anything anyone would want—it was remote, stark, run-down, and utterly depressing.

"But here . . . well, here, there's people. Ernest. Luke. Even you, when you're not complaining about your car." He smiled a little.

"I don't really *complain* so much as I—"

"I was thinking another week or so," he continued. "The thing is, I kind of need to be around people right now."

There was something in his voice that sounded a little unsteady. Worse, it sounded completely familiar. It sounded alone and in need of emotional support.

Tony swallowed and glanced down at the things he held in his hand. "I don't like being alone." He averted his gaze and reached for a new screw.

"I don't like it either," Libby said. "You can stay as long as you need, Tony," she said. He looked at her, his expression wary, as if he didn't trust her. "I'm serious. There's always something that needs to be done."

Tony reached into his soiled pocket and withdrew a cigarette. "Thanks. Then I should get to work," he said, and turned away from her. But he glanced over his shoulder and said, "Thanks, Libby."

Libby left him in the garage and walked back to the house. There was a nip in the air—it was too early for cold weather, she thought, but she could see clouds over the mountains across the valley.

She stood there, her arms around her middle, looking out over the valley. What was she doing here, really? Libby recalled a moment at Mountain View, in the haze of meds and fatigue. Someone—perhaps Dr. Huber, Libby couldn't really recall—had said that when something breaks, it's impossible to put it back exactly the same way. She remembered thinking that was such an odd thing to say, and that it had nothing to do with her. Unless they were talking about truck windows.

But now, Libby wondered if that's what she was doing. If she was trying to put the pieces of her life back together and they didn't fit. Alice and Max didn't fit with Sam. Homecoming Ranch didn't fit with weddings. She wasn't sure what fit anymore.

It was time she figured things out. For real. Not what she wanted, what was real.

A movement caught her eye—she saw the dust rising from the road as Austin and Gary's car drove up the road to the ranch.

It was showtime.

# SIXTEEN

There was a definitive change in the air; Sam could feel it weighing down on his temples and his throat. The sky was turning an icy blue, the color before a snow.

But it was too early for snow. It felt as if the earth were turning upside down and back onto itself—snowy autumns, fiery summers, dry springs. It was the same way Sam was feeling inside—twisted up and around, pulled in the wrong directions, the wrong things happening at the wrong times.

He took a hand off the wheel of his truck and tore the hat from his head, tossing it aside. He pushed his fingers through his hair, a nervous habit, and looked out the window at the gold meadows rolling by.

What he'd done in the Kendrick bathroom—kissing Libby, putting his hands on her body—reminded him of something he would have done when he was drinking. Something dumb, something indefensible. But then again, it was far different from a drunken grope, because unlike when he'd been drinking, Sam had known exactly what he was doing at the Kendricks'.

He couldn't figure out what was in his head. It wasn't as if he were going to sleep with Libby for the sake of sleeping with her—he wasn't that kind of guy. And he wasn't going to pursue any sort of relationship with her, either, for all the reasons that were so obvious to him. *The woman has issues,* he told himself for the hundredth time. Big issues. Bring-the-dogs-in-lock-the-door kind of issues.

If there was one thing he knew about himself, one definitive thing, it was that when he got involved with a woman who had big issues, everything went to hell.

It annoyed him to no end that he couldn't seem to get Libby off his mind, what with all her *don't check on me* and *happy medium.* But that smile and those blue eyes were stuck in his brain. Her earnestness had always appealed to him—no one could claim that she wasn't dedicated to a cause. Her sense of humor, too—she had one, in spite of her troubles.

Still, having feelings about Libby didn't mean Sam needed to act on it, for Chrissake's. It wasn't a mandate, it wasn't a siren call. And it didn't change anything.

He just needed to handle this the way he handled his life—keep his hands busy, his thoughts on benign things. Keep to himself, mind his horses, mind his life. Sam hated feeling unsettled. It made him want to settle himself, and in the past, the go-to for settling had been alcohol. He'd known for a long time that he was best all alone, best making birdhouses and checking on society's rejections, like Millie Bagley. The moment a woman entered his picture was the moment the wheels always began to fall off his sturdy little applecart.

The worst of it was that Sam had put Tony up at the ranch, which meant he couldn't exactly avoid Libby forever. Moreover, Tony had called him a couple of times since he'd been up there, feeling low. *I don't know what I'm doing with my life, man,* he'd said. *I just fixed a car for free, and I need the cash. What's the matter with me? I don't know how to be anything but a soldier, you know?*

Yeah, Sam knew.

*I don't want to go back out to the Beeker place, Sam. There's some pretty bad demons in the dark out there, you know what I mean? I hate it out there. I feel so alone and all I want to do is drink.*

Funny how Sam could find salvation in being alone, whereas Tony found only demons. Sam was the one who'd suggested Tony ask about staying on a little longer at the ranch. He understood how it felt when demons were crawling up your back. Tony needed to be with people to keep the demons off his back.

Sam had agreed to take Tony to an AA meeting tomorrow, which meant he'd have to drive up there and get him. If he could figure out a way to sneak in and steal Tony, he would. That's how messed up he was feeling about Libby Tyler.

This afternoon, he was headed home, but thought he would stop in the hardware store to see if T.J., the owner, might take Tony on, give Tony something to do, something to keep his hands busy. It was Sam's way of finding Tony his own version of birdhouses to build.

He reached Pine River and turned onto Main Street.

Pine River was once an old mining town that had been turned into a tourist destination. There wasn't skiing here; Pine River was a destination for summer tourists. They came to hike and to shoot the rapids, to bike, to camp. Any outdoor activity one could think of, one could find around this spot in the Colorado mountains.

The buildings along Main Street had been fabricated to look like the Old West—some of them legitimately so, some of them bad knockoffs. The UPS store, for example, had been made to look like an old hotel. Before that, it had been a standard stucco building with two front windows.

Sam was looking at the porch railing they'd recently put up when he happened to spot the little red car with the dented rear fender parked in front.

That was Libby's car.

He clenched his jaw and drove on to the hardware store.

T. J. was happy to see Sam, but he began to wince and make noises that sounded as if his lunch had disagreed with him when Sam brought up Tony.

"Tony D'Angelo, huh?" he said, and made a whistling sound through his teeth. "Ain't he the guy who scared everyone half to death at the Fourth of July thing?"

T. J. was referring to Pine River's celebration of the holiday. Before the fireworks, locals performed dance numbers and sang, and gave the obligatory speeches. That was the weekend Tony gave in to the call of booze. Sam hadn't been there, but he'd heard about it from some Pine River cops. Tony had been distressed by some speech, and had stood up, shouting profanities at the councilman, ranting about soldiers who had died in a useless war. They'd had to carry him off, and after some wrangling, had agreed to let Tony's girlfriend at the time take him home.

A couple of days later, Sam had gone out to check on him. It was divine intervention, he supposed, because he'd found Tony in his living room surrounded by empty beer cans and a bong. He had a gun pointed at his temple and was tearfully contemplating the end of his life.

"He's a vet, T. J.," Sam said. "He was having some issues, but he's doing pretty good now. He went to treatment, he's not drinking—in fact, he's rebuilding a couple of cars up at Homecoming Ranch without any trouble."

"I don't know," T. J. said. "I mean, I support our troops, I do. And I respect you, Sam. But I know you've had your troubles, too, so you might not be the most objective about this guy, you know?"

Sam thought maybe he was a little more objective about him than T. J., seeing as how he'd been through it, but he didn't argue. He shook his hand, and said, "Thanks anyway."

All Tony needed was a break. Just one. Sam believed in him.

He picked up a couple of things he needed before leaving and walked out, pausing on the walk to notice that the sky was even grayer than when he'd gone in. Gray was a perfect match for his mood.

"Hey, Sam, wait up!"

He turned around to see Gwen Spangler walking toward him. She was holding the hand of her son, who was dressed for soccer, and Sam instantly assumed the worst. "Everything okay?"

"Sure! Everything is great," she said cheerfully. "I just wanted to say hi. How are you?"

Sam liked Gwen. She had a short bob of blond hair and was wearing dental scrubs with a lot of smiling teeth plastered on them. "I'm good. How are you?"

"I honestly can't complain. I guess I *could* complain about how busy we are—it seems like we work all the time, but then again, someone has to pay the bills, right?"

"Right." Sam was lucky—he didn't worry about bills. He lived so simply that he'd actually amassed a sizable nest egg.

"I haven't seen you around," she said. "In fact, I don't see you unless . . . you know." She glanced down at Max. "When there's some drama in town." She gave him a lighthearted roll of her eyes. "Speaking of which, I hear she's determined to get on the Leo bandwagon and cause more trouble."

Libby's volunteering for the committee hadn't been at all like that. "She's known him a long time," Sam said, unwilling to discuss Libby in front of Max.

"Hey!" Gwen said. "*You* should join our committee! We're going to have a couple of single members." She waggled her eyebrows at him.

Joining a fundraising committee to meet women was about as enticing as a root canal. "I'm all booked up," Sam said.

"Oh, *sure* you are."

"Mom, let's *go,*" Max said, tugging on her hand.

"Yes, we don't want to be late again," Gwen said to the boy, and to Sam she said, "Jerry Baylor is the coach, and he does *not* like tardiness. Think about the committee!" she called over her shoulder as Max dragged her out to her car.

Sam watched Gwen strap Max into his booster seat, and then pull away, headed for the city's municipal park and soccer fields.

He looked the other way up Main Street, to the UPS store. The red car was gone.

He had a funny feeling. He debated following his instincts, but then again, he had meant what he said—no more hand-holding. He would not be her keeper. He'd done that enough in his life, and it never worked out for anyone.

Sam drove down the road to the turnoff to Homecoming Ranch. But as the clouds seemed to sink lower over the mountains, obliterating the view of the tops, Sam's resolve seemed to sink, too.

He turned his truck around and headed back to Pine River, cussing at himself the whole way.

# SEVENTEEN

Fat, heavy snowflakes were beginning to fall on the soccer field, creating a thin veil between Libby and the little boys running around chasing a soccer ball. Libby tightened her sweater and drew her knees up to her chest and wrapped her arms around them, annoyed with such an early snow.

She could see Ryan from her perch on a bench at the far end of the field. The only reason she knew it was Ryan was because she had seen him drive up in his truck. He was standing behind the fence that served as a backstop when the kids played baseball. His fingers looped into the chain links, just above his head, and he leaned against the fence, watching Max, calling out to him, encouraging him to run or to kick.

Libby tried to spot Gwen or Alice, but couldn't see them. Generally, Alice was beside the bleachers, practicing her dance steps. Sometimes, she managed to rope in a couple of friends to be her backup dancers, but this afternoon, Libby couldn't see any girls playing beside the bleachers.

She'd been sitting on the bench for about ten minutes, watching Ryan, watching the big flakes come down, and debating whether or not she should approach him. She didn't want Gwen to suddenly show up and call the police again. She could just picture Sam's dark expression that she was even contemplating it, but this was the opportunity Libby had been waiting for, the chance to speak to Ryan alone, to ask him where exactly they stood and if she could see Max and Alice.

Libby stood. She nervously pulled her braid over her shoulder and pulled her sweater together, folding her arms over it. She began to walk around the field toward Ryan.

He didn't notice her at first. He backed away from the fence, stuffed his hands into his pockets. But then he happened to turn his head, and he smiled.

A ribbon of anticipation ran through Libby. She believed in that moment that it was true—Ryan regretted what he'd done, and she felt an almost euphoric sense of vindication.

And then Ryan's expression changed. He looked back over his shoulder, and then pointed to the parking lot across the street, gesturing and directing her there. Libby hesitated, but Ryan's gestures grew urgent.

She changed direction, headed for the parking lot, darting across the street and between two parked trucks. She stepped out from between them and saw Ryan striding toward her.

He looked furious.

"What the hell, Libby?" he demanded, throwing his arms out as he strode closer. "Gwen and Alice are over there," he said angrily, jabbing at some point over his shoulder. "What if they saw you?"

"I'm sorry, I thought about calling, but I—"

"*Calling?*" he almost shouted at her.

Libby's gut turned sour. "I wasn't going to *call* you," she quickly amended. "I don't want to cause any trouble. But I need to speak to you," she said, taking a step backward.

Ryan gaped at her incredulously. "Speak to me? You're not supposed to speak to me!"

A snowflake plopped down on her eye, and Libby brushed it away. The sour feeling was turning nauseous. "I know, but I thought that—"

"You thought *what*, Libby?" he demanded angrily. "What crazy-ass thing did you think now?"

"*Daddy!*"

The sound of Alice's voice startled them both. She was skipping down the parking lot toward them, kicking up snow. Far behind her was Gwen, who was engaged in conversation with two women, and had not, apparently, noticed Libby. Libby reflexively stepped back in between the trucks before Gwen could see her.

"What did you think?" Ryan demanded, advancing on Libby and ignoring Alice.

"Stop it," Libby said harshly, as Alice paused to scoop up some snow. "You get to say whatever you want in parking lots, is that it? But I'm not allowed to speak?"

"I have no idea what you're talking about. You must be as crazy as they say."

Libby's pulse ticked up. She took a deep breath. "You told me twice, in parking lots, that you were sorry," she said. Alice was approaching, making Libby panic a little. "What does that mean, exactly?"

"What is the *matter* with you?" Ryan hissed, looking her up and down.

"I want to see the kids, Ryan. Alice has been calling—they miss me, too, you know."

Alice suddenly slipped into their midst and threw her arms around Ryan's leg. "Daddy!" she said gleefully, and then saw Libby. "*Libby!*" she shrieked, and darted around Ryan to throw her arms around Libby.

"What are you *talking* about?" Ryan exclaimed angrily.

Libby could taste the sourness in her throat now.

Looking baffled, Ryan stared at his daughter. "Alice," he said, crouching down beside her, "have you been calling Libby?"

"*No,*" Alice said emphatically.

The sourness in her rose up on a swell of humiliation. Libby suddenly understood, suddenly realized that her fantasy of a happy medium had impinged on her common sense. Her suspicions that Alice didn't have permission to call were right. Alice was generally a truthful child, but she was still a child. And yet Libby had pushed down those suspicions to have what she wanted—some contact with her.

"Alice," Ryan said, peeling his daughter from Libby's leg, "Don't you *ever* call her."

"I didn't!" Alice cried.

"Ryan, don't," Libby said frantically. "It's okay—I misunderstood."

"You misunderstood?" he said, rising up again to face her. He was angry; his brown eyes had gone almost black. "What part did you misunderstand, Libby? I've tried everything to get through to you. Alice, go to your mother," he said, pointing in Gwen's direction.

"Daddy—"

"*Go,*" he said more forcibly.

He turned back to Libby as Alice scampered away. "What the hell do I have to do to get through to you that it's *over*?"

"Good God, I know that it's over," Libby said. "I just want to see Max and Alice—"

"I thought I could appeal to you on the basis of friendship, ask you *nicely* to leave me the hell alone—"

"Friendship!" Libby repeated, rattled by the notion.

"Yeah, I know. Stupid," Ryan said, nodding angrily. "I should have known that wouldn't work. You're too damn needy."

Libby mentally stumbled over the grain of truth in that statement. That she was standing here, wanting something from a man who had so thoroughly wronged her was pretty good evidence.

Ryan shifted closer, glaring down at her, his glare oddly veiled by gently falling snow. "So let me tell you as plainly as I can—there is nothing left of us. *Nothing*. I don't want you anywhere near me or my kids, do you get that? Don't come around us! You're not their mother, you're not their aunt, you're *nothing*! You're nothing to them and you're nothing to me!"

That was a punch right in the soft belly.

"Here's the God's honest truth, Libby. The only reason I *ever* dated you is because I needed a goddamn babysitter. That's it—I needed someone to watch my kids. And you messed that up about half the time."

"That is not true," she said, her voice made breathless by such a vile statement. "I held this family together."

"Don't flatter yourself," Ryan spat. "Why didn't you tell Alice to stop calling? Why didn't you text me to tell me she was calling you? Because it's all about *you,* isn't it? You think you're doing something noble and worthy for my kids, and the truth is that you couldn't possibly be worse for them if you tried."

"Me?" Libby said, and suddenly shoved Ryan in the chest, surprising him. "If I was so bad for them, why did you leave them with me while you were betraying us, huh? You're saying these things to appease your own guilty conscience, Ryan. You know what a lying bastard you are"—Libby was startled by a hand to her shoulder; she whirled about, expecting Gwen—

"Good, I'm glad you're here, Sam," Ryan snapped. "I'm done. I'm done being nice." He shifted his gaze to Libby again. "You know what? You aren't going to see these kids again. *Ev*-er! Go babysit someone else's kids because mine don't need you around."

Libby felt sick with disgust. The depth of Ryan's cruelty astounded her. He'd put two small children in her care when they were two and four years old and had allowed her, *encouraged* her, to love them beyond measure. They were the two children who Ryan had allowed her to believe were the fabric of the life they would have together. And then he had abruptly removed them from her care for no reason other than her services as babysitter were over.

A flash of burning, impotent rage shot through Libby. Her skin tingled with it, just as it did the day she'd taken a golf club to his truck. She felt flush with heat, imagined that snowflakes were sizzling off of her. "You bastard," she said, her voice shaking. She tried to lunge toward him, but Sam's arm came around her and held her back.

"Yeah, come on, hit me," Ryan said.

"Go watch your son play," Sam said curtly, and forced Libby to turn partially away from Ryan.

"Handle it, Sam!" Ryan shouted.

"How do you sleep at night?" Libby yelled at Ryan.

"*Hush*," Sam said, and ushered her along, forcing her to walk through what was now a heavy snow. A heavy, white curtain now between Libby and the family she thought she'd built. The pain in her was real, the fury consuming her. "What are you *doing*?" she demanded, trying to twist out of Sam's grip.

"Don't talk," Sam said curtly. "Don't say a word. I'm so angry right now I could put my fist through a tree."

"*You?* I'm livid!"

"Don't say another word!" he said sternly.

"I deserve to see them! I earned that right!"

Sam suddenly stopped and glared down at her, his jaw tightly clenched. "Libby, don't talk. Not a word, not a *single word*." He resumed the march, striding across the parking lot to his truck, pushing her along in front of him. He opened the back door—where people in custody were placed—and put his hand on her head, pushed her inside as if she were handcuffed. When she was seated he said, "Sit there. Don't move, don't open your mouth, don't do anything but breathe. Is that clear?" He shut the door soundly.

She could hear the crunch of gravel and snow beneath his boots as he walked around the back. The crunch suddenly stopped, and she felt an abrupt *thud* on the side panel, as if he'd kicked or shoved the truck.

In the next moment he opened the driver's door and put himself into the truck and turned the ignition. He turned on the windshield wipers. He didn't speak, or look at her in the rearview mirror. He put the truck into reverse and backed out, then hit the gas so hard that the truck fishtailed a bit.

He drove to her car and parked just far enough behind it that a person could maneuver out of the parking space. He sat there, staring out at the falling snow, the bulge in his jaw flexing with each clench of his teeth. He made no move.

Libby sat quietly, her hands in her lap, swallowing down little swells of bitter disappointment.

Sam suddenly opened the door of the truck and got out. He walked around to her door and opened it. He pointed to her car and said, "Go home."

Libby looked at her car, then at him. "That's it? Don't you want to know what happened?"

"*No*," he said hotly. "Go home."

Libby stepped out of the vehicle, pulled her sweater around her, and ducked under his arm. She glanced back at him, uncertain what to think, but his icy stare was enough. His anger was coming off of him in waves, stinging her skin along with the cold and her own fury. She hurried to her car, and as she settled in the driver's seat she was aware that Sam was watching her, his head down, his arms folded, oblivious to the snow that was hitting his shoulders.

Libby put her key into the ignition and turned. But her car, which had purred like a kitten this afternoon when she'd driven into town, chugged and would not start. She paused, pumped the gas pedal a couple of times, and tried again. Nothing. "*No,*" she muttered, and slowly leaned forward, until her forehead touched the steering wheel, and closed her eyes. "*No no no no.*"

Sam knocked on the driver's side window, and when she rolled down the window, he said, "Pop the hood."

Libby did as he asked. Sam opened the hood and rooted around underneath. After a few minutes of that, he shut the hood again, walked back to the driver's side and said, "It's nothing that I can see."

"Okay," she said, nodding. "I'll figure it out—"

"No, you won't," he said flatly. "Get in the truck. I'll take you home and bring Tony back."

"Sam, you don't have to do that—"

He suddenly planted both hands on her open window and bent down, so that he could look her directly in the eye. "I'm taking you home. I told you not to speak. Nor should you look at me. But perhaps most importantly? Don't *argue* with me. This will go a whole lot easier for us both if, for once, you will do as I ask." And with that, he shoved away from her car and walked back to his truck.

Libby was not going to argue with a man who looked that angry. She quickly gathered her things—flyers, wedding toppers, ribbons, and her purse. She locked the car and with her head down, she ran back to his truck. She moved to open the rear door, but Sam impatiently gestured for her to get in the front passenger seat.

When Libby was in her seat, he drove, skirting around the back end of the soccer field.

Libby slid down in her seat and focused on her breathing. She could picture it—Ryan was probably telling Gwen what had happened. They were both getting into their cars, shaking their heads, wondering what was wrong with Libby. And because Libby had believed that a rat bastard like him could actually be *sorry,* she'd ruined any chance of seeing the kids. And because she'd tried to clarify it all, she'd created a strain and ruined the funny little thing between her and Sam.

A fairly spectacular day so far.

She took another deep breath. And another. She tried to summon that tropical beach, but it was nowhere to be found.

Libby glanced at Sam from the corner of her eye. He was staring straight ahead, squinting at the road before him. "Sam?"

"No."

She sighed and leaned her head against the window, wishing it weren't such a drive up to Homecoming Ranch.

As it turned out, the drive up to Homecoming Ranch was much longer than she might have imagined. Snow and a trailer sliding off the road blocked any chance of getting home.

"You can drop me at the Grizzly," Libby said.

Sam leveled a look on her. "Sit tight," he said, and got out of the truck, grabbing a coat out of the back seat and shoving into it as he walked up the road to meet the driver of the truck.

Libby pushed herself up, and hugged herself. It was freezing now, and the wind had picked up at this higher elevation, enough to bend the tops of the pines.

She watched Sam and a guy from one of the cars behind the trailer squat down next to the disabled truck to have a look. The snow was coming down really hard now, swirling around the men as they convened in the middle of the road. Sam pulled his phone from his belt and made a call. After more conversation, he walked back to the truck.

When he opened the driver door, Libby felt the gust of cold north wind on her face. "What are you going to do?" she asked.

"Take you to my place for now," he said, his gaze on his big side view mirror as he slowly backed up.

"What? *Why?*"

"A tow truck is coming, but it might take an hour or more in this weather. He'll need help. We're not going to get up to the ranch, anyway—John says the roads are icing up there."

John, she supposed, was the rancher. "Then take me back to town," she said.

"Look at the snow, Libby," Sam said flatly. "We're not going to town. We'll be lucky if we can get a tow truck up here."

"But I can't stay at your house," she said, the very idea giving rise to anxiety in her. There was a distance in his gaze that Libby did not like.

Sam ignored her. He slowly backed down the road until he could find a place to turn around. When he had, he headed down the road about a quarter of a mile, and turned onto a narrow dirt road. The truck bounced along, sliding a little on the corners, driving deeper into the canyon.

Libby knew Sam lived somewhere around Homecoming Ranch, but she'd never seen his house, or even knew that it was on this little country road. It sat at a bend in the road, a house of thick logs and masonry, charmingly nestled against snowy pines. It had a sloped green metal roof, and the window and door trims were painted green. The chimney was made of river rock. There was a screened-in porch to one side, and a couple of outbuildings around the place. On a post beside the drive, about twenty feet in the air, was what looked like a tiny replica of the White House. As they neared it, Libby realized it was a birdhouse.

Sam pulled up before the house and got out. He waited for Libby at the bottom of the steps and walked up with her to the door, pushing it and holding it open so she could pass.

She stepped into a darkened room; behind her, Sam flipped a switch.

His house looked like what Libby might have guessed—it was obvious a man lived here. There was a worn, braided rug that covered the wood floors, and a man's obligatory leather recliner. There was a nice leather couch and one small armchair, upholstered in plaid, that looked as if it might have been picked up at a garage sale, judging by the bare spots on the arms. There wasn't much on the walls—a painting of a windmill, another one of a mountain sky behind Pine River. And on one short wall, an impressive array of coats and jackets hanging from a line of hooks.

Beyond the living room, through a big archway, Libby could see the kitchen, and from where she stood, it looked to be a bit of a mess. Dishes were piled in the sink, and a pan was sitting on the stove.

"Bathroom is down there," he said gesturing vaguely to the end of the hallway on her left. Libby could see the white standalone sink, the neat blue rug before it.

Sam moved to the fireplace. He took a few logs from a stack he had to one side and put them in, building a fire. His cold demeanor was making the little house even chillier. Libby rubbed her arms and looked around. "Keep an eye on it," he said once the flame took hold.

When Sam had the fire going, he stood up and looked at her. His gaze moved over her in one long slide, making Libby feel self-conscious. What did he see?

"I'll be back as soon as I can." He started for the door.

"Wait!" she said anxiously.

Sam paused and glanced back at her, his expression impatient.

"What should I do?"

He shrugged. "Sit. Wait. Take the time to think about things." He picked up a hat. "Help yourself to anything in the fridge." He went out the door.

She heard him run down the porch steps, heard his truck start up again. She listened to him drive away. She stood there until she couldn't hear anything but the wind moaning around the house.

Libby slowly turned a slow circle in the middle of the room, concentrating on her breath. *Try to center yourself. Calm your heart.* She had a strong desire to lie down on the floor before the fire and curl up in a ball, let the day and her anger wash away from her.

Instead, she sat carefully on the edge of Sam's recliner, her face in her hands.

She could picture her mother, her hair neatly trimmed, her rings blinking at Libby as she stirred Splenda into her iced tea, looking annoyed. *For heaven's sake, Libby, what is the matter with you? What would ever make you think he'd let you see the kids? You've always been like that, always imagining things that just aren't so.*

Libby's hands curled into fists, her frustration with herself, with life, with everything that had gone on in the last twenty-six years bubbling up. Dr. Huber would tell her that her anger was justified, but her trust was misplaced. She would advise her to use the techniques she'd taught her—breathing exercises, word associations, change of scenery, and then remind her to take her pill.

All of that sounded inadequate for what Libby was feeling in that moment. Profound disappointment—with Ryan, with herself. With Sam. Overwhelming, bitter, bitter disappointment.

But if she dwelled on it, Libby knew she would sink deeper. Dwelling, brooding—that's what got her into trouble, that's how she'd found herself holding a golf club.

Libby abruptly stood up, and in doing so, knocked a magazine off the table next to Sam's recliner. She picked it up and looked at it. *Outside Magazine.* Not surprising. He was obviously a solitary man. He was the smart one.

She noticed the coats and jackets again, remembered that she was freezing. She grabbed a flannel jacket from the wall and slipped into it, pulling it close around her body, dipping her head to touch her nose to the fabric. It smelled like Sam, spicy and earthy and . . . safe.

*Get busy. Do something. Anything.* Whatever it took to keep her mind from spinning into an angry mush beneath what had been another brutal rejection by Ryan.

Libby walked into the kitchen and looked around. It was a man's kitchen, all right. The appliance population was small, and those he did have were the cheap varieties one picked up off the grocery store aisle. Pots and pans were stacked in the sink, and the counter looked as if it could use a good cleaning. In fact, the whole place looked as if it could use a good cleaning.

Outside the snow swirled in big gusts across a very big deck.

Just beyond the railing was another birdhouse. She couldn't be sure, but this one looked like a plane.

She leaned over the sink, peering through the gray light of the blizzard. Something moved in the meadow, something dark and big.

Libby walked down to the desk and leaned over it, squinting out through the window. "Horses," she said aloud. She glanced at the clock on the stove. It was almost five. What if Sam didn't come back in the next hour or so? It would be too dark to bring them in. There it was, the thing she had to do.

Libby went back to the wall of coats, exchanged the flannel jacket for a coat with a hood, and put it on. From there, she walked into the mudroom, which was attached to the kitchen, and began to root around for some boots she might pull on.

# EIGHTEEN

A hard wind was sending snow up in swirls and bringing it down sideways, making it hard to see as Sam drove up the road to his house. He worried about his horses and hoped he'd be able to find them in the snowy dark.

He pulled into the drive, turned the collar of his coat up, and hopped out. He walked around the side of the house to the meadow gate, trudging down to the barn to grab a lead. But as he neared the barn, he noticed the outside light was on. He didn't generally use that light. He opened the door to the tack room, walked through to the barn . . . and stopped midstride, staring with disbelief: His two horses were in their stalls.

The sorrel mare lifted her head, sniffing at him, then pawed the ground.

"Hungry?" Sam checked their feeders and filled them with hay.

A quarter of an hour later, he stepped out into the snow again. Light spilled out of the windows at the back of his house, illuminating his deck. He could see the faint impressions of where Libby had walked across the deck and down to the meadow. And he could see Libby at the kitchen sink now. It was obvious she would have to stay the night, and Sam was not happy about that. He was pissed off, and, worse, surprisingly disillusioned. He'd really believed . . . he'd hoped . . .

*What, Sam, that she was the one for you? Get over yourself.*

He hoped he could scrounge up enough food to offer her something to eat. He mentally catalogued the food in his kitchen. He wasn't much of a gourmand. Nor was he much of a grocery shopper. He kept a few staples around but grabbed most of his meals in Pine River.

Sam made his way to the mudroom, stamped his feet to dislodge the snow, then pulled his boots off and hung his coat up. He opened the door into the kitchen and was hit by an aroma so delicious that it took him aback. He wasn't used to that sort of smell in his house, and his stomach growled in appreciation.

He stepped inside the door and Libby suddenly popped into view. She had a dish towel tied around her waist, another one draped over her shoulder. He also noticed something else—his kitchen was clean. He couldn't remember the last time he'd seen it clean. And the fire was blazing, which meant she'd kept it stoked. "What happened?" he asked, hearing the reverence in his voice that something wonderful and transformative had happened to his house.

"Ah . . . nothing," she said uncertainly. "I cooked," she added, gesturing to the stove as if that weren't obvious. "I hope that was okay. I was starving and I figured you'd be hungry, too. You said help yourself," she continued, sounding apologetic.

"I did. It smells great. And you're right, I'm hungry." Now that he'd smelled actual food, he was ravenous. "Did you get the horses in?" he asked, unable to hide his surprise.

"Yes," she said. "I didn't know how long you'd be gone."

"Thank you."

She gave him a thin smile and turned back to the stove.

Thin as it was, Sam wasn't ready for smiles. He could hardly look at her without a wildly contradicting mix of emotions rifling through him.

"Do you want to eat?"

"Yes, I'd love to. I'm just going to wash up." He started for his room, but on his way out of the kitchen, he paused and looked back at her. Libby was watching him warily. "Don't think because you are feeding me that I am going to forget what happened today," he warned her.

Libby snorted. "Are you kidding? You have the memory of an elephant, and I didn't expect a little snow to change that. I hope you like turkey."

Sam debated mentioning how long that turkey had been in his freezer, and decided he was too hungry to worry about it.

In his room, Sam had to move a stack of books that had served as a doorstop in order to shut the door. A man living alone up in the mountains didn't need a lot of privacy.

He pulled off his shirt, felt exhaustion in his muscles and limbs. It had taken a lot of work to winch that truck out of the ditch, and then it had been a very slow trek down to the valley floor with the cattle bellowing behind in the trailer. The tedious drive back had given him plenty of time to think about the problem of Libby.

Sam sat on the edge of his bed, rubbed his face with his hands. What the hell did he do with her? He couldn't keep covering for her, couldn't keep allowing her to walk away from obvious violations of the restraining order. And there was something else. He didn't need this sort of drama in his life. It was the thing he'd learned in the course of his treatment and sobriety that he had to avoid. For a man who walked a tightrope every day—which he did—there was no place for anxiety and stress to go.

He'd been fully prepared to give her a dressing down, but then she'd brought in his horses, had cleaned his damn kitchen, and had *cooked* for him. When was the last time someone had cooked for him? Years? It made him feel almost strangely normal, and Sam didn't want to feel normal. Normal was deceiving. Normal made him believe things could be different for him.

He took a quick, hot shower, pulled on a long-sleeved T-shirt that said "Denver Rodeo" and some loose jeans. He combed his hair back and returned to the kitchen, bracing his arms overhead against the archway. "Smells good," he said. "What is it?"

Libby looked at the pot on the stove. "I'm not sure. I'm going to say it's Greek. But without the lamb. Or lentils. But it has turkey and peas and rice, and I made a great yogurt sauce, which was really hard to do seeing as how you have *nothing* in this kitchen. How do you survive? Anyway, it's not gourmet, but it should be filling."

To him, if it wasn't out of a microwave, it was gourmet.

"I also found some plates and bowls and set the table. There was a layer of dust on those plates," she said with a reproving look for him.

"Hey, I rinse them off before I use them." He looked at the small round table he rarely used. There were two place settings. It was a civilized meal, something this house rarely saw.

"Have a seat," she suggested, and prepared two big bowls of her invented dish. She smiled.

Sam looked at his bowl. She was not entitled to his smile, not even with the surprising gift of dinner. She was lucky she wasn't sitting in the holding cell in Pine River right now. But Libby's smile remained steady.

"Don't," he warned her, dipping his fork into her concoction.

"Don't what?"

"Don't even think of smiling at me after what you did today. I'm frustrated as hell with you." He put the fork into his mouth and almost slid off his chair—the Greek thing, or whatever she was calling it, was delicious.

"Yeah, well . . . I'm pretty frustrated, too." At his skeptical look, she insisted, "I *am.* You would not believe what I—" She stopped, shook her head, and picked up her fork.

"You what?"

She shook her head again. "Believe me, when I tell you, you'll be even more frustrated. And you'll get that look on your face—"

"*What* look?"

"*That* look," she said, making a swirling motion at his face with her fork. "The I-can't-believe-this-chick look. And you won't listen."

"Come on, Libby, I've listened to you," he scoffed. "More than once, I might add."

"I know, you have," she said. "You, of all people, have listened to me." She poked around her bowl with her fork.

He watched her a moment, wanting her to eat. He didn't like to see her so glum.

He forked another healthy bite. "This is delicious, by the way," he said. "You're an excellent cook."

"Spoken like a hungry man," she said with a rueful smile.

That was the thing that made Sam cave. He loved Libby's smile. It was one of the few things in life that made him feel good. He sighed, too, and put down his fork, his gaze on Libby again. He took in her hair, which she had pulled back, but several long tendrils of curls had drifted away. "I know you want to talk," he said. "But first, I want to know if you understand that I could lose my job by not taking you in for the violations? For covering for you? Do you understand that I have stuck my neck out for you more than once?"

"Yes, of course. Sam, look—I know I don't make sense to you. Or to anyone. And as much as I'd like to clear it all up, I never seem to find the right words to explain myself, you know? When you tell me that I make no sense, I understand why you're saying it. But in *my* head, I do make sense, and I find I am constantly trying to mesh what everyone tells me with what I feel. But today? Today was different. Today I fell for the hopes of an eight-year-old girl."

Sam was dubious. He focused on his food.

"I swear it," she said. "Here's what happened," she said, watching him closely, as if she expected him to cut her off at any moment. But Sam just shrugged and continued to eat his meal as Libby told him about Alice's phone calls. About how she'd believed the little girl—maybe not everything she said—but that Ryan knew she was calling and it was okay because he was sorry. "She just wanted to talk to me," Libby said. "She just wanted me in her life."

"And you wanted to believe her," he said. "Just like you wanted to believe there was some hidden message in what Ryan said in the parking lot that morning."

"You're right," she said, nodding. "You're so right, I get that now. I was stupid, and—well, you heard Ryan. He summed it up for everyone."

Sam had heard Ryan, all right. He really despised that man, the way he had treated Libby. He finished his bowl and leaned back, watching Libby continue to move her food around. "What do you think of Ryan now?" he asked, his voice betraying his disdain. "Still think he's the guy for you?"

She looked up at him, and Sam instantly regretted his tone. He could see the remnants of an old hurt in her. "No," she said quietly. "I think he's an even bigger ass than the day I picked up the golf club."

She suddenly reached for his wrist, wrapping her fingers around it. "All I wanted was a chance to keep Max and Alice in my life, and I just . . . *hoped,*" she said. She glanced away, and her fingers slid away from his wrist, back across the table, to her lap.

What was it about Libby Tyler that affected Sam so? Even now, after an afternoon of incredible frustration, he felt something stirring for her.

Maybe it was that he could see his own failures in her eyes. He knew all about useless hope, knew all about slicing pain that came with that moment of realization, when the world you had built on a hope came tumbling down like a tower of ashes. He couldn't help himself; he reached for her hand. It seemed to surprise Libby, but she turned her hand over, so that her palm was touching his, and wrapped her fingers around his hand, too.

"I'm starting to sound a little crazy to myself, you know?" she said softly. "I only know that one day, I thought everything was great, that we would always be together, and the next, it was like waking from a dream—it was all gone. And the worst of it was Alice and Max. I didn't know how to go from practically being their mother to being nothing. I didn't know how to not see them every day, or to not hear about their day, to not put them to bed. I guess I kept thinking it was a mistake, and somehow, I'd patch together a way we could still be together. I didn't get how a father could take someone those two kids cared for from their lives for no apparent reason. Did he even once consider their feelings or what they needed?"

"You just hoped too hard," Sam said. "You got too wrapped up."

"Obviously. But I never thought of hope as a bad thing. Do you think it is?"

"I'm really not the person to ask," he said. Sam felt antsy now; he didn't like thinking about how hard he'd once hoped. How he'd wasted so many good years and had even risked his health on a razor-thin hope.

Libby sighed and slid her hand out from under his, leaving his hand empty. "Alice and Max were babies when I met Ryan. They were sleeping weird hours and they were eating the worst things, and they wore dirty clothes, and half the time they had stuff stuck in their hair," she said, gesturing to her unruly mass of curls. "They were babies. And then they were *my* babies."

That, sadly, was Libby's downfall—those children had never been her babies. He had no doubt it felt that way to Libby, but they'd never been her children and they never would be. It was the crux of Libby's problems this summer—she couldn't let go of the maternal love she possessed for those children. Sam didn't have to point out the obvious. Libby knew it, even if her love blinded her to her actions.

"I met Ryan when I was working as a clerk in the sheriff's office. Did you know that?" she said wistfully.

Sam glanced up. "I remember."

"He came in to report some cattle loose up on Sometimes Pass," she said with a wan smile. "I thought he was really handsome, and we hit it off. He used to send me flowers, every Monday. They arrived like clockwork. Roses and marigolds, lilies, irises. You name it, he sent it."

Sam remembered it—the guys in the office had teased her, making kissing sounds and pretending to be her, acting silly when the flowers came. Libby was a good sport about it, always willing to laugh at her own expense.

"He took me to the places I'd never really been, like the Stake Out, and the little French bistro out on the Old Aspen Highway. No one had ever treated me like that. He told me his wife had misunderstood him, and that what he needed was a woman who could be his partner. He said Gwen hadn't connected with her own kids, and she'd left, taken off for Colorado Springs without them. He said what they needed was someone like me, someone who understood them, someone who could be a real mother to them." She laughed bitterly. "I guess he set me up, didn't he?"

Ryan had been fishing for a permanent babysitter, just as he'd told Libby today, and for that Sam reviled him.

"The thing is, he could have been straight with me about it from the beginning," she said. "But he knew what he had, because I was knocking on the door demanding entry, because I *wanted* a family. I wanted exactly what Ryan offered—a love affair, kids, a house, and a dog." Her gaze fell to her lap. "He said he loved me, and he loved how I had taken his kids in as my own, and he loved everything about our family. He said we would get married, and we would have more, and . . . and that's where I thought we were headed. I wasn't expecting the end. I never saw it coming."

Something tweaked in Sam's chest; it felt almost as if his heart was stretching a little. He felt for Libby, he truly did. "Most people don't see ends like that coming."

"Maybe not, but I've had more than my fair share of practice. I should have recognized what was happening."

"I don't follow."

"Like when I was eight," she said, lifting her gaze to his again, "my mom and dad got into some child-support tussle. She called his bluff and sent me out to California to live with him and Emma and her mother. Dad said, 'oh we're going to have fun, Libby. We're going to do this and that, and you'll be *so* glad you came,'" she said, with an airy flick of her wrist. "But really? My dad couldn't handle the responsibility of raising me and neither could Emma's mother. So he sent me back to Pine River. Only by then, Mom was with Derek and she was pregnant. Once the twins were born, I was the fifth wheel."

"Oh yeah?" Sam said, curious now. He'd met Mrs. Buchanan a few times and liked her. "Your mom seems really nice."

"Don't defend her, I'm on a roll," Libby said.

Sam couldn't help a small chuckle. "By all means, roll on."

"After that was Act Two with my dad," Libby said with a sigh. "I'll let you in on a secret—my dad was not a nice person. At least not to me." She paused. "I think he had a soft spot for Emma, though," she said thoughtfully. "Anyway, I tried so hard to know him, I really did. He wouldn't have much to do with me, besides an occasional dinner. And even then, he talked more on his phone than he did to me. And when he got sick, I thought I could help by taking care of him. He needed someone, right? I was willing to do that, but he wouldn't let me in. Not even for a moment," she said, with swipe of her hand.

"That must have been rough," Sam said, meaning it. His own father wasn't the warmest guy in the world, but at least Sam knew that in his own way, he cared.

"And you know what else?" Libby said, suddenly sitting up. "He *never* told me about Madeline. Even in the hospital, he didn't tell me," she said, punching the table with her finger with each word for emphasis. "He never told me about Homecoming Ranch. All I ever tried to do was be a good daughter to him, but I always felt as if I was bothering him when I showed up."

Sam didn't know much about Grant Tyler, other than he'd been a big man in Pine River. Luke had told him that Grant had tried to help Bob Kendrick out with a loan against the ranch when he needed the money for Leo. But Sam also knew that Madeline hadn't known him at all, much less that she had two sisters out in the world. Sam didn't know how a man could father children and then be so utterly irresponsible with their souls.

Libby pushed her bowl away and slid down into her chair, bringing one leg up so that she could prop her knee under her chin. "And then there was Ryan. Boy, oh boy, did I fall hard for him. Totally, completely, head over heels in love with him."

"We've been down this road," Sam said, because he didn't want to hear again how in love she'd been with Spangler.

"You know I got fired because of him, right?"

Sam didn't know it for certain, but he'd heard some talk. "How so?"

"When he . . . when he asked me to leave," she said, swallowing hard on those words, "I started getting calls from school. 'Who is picking Alice up today?'" she said, mimicking someone from the school. "It happened more than once. I started to worry about Alice and Max—Ryan couldn't keep in mind Alice's dance lessons or Max's soccer games. One morning, Alice called me because she couldn't find her backpack. It was eight forty-five and they were still at home and she didn't know where her dad was. I freaked out, I admit it," Libby said. "When I couldn't get him on the phone, I left work to go and see if they were okay."

"Were they?" Sam asked.

"Yes, they were fine," she said with a sigh. "The reason Alice didn't know where Ryan was is because his mother was keeping them. He'd gone on a hunting trip or something. I neglected to ask if anyone else was with them. But then, it happened again. The dance teacher called me one afternoon and said they were closing up shop but no one had come to pick up Alice. So I left work again." She sighed and rubbed her eyes. "The long and the short of it is, I couldn't stop worrying about the kids. I left work too many times to go and see about them, or to be at dance class or soccer, or just to make sure they were at school. I was fired for it. Me. Libby Tyler, the most punctual employee the sheriff's office had ever had. *God*," she groaned.

"Were the kids ever in true danger?" Sam asked.

Libby shook her head. "Nope. It was always me, assuming the world couldn't spin without me. Ryan kept forgetting, and I kept hearing about it, and I kept imagining the worst. The *worst.* I remember sitting at my desk imagining someone luring Alice to their car with a puppy while she waited for her dad to show up." She closed her eyes a moment. "I was a mess. Those two had been ripped from my life and I couldn't handle it. Mom told me I had to do something useful and stop worrying so much, and when did

I become such a worrier, and on and *on,*" she said. "When Dad died, and I found out about Homecoming Ranch, I thought, *this* is it! This is what I am going to do with my life! I have two sisters, and we can make this work!"

"You were thrown a pretty big curve ball," Sam agreed.

"I thought two sisters was the best thing to ever happen to me. I thought we were going to live as one big happy family up here. It never occurred to me that Madeline and Emma wouldn't want that." She gave Sam a sheepish look. "There you have it, Lone Ranger, my life in a nutshell. One long road of disappointment."

Those words resonated with him, because Sam had felt the same thing. So much hope put into a relationship, so much disappointment to come out of it. Disappointment in Terri, but mostly, disappointment in himself—for not seeing things he should have seen, for not being strong enough to fight alcoholism. He really wasn't that different from Libby.

"Look, I know it's been tough for you." He was forgiving her, and he couldn't stop himself. It was just too damn hard to be angry with Libby.

"You're right, Sam, I hoped too hard. When Ryan told me he'd made a mistake, I hoped that maybe it *was* all a mistake, sort of like a bad dream. What I wanted, really wanted, was for him to say that he was sorry. I wanted him to say it out loud and grovel a bit, but I really wanted to hear him say he was wrong so I didn't have to be wrong."

"Okay," Sam said, leaning forward and looking her in the eye. "I'll let you in on a secret—Ryan isn't man enough to admit he's wrong. Be that as it may, no more talk of it tonight, okay?" He didn't think he could hear another word without getting into his truck and going in search of Ryan, the snow notwithstanding. He picked up their bowls and stood. "I've got KP duty." He started into the kitchen.

"But isn't there something you need to say?" Libby asked.

"What's that?"

"What you're going to do with me. I mean, about the restraining order?"

That was a good question, and Sam really had no idea. But he wasn't going to do anything tonight. "Depends," he said. "Did you make dessert?"

A grin slowly lit Libby's face. "No. But I bet I could find something to throw together."

"Better make it good," he advised her. "It could be the difference between freedom and a little cooling-off time in jail."

"Wow." Libby stood, her body almost touching his. "In that case," she said, her gaze landing on his mouth and firing up his senses, "I really hope you have some sugar."

# NINETEEN

Libby watched Sam washing dishes, grateful that he'd let her talk, even offering a strong shoulder and a good ear. But give an inch and take a mile—Libby had dumped her entire life story on him, warts and all. Now, there was really very little Sam Winters didn't know about her. She hadn't told him that she'd once aspired to be a diplomat with spy privileges, but then again, she'd been ten years old.

Now, Libby wanted to know about him. She wanted to know what made him want to look after people no one else looked after. Or what romances in his life had taught him to kiss a woman so thoroughly she felt like she was floating. She wanted to know how he'd suddenly gotten so damn hot, and how she had failed to fully appreciate that in the past. She admired his trim waist, his broad shoulders, the way that loose pair of jeans rode low on his hips.

Sam noticed she was looking at him. "How about that dessert, Tyler?" he asked as he reached to put a pan away, revealing a glimpse of muscled abs.

"I'm thinking. You have to admit, your kitchen setup is pretty pathetic. You have cereal, and that's about it."

"Are you giving up? Opting for jail?"

"No way," she said. "But I'm going to have to resort to a poor man's dessert."

"Syrup and bread?"

"*No*," she said, horrified. "What sort of animal are you? Just stay here." She picked up a big salad bowl she'd found, and brushed against him on her way out.

She stepped into the mudroom, gasping with shock at the cold. She stuffed her feet into the oversized boots again, stepped outside and, using her bare hands, filled the bowl with snow. She came back in, hopping around a little to stamp the chill from her bones.

Sam was leaning against the clean counter when she returned to the kitchen. He took a look at her bowl and said, "Snow ice cream."

"Good guess!"

"Not really—it's just that I've been a poor man." He winked at her.

Libby grabbed milk from the fridge and measured it out, then looked in Sam's cabinet. "I can't believe you have vanilla extract. You have nothing else, but you have that. Why?"

He laughed. "Who knows?"

"It's curious, Mr. Winters. You know so much about me now, and yet I don't know anything about you. Hardly seems fair."

"Fair has nothing to do with it. You've made it my job to know about you. I'm being paid to know about you and to keep you from adding to the tale."

"Semantics. I think you are trying to avoid talking about *you* right now." She pointed a measuring spoon at him. "If we're going to be friends, I should get *some* details."

"Are we going to be friends?" he asked.

He was looking at her in a way that made Libby's pulse flutter. "Friends" sounded too soft for what she was feeling. She said, "It depends."

His smile was slow and easy, and Libby felt another shiver course through her. "There's nothing to know," he said. "Life is pretty boring up here."

"Come on," she said, measuring vanilla now. "We're stuck here. What else are we going to do? If you don't talk, then I guess I can keep talking about me and where my relationship with Ryan went wrong—"

"God no," he said, throwing up a hand and laughing. "Honestly, Libby, I'm not being coy. I go to work and I come home."

"Well. What do you do when you come home?"

He frowned a little as if he was thinking about it. "Putter," he said.

"That's so lame!" Libby said laughingly. "You're not playing the game correctly. Start at the beginning. Where did you go to school? When did you get married?"

She could see his entire body tense.

"I'm sorry," she said, turning her attention back to the ice cream. "I didn't mean to strike a nerve."

"You didn't strike a nerve," he said, but it was clear she had. He again tried to brush it off by saying, "It was a long time ago."

"Not that long," she said. "You were married when you started at the sheriff's office."

"Yep," he said, and pushed away from the counter. "I'm going to go tend the fire."

Libby listened to him rummage in the wood caddy, more curious than ever. She finished making the ice cream and put it into two small bowls. With a pair of mismatched spoons, she followed him into the living room and handed him one. "Thanks," he said.

"Welcome." She crossed her legs and lowered herself to the ground, sitting before the fire. Sam sat on the edge of the couch.

Libby's gaze flicked over him as she tasted the ice cream.

"What?" he asked, smiling uncertainly.

"Nothing."

"It's never nothing," he said.

"You're right. I was wondering what it is you don't want to talk about."

Sam groaned. "You're not going to let it go, are you?"

"Probably not. I'm curious."

He sighed.

"Here's a simple question, yes or no," she said. "Have you ever been in a situation where *you* hoped too hard?"

"That is not a simple question," he said. "But for the sake of peace, I probably did, yeah. Nevertheless, it was a long time ago, and I'd really rather not drag it all up again if it's all the same to you. I'm going to enjoy my poor man's ice cream."

"Sure," she said, and turned her attention to her ice cream. "Mind if I ask you something else?"

"About hope?" he asked suspiciously.

"No."

His eyes narrowed. "Against my better judgment, okay. Ask."

"What's it like, being in recovery?"

This time, Sam clanked his spoon into the bowl. "Wow. Talk about skipping the salad and going right for the meat." He put aside his bowl. He leaned forward, rested his hands on his thighs. "Libby . . . if I give you the Sam Winters rundown, will you stop asking so many questions?"

Libby thought about that a moment. "I don't know if I can make that promise for all of eternity . . . but I could probably stop for the night." She winked.

"I'll take what I can get. So move over," he said, nudging her with his foot, then dipped down, settling in front of the couch, his legs long in front of him, crossed at the ankles. "You want to know the truth about me, huh? Okay, here goes. I'm an alcoholic. I've been sober for three years and thirty-two days."

"Congratulations," Libby said, uncertain what else to say.

"Thanks."

"That must have been really hard," she said.

"To quit?" he asked, and Libby nodded. "Yes," he said. "It was the hardest thing I have ever done."

"Is that why you . . . you know, split up with your wife?"

His gaze wandered over her face, and yet he didn't seem to be looking at her, but rather something only he could see. "Alcohol was a huge problem in my marriage. On both sides."

This was a whole new side to Sam Winters. Libby placed her bowl in his, put them on the end table, and turned to face him. "I'm a good listener, too."

Sam chuckled. He casually touched the back of his hand to her face. "No you're not. You're possibly the worst listener I've ever known. But I'll tell you anyway."

He told her how he'd met his wife in college. Terri was her name, he said. A free spirit. Sam said he'd been enthralled, that he'd never known anyone like her. "We fell in love, and after college, we moved around to various jobs. She was always looking for a big cause to get involved with."

When the jobs had ended up leading them nowhere, Sam brought her to Colorado Springs and joined the ranks of law enforcement, and eventually they ended up in Pine River. Terri, he said, had trouble keeping a job because she couldn't stay sober, and by that point, he wasn't much better.

"It snuck up on us," he admitted. "I'd never been much of a drinker. My dad drank, and I didn't want to be like him," he said, shifting his gaze to the fire. "It made him as mean as Millie Bagley."

"Oh wow," Libby said. "I'm sorry. He was an alcoholic?"

"I'm sure," Sam said. "But I never really thought of him that way. To me, he drank too much, that was it. I never thought of it as a disease, or that it could happen to me. And when I started drinking, it didn't seem like a big deal—a drink here or there, that was all. I guess I fooled myself. I remember justifying it by telling myself it wasn't like I had to have it. I had myself convinced I was very different than dear old Dad, you know? Terri and I drank to unwind after class. She'd binge drink on the weekends, but you know, it was college, and a lot of people did that. I was naïve." He glanced at his hand.

There but for the grace of God, Libby thought. When she first started working at the sheriff's office, there had been some wild parties. On a couple of occasions, she'd had far too much to drink. She'd even known in the moment she was drinking too much, but alcohol had a way of making her believe she was okay. "When did you realize you had a problem?"

"Not until it was too late," Sam said with a snort. "By the time I graduated and we got married, Terri and I would have a drink at the end of the workday together. And then, it began to roll into the dinner hour, changing to wine. And somewhere along the way, it became a cocktail, wine with dinner, brandy or port after that."

"That doesn't sound so bad," Libby said. "I know a lot of people who relax with a few drinks."

"They're probably not alcoholics," he pointed out. "I remember the first time I put whiskey in my morning coffee. I remember standing at the kitchen sink telling myself it wasn't that big of a deal. That was my life—a constant state of rationalization. I refused to acknowledge that my life and my marriage were unraveling into one tangled string of drinks. Terri and I were of one mind—any excuse for another drink."

It was hard for Libby to imagine it. It was hard to look at Sam, a stand-up guy by anyone's measure, and imagine him in the grip of addiction.

"I tried to talk to her about it. I told her we should get help, but it's easier to talk about than it is to do." He paused, glanced at his hands again, stretching his fingers wide. "I tried to stop drinking. I tried to be a good husband even though Terri had abandoned any pretense at being my wife. She drank in front of me, and I couldn't vanquish the temptation to drink with her. I was losing everything. I knew it, I could see it, and still, I couldn't stop drinking."

"Wow," Libby said softly. "I'm sorry, Sam. It must have been so difficult for you."

"You have no idea," he said with a wry laugh. "I tried everything, but I still found myself pulling off the side of the road while on patrol and digging a bottle out from beneath the seat."

Libby knew something like that had happened—everyone knew Sam had been drunk on the job. But looking at him now, the strong, kind man that he was, she couldn't picture it. She couldn't guess how hard that must have been for him, to be that strong and yet unable to defeat his biggest adversary.

"I started missing work with some pretty spectacular hangovers. When I was at work, I chewed gum like a maniac to keep the smell from my colleagues, but they knew. Everyone knew. I've smelled it on drunks myself—once alcohol gets into your blood, there's no masking it.

"It caught up with me. At the time, I thought it was the end of everything, but it ended up being my salvation. If it hadn't caught up with me when it did, I could very well be dead now."

That was painful and sobering to hear. "What happened?" Libby asked. "I only know that you were asked to go."

"Nothing splashy, no wrecks or shootings, thank God," Sam said. "What happened was that I picked up a kid for burglary. Caught him right there, with the stuff in his truck. But I was drunk, and the paperwork was incoherent, and so was I. The kid was savvy, too, and he kept accusing me of being drunk. Loudly. Yelling at other officers that I was drunk, and he was right. I had plenty of excuses for it—long shift, no sleep, whatever—but it was apparent to everyone by then. I was a drunk."

"And the sheriff fired you?"

"No," Sam said with a shake of his head. "What he did was give me a chance, and for that, I will always be grateful. He called me into his office the next day. I'll never forget it; all the top brass were there. His chief deputy, the head of human resources, the attorneys. Basically, he gave me an ultimatum: either I went for treatment at the facility the department had already arranged and get sober, or I would lose my job. Plus, he said he would see to it that I never worked in Colorado law enforcement again. But if I did as he asked and went for treatment, maintained sobriety, and proved I could be trusted, he'd find a job for me. He kept his word—that's why I have this position now."

"Oh, Sam," Libby murmured. "It was brutal, wasn't it? Treatment, I mean. It's such a depressing place to be."

"It is definitely that," he agreed. "The drying out wasn't as bad as the therapy, and facing things you don't want to face. All those old childhood hurts and traumas you didn't even know you had, but somehow drink to numb them. I never knew what an issue I had with my old man until I went to therapy, for example."

Libby smiled ruefully. "I remember lying on this cot. I felt like I was literally on the floor, and I kept telling myself, if I could just peel one shoulder up, just one, I could get up and make it right. But there was some invisible weight on me and I couldn't even do that."

Sam took her hand in his. "I know, it was hard as hell. But in the end, I can say it was the best thing to happen to me. The sheriff was being a friend, and to tell you the truth, I was actually a little relieved. I was at the bottom, and I knew it. I just didn't know how to crawl out of that hole, and he offered me a rope."

"What happened to Terri? " Libby asked.

Sam's expression changed. He looked sad. "She still refused to admit she had a problem, or quit, even though she was going through a fifth of vodka a day. And when I came out of treatment ninety days later, sober, and ready to reboot my life, she wouldn't stop drinking. She wouldn't or couldn't do that for me, or for herself. And I . . ." He closed his eyes as if the memory pained him. "I left her. I couldn't stay married to her. It was either me or booze, and she chose booze. I chose sobriety."

"Heartbreaking," Libby murmured.

Sam smiled and lazily traced a line down to her wrist. "You know when you go to a concert in the park, and everyone is sitting on blankets, but it seems there is always one person up front, totally into the music, dancing alone, like they are the only person there?"

Libby nodded.

"Well, that was Terri. When I first met her, I thought she was a free spirit, a woman who danced to her own beat and didn't care what the world thought. But now I look back and see that she was dancing for attention. She was always dancing for the attention, and not because she was moved by some artistic spirit. Alcohol gave her attention. Not all good, but attention all the same. And whatever had been between us had drowned in the booze a long time ago."

He glanced at the fire.

Libby laced her fingers with his. Her problems with Ryan and the kids felt so small in comparison to what Sam had been through. "Have you had a drink since?"

"Once," he admitted. "A couple of months after treatment when I was living in the halfway house. But I had a sponsor who shook me up and got me back to meetings, and I haven't had a drink since that day."

"But that's great," Libby said.

Sam gave her a patient look as if he'd had this conversation before. "It's okay, Libby, but it will never be great. Every day I go without drinking is a victory, and it's always going to be that way."

He sighed, leaned his head back against the couch. The recounting of his past had exhausted him.

"Thanks for confiding in me." Libby turned around, leaned against the couch beside him, and stretched her legs out next to his and folded her arms across her middle. Sam had his own private demons, just like her. The difference between them was that he was better at controlling his demons now than she was. "We're not that different, are we?" she mused.

She heard the chuckle deep in his chest. "I guess not."

She liked being next to Sam. She liked feeling his warmth beside her. She liked that they were kindred spirits. Sam might not see it that way, but Libby did. They were two people who hadn't coped with life's messiness as well as they would have liked, and paid a price most people couldn't imagine.

They remained side by side, nothing but the sound of the fire crackling in that room, surrounded by the moan of wind through the eaves. On the floor of his small house, Libby felt strangely content. There was something very comforting about being here, with him. She could forget she'd made a mess of things with Max and Alice, or that she was broke, or that she didn't have a clue what she was going to do after Gary and Austin's wedding. This was where she was supposed to be tonight, away from the world, with someone who understood her better than she had even realized.

Sam shifted a little, and Libby reflexively put her hand on his arm, as she might have done with one of the kids, or with a friend.

But when she touched him, she felt Sam still. She turned her head to look at him.

He was looking at her, too, his gaze questioning.

Libby moved her hand. "I'm sorry," she said. "I forgot for a moment that we are captive and captor." She smiled. "You're a good guy, Sam. It's funny, but you've seen more of me than anyone else has ever seen. The real me, I mean. You've been more of a friend to me than . . . than anyone. Did you know that?"

"There's the friend thing again," he said, his gaze sliding down to her mouth. "Are we friends, Libby? Because I like kissing you too much to be a friend." His gaze slid right on down to the sweater she was wearing. He cocked his head to one side, studying it. "I think I ought to take you in and let you sit a night in a holding cell, but I can't seem to make myself do it."

"I won't argue."

"Good call," he said, and slowly lifted his gaze, piercing hers with his sea-colored eyes. "We're not friends, Libby."

"No?"

"*No.*"

His gaze was smoldering, and Libby was ignited by it. She shifted around, onto her knees, facing him. "Then what are we?"

"I don't know. That's what scares me," he said with a wry smile. He touched her waist, his hand sliding around to her back.

"Do I scare you?"

He shook his head.

"Then you're the only one."

Sam began to pull her toward him.

"Sometimes, against my better judgment, I feel things about you, Sam Winters."

"Oh yeah?" he asked, and casually caressed her back. "What sort of things?"

"It's hard to explain." She touched his chin, traced her finger along the jawline, feeling the stubble of his beard. "Because sometimes it feels really pissed off. But other times, it feels warm and fuzzy and . . . tingly."

"I like tingly," he said, and leaned forward, touching his nose to her hair.

"But I'm pretty sure tingly is not something one should feel for one's arresting officer."

"That's true." He brushed her hair from the side of her face and touched his mouth to her neck, sending a hot tingling flush down Libby's body. "And then again, I haven't actually arrested you." He cupped her chin with his hand, kissed her cheek, and then the corner of her mouth. A swirl of tingling flared across her skin, and she sighed with longing as she turned her head to kiss him. She didn't care if he arrested her or not. Tonight, in the middle of this blizzard, she only wanted to feel his arms around her.

Sam lifted his head. He studied her a moment as he stroked his thumb across her bottom lip. "I thought we weren't doing this anymore."

"That might have been a hasty decision," she said.

"This is a dangerous path we're on, Libby Tyler. Are you sure you want to slide down it?"

She touched two fingers to his lips and smiled. "I'm sure."

"*Good*," he said, and grabbed her, dragging her across his lap to kiss her.

His hand slid down to her hip, squeezing it. Libby's hand was still on his chest, caught between their bodies. She could feel the beat of his heart melting into her pulse. She moved her fingers across his nipple, felt it harden beneath her touch. She nestled closer, wanting to feel the heat of his body seep into her skin.

Sam's tongue was in her mouth, sweeping over her teeth. He nibbled at her lip, filled his palm with her breast, kneading it, and then tucked his hand underneath her sweater. His rough skin against hers aroused her, made the tingling in her spread to all her limbs. She was aware of her body dampening, her pulse throbbing at her temples and in her groin. All her second thoughts washed away from her. No matter how they'd come together, no matter anything else, this felt right, as if she belonged on his lap before a fire, his hands on her body, his tongue in her mouth.

He shifted again, rolling onto his side, and putting Libby on her back before the fire. He moved over her, holding himself above her, taking her in, his gaze wandering all the way down to the socks on her feet, then up again, to the funky sweater she wore. With the palm of his hand, he moved slowly from her chest, over her breast, down to her belly, and to the top of her skirt. He kissed her softly on the hollow of her throat and moved his hand again, down to her knee, then up under her skirt, his fingers sliding up so softly that a shiver of anticipation ran deep into her veins.

He languidly caressed her inner thigh, stoking a fire deep in her groin. "This is crazy," he said roughly. "*You* make me crazy. I don't know what it is about you, but you make me crazy." He kissed her neck and slid his fingers up between her legs, sliding over the silk of her panties.

His touch reverberated through every limb. She sighed as she thrust her fingers in his hair. Sam stroked her over the fabric of her panties, then dipped one finger beneath them, into the damp heat. She could feel his cock hard and long against her leg, and she imagined him sliding into her, his hips clenching with the effort to restrain himself. Her eyes fluttered shut at the erotic image, her thoughts devoid of anything but him and his touch, of the way he could tantalize her with just a stroke or swirl of his fingers.

Sam was kissing her wildly now, his finger sliding up and down and into her body, pushing her to the brink.

He moved again, this time pulling her up, his hands on her rib cage. Libby was quick to discard her clothing, baring her breasts to him. Sam made a sound of pure hunger as he took a breast into his mouth, his tongue flicking against the peak, his teeth lightly teasing her.

She heard panting—*she* was panting. She fumbled for the waistband of his jeans, desperate to feel him in her hands, and he was eager to oblige her. Through some feat of athletic prowess, he managed to keep his mouth on her while kicking off his jeans. He paused to remove his shirt, then shifted over her again, eagerly yanking at her skirt and panties, pulling them from her body.

Just looking at him made Libby shudder with desire. He was magnificent, his eyes shining hungrily in the gold light of the fire. His arms and chest were muscled and hard, his waist lean, his hips powerful. He began to stroke her again, his eyes locked on hers, his breath coming in long, deep draws. He hadn't even made love to her and Libby was flying. She pressed against him, wanting more as a furious, demanding rhythm thrummed in her. He began to suckle her breast at the same time his thumb began to swirl around her clit.

Libby arched her back, her hands seeking his flesh and his cock, feeling it hard and hot in her hand. She circled him with her arms, lifted herself to his chest, then forced him down with her, bringing him to the ground and moving her legs so that he could nestle between them.

His body was damp with the perspiration of restraint. Libby's blood simmered just beneath the surface of her skin, and each time his hand caressed her, she felt a ripple in her veins. She had passed the point of no return, had surrendered her heart to him.

Sam groaned as Libby swept her hands down his body; his mouth moved to her jaw, and he trailed a path with his tongue to the hollow of her throat, then down to kiss the crevice between her breasts. His kisses turned tender, his mouth soft and wet against her skin.

"This is not what I intended," he said as he shifted between her legs, the tip of him against her wet opening.

"Me either."

"I don't know what to do with you," he said, his voice rough. "You're beautiful, you know that?" he asked as he kissed her cheek and nuzzled her neck.

*Beautiful.* He thought she was beautiful. Libby smiled with pleasure. He had teased her body to a precipice, and she wanted to leap off that cliff, to fall with him. He lifted himself up, his gaze on hers as he slid into her, easing himself in, his strokes gentle and slow, lengthening. It was exquisite torture, so pleasurable, so maddeningly tantalizing. Libby adored the feel of him inside her, the way her body claimed him, drawing him in, and lifted her hips.

But then Sam began to stroke her clitoris in time with his body's slide in and out of her, and she could feel a monstrous release swirling around in her, gaining momentum, pulling her closer and closer to the edge of the cliff. She could feel that she was pulling the same sort of release from him, and when she couldn't take it another moment, when she went tumbling off that edge, and her body convulsed around his flesh, Sam came with her, falling just as hard, shuddering forcefully to his end.

They were both panting; Sam slipped his arm around her waist and maneuvered them onto their sides. She felt a strong connection to him, and she wondered if it was real, or if it was the afterglow of lovemaking that made her feel so entwined with him. But she was quite sure she'd never felt such an explosion of joy and tenderness all at once.

When his body slipped from hers, she rolled onto her back, her eyes closed, remembering every moment of it.

"You're smiling," he said, and she felt him trace a line from her chest to her pubic bone.

"I am," she said dreamily. "I'm smiling like I haven't smiled in a very long time. Are you smiling?"

"Like a damn clown," he said, and Libby giggled with delight.

# TWENTY

They ended up in Sam's bed at some point—he couldn't really recall exactly how it had happened, only that her hands had been on him again, her lips driving him crazy, and he was fairly certain he'd carried her. Other than that, he had no memory of anything except what they had done in his bed, and the way she had taken him into her mouth, her lips and tongue swirling around the tip until he couldn't stand it another moment and had dragged her on top of him to ride.

He remembered the way her long curly hair fell around her shoulders, teasing her nipples. He remembered how she had tossed her head back the moment she came, and how he'd had to hold her hips to keep her from falling off when she did.

He remembered what it felt like to be inside of her, and how he'd been surprised by just how much he had missed the feel of a woman. She was like faerie dust, turning him upside down and shaking out all sorts of rusty, dented feelings that were now busily buffing their way clean and new.

Morning light crept into his bedroom and Sam winced as he glanced around. It looked like a caveman lived here, someone with no one in his life to make him care. Clothes were scattered about, his shoes landmines on the floor in the dark. There was a layer of dust on the bureau—what he could see of it, anyway. Most of the surface was covered by magazines and papers.

Libby was on her stomach, her hair covering her face, her back trim and smooth, her hips heart-shaped.

He had imagined being with her, of course he had. He was a guy—it came with the territory. He'd imagined it a lot, actually, but it had been more of a longing instead of testosterone-fueled lust. He leaned down, kissed her back, and smiled when she groaned. He could feel his body waking to the woman in his bed, and he was sliding down the sheets, his hand on her hip, when his phone rang.

*Damn it.* With a sigh, he rolled over, picked it up off the nightstand. "Winters," he answered, and pushed his fingers through his hair.

"Sam . . . I'm . . . it's bad."

It was Tony, and Sam sat up. "What's up, buddy?"

"I don't know," Tony said tearfully. "I was watching it snow last night, and Ernest, he was having a beer, taking some time off, and I wanted one bad, man, so bad, and I started thinking, I didn't have this drinking problem before Afghanistan, this wasn't me, and now I'm a basket case. I get all nervous about shit that don't even matter, and what, I'm supposed to spend the next forty years without a *beer*? I don't care anymore, Sam. I don't care—"

"Hey," Sam said, and swung his legs off the bed. "First of all, you're down because of the weather. You know that, right?" He had no idea if that was true—he was grasping. He stood up, moved the curtains at the window aside to look out. There were several inches of heavy snow on the ground. But it was sunny, which meant the melt would be quick. Sam figured he could have his road cleared by midmorning.

"They've done all kinds of studies about it," he said into the phone. "First cold snap, dark skies, big snow—people feel hopeless."

"I haven't heard that," Tony said skeptically.

Sam turned around, searching for something to put on. Libby was sitting up, the sheet barely covering her. She blinked sleepily at him, using one arm to sweep back curls.

"No, no, it's definitely true," he said. "Have you slept?"

"Nah, man. I can't sleep when I'm like this."

"Yeah, well you need to get some sleep. The snow is going to melt, dude. We'll get the roads cleared and then you and I can talk."

Libby picked up a sweater and held it out to him. Sam grabbed it.

"There's nothing to talk about. It's useless. I'm not a man anymore, I'm a *thing*. I can't support myself, I am missing half my body, and I can't have a goddamn beer—"

"Tony, you're a man," Sam said sternly as he hopped on one leg to pull on a pair of jeans. "Look at what you've done in the last week. You fixed Libby's car, you fixed that old Buick. Do you know how many people could do that?"

"I fixed that fence, too," Tony said, speaking as if Sam knew what he was talking about. "That's not easy to do with a fake leg."

"It's impossible," Sam agreed, and paused briefly to pull the sweater over his head. "You're on the right track. Sometimes, those voices start talking to you, and it's not easy. It's just the weather, trust me. Do me a favor. Go to bed, get some sleep. I'll be up this afternoon."

He heard Tony's sigh. "Okay," he said at last. "Okay, yeah. I feel pretty wasted, now that you mention it."

"So you'll get some sleep and wait for me?"

"Yeah," Tony said, and he yawned.

"Tony . . . give me your word."

"I give you my word," Tony said.

Sam resisted a sigh of relief. He knew what it was like when the doubts started creeping in, how easy it was to give in to the whispering in your head. "I'll see you later." He hung up.

"Is Tony okay?" Libby asked.

"For now," Sam said, worried. "He doesn't sound good. He gets down sometimes, and he's tempted to drink." Sam felt the slight swell of nausea he always felt when he thought of how far and hard that fall would be. "Or worse," he added grimly, because with Tony, he didn't know. "I'm going to shower and see if I can get up there to talk to him," he said.

"I'm going with you," Libby said. She leaned over the bed, reaching for clothes. Libby pulled one of his T-shirts over her head and stood up.

Sam caught her wrist and pulled her to him, into his chest. His arms went around her. It had been so long since Sam had been involved with a woman who wasn't Terri that he had forgotten how these things went. "I had a great time last night."

"You and me both, Lone Ranger."

"I'm not sure where it leaves us," he said, smoothing her unruly hair. "You're still half nuts. And I'm still a deputy with a responsibility to enforce the law."

She laughed. "That makes it doubly exciting."

Sam ran his hand down her arm, and said, "What I'm trying to say is, it's been a long time since I . . ." Since he'd what? Slept with a woman? Become emotionally attached to a woman? Wanted something more from a woman? He felt suddenly awkward. Rusty. A little old.

Libby caressed his cheek. "Well, generally, I think that when two people come together, they hang out and see what develops."

"Is that what you want?" he asked. "Because I'll be honest—I don't want to be the rebound guy."

"The rebound—" She suddenly laughed, rose up on her toes and kissed him. "You're not the rebound guy, Sam. You're the guy who caught me when I fell. That makes you the *hero*," she said, poking him in the chest.

He caught her hand and held it against his chest. "I'm no hero, Libby," he said. "I'm the opposite of that. I've worked hard to maintain my sobriety, and like I told you, it's never easy for me. It's hard for me to convey just how difficult it is."

"So what are you trying to say?" Libby asked uncertainly.

Sam wasn't really sure. He had an indistinct feeling of unease crawling in beside the happiness and elation of human affection he was also feeling. He hadn't been with anyone in a long time. He certainly hadn't tested his emotional fortitude fully sober. He thought he might really love Libby, but he also feared she could derail this thing between them. "I want to try us. I want it more than anything. But I can't have a lot of chaos in my life, Libby. It's taken a long time for me to understand that chaos—uncertainty, drama, all of it—is as dangerous to me as alcohol."

She tugged her hand free of his, and put her arms around his neck. "I *knew* you didn't get around much. Okay, I swear, no chaos."

She didn't understand him, he could see it in her smiling eyes. "I'm serious, baby. I have my own demons and I can't carry more."

"Sam." Her voice was softer now, her gaze sympathetic. "I hear you. And I promise—no chaos. I just want to see where this goes, and I am really glad you want the same thing. But right now, today, you have to do something about Tony." She kissed him.

Sam's heart told him he should try again, find better words to convey what he was trying to say, to make her understand what he scarcely understood himself. But his body was waking and silenced his heart. "Don't you need a shower?" he asked, nuzzling her neck.

"I *do*," she agreed, and put her feet on top of his as Sam walked them into the bathroom.

He lingered in the shower with her longer than he should have, but he finally made himself get out and dress. Libby stayed behind, washing her hair.

Sam checked on his horses and fed them, then took a shovel, cleared a path out to the meadow, and sent the horses out. When he returned to the house, he found his coffeemaker on, and made himself a cup.

With coffee in hand, he walked back to his bedroom, but Libby wasn't there. He returned to the kitchen and looked out over the deck, thinking she'd perhaps gone down to the barn. He saw her footprints, all right, but they didn't lead to the barn, they led across the deck, down to his work shed.

Sam's heart made a tiny leap to his throat. Dirk was the only person who had seen his work shed, and even that had made Sam uncomfortable. There was something about the birdhouses that made him feel vulnerable, that set him apart from the world, and he wasn't quite ready to open up that side of him.

He walked outside.

Libby was standing just inside the shed, wearing his down jacket and his Wellingtons. She was looking up, to where he'd hung a galaxy of birdhouses—the sun, the moon, a few of the more recognizable planets. When she heard him step in behind her, she turned around, her blue eyes bright. "Look at all these birdhouses!" she exclaimed, as if she'd just discovered a treasure.

"Yeah," he said sheepishly, and shoved his hands into his pockets.

"Where did you get them?"

"Where did I . . . I *made* them."

She gasped and looked around again. "You're kidding. You *made* them?" She reached out, her fingers gliding over his replica of the *Hindenburg* blimp. "By yourself?"

"No, forest gnomes helped me. Yes, by myself."

"Sam! They're *amazing*! Do you sell them?"

"Nah, it's just a hobby."

"But they're remarkable! Look, it's the Capitol—and the White House!" she exclaimed with delight, rising up on her toes to examine that one.

Sam thought of the hours he'd spent in here, when his thoughts would meander to vodka and then back to the work at hand. Every piece of wood, every bit of tin, every hole he'd drilled and every design he'd carved on those birdhouses represented one more step away from alcoholism, one step closer to sobriety. They were the monuments to his struggle, to the progress he'd made, and a reminder of how much work he would throw out if he ever drank again. He needed these birdhouses, and that was his dirty little secret. He needed to see them and touch them in order to stay on his path.

Libby stooped down to peer at the Eiffel Tower, which Sam considered one of his better pieces. "How do you know how to even do this?" she asked, her voice full of awe, which, Sam thought, gave him no small amount of pleasure. "You really should sell them."

"No," he said instantly. "They're for me."

"But . . ." She stood up and turned in a slow circle. "There are so *many* of them."

"I know. But every one of them means something to me."

Libby gave him a questioning look.

"Every single one of them represents a bottle I didn't drink, Libby. They are for me."

He could almost see her questions whirling about in her head.

But she apparently understood that they were important to him because she said, "Well, they're wonderful. I love them. If you're not going to sell them you might want to think of building a bigger shed." She laughed. "I love them so much, Sam. I love them even more now that I know they are little pieces of you."

He was surprised at how good her praise made him feel. He was reminded of an ugly Sunday afternoon when, in a vodka-infused haze, Terri had called him a worthless whittler. Mostly, those sorts of insults rolled off his back, but perhaps it had been the venom in her voice or the fact that Sam had believed himself fairly useless at the time that had made that insult stick with him all this time.

"I should plow the road. We should be out of here by this afternoon. I'm sorry that I don't have any food to speak of."

"I'm good," Libby said airily. She slipped her hand behind his head, pulling it down so that she could kiss him.

Sam couldn't resist her. He put his hand around her waist, pulled her into his chest and kissed her a little more deeply. He lifted his head. "Be good," he warned her.

Libby laughed, the sound of it warm and light in that shed. "Don't ask for the impossible."

A tiny bell of warning clanged somewhere in Sam's head again but he ignored it, and left Libby standing in his private sanctuary.

# TWENTY-ONE

When Sam dropped Libby off at the ranch that afternoon, Libby wasn't sure who was more eager to greet her, the dogs or Madeline.

"Hey, Sam," Madeline said, smiling coyly, her gaze sweeping over him.

"Madeline," Sam said. "Hi, Tony," he added, looking over Madeline's shoulder.

Madeline didn't turn around. Her laser-sharp gaze had shifted and was drilling a hole right through Libby.

"Sorry about the car, Libby," Tony said. "It's probably the belt. Those old cars, the belts can go like that," he said, and ran both hands over his crown, lacing his fingers behind his neck. "I should have taken a closer look."

"It's no big deal, buddy," Sam said. "Come on, let's go to town and check it out."

Libby didn't care why her car hadn't started. If it had started, Sam never would have made her get into his truck. Her life would be vastly different this morning, and not in a good way. She couldn't help but smile at that.

Sam said to Madeline, "I'll be back to pick up the horses this evening."

"Great. Thank you, Sam," Madeline said, her gaze still on Libby.

Sam put his hand on Tony's shoulder and started him toward his truck.

Libby watched him walk away. But when she turned toward the house, Madeline's close proximity startled her.

"Oh. Sorry," Libby said and tried to step around Madeline, intending to walk up the porch steps to the house.

But Madeline put her hand on Libby's arm. "Not so fast, Libby Tyler. You sure are smiling a lot for someone whose car broke down in the middle of a freak blizzard. So where were you last night? At the Grizzly? Or in jail?"

"Geez, Madeline, you're worse than my mother," Libby said, and jogged up the stairs to the house.

"What do you expect? You come home wearing a shirt way too big for you and a big fat smile on your face!" Madeline shouted after her, and jogged up the steps after Libby, with the dogs on her heels.

Libby looked down at the long-sleeved T-shirt she'd borrowed from Sam. "Oh. Right." She walked into the house and let the screen door bang behind her.

"So what's the big secret?" Madeline said, following her with the army of dogs. "Why can't you tell me where you were or why you're so happy all of a sudden?"

"Am I?"

"Yes!" Madeline insisted. "You've stomped around here since you came back from Mountain View, and today, you're all smiles and giggles."

"You'd stomp around, too, after a week at Mountain View, trust me. I don't know why I'm happy, Madeline. I guess the first snow of the season does that to me. I love it. Don't you love it? All that time in hot and humid Florida, don't you love the first big snow?"

Madeline's eyes narrowed. "It's my *first* big snow," she said. "And it's very cool. Unfortunately for me, Luke ruined it by reminding me that we have a ceremony to stage in a few short days and it will be muddy."

*The ceremony.* Libby groaned—she hadn't thought of it in the last twenty-four hours. "Not to worry," she said. "We can spread straw around. And the horses are going down to Sam's tonight, right? We'll have it cleaned up in no time at all."

Madeline cocked her head to one side. "What about *you*? Going to Sam's tonight?" She arched a brow.

Libby smiled. "You should really consider a career in police interrogations. We were stranded by the snow, just like you."

"So obviously you were stranded at Sam's house," Madeline said, folding her arms. "Instead of, say, the Grizzly. Because that would make more sense, you know. Your car broke down in town, not at Sam's."

Libby suddenly burst into laughter. "Okay, so what if I was at Sam's last night? You've been telling me to move on, haven't you?"

Madeline's eyes widened. And then her face broke into a wreath of smiles as she abruptly grabbed Libby by the shoulders and swung her around. "*Libby!* You and Sam? *Really?*"

"Me and Sam," Libby said, happy to share some news with Madeline for once that wasn't bad. "Ohmigod, I'm giggling."

"That's fantastic!" Madeline cried, flinging her arms wide. "We *love* Sam!"

"We? Who's we?"

"Me and Luke, of course. And Leo and Bob. And Dani, for that matter. We've all been rooting for him."

"Wait, what?" Libby asked, her smile fading a little.

Madeline clucked her tongue. "It's obvious that Sam has a thing for you—"

"A thing for me!" Libby exclaimed.

"Oh come on, you know that," Madeline happily scoffed.

"No, I—I didn't think it was a *thing*," Libby said uncertainly, but suddenly things were beginning to make sense.

"Oh, sure," Madeline said. "I don't know. I noticed it when I first moved to Pine River. Remember that night we were in town for First Tuesdays?"

Libby thought back to that night. Madeline had just moved to Pine River to be with Luke, so she and Libby, in an effort to form a sisterly bond, had gone to take a look at some of the crafts that were sold in town on the first Tuesday of every month through the tourist season. Libby remembered that night very well, but not because of Sam. That night, she'd seen Ryan and the kids with Gwen. She'd been surprised by it, and had assumed it was a visitation agreement. She remembered how agitated Ryan had been when she'd approached them to say hello to the kids.

"Sam was there, remember?" Madeline said.

"He was?" Libby asked absently. Another memory began to come back to her. A smile, a black collared shirt. "Right . . . I remember now," she said. "He was talking to you, asking about your move from Orlando."

Madeline laughed. "He may have been asking about me, but the whole time he was looking at you. But you were obsessed with Ryan. I am *so* glad you are over him. You are, right?"

Something hitched inside Libby. She *was* over Ryan. She'd been over him a long time now, and had allowed herself to believe that, for the sake of Alice and Max, she could possibly reconcile with him if necessary to have them in her life. But last night with Sam had been so incredible that Libby couldn't imagine how she'd ever believed that.

Madeline was still watching her, still smiling. Libby groaned. "Try not to take flight with joy, or you'll hit your head on the ceiling. And geez, stop smiling like that. Seriously, *stop,*" she said, giggling at Madeline's goofy grin. "Who knows where this will go?"

"Okay, okay," Madeline said gleefully. "I'm sorry. I'm acting just like my friend Trudi, and she drives me nuts. I'm just really happy for you."

Libby felt another hitch inside her. It felt as if this wasn't the first time Madeline had expressed these feelings about her—just not to her.

"Oh, by the way, I'm making chili!" Madeline announced. "I'm going to ask Sam if he wants to stick around for it, if that's okay with you."

"Madeline!" Libby lightly protested.

Madeline giggled and passed Libby on her way to the kitchen. "He's already going to be here, Libby! He'll be hungry after they load the horses. Don't worry, I promise I won't be a nuisance."

Libby had her doubts about that.

The chili dinner turned out to be something of a party. Madeline invited everyone—Ernest and Tony, Luke and Sam. She'd even decided to assign seats at the dining room table. A first at Homecoming Ranch, and Libby knew exactly what her sister was up to—she was orchestrating a date for Libby and Sam. That was Madeline for you, assuming that things weren't being done correctly if she wasn't the one doing them.

Madeline's chili was good, surprisingly so. Over dinner, Libby and Madeline told the guys about the plans for Gary and Austin's civil ceremony. The talk then turned to people around town.

"Luke, how's Leo?" Sam asked. "I heard yesterday that he'd had another seizure."

Luke sighed and shook his head. "We thought we had that under control with a new combination of medicines. While we were in Montrose, they found he had some fluid on his lungs."

"Oh no," Libby said. "Is he home?"

"Not yet. He's due to be released tomorrow if all goes well."

The news about Leo was never good. This summer he'd suffered from uncontrollable seizures, and Libby had heard Bob Kendrick say he would need a feeding tube before long. "I can't wait to get started on the fundraising for him," she said, more to herself than to anyone in particular.

That was followed by a bit of an awkward silence. Ernest and Tony seemed to be more interested in their food. But Madeline, Luke, and Sam looked anywhere but at her. "What is it?" Libby asked, looking around at the three of them.

Madeline and Luke, she noticed, exchanged a look, and Luke's jaw tightened, as if he were biting back words. She looked to Sam for help understanding what everyone was so quiet about.

"I think," he said, looking at Madeline and Luke, "there is a slight concern about your participation on that committee since Gwen Spangler is heading it."

Libby ignored the little catch in her heart. "Good for Gwen," she said, a tad too dismissively. "Just out of curiosity . . ." She picked up her spoon and dipped it into her bowl, "Why *is* Gwen chairing it?"

"She wants to help," Luke said. "The Methodists have a ladies group that chooses a cause every year, and this year, Leo is their cause."

"Well, I like a good cause, too, and I can't think of a better one than Leo. This means that Gwen and I are on the same page."

"But still," Madeline said, "Maybe it's not a good idea, given everything that's happened."

Libby spooned some chili. "Okay, everyone, lighten up, will you? I get it, I understand your concern. But nothing is going to happen. I've known Leo all my life, and this isn't about anything but helping him." To their skeptical looks, she said, "I swear it."

"What's the big deal?" Tony asked casually.

No one looked as if they wanted to answer that. Madeline said, "Libby's had some issues with a couple of people in town." She waved her hand as if it were a trifling thing, but her voice belied that gesture.

Tony snorted. "You wouldn't believe how many *issues* I've had in Pine River. This is what you do," he said, pointing his spoon at Libby. "You fall down, then you get back on the saddle and you move the hell on. Am I right, Sam?"

"Yep," Sam said.

"That's what you do," Tony said to everyone else.

"I agree, Tony," Libby said. "And that's exactly what I am trying to do."

"You turn the page," Tony continued. "Turn the page and go on. I had this friend," he continued. "We called him Frick, because he was always hanging out with this dude named Franken, something like. Frick and Frank, right? We were all stationed in Afghanistan together, the Helmand Province, and Frick and I, we were wounded by the same IED. Killed Franken," he added casually, as if Franken had caught a bad cold instead of losing his life. "Anyway, we come back to the States, me missing a leg and Frick missing both arms below the elbow, and he finds out his wife has moved on. Only she forgot to tell him."

"Oh my God," Madeline said. "How awful."

Libby couldn't imagine surviving a bomb, losing limbs, only to find out that everything had exploded at home, too.

"Well old Frick, he was stubborn, and he tried to get her back but she wouldn't come. She didn't like him without his arms, you know? Like that changed the man or something." Tony made a sound of disgust and shook his head. "Let me tell you, Frick took that shit hard. I said, buddy, turn the page. Life goes on."

No one spoke. They waited for Tony to continue, but Tony shrugged and leaned over his chili.

"So?" Libby said. "What happened?"

"Huh?" Tony looked up. "Oh, he killed himself," he said. "Had his toe on the trigger."

Libby gasped and exchanged a look of shared horror with Madeline.

"It wasn't just his wife, you know," Tony said. "He might have gotten over that. But it was the no arm thing, too. No job, no woman—that can really get to a man." He helped himself to more chili. "I would have helped him, but at the time, I was sleeping on my mom's couch."

He ate his chili and looked around the table, realizing only then what a rapt audience he had. "Oh, hey," he said. "I didn't mean to bring you all down. Shit happens. There's just not enough places for guys like us. It's not like anyone comes back from war in good shape, you know?"

"We get the horses now?" Ernest said to Luke, and both Luke and Sam were more than happy to have an excuse to leave the table. Even Tony, shoveling in a few more bites as he came to his feet, wanted to help. "This thing works like a charm on the snow," he said proudly, patting his prosthesis, and walked out behind the other men.

Libby helped Madeline clean the kitchen; by the time they'd finished, the men had loaded the horses into the trailer. Sam met Libby on the porch, his hands deep in his pockets against the chill. Everyone else had disappeared inside.

"I should go before the roads ice," he said, and put his arms around her. "You're shivering."

"I don't want you to go," she said into his coat.

"The horses need to be fed. I'll call you tomorrow, okay?"

"Okay," she said, and lifted her face to his. He kissed her, his hand cupping her face, his tongue and lips teasing hers, warming her up. When he let go of her, the cold air sank into the space where he'd just been.

He walked down the steps, but paused on the bottom and glanced back up at her. "Are you sure about the committee, Libby? Madeline has a point."

Libby sighed. "Sam . . . I'm sure. It's like Tony said—I've turned the page."

She didn't like the doubtful way Sam looked at her.

# TWENTY-TWO

You've probably heard by now that I had another seizure, first one in about two months. I don't remember it. One minute I was watching *Biggest Loser* and rooting for the cute chick, and the next minute, I woke up in the hospital. I was *pissed.* I don't have time for hospitals; I have a van to acquire.

The only good thing about hospitals is the hot nurses. It's like bellying up to a buffet of women. But get this—this time, I woke up to a *guy* nurse. Yes! A *guy*! I said, "No offense, dude, but I am getting you reassigned. I don't pay to look at a guy's mug while I'm in here."

The nurse said he understood, but he was putting a catheter in while he was talking and that made our little chat sort of awkward. Ruined my whole trip, if you want to know the truth.

But the good news is, I ran into Dante. Dante is a seventeen-, eighteen-year-old kid who has cancer. We usually run into each other when he's doing chemo and I'm having some doctor tell me I need a feeding tube and after that, probably a breathing machine, and other crap that I don't listen to unless Dad gets upset about it.

Which he does, a lot. He's getting soft in his old age. I tried to get him to watch the *WWE* with me, but he said he didn't like wrestling. Who doesn't like wrestling, I ask you? Chicks and old men, that's who. Give me some six-year-old boys or some thirty-year-old men, and it's a party when the *WWE* is on.

Originally when I met Dante and they had said maybe he didn't have that long, he and I were going to use his trip from Make-A-Wish Foundation to go to the Broncos game. But Dante totally blew that by going into remission. He said he was super sorry, that he wanted to go as much as me, but I have my doubts about that. I told him not to sweat it, that I would work my magic to get us the tickets. You know all about that already, so I won't bore you with the riveting details of my genius this time.

Yes, Marisol is right, I like to hear myself talk, especially if it's about me. But in my defense, there's nothing very interesting going on in Pine River. I mean, I'm it.

Anyway, I'm back in Montrose with a guy nurse, and I saw Dante walking around with an IV, and I said, "Hey, what are you doing back here, trying to get a date?" Turns out, Dante's cancer is back, and that sucks. But on the other hand—and this may sound selfish—the only time I get to see him is when he and I are both in Montrose, him getting chemo, me getting some nurse eye candy.

I am happy to report that Dante is feeling pretty good and he is totally stoked about the game. I told him about the van we're going to get—red, with twenty-inch chrome wheels, and some kick-ass flames painted on the side. But Dad was sitting there, and as he is the King of Wet Blankets, he tried to tell Dante that we weren't painting flames on the van. I winked at Dante and told him later that Dad doesn't know I've already got that lined up from a buddy I went to school with. Dad thinks it's weird to drive me around in a red van with flames on it, but he's, like, fifty- or sixty-something and is out of touch with sexy.

Anyway, I could see I was getting Dante's hopes up with this talk of the van, and he said, "Dude, you're going to be like the *sickest* wheelchair in the nation!" He didn't mean sick like MND sick, he meant sick as in totally cool. So now, I have to deliver, and I'll be honest, I'm a little worried about it because the Methodist ladies are a little slow on the uptake.

They started off by selling raffle tickets for things like dinner and a movie. It doesn't take a genius to know they're never going to get me a van like that, right?

That's okay, I'm on it, using my considerable brain capacity to think things through. One day, Luke comes home or over—who knows if he lives here or not anymore, right? Get married already!—and he says, all serious, "Dude, you better have a tight rein on that committee."

Like I don't. Like I am going to entrust my van to a bunch of women. Don't make me laugh. Seriously, what do women know about vans? Nothing, that's what. Now, don't get your panties in a wad, it's just biology. You wouldn't trust me to choose the new furniture for your living room makeover, would you? I rest my case.

I said to Luke, "I've got my fingers all in that pie, bro. We're working on a silent auction. I just need a little help rounding up some excellent prizes."

He said, "Like what?"

"Helicopter skiing," I said. Honestly, it just popped into my mind, but that's what happens with MND, brilliant and clever thoughts are constantly firing away.

But Luke was like, "Helicopter skiing!" As if he totally wouldn't do that. Of course he would. I never knew anyone who was as fearless as Luke. He said, "Where are you going to get that?"

I said I didn't know, but the Methodists weren't going to find helicopter skiing, and that was a problem because this auction needed some *pizzazz* to get the van.

And Luke said, "Well, I think you're going to have a bigger problem than a lack of pizzazz, Leo. Libby Tyler has joined the committee."

Now, see, this is where the wheat is separated from the chaff. While everyone else might see a problem, I see something totally *awesome.* In fact, I can't believe I didn't think of it before! What that committee needs is a little bit of all-American competition, so I was totally pumped when Luke told me that. He wanted to know what I was grinning about, and I told him I was going to turn Libby and Gwen loose on each other, and he said I was an idiot, that there was nothing worse than two women in a catfight. I said I thought it was sexist to suggest that women in competition were automatically a "catfight," only because I heard that on the Katie Couric show. Between you and me and the wall, there is nothing that turns me on more than two women duking it out.

Yeah, okay, there might be something that turns me on more, but this isn't that kind of story.

So Luke goes on, telling me what I knew about women he could put on a postage stamp, and, of course, in waddles Marisol, and *she* has to get in on the act and agree.

"You don't think before your tongue moves," she said, pointing a finger at me.

I said, "Pile it on, bitches. You can't touch this," and if I could point, I would have pointed to me. But they knew what I meant and Luke said some very mean things to a guy in a chair, which, in hindsight, totally makes me laugh.

The thing that really chaps them is that they know I'm right. Just like I knew Sam was hot for Libby, I know that this is going to work. It's going to be the best fundraiser *ever.* And when you see my van flying by with some killer flames and twenty-inch chrome wheels, you can wave and say, *there goes a genius.*

# TWENTY-THREE

Libby was happy, in a way she had not been in a very long time. Jubilant. Buoyant. A walking, talking Alka-Seltzer, bubbling and fizzing with happiness. Funny how these things went, how you could believe you were relatively happy, that you were doing okay, but then something would change, and suddenly, *real* happiness was sliding over you in big, gelatinous waves, oozing into all the corners of your life.

That was how it went for Libby. With Sam, she was happier than she'd been in weeks, months, maybe even years. He was attentive and caring and funny and strong and . . . well, she could go on, but the point was, Libby felt as if she had at last reentered her life, had opened the door and walked through to the big wide world out there instead of hiding in the shadows of the past. Since Sam and she had come together, Libby could feel herself changing. She could feel it in her bones, could feel the layers of disappointment sloughing off of her, being replaced by fresh new hopes and dreams.

She still had her problems—her bank account was whimpering, and she hadn't had time to focus on her plan to drum up more events. She missed Alice and Max like she would miss an arm, thought of them all the time, debated calling them, tried not to think about them. That was hard, and some days, impossible. Admittedly, Libby was still finding reasons to go into Pine River just about the time school was letting out, and from a distance, would watch Alice skipping out with her best friend, Sasha. Or see Max with a soccer ball kicking and dipping his way to the field for afterschool practice.

Libby had come to accept that if she could just *see* them, if even at a distance, and know they were okay, she could live with not holding them. And it didn't hurt that in the back of her mind, she believed that in working on the committee for Leo, she might see the kids. It stood to reason that if Gwen was heading the committee meetings, there would be times when she would either have Alice and Max in tow, or perhaps the babysitter would drop them off. And Libby would see them.

Just see them. Not wave at them, not carry on conversations with them. Just *see* them and know they were happy and whole.

It was a small hope, a secret hope, but it helped Libby cope with the reality of her relationship with the children she loved.

In the meantime, she was thankfully and exceptionally busy in her new relationship with Sam and putting the finishing touches on Austin and Gary's ceremony.

She was amazed at how happy Sam made her. It all seemed so easy for him, too. It was in the little things—the way he looked at her as if he longed for her, even though she was standing right before him. Or how his smile was full of fondness, or how he laughed at her jokes, even the bad ones. It was in the way he didn't seem to mind that she liked to talk about things—anything and everything.

What perhaps meant the most to Libby besides Sam's affection for her was that she didn't sense any judgment from Sam. She didn't sense anything from him but interest in who she was and in what they could become together. That made her happy. They *were* good together.

Libby tried not to compare Sam to Ryan, but she couldn't help it. At the end of every day, Ryan had been more concerned if Libby was listening to him than with anything she had to say about herself. Nor did Libby recall ever feeling as if Ryan understood her completely. At the same time, she'd assumed that it was male-female discord every other couple experienced at one time or another.

She didn't feel that discord with Sam.

Dr. Huber had subtly pointed this out to her once. "Don't you think," she asked, "that a relationship should be a give and take of the good, the bad, the mundane, and the exciting for both parties? Doesn't that create balance in a relationship?"

Libby had never given that notion much thought. She knew that Ryan had so much on his plate—an ex-wife to deal with, a propane business that was suffering from the economy like everything else—and while those words sounded good, Libby thought that Dr. Huber was a little blind to the realities of working-class people.

But Dr. Huber had been right, and Libby had been shown once again how she had lived with blinders.

Not this time. Libby stole every moment she could to be with Sam, and every moment spent in his company—talking, making love, laughing—was another moment she felt her life gaining strength and direction.

The day before Austin and Gary's wedding, the weather turned cold and wet, and the skies began to spit bits of icy rain. Libby's happiness shrouded her like a cloak when several guests decided not to make the trek up to Homecoming Ranch for the ceremony for fear of being stuck by another early blizzard.

The few that did drive up from Durango and Colorado Springs sat shivering in the barn, no matter how high Luke cranked the space heaters. Gary and Austin's little dogs had muddied feet, and one of them planted his paws on Gary's trouser, sending his mother, Martha, into an orbit of displeasure.

In spite of the hard work Libby and Madeline had put in, and how happy Austin and Gary seemed to be, Martha's sourness about the event—and the lack of dazzle, given the elements—rubbed off on Madeline.

"I don't see how this is ever going to work," she said at the end of the night when the guests had left. "It's too far out, and too many things can happen. Unless we build a hotel with a big ballroom, this ranch is never going to work as a destination event place."

"We have two cabins—" Libby started, but Madeline was quick to cut her off.

"Two *empty* cabins. Two empty cabins that we paid to have built so that people would stay *in* them. Which they did not do because we are too far away from anything, the weather is too unpredictable, and, Libby, please, God, admit it, this is not going to work."

"Okay," Libby said, defeated. "I admit it." What Madeline was saying was true. But Libby had put so much hope into Homecoming Ranch. She'd hoped too hard, just like she'd hoped too hard with Ryan. She could admit defeat in the event business, but she wouldn't declare Homecoming Ranch defeated. She'd come too far with it. There had to be another way to make it viable.

Libby refused to let Madeline's pessimism dampen her spirits. She felt nothing but optimism for the future. This was exactly the sort of setback that would have put Libby on the floor only weeks ago, but everything had changed since then. She was bone-tired from the work of getting a muddy ranch ready for a wedding, from the stress of not knowing where her next paycheck would come from, and still, she felt as if she were floating around on little puffy white clouds.

When she wasn't at Homecoming Ranch, she was at Sam's place, watching him craft birdhouses, even though he said that made him self-conscious. Or cooking for him in his underwhelming kitchen. The day after the disastrous wedding event, Sam even talked her into riding out to check on mean Millie, who told Libby to get off her property or she'd shoot her. Libby had laughed at the threat. She felt too invincible to be brought down by the likes of Millie Bagley.

She really appreciated the way Sam cared for Tony, too. Now that Ernest had brought the cattle down from the forest leases, he was ready to drive them down to one of the valleys for the winter. Tony had tried to help him, but his artificial leg had proved to be a problem.

"He really hates that he can't do all the things he used to do," Sam said. "I keep telling him that he had twenty-seven years to get used to the leg he lost, and he needs more than a year to get used to the new one."

Sam was diligent about checking on Tony and building him up, and Libby truly admired the way Sam had shouldered the responsibility in a way that no one else had. Or would, given the opportunity. But that was Sam—he was the towering tree among them, strong and protective and supportive. Sometimes, Libby wondered if he was trying to make up for what happened with Terri. Trying to erase those years by doing something good and really helping people instead of merely talking about it.

Whatever his motive, Libby wanted to be more like him. She wanted to help. So when Tony told Libby one afternoon that he was sad all the time, she asked him if there was someone he'd like to talk to. She had in mind someone like Dr. Huber, but Tony said, "My buddy Justin. He's in Denver. I told him maybe he could come out here for a few days."

"He's more than welcome," Libby said. "Luke goes to Denver from time to time—maybe he could bring him. Tell him to come on."

If Libby was this happy, she thought Tony deserved to be happy, too.

Madeline wasn't quite on board with it, however. "God, Libby," she said, rubbing her temples. "We can hardly pay bills. We can't pay these guys, we can't really feed them—we just don't have the money."

"Then I'll stop by the food bank," Libby had said calmly. "I'll handle it, Madeline. Don't worry."

"I can't help it," Madeline had said wearily.

When Justin showed up, and he and Tony puttered around the ranch, fixing this or that, it really seemed to help perk Tony up. And it gave Libby an idea.

One night, she lured Sam to the ranch with the promise of lasagna. Before dinner, she took him up a muddied path through a stand of cottonwoods to Mrs. Kendrick's garden. The garden was concealed by shrubbery. Inside the garden was a hammock stand, an old stone bench, and some empty clay pots. Tony and Justin had recently cleaned up the flower beds, digging out the weeds and debris.

"A little late in the season for gardening, isn't it?" Sam asked, looking around.

"Yes," Libby said. "But it will be less work in the spring. There are a million jobs like this at Homecoming Ranch," she said.

Sam laughed as he stood behind her. He put his hands on her shoulders and rubbed. "There's a million jobs like this around every place in the mountains."

"Right," Libby said, and twisted around in his arms. "Therapeutic work. Things to do with your hands."

Sam looked at her curiously. "I have a feeling there is a message here."

"What if," she said, "veterans who needed a place to stay, to learn how to be in the world again, came here? What if we made this a therapeutic place for them?"

Sam looked around the garden.

"We have the bunkhouse. We even have two cabins. We could have several up here at a time."

"Something like that would take money," Sam pointed out. "Money you don't have," he added, touching his finger to her nose.

"I thought of that," she said, and slipped her arms around his waist and laid her cheek against his chest. "I've done a little bit of research into rehabilitation for vets. I need to do more, a lot more, and talk to some people—but I've learned there is the possibility of grants and donations to help."

Sam didn't say anything. Libby felt a twinge of disappointment. No doubt he was thinking it was too impossible, too far-fetched. She lifted her head and risked a look up at him and was surprised when Sam smiled.

"I think it's a great idea. Don't get me wrong—it will be hard to execute, and you'll need a good plan for it . . . but I think you might be onto something," he said, looking around at the neat little garden, nodding his head.

"Thank you!" Libby said, and squeezed him in a hug.

"For what?"

"For not shooting it down." And for giving her something to think about, something on the horizon to look forward to.

Unfortunately, there were other worries that needed her immediate attention. It was clear to her that she would have to get a job, but before she was submerged into the ocean of working long hours for little pay, she really wanted to help Leo get that van.

Finding out the schedule of the committee meetings proved to be the most difficult thing of all—no one seemed to know when or where they were.

She finally managed to get hold of Deb Trimble one morning to get to the bottom of the mysterious committee meeting times. Deb didn't seem very happy to hear from Libby, especially when she knew the reason for the call. "Ah, well," she said, in a sing-songy voice. "I'm not sure the next meeting has been set."

"Next?" Libby said. "You mean there's already been one?" No one had called her in spite of repeated inquiries.

"We've just started," Deb quickly clarified. "It's been a lot of email, that sort of thing."

"There's an email loop?"

"Ah . . . no. Not a loop," Deb said. "Informal."

Libby frowned at the wall before her. "So . . . do you think in the emails someone might have mentioned the time and place of the next meeting?"

"I guess I remember something about it," Deb said. "Let me look."

A moment later, she told Libby the next meeting would be held Wednesday at noon at the church. That was the time the women's group met every week—Libby knew this because Dani went every week. Which meant that it wasn't a very hard meeting time to remember or to pass along.

Libby knew what was going on, and she wasn't going to be put off.

"Everyone is coming back with their ideas of fundraising activities, and we're going to vote on what we can realistically pursue in the next two months," Debbie said. "There are a lot of good ideas already, Libby. A *lot*."

"Great!" Libby said confidently. "I've got a couple of good ideas, too."

"I'm sure you do," Deb said, and Libby chose to ignore the strain of sarcasm in her voice. She'd never had any issue with Deb Trimble and she wasn't going to create one.

On the day before the meeting, Libby met her mother for coffee in Pine River.

She hadn't seen her mother in weeks, as her mother's life revolved around the twins' school and her work as a designer with Claire's Fine Furnishings.

Stevie Buchanan was wearing leggings and boots and a thick sweater with a cashmere scarf around her neck. Libby was wearing a similar outfit—but her boots were a bit scuffed and her sweater not as elegant. Her mother had the same unruly hair as Libby, but she paid to have it straightened and wore it short. Libby held her mess back with a headband.

Her mother gave Libby a tight hug, held her out at arm's length and looked at her. "You look great, honey," she said, nodding approvingly. "You've put on a little weight since Mountain View."

Libby wasn't certain that was a compliment.

"So?" her mother said, smiling, as she picked up a menu. "I heard at the salon that you've been stepping out with Sam Winters."

"Stepping out?" Libby laughed. "That's so nineteen-twenties, Mom."

Her mother waved a hand at her. "Come on, tell me *all*," she said with a smile. "Well, not *all.* I don't want to hear the details of your sex life."

"Mom!"

"Oh, please. You're almost twenty-seven. Let me tell you, I always thought that man was a *hunk*. So how did this thing get started between the two of you?"

"You really want to know?" Libby asked, and leaned forward, as if she was going to share a delicious secret. "He almost arrested me for violating the restraining order."

Her mother gasped. "*Libby!*" she cried. "Good Lord!"

"It's true!" Libby said laughingly. "I wasn't really *violating*—well, okay, technically I was." Her mother opened her mouth to protest, but Libby held up her hand. "Mom, spare me the lecture, please. I've heard enough from Sam and Madeline."

She told her mother about the things Ryan had said, and Alice's phone calls. She explained how she wanted more than anything to hear Ryan say he was sorry. She repeated the awful things Ryan said in the parking lot by the soccer fields, how angry Sam had been, and how the blizzard had put them together, given them a chance to talk, and . . . and now, she was happy. Utterly, completely, happy.

Her mother listened attentively, nodding as Libby talked, her brows rising up only once or twice. When Libby had finished filling her in on the last few weeks, her mother settled back against her chair, sipped her coffee, and put down the cup. "Libby, I'm happy that you're happy."

"Thanks, Mom."

"And I don't want to point out the obvious."

Libby sighed heavenward. Here it went—her mother could never just be *happy* for Libby. There was always a but, always a warning, always a little black cloud to cast over her. "Then maybe you shouldn't," Libby suggested.

"What kind of mother would I be if I didn't say it?" her mother asked cheerfully. "You have a long history of creating impossible expectations for people and things and being terribly hurt when they don't work out."

"Mom—"

"*Anh*," she said, throwing up a hand to keep Libby from disagreeing. "I'm serious, honey. From the beginning, this whole business with Ryan was one long impossible expectation that ended badly. Do you remember I warned you that he had a reputation around town?"

"You also told me the boy I crushed on in the fifth grade was bad news."

"And I was *right*," her mother said triumphantly. "He's probably doing time somewhere right now."

"You have never been happy with my choice of boyfriends."

"Well, I'm happy with the choice of Sam Winters. Ryan . . ." She waved her hand. "It doesn't matter, it's all in the past. I just don't want you to place some overly idealistic rosy picture on what's happening between you and Sam right now. He has a history, as do you."

"Thanks for the reminder," Libby said evenly. "Because God knows I might have forgotten I spent a week in Mountain View this summer if you didn't constantly remind me. Mom, I need to go. I'm going to be late to my meeting."

"Oh, Libby," her mother groaned. "*Why* did you volunteer to be on this committee? Of all the charitable things you could volunteer your time for, did it have to be Gwen Spangler's committee?"

"It's not *Gwen's* committee, it's Leo's. And why did Gwen have to end up working on a cause for Leo? He is my friend, Mom. His brother is marrying my sister. Everyone seems *so concerned* about Gwen," she said with mock worry as she fished her wallet from her purse.

Her mother waved her off the wallet and reached for her own. "I'll get this, honey. I mean that you're making it awkward for everyone because of what you did."

"Great, I can add awkward to the list of things I have to worry about. You know what really gets me, Mom? I had one bad summer, and now I'm the town menace."

"No, you're not," her mother said. "But you have to understand that no one will ever be comfortable with you and the Spanglers in the same room again."

"So, what, I should live in the mountains and never come to town?"

"No," her mother said patiently. "But maybe you should let Gwen have this committee."

"Have some faith, Mom!" Libby said irritably.

"Libby, honey," her mother said. "I have faith in you. But I worry. Sometimes, you're not the best judge of people."

"Oh my God," Libby muttered.

"You've worked so hard to come back from the events of the summer, to come back to *you,*" she said, gesturing to her. "I don't want to see anything happen to ruin that for you."

Libby was sick of everyone being so worried for her. "I'm fine, Mom. Really. I am." Libby leaned over her mother to kiss her cheek. "Thanks for the coffee. I'll talk to you later."

As she walked out of the coffee shop, Libby shook her head. She had worked hard. She was trying to improve herself. But she wasn't going to sit back and not be part of this town.

# TWENTY-FOUR

The Methodist church was a turn-of-the-century, redbrick building that smelled musty. The wooden floors creaked underfoot, which Libby discovered as she walked along the confusing maze of hallways, looking for the meeting room. She was late; her clomping about would announce her to everyone. So much for sliding in and taking a seat in back.

She saw the open door before she reached it, heard the sound of female voices rising up. She composed herself, put a smile on her face, and poked her head in.

The moment she did, everyone stopped talking and all heads swiveled in her direction. “I’m sorry I’m late,” she said apologetically, and looked around for a seat. Dani Boxer, bless that woman, instantly pulled out an empty chair next to her. “Come sit here, Libby,” she said, as if she’d been expecting her.

Libby gratefully took that seat and kept smiling as she met everyone’s eye around the table. Deb Trimble was there, for course, her hair recently dyed a new shade of red. So was Karen Miller, who wore an Indian blanket around her shoulders. Barbara

Perkins and Michelle Catucci were also in attendance, as was the ancient Mrs. Freeman, who had taught Libby tenth-grade English. She had a cotton-top head and smiled distantly at Libby.

Gwen was dressed in her dental hygienist scrubs. A row of toothbrushes carrying musical instruments marched around her torso. Her short, blond hair was pulled into a little ponytail, and held back by a pair of sunglasses on top of her head. She was wearing a big sparkly ring—a sapphire, it looked like. Libby wondered if it was an engagement ring.

Gwen did not look at Libby, but kept her gaze on her notes. But Libby was acutely aware that every other woman in that room was watching her and Gwen, and she could almost feel a collective shift forward in anticipation.

"Could we please get started?" Gwen asked, lifting her gaze from the paper before her and looking down the table. "A bit of good news first—we have raised forty-two hundred dollars so far."

"Ooh," said Mrs. Freeman. "That's a good start!"

"I think we should give ourselves a round of applause," Deb Trimble said, already clapping.

The group applauded themselves, Libby perhaps a little less enthusiastically than the others. Forty-two hundred dollars didn't sound that great to her; they needed so much more.

"All right!" Gwen said. "Let's get through this agenda so we can all get back to work. I assume most of us have to get back to work, anyway," she said, and Libby was certain that her quick glance up was directed at her.

"So let's talk about the silent auction," Gwen said. "What have we been able to round up for bids?"

Deb Trimble raised her hand. "My husband was able to get the golf club over at Corita City to donate one annual membership. That's a fifteen-hundred-dollar value."

"Oh, that's fantastic!" Dani said, and everyone congratulated

Deb, who was eager to accept their praise. And so it went, the announcement of donations the women had arranged. It was great, Libby thought, really great . . . but none of the things mentioned—the golf membership, free guitar lessons, a new sewing machine—were enough to bring in the amount needed to buy Leo a van in time.

The talk shifted to when the silent auction would be held. Dani had volunteered the Grizzly Lodge. They batted around a few dates and finally settled on one a month down the road. When that was done, Gwen began to stack her papers. "Thanks, ladies!" She glanced at her watch. "We got a lot accomplished today."

"Ah, excuse me?" Libby said, raising her hand.

Gwen tried not to look at her, but Dani said, "Oh, Libby, you've got something?"

"Okay," Gwen said, and looked down at her paper. "Libby?"

"I thought maybe we could organize a race."

"A race!" Karen said, as if she wasn't quite sure what that meant.

"A run. Everyone is running these days, right?"

"Not me," Barbara said, folding her arms over her chest. "I don't run unless someone is chasing me." She laughed as if no one had ever said that before.

"But a lot of people do," Libby said, and inched forward on her seat. "I talked to the manager at Fleet Feet, the running store out on the Old Aspen Highway? They've organized a lot of races and said they would be happy to help with a fundraiser. The way it works is that we ask runners to pledge to raise two hundred dollars each. If we can sign up five hundred people, that's one hundred thousand dollars. After the race expenses are deducted, there would still be at least seventy thousand to contribute toward the van and more. And it's something we could do fairly quickly."

"Sounds like a great idea to me," Dani said.

No one else said anything. Gwen was watching Libby curiously, and Libby couldn't tell if she was interested in what Libby had to say, or merely amused.

"I don't know," Deb said, shaking her head. "That's a lot of money to ask someone to raise. I can't imagine there are five hundred people in Pine River willing to run very far."

"A 5k is only 3.1 miles," Libby pointed out.

"I think it will be too cold," Mrs. Freeman said with a grimace. "It's already so cold," she said, pulling her sweater a little tighter.

"We don't really have enough time to organize a race," Michelle said. "You need sponsors and a course."

Libby pulled a paper from her purse where she'd jotted some notes. "Fleet Feet has done this before. We just need to help organize it. They also have a course they've used that is the right distance. I've made a list of potential sponsors."

"I say we add Libby's idea to the list," Dani said.

"Maybe if we had more time," Barbara said uncertainly, "but it just seems too ambitious to me."

"There's nothing wrong with ambitious," Libby said. "If we all pulled together, we could do it, and raise some good money."

"It feels like too much for this group," Gwen said firmly. "None of us has ever done anything like that, am I right?" she asked, looking around. "Have you, Libby? Have you ever put together a race to benefit a charity?"

"Ah . . . no," Libby said. "But I think I could do it."

"Right now, I think we have enough on our plate." Gwen stacked her papers and stood up. "And, we all have to get back to work. When's our next meeting, Deb?"

"Friday. We'll meet at the Grizzly so we can have a look at the banquet hall for the silent auction."

Everyone stood, leaving Libby sitting at the table, her idea effectively dismissed. Pushed aside. Ignored.

She pasted a smile on her face, pushed down that whisper of anger that was trying to take hold. *Deep breaths. Tropical paradise.* She stood up. "Deb, can I bring anything to the next meeting?" she asked as politely as she could make herself speak.

"No thanks, we've got it covered."

Libby nodded, slung her purse over her arm, and walked out of the meeting room while the others lingered to say good-bye.

She walked straight to the ladies' room, and into a stall. She sat down and braced her hands on her knees, taking deep breaths, trying to quell her anger before she said or did something she'd regret. Before she could manage it, she heard the door open, and two entered.

"Anyway, he said it was a joke."

That was Deb Trimble speaking.

"He said they knew it was going to be a disaster, but it was too late to do anything about it. So off they went and got married in a barn."

Libby's mouth dropped open.

"A *barn.*"

She recognized Karen's voice over the sound of water running.

"Yes," Deb said with a snort. "A *barn* wedding. I guess that's the kind of thing they do in California, but not here. And Gary said it was all so disorganized, as if it hadn't been thought through."

That was not true! If there was any disorganization, it was because Austin and Gary kept changing their minds! And Gary! He'd seemed so happy, and he and Austin had been totally on board with the barn setting, had both said it was a really cool idea.

"Well, you know, what can you expect?" Karen said. "It was probably a little too early to jump into something like that after her breakdown."

"Yes, probably," Deb agreed.

"My aunt had a breakdown when I was a girl. They just need a little time to recover, you know?"

*They.* As if the people who reached a breaking point were a different class of person. Deb and Karen probably thought that she needed to be wheeled into the sun every afternoon and have poetry read to her instead of returning to her life.

"I think I'll speak to Gwen," Deb continued. "I don't know if it's a good idea that she plans a big race, either. I heard she's been driving by Ryan Spangler's house."

"Oh no. But you know, Deb, it might be best if she goes off to plan something on her own so we don't have any issues with the auction."

"That's true," Deb said, and Libby heard the door open. The ladies walked out of the bathroom.

A month ago, Libby's anger would have exploded. Today, she felt as though if she just kept breathing, she could keep it under control. She *had* to keep it under control. She couldn't possibly give them anything else.

But she wasn't giving up on that race, especially now.

When she felt as if she could walk out of the church and smile at whomever she encountered, she left. In her car, she found her phone at the bottom of her purse and dialed a number.

It rang three times before Emma picked up with a lazy, "Hello."

"Emma!" Libby said, surprised to have reached her. "It's Libby. I can't believe I got you."

"What's wrong?"

Libby could count on one hand the number of conversations she'd had with Emma over the last couple of years, and Emma never once asked about her. Emma never said much of anything other than *no* and *leave me out of it.*

"Nothing is *wrong,* but . . . but I need your help."

"I'm not going to come out in the middle of nowhere and plan weddings, Libby," Emma said. "I've told you that. It's not worth my time. Or yours, for that matter."

"This isn't about a wedding, it's about me," Libby said. "I need to put on a 5k race in two months' time and make some money from it."

"Why?" Emma asked suspiciously. "Did you do something?"

"Do something?" Libby repeated, confused. "Like what?"

"Like a drug deal gone bad," Emma casually suggested.

Libby pictured her sister somewhere in Los Angeles, her long, blond hair slick and shiny, her bee-sting lips, her skinny legs in skinnier jeans. "I don't do drugs."

"Oh, right, of course not," she said, sounding disdainful. "Middle America does not do drugs. Or so they say." She snorted. "So why do you need the money?"

"I am trying to raise money for Leo Kendrick. You know, Luke's brother? He's in a wheelchair and needs a new van."

Libby could hear the clink of glass and voices in the background. "You don't need me for that," Emma said. "It's easy. Get a couple of sponsors to make T-shirts and buy some trophies, and voilà, there's your race."

"No, this has to be done right."

"So do it right—"

"No! Emma, listen—here is the real reason I need you," Libby said flatly. "The real reason I need you is because this summer, I had a nervous breakdown and spent a week in a mental institution, okay? They call it Mountain View Behavioral Health Center, but that's what it is, a place where they lock the doors at night and give you pills to help you sleep. And the other women on this committee think I can't do this. They all think I am too crazy to do it. But I'm not, Emma. I want to prove I'm not. *That's* why I need you."

There was silence on the other end, nothing but the sound of a car driving by.

"Well, well, at last, something interesting to come from Pine River. Tell me about it," Emma said.

Libby told her. And a half hour later, she was smiling and still in a bit of shock, because Emma had agreed to come and help her.

# TWENTY-FIVE

If there was a lesson Sam had learned in his years of recovery and sobriety, it was that you could never take anything for granted. And that there was no rhyme or reason to why an addict or alcoholic would return to drinking or drugs.

He'd known a guy once who had been sober for six years. His name was Rick, and he was solid, he had it beat. Rick worked as an accountant, dated a beautiful, sexy woman, and liked golf. To Sam, he moved through life with ease. Rick had told Sam more than once that his addiction wasn't a problem, that once he'd turned away from the Oxycontin, that was it—there was no turning back.

He said, like Tony had said the other night, he'd turned the page.

But then one fall the Colorado Rockies baseball team blew a pennant race, and Rick turned another page. Only he went in the wrong direction and took a bunch of pills, and just like that—like *that*—he fell off his sobriety.

It could happen in the blink of an eye.

Sam worried for Tony. To an outsider, it would seem that things were looking up for Tony. At Homecoming Ranch, he'd struck up a friendship with Ernest Delgado, and was doing some odd jobs around the place. Luke told him that Tony had been helping make some repairs and that he was pretty handy with a hammer. Just like Libby, Luke told Tony he could stay as long as he needed. They'd even try and pay him a little something.

But then Tony's friend Justin left for a job down in Texas, and Tony seemed to sink. He told Sam he liked the work okay, he liked Ernest, and liked being around people and animals. But Tony also worried about his missing leg. He feared that no woman would ever want to take that on. Sam pointed out he'd had a bunch of women take it on, but Tony shook his head, said they all took off after they found out what was involved in taking care of the stump and the prosthesis.

"That might be the kind of woman you keep company with," Sam said. "But there are lots of great women out there who wouldn't care about a leg."

"Like hell there is," Tony said.

"At least you've got a place to stay," Sam reminded him, but Tony just shrugged. "I don't want to be a damn charity case. That's all I am, a damn charity case."

That simply wasn't true. Sam assured Tony he was pulling his own weight around Homecoming Ranch and then some, but Tony wouldn't hear it. Sam tried to convince Tony to call one of the military hotlines for mental health, but Tony scoffed at that. "So they can give me a pill and a Band-Aid? No thanks."

Tony talked a lot about the desire to drink, about the struggle to keep from helping himself to Ernest's beer. Sam understood that all too well, and he felt prepared to talk him through that, to make sure he attended his meetings and kept busy. Sam called

Tony twice a day. He did everything he knew to do to support his sobriety.

But when Tony started to talk about killing himself, Sam felt out of his league.

He worried.

He worried about Libby, too, but it was a different sort of worry.

Libby was bubbly and happy, content in their new relationship. She made him happy. There was something to be said for ending a long day with a pair of shiny silvery blue eyes and a pretty smile. She was always happy to see him, throwing her arms around his neck with a happy kiss. "Hey!" she would say, "How was your day? Do you like lasagna? I hope so, because I made a huge batch of it."

These days—busy and full, but easy—made Sam feel like he had finally reached the place he'd been searching for, a place he could relax. He felt safe in his new relationship.

But his time with Libby wasn't without little niggles of worry here and there. She told him about her first fundraising committee meeting and the things she'd overheard in the bathroom at the Methodist church. She told him how awkward the meeting itself had been, and how no one seemed to want to hear what she had to say.

"You knew it would be tough," he reminded her.

"But I thought that once they saw me and heard my ideas, they would understand that I am there just to help." She frowned thoughtfully. "Do you think that Gwen is being spiteful?"

Sam didn't think Gwen was the type, but then again, women had their own code of conduct that he didn't understand. And it did seem to him that all the grunt work was falling to Libby. Somehow, she was the one running all the committee errands. "I have the time, you know, since I'm not working."

As far as Sam knew, a couple of the women on that committee didn't work, either, but it was Libby who took care of the printing, of picking up the silent auction items. Anything that needed to be done, Libby ended up doing. She had always been the type to raise her hand and volunteer first, and ask questions second.

Still, she was very determined in this particular venture, and Sam couldn't help wondering if there was more going on than her desire to help Leo. He feared that perhaps Libby hadn't let go of the Spanglers. It just seemed too easy after all she'd been through.

He was happy that at least she was putting her energy into a new direction for Homecoming Ranch. She had sworn him to secrecy about her plans. "I have to have the plan together before I tell Madeline. The more t's that are crossed the better." She'd laughed at that.

The days flew by, running together.

One night, when Sam came home from breaking up a fight at a Tanner Creek campsite, he walked in to the smell of sizzling steaks. He and Libby were not officially cohabiting, but they were spending most of their time together, either at his house, or at the ranch. He was getting used to the smell of actual food emanating from his kitchen. A bowl of salad was on the table, too, and a pie was cooling on the counter. "Wow," he said as he took off his coat. "What's the occasion?"

Libby was wearing an apron and a T-shirt that said "Pine River Chamber of Commerce" on the back. "You don't know?"

"No clue," Sam said and bent his head to kiss her.

"I'm a free woman, Lone Ranger. As in, no more restraining order. It expired today." She did a little hop as she went back to the stove where something was cooking.

"That's great," he said. "Fantastic news. I'm so glad that's behind you."

"Me too!" she said cheerfully.

Over dinner, they talked about his work and the interesting things she'd read about veteran rehabilitation centers that afternoon.

Later, they were lying on Sam's couch, watching the fire. Her head was on his shoulder, her leg draped over his. "What are you doing tomorrow?" he asked her.

"I'm driving up to Aspen to pick up a contribution to the auction. Deb Trimble said that Gwen asked her if I would. Gwen won't ask me herself."

"She's probably a little leery of you."

"She shouldn't be. I've done nothing but work my tail off for that committee."

Sam stroked Libby's hair and brushed the end of one long tress against his cheek. "Maybe she wonders about it like I do," he said.

"About what?"

"About your dedication to that committee."

He felt Libby's body stiffen. She slowly pushed up and twisted around to face him. "Why would you say that?"

"Because of the proximity to Gwen." He shrugged. "I guess I wonder if you are really over that part of your life. If you have turned the page, so to speak."

She looked surprised. "Sam . . . of course I have. Isn't it obvious?"

"It's obvious that you want to," he said sincerely. "But it's a big turnaround in just a few weeks."

Libby leaned back. "Don't you trust me?"

He didn't know how to answer that. He wanted to trust her. He wanted more than anything to trust her completely. He *needed* to trust her. "Yeah," he said. "I do."

And that's what scared him.

Libby pulled herself up and kissed him. “Good. Because you have nothing to worry about. Even if I saw the kids, I wouldn’t do anything.”

She kissed him again, but something in her statement registered in Sam’s mind. And as Libby’s mouth began to move down his body, her fingers following the wet trail, he knew something was off in that statement. But his thoughts were lost in a haze of flesh and kisses, of fragrant skin and soft, dark hair, and it wasn’t until the next morning he realized what it was that bothered him. *Even if I saw the kids, I wouldn’t do anything . . .*

Sam had not mentioned the kids. Libby had. And that statement sounded as if she had thought about seeing those children.

He tried to give her the benefit of the doubt. To his dismay, he couldn’t do that completely.

Sam was also worried that Libby’s sister Emma was going to disappoint her. That she’d been in contact with the elusive Emma was a surprise to everyone. One evening as they had dinner with Luke and Madeline, Libby announced that Emma was coming to help her.

Madeline had almost spilled her wine when Libby said it. “*What?*”

“I called her,” Libby said. “I really want this race to be a success, and Emma knows how to organize them.”

“You called her and asked her to come help you and she said yes? Just like that?” Madeline asked.

“I know, I was surprised, too,” Libby said. “I thought it was worth a shot—”

“I mean, we’ve been *struggling* here, needing her help, and out of the clear blue, she decides to come help with the race?” Madeline continued incredulously. “That is . . . so wrong.”

“It’s a fundraiser for Leo’s van,” Libby reminded her.

"That's great, Libby," Luke said, and looked meaningfully at Madeline.

"I know, but . . . but we have needed her and she couldn't care less."

Madeline seemed bothered by it all night.

Later, when Sam drove Libby back to his house, he asked, "So what's going on with Emma? Why is Madeline upset?"

"Oh," Libby said, with a flick of her wrist. "Emma is . . . Emma. She and Madeline didn't exactly hit it off when they first met." She smiled ruefully. "She's a very hard woman to understand, so I don't blame Madeline for that. But I don't take it as personally as Madeline."

Libby's attitude was short-lived. As the days piled on top of one another, and Libby couldn't get Emma on the phone to firm up her plans to come, Libby began to take it personally, too. Emma's silence was hurtful, and while she didn't say it, Sam could see that Libby was bewildered by it.

He hesitated to ask about the race, but finally asked one night as they were cleaning the kitchen at the ranch. "How is the race shaping up?" he asked.

"Ugh," she said with a shake of her head. "It's harder than I thought it would be. I could really use some help." She tossed down the rag she was using to wash dishes. "I don't understand why Emma won't call me back."

"You might have to accept that she's not coming," Sam suggested, but the moment the words left his mouth, he saw the flash of emotion across Libby's face.

"She'll come," she said. "Maybe I wasn't clear enough about the time line."

"Is there some way I can help?" he asked.

"Really?" Libby asked hopefully. "I really need to do this, Sam. They think I can't. They think that I'm nuts." She pressed her lips together and shook her head. "It's a great idea, right? And I think it's the only thing we've got to raise enough money in a short amount of time."

"It's a great idea," he agreed, wrapping her in his arms.

Sam wanted to make things better for Libby. But in some ways he felt powerless. Her issues seemed as complex as his own, scars that were formed over time, that ran too deep to clear up with simple encouragement. His heart warned him, told him that she wasn't ready for this relationship, but Sam's heart had already split open, had already let her in, growing new from the inside out.

Libby had said once that no one let her in. Well, he had let her in.

He had fallen in love with the curly-haired, blue-eyed woman. She'd brought a lightness to his life that he had desperately needed. Libby was his daily dose of effervescent happiness. She teased him, cajoled him, made love to him. She made him feel alive in a way he couldn't remember ever feeling. Their connection felt as if it were on an elementally cellular level.

On the eve of the silent auction, Libby was more distracted. There were dozens of little details that seemed to fall to her. Sam had seen some of the silent auction items and thought the group would be lucky to raise ten thousand dollars.

"How about I drive you in tomorrow? We'll swing by the city offices and get a permit for the race." That was something he could do to help her, pull some strings with people he knew at the city.

"Don't you have to work?" she asked.

"Yep. But I'm going out to Trace Canyon to talk to a man who might be hiring ranch hands. See if he wants to take on Tony."

"I thought Tony was going to help Ernest rebuild a fence."

Sam laughed. "How long do you think it takes to build a fence?"

"I don't know. It would take me a year, and that's if I had a clue what I was doing. Maybe I should take my own car, Sam. We have a lot to do tomorrow before the silent auction and I don't know how long I will be."

He caught her by the waist, pulling her into his chest. "I thought you *liked* riding with me," he said, and kissed her.

"Just seems a little convenient, deputy," Libby said, dropping her head to one side so he could kiss her neck. "I think you might want to take advantage of me. Or make sure I stay out of trouble."

"I know you're going to stay out of trouble," he said. "Because you'll have me to answer to if you don't." He put his hands on her waist and lifted her up; Libby wrapped her legs around his waist.

"That doesn't scare me," she said, smiling.

He turned around, put her on the edge of his bed and filled his hands with her breasts. "Don't tempt me."

Libby grinned and put her arms around his neck. "I love it when you get all stern."

"I'm about to get very stern," he said, and dipped his hand into the waist of her jeans and nudged her back, crawling over her, his body already thumping with want. Libby closed her eyes and sighed, and as usual, Sam forgot his niggling worries, let them float off to that place all worries went when he was making love to Libby.

# TWENTY-SIX

The afternoon of the silent auction, Libby went into town early to help set up. Libby had to hand it to Gwen—she'd done a great job at putting the silent auction together. They anticipated a full house. Everyone in Libby's life would be coming. Sam of course, as well as Madeline and Luke. Libby's mother and her husband planned to attend as well. And naturally, the guest of honor, Leo, would come with the rest of the Kendricks and Marisol and Javier.

Libby dressed in her best outfit—sleek black pants, a silky red top, and the black boots her mother had given her last Christmas. She was excited to announce the 5k race tonight. With Sam's help, she'd gotten the permit from the city to close the same streets they'd used for a race last spring. Fleet Feet, the local running shop, was going to sponsor the race and had arranged for a local construction company to subsidize the cost of the T-shirts. Libby needed more sponsors to help pay for the race trinkets, the food, and the city costs for cleanup and crowd control, but she was optimistic that Michelle would make good on her promise to convince the bank to provide some support.

Still, Libby tried to raise Emma one more time before she set off to town and the Grizzly to set up for the night's event.

*You've reached Emma Tyler. Obviously, I'm not here. Leave a message. Or not.*

"Charming," Libby muttered. At the beep, she said, "So, Emma . . . just wondering what the hell? You said you'd come and help me. I thought that meant you'd actually come to Pine River and *help* me. Would it be so hard for you to pick up the phone and tell me you're not coming? Seriously, Emma—look around LA for your manners. Oh, FYI, don't bother coming now. I've put the race together and turns out you were right. I didn't need you." She clicked off.

The parking spots outside the Grizzly were filled with committee member cars. Inside, Libby walked in to complete chaos—everyone was stepping around everyone else in a frantic attempt to set up the auction items and tag them with the pretty handwritten calligraphy Karen had done.

Gwen in particular seemed a little frantic.

"She's got her kid's dance recital at five-thirty, and then the cocktail party starts here at six," Karen explained when she caught Libby watching as Gwen dressed down one of the waiters on hand for the evening. "She doesn't have a moment. In fact, she will miss most of the cocktail party to see her daughter's dance recital, get dressed, and get back here in time to emcee. She's just a little stressed," she said laughingly.

Libby remembered the promise she'd made to Alice, that she'd try and make her recital. More than anything, Libby wished she could see Alice dance. Of course, that was out of the question, given her relationship with Gwen and Ryan.

She still missed Alice and Max so much. Sometimes, she could feel that ache in her bones. Sometimes, she would be awakened by the sound of one of them calling her name, a waking dream. Libby had not seen Alice or Max once in the last month, other than those times she drove by the school. They'd never come with Gwen to the meetings. No one had ever dropped them off to meet their mother.

Libby turned away from Karen now, imagining Alice in her dance costume, a purple butterfly. She could picture her practicing the twirls and dips and bows she would be required to make, over and over again, up and down the hall. She could see Max behind her, his imaginary gun pointed at his sister, diving behind the hall table to hide.

Libby pulled out the next auction item.

"Gross," Karen said, looking over Libby's shoulder. Libby looked at what she held in her hand. It was a stuffed quail to be set up with the hunting-lease display. Someone had already turned on an iPad which rotated pictures of happy hunters with dead bucks.

"You know, I have to say, you've done a really good job," Karen said to Libby as they arranged the items.

She said it as if she had been expecting the complete opposite, and Libby could feel herself coloring. "Thanks," she said. She wanted to tell Karen that she always did a good job, and one bad summer did not define a person.

"I never put much stock into the talk that was going around town," Karen said, her voice lower. "My first husband cheated on me, and let me tell you, it was a good thing he got to the butcher knife before I did. Okay, I've got to go help Deb get that sewing machine out of her car."

Libby appreciated the vote of confidence.

The setup for the auction ran a little longer than they expected, and at the end, most everyone was hurrying out the door to dress for the evening. Libby had come dressed, as a drive back to Homecoming Ranch wasn't practical. At four-thirty, only Gwen, Dani, and Libby were left.

The room looked just about complete. Libby was thinking of popping into the Grizzly Café for some coffee when Gwen suddenly gasped, startling Dani and Libby.

"The posters!" Gwen cried. "The big posters for the stage! They're our displays!"

"Posters of what?" Libby asked.

"Of the van, of *Leo*. We had a big display made so everyone can see why we are raising money," Gwen exclaimed, and began to search her purse for her phone. "They cost us a *lot* of money. They're at the printer—I have to pick them up by five!"

"You've got time to make it," Dani said, looking at her watch.

"No, no, you don't understand. They're huge! I need Ryan's truck to get them, and he's at work." She jabbed at the number pad on her phone, calling the printer. She explained the situation and asked if anyone could deliver the posters. Her shoulders sagged. "They don't have anyone who can come. I have to go get them."

"Well go get them, Gwen," Dani said. "Libby and I can finish up here."

"I *can't* go and get them. My kids are coming here. The babysitter is dropping them off and I have to get them to the school, because Alice has her dance recital today."

Libby managed to suppress a small gasp of delight.

"Libby, please go and get the posters," Gwen pleaded.

"Me?" Libby asked. "My car is much smaller than yours."

Gwen looked frantic. "I don't know what to do." She chewed her bottom lip, thinking.

"Now, Gwen, run and go get those posters," Dani said. "We'll be here. We can look after a couple of kids for a few minutes."

Gwen's head came up at that, and she leveled a brown-eyed gaze on Libby.

"Hey," Libby started, but Dani quickly interceded.

"Libby has worked really hard on this committee, Gwen, and she hasn't said one word to you about the situation between the two of you. It will be fine."

Gwen was still looking at Libby, clearly debating it.

Libby made a sound of exasperation. "Come on, Gwen—what do you think I'm going to do?"

Gwen didn't answer that exactly; she just shook her head. "Right. Okay. I'll be back in half an hour." She grabbed up her purse and hurried out the door.

"Thanks, Dani," Libby said.

"Think nothing of it. Whole thing is pretty darn silly if you ask me. I know you wouldn't do anything."

Libby was not going to be bothered that Dani didn't sound very certain of that.

They continued working to set up the last item—a sewing machine—which had come with a display of things the owner had made on a similar machine: baby clothes, doll clothes, a work shirt. A quarter of an hour after Gwen had left, Libby heard Max and Alice coming down the hall to the banquet room, both of them running, Max shouting at Alice to slow down.

They burst into the room at once, Alice stopping to look wildly about, and Max running straight to Libby. He threw his arms around her, turned his beaming face up to her and said, "I got a *goal*!"

"No way!" Libby cried. "High five!"

"Where's my mom?" Alice asked breathlessly. "I need to talk to her."

"Alice!" Libby said, holding out a hand to the girl.

Alice ran to her, threw her arms around her waist. "*Libby*! We have to go! I don't have my costume! Everyone else has their costume!"

"I'm going to be goalie, Libby!" Max cried, vying for Libby's attention.

"You are? That's such an important position," Libby said.

"Libby!" Alice shrieked. "Mommy forgot my costume! I have to get it because *I'm the butterfly*!"

"Okay, calm down, sweetie, we'll figure this out. Where is it? At school?" Libby asked, running her hand over Alice's head.

"No! It's at home! Mom forgot!"

"Oh my goodness," Dani said. "I'm pretty sure the recital begins in about forty-five minutes."

"You'll have to take them," Libby said to Dani. "I shouldn't."

"No, *you* take us Libby!" Alice cried, tugging at her hand. "You know where to go. But we have to go *now*."

"Alice, honey, I can't," Libby said, wincing at the distress on the girl's face. "But Dani will."

"Okay, where do they live?" Dani asked.

"Vista Ridge subdivision, on Canton Way. It's in the back, up that big hill. You know that hill, right?"

"No," Dani said, frowning. "I don't even know that subdivision. I never go out that way."

"It's easy," Libby said as Alice tugged on her hand. "Just enter through the north gate and take your first right. At the stop sign, you're going to want to go left—"

"I need to write this down," Dani said, and patted the bun in the back of her head, apparently looking for a pencil. "What did I do with that pencil?"

"Libby, you *have* to take me. She doesn't know how to take me," Alice pleaded.

"Do you have GPS?" Libby asked Dani.

"Lord no! My truck doesn't have any fancy bells and whistles, but it's paid for."

Alice, sensing impending doom, began to cry. "The teacher won't let me do my dance if I don't have my costume!"

"Let's call Mommy," Dani suggested. She took her phone off the counter and punched in Gwen's number. A moment later, they all heard Gwen's phone ringing at the podium, where she had inadvertently left it.

"I guess I can call Ryan," Dani said. "Do you have his number?"

Libby knew his number, but in that moment, she'd not admit it, not be accused, however thinly, of stalking him.

"*Lib-beee*," Alice said tearfully.

It was a dangerous thing to do, but Alice's distress was unbearable. "Don't call Ryan," she said to Dani. "I can take them. It will take us thirty minutes round trip, tops."

Dani looked at the kids, then at Libby. "I don't know," she said uncertainly. "Gwen wouldn't like that."

"I know, Dani, but she doesn't have her phone, and clearly this is an emergency."

"Well . . ." Dani said, clearly unsettled with Libby's suggestion.

"I'll be quick," Libby said. "I know exactly where they live. I know where Ryan keeps the extra key. Alice can get it; I won't go in the house—"

"Okay, go," Dani said with a wave of her hand. "I'll tell Gwen what has happened. But come right back, Libby. Promise me you'll come right back."

"Dani! Of course I will," Libby said, and turned a bright smile to the children, thrilled to have a few stolen moments with them. "Come on, guys! We have an important mission and we have to hurry!"

Because she had no booster seats for them, Libby put Max in the middle of the back seat. Alice was big enough to ride beside her brother.

Max was concerned. "I'm *supposed* to have a booster seat," he insisted.

"I know, but just this once, it's okay," Libby assured him. "We have to hurry before Mommy gets back."

With the kids buckled in, Libby drove with one eye on the road, and one eye on the rearview mirror so she could see their faces—Alice's worried stare out the window, Max's intent study of the back of the console between the front seats and his ability to reach it with his foot. She chatted happily with them, asking about school, about their friends. It felt like the old days, when they were a big happy family, when Libby would pick them up from school and hear about their day, then bring them home and prepare dinner for the four of them while Max played and Alice danced around the kitchen, repeating everything her friends had said that day.

Today, Max was desperate for Libby to know about his new game. Alice talked over him about her beautiful butterfly costume and the fairy costume that her best friend Sasha would wear. She smiled in her rearview mirror. "Hey, you two. You know how much I love you, right?" she asked.

"Yes," they said in unison. The question was familiar to them, their answers automatic.

It felt as if the last few months were falling away, as if nothing had happened, as if Libby had never been separated from them. It felt as if things really *could* go back to the way they were, as if Libby really could have her family back, right here, today.

# TWENTY-SEVEN

When Sam pulled onto Main Street, he knew something was wrong. He was used to seeing a Pine River cop parked outside the Grizzly Café, but this late afternoon, there were three of them.

He parked and walked to the Grizzly Lodge, bile rising in his throat. When he saw Gwen standing at the entrance of the lodge, talking with two police officers, he knew, he just knew, and his heart sank.

"Sam!" Gwen shrieked when she saw him. "You have to help me! Libby has taken the children!"

"What?" He could imagine many things, but kidnapping was not one of them. Libby's misdeeds were generally more out in the open than that.

"I had to go get the posters, and I *told* Libby and Dani that my kids were coming. Alice has a dance recital at five-thirty, and I said I'd be right back. But when I came back, they were all gone! Where are they? Where could they have gone? She *took* them!"

"Gwen, calm down," he said, putting his hands on her shoulders. "Where's Dani?"

"Her chef said she had to run to Walmart because the produce truck never arrived. And she won't answer her phone! But Mrs. Ramsey *saw* Libby put my kids in her car and drive off! She *saw* her, and she *heard* Libby tell them to hurry before I came back!"

Sam glanced at the woman who was standing with John Powers, a police officer he knew fairly well. "You saw them?" he asked Mrs. Ramsey.

"Yep," she said, scratching her arm nervously. "I watched her put those kids in the backseat. She didn't even have a booster for the boy. She told them they had to hurry before their mommy came back. Then she just drove off, pretty as you please."

"Did anyone call her?" Sam asked, taking his phone from his pocket.

"No," Gwen said. "I don't have her number! Why would I have her number?"

"Gwen . . . calm down," he said. A thousand thoughts rushed through Sam's mind, not the least of which was that he should never have let his guard down. He should have kept to himself, should have left his heart shuttered. Right now, he felt gutted. He'd let Libby in, had let her into the crack in his heart, had wrapped himself and his hopes around her. This was a bone-crushing disappointment.

He punched her number into his phone and waited for it to connect. What stung was that he'd told her that this was the one thing he couldn't bear, the one thing that he had to avoid. If he couldn't trust her, if he couldn't believe in her judgment, that she would not take everyone on an emotional rollercoaster, he couldn't maintain the relationship. The lack of basic trust was what weakened him, sapped him of his strength, and for the sake of his own sanity, he could not have it in his life.

"She took my kids!" Gwen cried. "She may be halfway to Mexico by now!"

"Mrs. Spangler, you need to calm down. You're jumping to conclusions. We don't know anything yet. We need to speak to Ms. Boxer, but in the meantime, we've got units looking for Miss Tyler right now," John Powers said calmly.

Libby's cell phone began to ring.

"I am not going to calm down! She stole my *kids*!" Tears began to slide from Gwen's eyes. She pressed a hand to her heart and bent over with despair.

"Hey! That's her!" Mrs. Ramsey said suddenly. All heads swiveled around as Libby's little red car slid into a vacant spot at the end of the block.

Sam clicked off his phone.

A moment later, Max appeared, running down the sidewalk, leaping to hit the top of each parking meter as he passed it. Behind him was his sister, holding a purple frilly dress over her shoulder, running toward Gwen.

"Mommy! You forgot my costume!" she shouted.

"*Ohmigod*," Gwen cried and rushed toward her children, her arms outstretched, falling down on her knees to gather them to her.

With her purse over her shoulder, Libby hesitated at the sight of Gwen on her knees. She had her phone in her hand and lifted her gaze to Sam.

Sam couldn't look at her. If she thought he would save her again, cover for her, pull her back from the edge, she was mistaken.

"I'll go have a chat with her," John said, and walked forward to intercept Libby.

"*No*," Sam heard Libby say. "No, that's *not* what happened. Alice forgot her costume and her recital is in twenty minutes," she said looking at her phone. "You don't understand how much dance means to her. If we hadn't gone for her costume, she wouldn't have had it in time. Dani will tell you," she said, looking around. "Dani was here, she agreed, she said I should take them to get Alice's costume. We tried to call Gwen, but she forgot her phone."

"You should have left a note. Maybe called her husband," Officer Powers suggested.

"But there was no time!" Libby said sharply. "And Dani was going to be here! I don't get this," she said gesturing to Gwen. "I was *helping* her, not hurting her. There's Dani!" she cried, pointing up the street. "Dani, tell them! Tell them we agreed!"

Sam looked over his shoulder as Dani came hurrying down the street carrying several plastic Walmart bags. "Oh *no,*" Dani said, stopping on the sidewalk, her broad shoulders slumping. "Oh dear, this is *all* my fault. Our order of salad greens didn't arrive, so I had to run down to Walmart, and there's a wreck on the highway. You know how it is around here, there's no way to get back across town by the old highway—"

"Dani," Libby impatiently interrupted, "just tell them that you and I agreed it was best that I take the kids when we couldn't get hold of Gwen."

"Alice forgot her costume," Dani said, nodding. "And Libby wanted to take the kids. She said it would be quicker."

Libby gasped. She looked at Sam. "I did say that, but *after* we tried to call Gwen and couldn't get an answer."

"Well, maybe so," Dani said uncertainly, her brow furrowing with thought. "I just know that there wasn't any time, and Libby didn't want me to call Ryan, so yes, she said she would take them and I said I'd be here to tell Gwen. And I meant to." She turned to Gwen, who was standing again, a firm grip of each child's hand. "I'm so sorry, Gwen," Dani said. "But the produce truck didn't come, and I didn't know what else to do."

"See?" Libby demanded of Sam. "I didn't take her kids!"

Sam's heart had already begun sliding out of his chest because the damage was done. No matter how good her intentions, she should never have taken those children, and the most distressing thing was that Sam didn't know if Libby even understood that.

Dani was consoling Gwen, who was, understandably, unhappy that Dani had agreed Libby should take her kids, and John Powers was trying to diffuse Gwen's unhappiness by pointing out it was all a misunderstanding.

"Oh, I know," Gwen said angrily. "It's always a misunderstanding with Libby Tyler! Everyone in town knows that."

"Mom, we have to *go,"* Alice said, pulling on her mother's hand. "We're going to be late!"

"We're already late," Gwen said angrily, and glared at Libby. "Thanks a lot, Libby. Now, we're late for Alice's dance recital. You *knew* I wouldn't want you to take them. You could have come to the printer's and intercepted me, for heaven's sake. There are a hundred other things you might have done than put my children in your car and take them from here."

Libby looked shaken. She pushed her hair from her face. "I meant only to help Alice," she said again. "And you, Gwen. She needed her costume in a very short time."

"Right," Gwen scoffed, and took her kids by the hands. "Come on, kids, we're late."

Sam didn't hear what else John said to Gwen as she began ushering her children to her car, because a white van with the faded words *fresh baked* rolled up to the curb, its engine making a clunking noise. Leo had arrived for the auction.

"Step aside, mere mortals, the star is here," he called out as his dad wheeled him out of the back of the van. He was wearing a suit that hung awkwardly on his bent body, dark sunglasses, and a silk scarf around his neck. His useless feet were encased in black leather shoes polished to a high sheen. He was smiling crookedly, one arm bent at an odd angle against his chest. He looked like a rock star.

"Let's *do* this," he said happily.

"Sam, I—"

"Now is not the time," Sam said curtly, and went to help Bob get Leo inside the wheelchair-resistant Grizzly Lodge, with Marisol walking behind, huffing and puffing with one hand on her belly, one hand carrying a black bag of the medicines and things Leo would need for an evening away from home.

When they finally had Leo situated—just inside the door of the banquet hall so that he could greet people as they entered and encourage them to bid as only Leo could do—Sam walked outside for some air. He wished he had some aspirin. His head was pounding, his throat dry.

He hesitated when he saw Libby pacing the sidewalk. She stopped when Sam walked out, her legs braced apart, her hands on her waist. "You didn't believe me," she said flatly. "I could see it on your face—you thought I had done something."

He didn't answer her; he feared the torrent that would come out of his mouth if he did.

She gaped at him. "You don't *trust* me." Her eyes widened and she took a step back. "Wow. You're just like everyone else in this town—you don't trust me."

He looked at her mouth, at her body that had quickly become almost as familiar to him as his own. He looked into the pale blue eyes that had captivated him so long ago. He didn't know what he thought or felt. He only knew that the inability to trust her was his kryptonite. He'd tried to make her understand that he'd worked hard to distance himself from the things that made him drink. He didn't understand exactly how it all worked in his head, he only knew that misplaced trust had always been an issue with him. If he couldn't trust he was in the right place with the right person, if he couldn't trust his own instincts, he was prone to numbing his doubts with alcohol. It didn't matter that he could reason through it. It didn't matter that it didn't make sense to him. The only thing that mattered was that reason did not subdue the desire to numb the mistrust.

It was a high wire he walked, and Sam would never jeopardize his sobriety. Not even for her.

"Should I believe it is only coincidence that once again, you have inserted yourself in the middle of the Spanglers' lives without invitation?"

She looked as surprised as if he'd struck her. She took another step back. "I can't believe this. I trusted *you,* Sam. I opened up to you, told you everything. I told you the truth. But you're going to believe Gwen Spangler instead of me."

"I don't have to believe Gwen. You took the kids, Libby. There's no debate in that. And you had no right."

Libby stared at him, her hand clenching and unclenching. She suddenly turned around, started walking.

"Where are you going?" he called out to her.

She quickened her step, going as fast away from him as she could.

Sam resisted the urge to go after her. Right now, he needed to think, to find his bearings. He'd made a commitment to this fundraiser, and he wasn't going to let Leo down because Libby had let *him* down. He made himself turn around and walk back inside to the silent auction with his pulse pounding angrily in his ears. He heard a phone ring, but it took him a moment to realize it was his. By the time Sam dug it out of his pocket, the call from Tony had rolled to voice mail.

Sam tucked the phone back into his pocket. He couldn't talk to Tony right now. He had to think, to calm down. He would call Tony later when he'd cooled off.

# TWENTY-EIGHT

Libby walked blindly into the Stake Out. She didn't know where she was going, other than away from Sam, and found herself at the bar, still seeing Sam's cold and distrusting expression before her. It was the worst sort of feeling—as if someone had pummeled her heart and left it bleeding.

"What can I get you?" the bartender asked.

"Water, thanks."

The bartender walked down to the other end of the bar to get it.

Libby picked up a coaster and began to twirl it through her fingers. She was angry. With Gwen, for one. After all this time working on the committee, Gwen couldn't possibly believe Libby would steal her children. And just what did Gwen think she would do? Run with them? *Harm* them? It was infuriating.

Libby was also angry with herself, for having taken Alice and Max to get the costume. It was a dumb thing to do, and even though Libby hated to see Alice upset or disappointed, it was not her place to soothe Alice's wounds. *It was not her place.*

It was so painful to admit that to herself. Libby had believed that she'd come to terms with it, but today had proved to her she hadn't at all. She had jumped at the chance to be with them. She had been so happy to be the one to fix things. She hadn't come to terms with anything.

But what made her so angry that she could not keep from taking tiny little gasps to calm her racing heart was that Sam didn't trust her. She'd made a mistake. Okay, another one. But how could he not understand what was in her heart?

"Here you go," the bartender said, putting a glass of water before her. He slid a shot glass in beside it.

"What's that?" Libby asked.

"The guy down there sent it. Said to tell you it would cure what ails you."

Libby looked down the bar at the man. He lifted his beer bottle to her.

"Take it back," Libby said. "I don't want it."

The bartender shrugged and picked it up, made his way back down the bar.

Libby sipped her water, seeing Sam's clenched jaw, the hard look in his eye.

"Give it a try, at least."

Libby turned to see who'd spoken. The man from the other end of the bar was standing beside her, smiling down at her. "You look like you could use a friend. What's your name?"

Libby snorted. "Don't get too close, pal," she said. "I have been known to pick up a golf club and go off on a man's truck."

He laughed. "That's my kind of woman," he said, and slid onto the barstool next to her.

The silent auction went fairly well, Sam thought, but in the end, there were a couple of items that were taken to the podium for open bidding. Sam bid on the hunting lease—he had no intention of using it, but then again, he couldn't see vying for a sewing machine. In the middle of the auction, his phone rang again. It was Tony.

"I've got five hundred. Who will make it five fifty?" Gwen said, scanning the crowd. Somehow, in spite of the mess of the afternoon, she had changed into a black sheath and looked very good and poised. "Five fifty?" Gwen asked.

Sam raised his hand.

"Great. Have we got six hundred?"

Jackson Crane raised his hand. "Six fifty," he called out and grinned at Sam. "No offense, big guy, but I want the lease."

"Six fifty," Gwen repeated.

"Make it seven, Gwen," Sam said, and smiled at Jackson. "It's a fundraiser."

The crowd laughed.

Jackson did, too. "All right, all right. Eight hundred dollars, Gwen. And if I don't get at least a squirrel, I'm suing Jack Wolzniak," he said, turning around to look at the man who had put the lease up for auction.

"Eight hundred fifty?" Gwen said to Sam.

He shook his head. "Let Jackson have it. I'd hate for him to miss out on a squirrel this season."

Everyone laughed as Gwen declared, "Sold to Jackson Crane for eight hundred dollars! Ladies and gentlemen, that brings us to the end of our auction tonight." She stuck glasses on her face and glanced down at a piece of paper someone had just handed her. "This is great news. We've raised fifteen thousand dollars to date! Leo, would you like to say something?"

She stuck the microphone in Leo's face. "I'd like to say thank you to everyone," he said. "This means a lot to me. Many of you know that football has always been important to me, and in fact, I was playing football at the Colorado School of Mines when I was diagnosed with MND. I had hopes of playing in the NFL like I guess all boys do. Well, I obviously can't do a lot of what I used to do, but by God, I can still coach the Broncos!"

A wild cheer went up from the crowd.

The auction was completed, and the evening began to wind down. Sam walked outside of the banquet hall to return Tony's call. But there was no answer. He found that odd, as Tony had called him only minutes ago. He grabbed his coat from the hat-check and walked outside to try again.

On the second try, Tony picked up. And he was crying. "Sam," he said. "You've always been a real good friend to me."

Sam's pulse quickened. "I still am, Tony."

"Yeah, but . . . I just wanted to *thank* you," Tony said, his voice tearful and thick.

"You okay, buddy?" Sam asked, but his heart had started to race with apprehension. He began striding toward his truck.

"I'm just thinking about everyone who has tried to help me."

"I'm coming up there," Sam said. "Let's go over them together."

"Nah, man. I'd rather be alone."

Panic flooded Sam. "Tony, goddammit, I'm coming up there. Just hang on. I'm in Pine River right now. Give me twenty minutes. You *owe* me twenty minutes!"

"Don't bother," Tony said. "I'm not worth it. You waste all this time on me and I'm nothing . . ."

"Twenty minutes, Tony!" Sam said sternly, and clicked off, quickening his step. His mind was on Tony, his thoughts up in the mountains, away from Pine River. He didn't notice the waitress from the Stake Out until he almost collided with her. "Oh hey," she said. "Hey, I know you. You've been in the Stake Out with Libby Tyler, right?"

"Yes," Sam said. "Why?"

The girl glanced back at the Stake Out. "She's pretty drunk. And there's this guy, Tom Veranno, who keeps buying her drinks. He's a dog. I tried to talk her into leaving but she wouldn't listen to me."

Something hard and unforgiving snapped inside of Sam. "Thank you," he said, and changed direction, heading for the Stake Out.

The bar was crowded for a Thursday night, but then again, the Stake Out was the destination for hungry singles in Pine River. As Sam pushed through the crowd, he could smell the booze, and there were dirty glasses on the bar, empty shot glasses, empty beer glasses. Two bartenders were walking quickly back and forth behind the bar, carrying four or five drinks at a time.

It never ceased to amaze Sam how the smell of alcohol and cigarettes could make him yearn so for a drink. He could feel the desire rising up like leavened bread, suffocating everything else inside him.

He saw Libby instantly. She was laughing at something a man was saying. A man who was practically on top of her, his eyes fixed on her breasts. Sam walked around to where she was. Her back was to him, so he put his hand on her shoulder. "Come on, Libby, let's go home," he said.

She jerked around, her eyes wide and bloodshot, and she teetered on the edge of her stool. "Home! Where's home, Sam? Wait, don't answer that. I don't *want* to go with you," she said, jerking her shoulder out from underneath his hand.

"Hey, pal, the lady doesn't want you around. So take a walk," Tom said, standing up from his barstool. He was several inches shorter than Sam.

"I'm not taking a walk," Sam said. "I'm taking her home."

"Don't be like that," Libby said. "Tom's been really nice to me."

"Yeah, I bet he has," Sam put his arm around her waist and made her stand up. "Where's your purse?"

She looked around her. "I don't know. Oh. There it is." She slid down to get it from where it had somehow ended up on the floor.

"Dude, I said, leave her alone," the man said, and when Libby dipped down, he put his hand on Sam's arm. Sam swung so fast he surprised himself. He connected with the man's jaw and sent him tumbling to the ground.

Libby popped up, gasping with surprise. "*Sam!*"

"I'm calling the cops!" the man said angrily, clambering to his feet.

"I *am* a cop." Sam grabbed Libby by the hand. "Let's go." He yanked her away from the bar and stalked through the crowd, pulling her along behind him. Everyone had turned to see what the commotion was, and several stepped out of their way as he marched through. Libby stumbled along behind him.

With every step, Sam felt his belly churn. He hated this. He hated scenes, he hated drunks. And he especially did not care for the woman he loved to be so drunk. Yes, he loved Libby, of course he loved her, he'd always loved her. And to see her like this was beyond maddening to him.

She said nothing until he opened the passenger door of the truck. She turned around then, swaying on her feet, and said, "I'm sorry."

"You're always sorry, Libby. Get in."

"No, really. I'm *really* sorry. More than I am ever sorry about anything, because, I, you know, I *love* you, Sam."

Sam rolled his eyes. He knew all about drunken proclamations of love and the promise to do better. "Get in," he said, and helped her inside the truck. He walked around to the driver's side, stepped in, and started the truck.

Libby slid down in her seat. "I thought you loved me, too."

He wasn't going to respond to that. He'd been in this situation too many times to count, and it left a bitter taste of resentment in his mouth that he should be here again. There it was again, the overwhelming desire for a drink.

"Okay, you're mad, but what was I supposed to do?" she demanded, banging her fist on the console.

"I assume you are talking about taking those children," he said sharply. "You were supposed to let someone else handle it, that's what. Let it be Gwen's problem, and not yours."

She slid deeper in her seat. "I know. You think I don't know? But Alice would have been *crushed*," she said, saying it with so much conviction she almost tipped over.

"And she would have survived," Sam said curtly.

"That's not—"

"*Stop,*" he said angrily. "I don't want to hear it."

"Fine," Libby snapped and folded her arms across her middle.

Before Sam turned off onto the road up to Homecoming Ranch, she had passed out.

# TWENTY-NINE

It was already noon by the time Libby made her way downstairs, one hand on her throbbing head, the other on the handrail. She felt awful, like she'd been dragged back from the brink of hell. Libby was not a drinker beyond the occasional glass of wine with dinner. She couldn't remember the last time she'd even drunk liquor.

She'd drunk what felt like bottles of it last night.

Madeline was sitting at the kitchen bar, papers strewn in front of her when Libby stumbled in. "So you're alive," she said simply.

"Debatable," Libby said. She shuffled to the coffeemaker and turned it on. "I guess you know Sam brought me home."

Madeline snorted. "I know. It took the both of us to pour you into bed."

"That bad, huh?" Libby asked with a wince.

"Worse," Madeline said, sounding sympathetic.

Libby groaned. "I was so stupid last night, Madeline. Where is Sam now?"

"I don't know, probably still in Montrose," Madeline said.

"Montrose?"

"You weren't the only one to get rip-roaring drunk," she said. "Tony, too, apparently. After Sam got you upstairs, he went down to the bunkhouse and found Tony, several empty beer bottles, and an empty pill container."

Libby gasped. "Is he all right?"

"He lived," Madeline said. "I don't know what he took, but it wasn't lethal. Sam rushed him to the hospital in Montrose. Irony of ironies, they are sending him to Mountain View today."

"*Ohmigod.*" Libby sank onto a barstool and buried her face in her hands. Tony had seemed so upbeat last week after Justin's visit. "What happened?"

"Who knows?"

"I should go," Libby said, her mind racing ahead. She could help Sam, could talk to Tony. "I can help."

"I don't think you can, Libby," Madeline said. "You want my advice?"

"No. No, wait," Libby said, squeezing her eyes shut. "Yes. Yes, I want your advice, Madeline. I do."

Madeline frowned dubiously.

"Look, I've managed to screw up maybe the best thing to ever happen to me. I need every piece of advice I can get, if I like it or not."

Madeline slid off her seat at the bar and picked up her papers. "Okay. If I were you, I'd lay low a couple of days. And then I'd think about getting some help for *you,* Libby. Remember when you came back from Mountain View, after you'd had all those talks with Dr. Huber? That really seemed to help you to be able to talk about things. I would do that."

"You're right," Libby said. "Good idea."

"But I would not go and find Sam. Not now."

Libby could feel her heart begin to split open, a soft tear, spreading like a spiderweb down the center. "Why not?" she asked.

"Because . . ." Madeline glanced heavenward a moment, then at Libby. "You know, I really disappointed Luke one time. Like . . . *really* let him down. And he told me—Well, he said a lot of things. But basically he said he was in our relationship for the long haul, but he wasn't in it to be jerked around. I'm guessing the same is true for Sam. I know he is crazy about you. He's been crazy about you for a long time. But he's not *crazy*, if you know what I mean."

Libby knew exactly what she meant. Sam could be the one for her, but not if she kept stirring up the dust. Even if she didn't intend to stir the dust, she'd still done it, and the only way to keep that from happening was to stay away from all the Spanglers. "I know what you're saying is right, Madeline. It's what I have to do. But I love Alice and Max so much," she muttered.

"I know," Madeline said. "Seriously, I know how much you care for them, and how difficult it must have been for you to lose them. I can't imagine how hard. But Libby . . . if you really love them, you really have to let them go. It must cause them heartache, too. Do you think they want you and their mother and father to be at odds? They will always care about you, but at the rate you're going, they will end up resenting you. You don't want that, do you?"

"No," Libby said wearily. "Of course I don't."

Madeline came around the bar and surprised Libby with a sisterly arm around her shoulders. "I've been there," she said to Libby. "I've lost people from my life that I loved, and I know how it hurts. Just don't lose Sam. He's one of the good guys. Chill out, work on yourself, and my guess is he'll come around."

Libby didn't know if that was true or not.

As the day passed, she waited to hear from him. She kept thinking she'd see his truck driving up the road to the house.

He didn't come.

So Libby tried to reach Sam by phone. It rolled into voice mail.

That afternoon, Madeline gave Libby a ride into town to get her car, left at the Grizzly Lodge. Libby went inside to speak to Dani.

Dani was busy behind the counter, but in spite of everything that had happened, she still had a smile for Libby.

"How did it go last night?" Libby asked.

"It was *great,"* Dani said. "We're halfway to our goal. Leo was very happy. I think it tired him out something awful, but he left with a smile on his face." She looked slyly at Libby. "Where were you?"

Libby shook her head. "You don't want to know. Dani . . . I am sorry about yesterday. I thought I was being helpful—"

"Well of course you did, hon. I'm sorry, too. I want to tell Sam that the more I thought about it, the more it seemed it was my idea, but he hasn't been in."

Libby could picture him in his work shed, making birdhouses. "It wasn't your idea, Dani. It was mine. But thanks for trying to help." She smiled sadly. "I'll see you."

The next afternoon, Libby drove to Mountain View to see Tony.

He was sitting on a bed, staring vacantly out the window. "Wow," Libby said. "You look like hell."

"You don't look much better," Tony pointed out.

"Tell me about it." Libby sighed and sat on the edge of his bed, sitting cross-legged where his leg would have been. His prosthesis was beside the nightstand. "We miss you, Tony," she said. "You have to come back. Ernest is moping around. Madeline and I have no one to cook for."

Tony rolled his eyes and kept his gaze on the window.

"You're part of us now," she said. "So you have to come back, Tony. Besides, I have big plans for us."

"Another wedding?"

"Nope. No more weddings. Something more useful than that." She told Tony her idea to create a safe place for vets like him. A therapeutic place where vets could come and get help while they prepared to reenter their lives. "You'd be a critical part of it. I can't do it without you."

Tony looked at her with dull eyes. "I don't know. I'm not much use to anyone."

"That's not true. You're a big help to Ernest, and that's just the start."

He slid a look to her. "Has he hung that broken barn door yet?"

"No," Libby said. "He needs help and Luke has been too busy to help him."

Tony shifted his gaze back to the window. "I'll think about it."

When the nurse came with some meds and some food, Libby put her hand on the stump of his leg. "I'll be back in a couple of days, okay?"

"Tell Ernest not to try and hang that door by himself, just to hold on," Tony said.

Libby smiled. "I will."

On her way out, she stopped by the office. Rosie, the receptionist was sitting behind her desk. "Oh . . . hi," Rosie said. "It's Libby, right?"

"Yes . . . Libby. Is Dr. Huber in?"

It happened that Dr. Huber was in, and she was happy to spare a few minutes to see Libby.

Dr. Huber smiled sympathetically when Libby told her what had happened since leaving Mountain View. "Take your meds,

Libby, and give my friend Linda a call," she said, jotting down the name of a therapist who lived near Pine River.

As luck would have it, Linda Walker had time to see Libby the next afternoon. She had a warm smile and piercing blue eyes. Her office was decorated with windmills—pictures, paintings, and one replica on her desk.

Libby explained her life to Linda, glossing over some details, stumbling over others. Linda's smile remained steady, and when Libby finished, she said, "I think I can help you. Shall we start on Tuesday?"

"I don't have a lot of money," Libby said apologetically.

"That's okay. We'll work it out."

Libby thanked her. On her way out, she asked about the windmills.

"Oh, those," Linda said, looking around the walls. "I don't know, I just like them. They spin with the wind. I sort of like that idea, spinning with the wind, letting life carry us along instead of trying to carry life on our backs, you know?"

Yes, Libby knew all about that, and thought she and Linda would be a good match.

Tony was released from Mountain View a couple of weeks later with a new bag of meds and a slightly more positive outlook than he'd had prior to arriving at the facility. Libby made the drive to get Tony and bring him home. When she arrived to pick him up, he introduced her to two other war vets, Jason and Doug. Doug had also been a patient at Mountain View. Jason was merely homeless. Libby brought all three men back to Homecoming Ranch.

"What are we doing here?" Madeline whispered as Ernest showed the men around. "Are we starting a camp for veterans?"

"We could do worse things," Libby said. "Like weddings."

Madeline blinked. And then she laughed. "There will be at least one more," she said. "Luke and I are setting a date, and we have so much to do!"

Madeline wasn't kidding—now that she and Luke had decided to make their relationship official, she was engrossed in the planning for it. Libby was just as busy, getting ready for the 5k race, which would be held Thanksgiving morning. She was waiting on some information from the Veteran's Administration—once she had that, she'd be ready to talk to Madeline about her ideas for Homecoming Ranch.

Funny how these things worked out, Libby thought. At night, she could see the lights on in the bunkhouse and could imagine the three men under Ernest's watchful eye, who, surprisingly, had taken a liking to his role as a sort of den mother. The three men liked to keep busy during the day, and Ernest put them to work finishing a third cabin.

The rhythm returned to their days, and while Libby kept busy working on her plan and the race, Sam never left her thoughts. He consumed her, filling her up with worry and regret. She missed him, missed his smile, his easy manner. She missed the way he made her feel—attractive, special . . . like he'd never let her go. She mourned the bond they'd shared, that deep connection to someone in this life who understood the private hell she'd suffered. Libby's disappointment in herself sickened her—with one single lapse of judgment she had jeopardized the best thing to happen to her. It was real this time, and she'd blown it. She had let him down in the worst way, and in doing so, had let herself down.

Had it not been for Linda Walker, she might have submerged herself in her disappointment and lost herself again. But it was worse than that, so much worse—she couldn't imagine the depth of Sam's disappointment. He had been the one to believe in her when no one else would. He had been there for her, propping her up, loving her, and she had let him down. She would never forgive herself if she had somehow compromised his recovery. She wanted to apologize to him, to make him understand how much he meant to her, if that was even possible.

She debated going to see him, but honestly, Libby didn't know if she could bear to see the disappointment in his eyes. Or worse, that dark, cold look he'd given her the night of the auction. And then again, she feared she would never see him again if she didn't.

With no clear solution, she just kept working and brooding, and seeing Dr. Walker, looking and hoping for the right answer.

One afternoon, Libby was in the dining room reviewing the information the Veteran's Administration had sent her about potential grant opportunities when the sound of a vehicle drew her attention. Libby's heart leapt with hope as it did every time she heard an unfamiliar vehicle on the road: *Sam.*

She jumped up and hurried to the door. Madeline appeared from the kitchen. "Who's that?" she asked.

The car that pulled into the drive was not Sam. It was not a car Libby recognized. The driver's door opened and from it emerged a very thin woman with long, sleek, blond hair. She stepped out of the car and tossed a leather tote bag over her shoulder, and marched around the car and up the stairs. She opened the door to the house and walked in.

"I'm back, bitches," she said, and moved past a stunned Libby and Madeline into the living room.

Madeline shot an accusing look at Libby. "Am I hallucinating? Or is that Emma?"

"It's Emma," Libby said, and followed Emma into the living room. "Emma?"

"What?" Emma said, and flopped down on the couch.

"Don't you *call*?" Libby asked. "You just show up without a word of warning?"

Emma's green-eyed gaze flicked over Libby. "You look like hell. They still calling you crazy in town?"

"How do you know that?" Madeline asked.

"Libby told me," Emma said, and shifted her gaze to Madeline, giving her the once-over. "For someone who couldn't wait to get the hell out of Dodge, you're still hanging around, I see."

Madeline folded her arms. "I think you mean I'm still being responsible."

"Nope. That's not what I meant," Emma said.

"Wait," Libby said, throwing up her hands before Emma and Madeline could begin to argue. "Emma, why are you here?"

"*Why?* I told you I'd come help you."

"But that was more than a month ago!"

Emma shrugged. "I had some things to do. So when am I going to meet the guy who needs all this fundraising?"

"Who, Leo?" Madeline asked, looking a little horrified.

"Yes, Leo." Something wasn't quite right with Emma. She seemed far too casual, and yet, she kept glancing past Libby and out the front windows as if she expected to see someone coming up the drive. "Is he around?"

"No," Libby said. "He lives in Pine River."

Emma looked around the room. "Well then, do you have anything to eat?" she asked, and pressed a hand against her concave belly. "It's a long drive from Los Angeles."

"You drove from Los Angeles without eating," Madeline said, her voice full of disbelief.

"I'll make you something," Libby said.

"Libby!" Madeline cried. "Emma just waltzes in here without a word and you're going to cook for her?"

"I didn't waltz in without a word," Emma said. "I told Libby I was going to come and help her. So I'm here to help. Try not to get your panties in a wad because, apparently, we're going to be stuck here together for a little while."

"Oh no," Madeline said.

"Oh yes," Emma said.

Emma chose the room at the end of the hall with a view of the forest. It had been a study at one point, and was as far from the rest of the house as one could possibly get. Libby helped bring her things in while Madeline hightailed it into town to be with Luke.

Emma's things consisted of the tote bag she would not let out of her sight, and a small suitcase, which she pointed to for Libby to carry. "So Madeline's really going to marry Luke Kendrick, huh?" Emma asked as she examined herself in a faded mirror. "He's hot."

Libby hoped Emma wasn't one of those women who stole boyfriends and husbands. She certainly had the looks to pull something like that off if she wanted. That was the thing about Emma—even though she and Libby had known each other for years, Libby didn't really know her at all.

Emma suddenly swung around and looked at Libby. "What about you? Where's *your* boyfriend?"

"Who, Ryan? The one who dumped me?"

"No, not him," Emma scoffed. "He's a dick. If you're still with him, no wonder everyone thinks you're batshit crazy."

"Please don't sugarcoat your opinions on my account," Libby said drily.

"Okay, so who is the guy that has you all sad looking?"

"God, is it so obvious?" Libby asked, pressing her hands to her cheeks.

"It's always a guy who takes the sparkle out of us," Emma said. "Just zaps it right out," she said with a snap of her fingers, then whirled around and fell backward on the bed. "So tell me."

Libby told her. She told her about Ryan, and how Sam had been there for her, saving her from herself more than once. She told Emma what had happened the last night she'd seen Sam. She told her how she'd been moping around for the last couple of weeks, seeing a therapist, making plans, working the race, but feeling numb and empty and missing him, missing him so deeply.

When she finished, Emma sighed, stacked her hands behind her head and said, "Far be it from me to ever tell another woman how to do her business, but for shit's sake, Libby, go *talk* to him. At least tell him you're sorry. He's probably in some bar drinking right now because he misses you so."

"I don't think so—he's a recovering alcoholic."

"Oh great, it just gets better," Emma said. "Then maybe he's hoeing weeds, I don't know. Just go *talk* to him."

"It's not that simple," Libby said.

"Why not?"

"Because he won't return my phone calls," Libby said. "And I don't want to push him into a confrontation. Especially since that worked so well with Ryan."

Emma waved a hand at her. "You have to. Men are notorious for not wanting to talk about feelings. You have to push them up against the wall sometimes."

"But if I push too hard, I could lose him," Libby argued.

"Sounds to me like maybe you already have. And if you haven't, and he gets all bent out of shape and weepy about it, then who cares? You don't need a fragile little flower as a life mate."

She had a point. The next morning, Libby drove to Sam's house.

# THIRTY

Sam knew the sound of Libby's car—he'd heard it a few times over the last couple of weeks, motoring down the road into town, and back up to the ranch again. Every time he heard it, he wondered if she would stop.

Every time, he hoped she wouldn't, a hope that was quickly followed by a contradicting hope that she would stop. Sam was clearly and annoyingly conflicted. He missed Libby so much, but his apprehension about her was powerful.

After the near-disaster with Tony, Sam had been badly shaken. He'd thought he had a grip on Tony, that Tony was getting better. He'd worried that Tony would drink—but to take those pills? Sam had been caught off guard by it. He'd thought they were past that.

When he'd found Tony that night, he'd grabbed up the empty pill bottle, had somehow gotten Tony to stand, then had driven recklessly back to Pine River, where he'd paced the halls, every step just one away from a drink to dull his fear, until the doctor told him Tony was going to make it.

Sam wasn't angry with Libby for what had happened to Tony. Sam understood better than most how things could happen that made a man want to drink, and that was what happened to Tony. Sam was angry with Libby for being unpredictable in her emotions, and for letting emotion cloud her judgment.

He recognized that was an impossible standard to put on anyone. He understood he needed too much from her. It didn't make losing her any less painful.

After that night of so many near-misses, Sam slid back into his solitary existence, keeping his distance from others. But Libby dominated his thoughts. The ache of missing her, of wanting her, would not go away, no matter what he did. At least at home, he was safe. He needed sameness. He needed black and white. He couldn't risk her, not now.

He had meant to tell her this, to explain why he was breaking it off. At first, he'd been too angry to speak to her. And as each day passed, it became a little easier to ease away from the love he'd had and simply turn his back. Too easy. He was surprised that he, of all people, who valued integrity and honesty above all else, could just walk away.

So when he heard her car slow and turn on the road that led up to his house, he groaned. That was the thing about mountain valleys—one could hear people coming literally from miles away. Sam could have stopped what he was doing, cleaned up, met her out front and turned her away, but instead, he kept working on his latest creation—a birdhouse made like a Japanese pagoda.

Libby's car stopped. He heard her knocking on his door. A moment later, he heard her walking around his house, her feet on his deck, coming closer to his work shed.

He knew she was at the door, standing behind him, and still, he didn't turn around.

"You've come this far, you may as well come in," he said.

"Thank you," she said, and her voice slid over him like warm honey. He felt her step in deeper, could feel her presence fill up his shed.

"What are you making?" she asked.

"Japanese pagoda." He took a breath, put down his tools, and turned around to face her. His heart caught, midbeat, at the sight of her, the curly black hair framing her face, the jeans hugging her body and tucked into rain boots. She wore a tight sweater, and it seemed to him that she'd lost a little weight. Her eyes were two little shimmering pools.

"How are you?" he asked.

"Ah . . . okay, I guess," she said, and nervously shoved her hands into her back pockets. "How are you?"

"Okay."

"You don't pick up your phone these days."

"I've been busy." *Busy missing you.*

She nodded, pressed her lips together. "Well, I guess I should just say what I came to say," she said, sounding resigned. "I came to apologize, Sam. I have tried to think of the right words that would convey just how sorry I am for everything, but I can't seem to find them. Nothing seems adequate. Sorry doesn't begin to cut it, I know it, but that's all I have. So I'm sorry," she said, and her eyes began to glisten with tears. "From the bottom of my heart, from the depth of my soul, I am deeply, truly, sorry."

That apology broke his heart. "I know you are, baby," he said quietly, and Libby's eyes welled even more.

"I've started seeing a therapist," she said. "She's helping me a lot. She likes windmills, and she says that we should let life carry us . . ." She paused, gave her head a slight shake. "She's really helped me to understand what I did was wrong, and better yet, to understand why I do things like that."

"That's great," he said. He could feel his chest constricting around his heart, squeezing it. This was not what he wanted—what he wanted was to wrap his arms around her, feel her breath in his ear, her body warm and soft against his.

"Since you won't return my calls, I came up here to tell you this. It's important to me that you know how sorry I am, and how . . . how much I love you, Sam."

Sam couldn't help himself; he reached out and stroked her wild hair, recalling the feel of it on his face when they made love. His heart squeezed again, and he dropped his hand.

She mistook that caress for encouragement. "Things are better now," she said. "I've been working on a plan for the ranch, I'm working on the race. I think I am finally to a place where I can manage my . . ." She made a gesture at herself. "My anger and disappointment. The past is not important to me anymore. *You're* important."

He pushed his hand through his hair. "I'm glad to hear it. But I can't be with you, Libby. Not because I'm mad or disappointed, but because I'm an alcoholic," he said, and pressed his hand to his chest. "I told you once that I walk a tightrope every single day of my life. It's the truth. The only difference between me and Tony is that, somehow, I managed not to pick up a bottle again. And when you . . . when you took those kids," he said, swallowing down the bitter reminder of that evening, "I felt an urge to drink that I haven't felt in a very long time. I felt myself inching closer to a drink, to drown the anxiety. And because I went into the bar to get you, to rescue you again, I didn't get to Tony in time. Maybe if I had, I could have helped him. I might have at least stopped him from picking up the booze and the pills."

"Don't say that," Libby whispered, her voice breaking.

"But it's true, Libby. I let Tony down, I let myself down. I know what I need. I need an even keel. I can't rush to everyone's rescue anymore. I can't save every soldier who wrestles with demons. The only thing I can do is save myself, one day at a time."

"You didn't have to save me," Libby said. "You don't ever have to save me. You could have let me take the fall for once instead of coming to my rescue."

"What, and let you be arrested? Let that man talk you into going home and doing God knows what?" he asked skeptically.

"Maybe," she said with a shrug. "Actions have consequences, but you didn't allow me to have them."

Sam laughed with surprise. "Next time, I'll be sure and let you have them."

"You're missing the point," she said. "Sometimes, people need to fall on their faces so that they can get back up. They need to lie on the floor of Mountain View and try to peel their shoulders up. It's not your fault that Tony tried to take his own life. It's not your fault that I took Alice to get her costume or tried to talk to Ryan."

"I know that, Libby," he said patiently. "But this is a matter of trust between us. Of stability. Do you understand that?"

A tear slipped from her eye, and Sam couldn't help himself; he stepped forward, cupped her face in his hands. "Look, I'm not asking you to change or to be something you're not. But I can't be with someone who is impetuous, because *I* can't survive it. I know that about me."

She grabbed his wrist and wrapped her fingers tightly around it. "Maybe I am impetuous from time to time, but I'm just me, living my life as best as I know how. Sometimes I make mistakes. Sometimes I fall. It's called life, Sam."

But it wasn't his life.

"I love you, I do, I love you," she said earnestly. "I was numb before I met you, Sam. I wasn't really breathing until I met you. You helped me find my way, to feel as if I was living again, really living. I still love you, I miss you every moment, and I want to be with you."

Sam kissed her forehead, then freed himself from her hold. "I can't, Libby. I've worked too hard and struggled too long to risk it."

He stepped back, turned to his Japanese pagoda. He waited for her tearful promises, or at least the sound of her retreat.

But Libby said, "So this is the old *It's not you, it's me* speech, huh?" she said, her voice low and shaking. "You know what, Sam? These last two weeks, I've been so worried about how disappointed you must be. But I suddenly get it—you're just a coward."

Sam's pulse leapt. He slowly turned around. "What did you say?"

"You heard me," she said angrily. "You're a *coward.* You're so afraid of disappointment, of being hurt, of *living* that you hide up here with your birdhouses and pretend that you're doing some noble thing!"

Her outburst stunned Sam. "Are you really going to stand there and lecture *me*?"

"Yes! At least I *own* my weaknesses. At least I *try* and face them. But you don't even do that! Yes, you're sober. Yes, you've fought a long, hard battle, and you have to keep fighting for the rest of your life. I get that, I admire that. But you know what, Sam? You hide behind it!" She lurched forward, her gaze piercing his. "Because *you* are a coward," she said, poking him hard in the chest with each word.

He caught her finger in his fist. "You have no idea what I'm talking about."

"Yes I do," she said, jerking her hand free. "We've both made mistakes. We've both paid huge prices for them. But I'm not afraid to try again, Sam. What I'm afraid of is *not* trying, of ending up in some tiny little shed making birdhouses for the rest of my life instead of finding love and happiness and discovering what it is

I've been stumbling around and looking for. But you? You will hide in here and occasionally go out to check on people who are far more damaged than you, so that you can keep patting yourself on the back, telling yourself you're doing the right thing by *hiding*! Well guess what, you're in luck!" she cried, casting her arms wide. "You don't have to check on me ever again, because I don't have any use for cowards." She fled then, running across his deck.

Sam stood where she'd left him, trying to find his breath. He felt as if she'd just rammed a fist into his gut, had knocked his feet out from beneath him. He slowly turned back to his pagoda. He took a deep breath. And then another. And then he picked up the hammer and smashed his pagoda to pieces.

# THIRTY-ONE

Libby drove in a blind rage back to Homecoming Ranch, going much too fast on the gravel road up to the house, so that her car bounced and landed sideways a couple of times.

As she barreled into the drive, Tony limped out onto the lawn, his eyes wide, and watched her car slide to a stop before the house. "Hey, *hey*!" he shouted, waving his hand at her. "What are you doing? I've worked hard on that car, and you're going to ruin it driving like that!"

"Sorry," Libby said, and waved at Jason, who had wandered out of the garage to see what the commotion was about. Inside the garage, Libby could see Ernest's old work truck, up on blocks.

"What's going on?" Jason asked.

"I'll tell you what's going on!" Libby shouted. "It's a new day at Homecoming Ranch. Stay tuned, guys!"

She ignored their looks of surprise and jogged up the steps, bursting into the house. She stood in the entry a moment, her fists curled, her breath coming in furious, angry gulps. She hated Sam, hated him for being so damn afraid of life.

"What is going on?" Madeline called out, appearing at the top of the stairs. "Has something happened?"

"I need to talk to you and Emma," Libby said, and stalked into the living room, starting a bit when she saw that Emma was already there, lounging on the couch in a long sweater and a pair of thick tights. She looked amused as Libby passed through to the dining room, gathered her papers, and returned to the living room.

Madeline came in behind her. "What the hell has happened?"

"You sound like you think she's had another nervous breakdown," Emma said casually.

Madeline sighed and rolled her eyes. "Emma, you don't know what all has gone on here—"

"Yeah, but I don't think she's had another *breakdown*—"

"Hey. Please," Libby said, holding up her hands. "I need to talk to you both. I've been doing some thinking. And some study and research and talking to people. I think I have a great idea for what to do with Homecoming Ranch."

Both of her sisters groaned and fell back against the couch, as if they'd had this conversation dozens of times before. Which, perhaps they had. But Libby wasn't going to stop now. Sam's rejection was a huge blow. She'd always believed herself to be stable and trustworthy—at least she used to be. But he was right, in the last months, her irrational anger had clouded everything. Everything! She was guilty of the same thing she'd accused Sam of: hiding. Only Libby had hid behind her anger. She had refused to face reality or deal with it until it bubbled out in angry outbursts.

"Do we really have to have this conversation?" Emma sighed, her eyes closed now.

"What's wrong, Emma?" Madeline said. "One time too many for you? Try a dozen times. Try living out here trying to make sense of this place," Madeline said.

"Jesus, Madeline, are you going to hold a grudge forever?" Emma asked.

Things were going to change in Libby's life. This morning's conversation with Sam had been a turning point. He was always talking about turning the page, and she was doing it. Libby could feel it in her, could feel the sludge turning over to new, clean waters. "Seriously, can you guys snipe at each other later? Listen—did either of you ever see *The Bachelor* episode where the guy chose one girl, but then spent some time with her, and later, chose the runner-up?"

"*What?*" said Madeline and Emma in unison.

"Never mind," Libby said with a wave her hand. "What I am trying to say is that we can't turn Homecoming Ranch into a destination-event place, agreed? We tried, but we all know they're laughing at us in Pine River for Austin and Gary's wedding—"

"*What?*" Madeline said, sitting up. "Who's laughing?"

"It doesn't matter, Madeline. I've been doing some investigating, and I've put together a business plan for something that is worthy of our time and attention."

"Do tell," Emma drawled.

"Tony is doing pretty good out here, right? And now he's got his friends, Jason and Doug. We have the bunkhouse, and we have three cabins."

"So?" Emma said.

"So . . . what would you think of making Homecoming Ranch a rehabilitation center for war vets?"

Neither Emma nor Madeline spoke. They stared at her as if they thought she was truly crazy.

"Think about it," Libby rushed ahead. "There is always work to be done, and these guys really respond to having something to do. I talked to my therapist—"

"You have a therapist?" Emma interjected.

"Yes, I have a therapist," Libby said impatiently. "I talked to her about the sort of things we could do, from cognitive therapies, to desensitization training, to even equine or dog therapy. She also said there are a lot people around here who would volunteer their time to help."

Madeline, always practical, shook her head. "But how do we *pay* for something like that?"

"We solicit funds. We apply to the federal agency for grants that exist for his very thing. But to start? I have a business plan written up. And I am not taking no for an answer from Michelle again."

Emma slowly sat up. "Who's Michelle? Whoever she is, I don't care. This idea sounds much better to me than a bunch of weddings. I like it. I like it a lot."

Libby looked at Madeline. "What do you think?"

Madeline looked at Emma, then at Libby. "I don't know," she said. "For me, it would depend on the funding. If we can't get funding, there is no point in talking about it, because we are surviving on fumes as it is."

"We just raised fifteen thousand dollars for Leo Kendrick's van in one silent auction," Libby said. "And that was without any real campaign. It was people asking people to donate something we could bid on. Imagine what we'd be able to raise if we had a *plan.* And you know what? I am going to prove it with the 5k race we are doing at the end of this month."

"I'm in," Emma said.

Madeline looked at her with surprise. "Geez, Emma—do you mind at least telling us why, after months of silence, you're suddenly on board? And *here*? And do you plan on sticking around this time, or disappearing again?"

"Who knows?" Emma said. She stood and stretched her arms high overhead. "For the moment, I'm in." She walked out of the living room into the kitchen.

Madeline stared at Emma's departing back.

"Madeline, let's try it," Libby said. "We have nothing to lose by trying."

Madeline sighed. She rubbed her temples a moment. "Okay," she said, and looked up. "But prove that we can do it, Libby. Prove to me that we can raise funds to support this . . . camp, or whatever we're going to call it. And I want to see that business plan. I want to know what we're in for."

The sound Libby imagined was her page being turned. "We're going to call it Homecoming Ranch, because that's what it is—a homecoming." She handed Madeline her papers. "It's all there."

The first thing Libby did was call and arrange a meeting with Michelle. She was prepared for resistance, for disdain, for a flat-out *no.* Nevertheless, she dressed in her best outfit, stuffed her presentation into a briefcase she'd borrowed from Madeline, and marched into the bank as if she took out loans all the time.

Much to her surprise, Michelle loved the idea. "It's a *great* use of the ranch," she said as she pored over Libby's presentation again. "Personally, I think this is something our community would get behind. But in order to lend you money, I am going to need to see some sort of plan for how much you anticipate in fundraising and federal grants in one-year, two-year, and three-year outlooks. Come back with more details, and we'll see what we can work out."

Libby walked out of the bank feeling as if she were walking on air. She stopped on the sidewalk and pulled out her phone to call Madeline and give her the good news when she saw Gwen Spangler walk out of a dress shop. Gwen saw Libby at the same moment, and she instantly turned the other way.

"Gwen!" Libby shouted.

Gwen walked faster.

Libby ran to catch up. "Gwen, please," she said. "Just give me a moment. One moment."

Gwen's shoulders sagged with a heavy sigh, but she turned around. "What, Libby?"

Libby hadn't really thought through exactly what she'd say when she saw Gwen again, so she said the simplest thing that came to mind. "I'm sorry. I am so very sorry for scaring you. I should never have taken Alice to get her costume. But, Gwen, you know me. I would *never* in a million years harm one hair on either of their heads."

"Okay, you're sorry," Gwen said, and turned to go.

"Can I just . . . Gwen, wait. *Please.*"

Gwen sighed and turned partially toward her. "What?"

"Here's the thing, Gwen," Libby said, taking a cautious step forward. "You have two exceptional children. Beautiful, exceptional children. And I . . . I love them so much," she said, alarmed that her eyes would water so quickly. "There is a huge gaping hole in my heart where they were, but I want you to know that you don't have to worry about me anymore." A tear slid down Libby's cheek, and it appalled her. She swiped at it. "Ignore the tears, will you? Anyway, I know I should have let go the minute you were back in the picture, and I didn't. I have no excuse but that I was bruised and I loved the kids so much, and they were suddenly ripped from my life, and I . . . I couldn't deal with that. It didn't help that Ryan wasn't exactly straight about what was going on, or that I never saw it coming, or that I was apparently the only one in Pine River who didn't see what was happening between you and him . . ."

God, she was mangling this. She sighed.

"Look, I made some horrible decisions. I'm not offering an excuse. I only wanted to tell you that I am sorry. And that I love your children."

Gwen folded her arms. Her eyes narrowed. Libby expected her to say she was going to call the cops. But she said, "Are you being real with me now?"

"Yes," Libby said, nodding. "Completely."

"Well then this is the first sane thing you've said since I came back to town," Gwen said.

"It is?"

"My kids have missed you, too, Libby. Honestly? I think part of me didn't want them around you because of that. Do you know how many times I hear Libby this or Libby that? Do you know how guilty I have felt that I had to leave them to go and get my license? I thought Ryan would take care of them. I thought he would live up to the promises he made, but I should have known he wouldn't or couldn't do it by himself."

Libby's heart began to swell with relief. She couldn't suppress a small smile.

"And you're right, Ryan isn't the most truthful guy in town. I wondered what bullshit he fed you."

"He knew how to play me, no doubt of that," Libby agreed.

Gwen smiled a little. She glanced down at the ground a moment. "I thought you had some real hutzpah showing up on my committee."

"I've known Leo since we were little, Gwen. I really—"

"No, Libby, I mean that I kind of admired you for it. Made me mad as hell, but I admired you for having the courage."

"I wish you hadn't been afraid of me," Libby said. "I would never hurt Alice or Max."

"Oh, I know," Gwen said with a flick of her wrist. "I was just *so* pissed off." She looked curiously at Libby. "Thanks for being honest," she said.

Libby nodded. "I just wish I'd said this weeks ago."

Gwen looked down the street and said, "I hope you and Sam work it out. He's a great guy."

That surprised Libby. "How . . . ?"

"God, Libby, everyone knows," Gwen said. "This is Pine River. You tie your shoelace wrong or pick up a golf club and everyone knows." She smiled a little at her joke and glanced at her watch. "I've got to run. The Methodist's Women's Group is meeting this afternoon. We're still looking for ways to raise money. Are you still doing the race?"

"It's going to be a Thanksgiving Day turkey trot," Libby said proudly. "We'll be putting posters around town later this week."

"Well . . . good luck. See you around town." Gwen turned and walked away.

Libby smiled heavenward. *"Finally,"* she whispered. Finally, a few things were going her way.

# THIRTY-TWO

I'm never one to complain, no matter what Marisol says, but this has *not* been my month. First, the Methodists worked hard and raised about eighteen thousand dollars, all told. I know that sounds like a lot of money to *you,* but it's not *van* money. I hate to say it, but my last shot at getting my van before the big game is Libby Tyler's race on Thanksgiving Day.

At first, I didn't have much hope of that working out, either, not after what happened the night of the silent auction, and I don't mind saying that all those police officers really detracted from my spotlight. Don't judge me—it's not like I get the spotlight very often.

It's not that I think Libby can't pull it off, because I don't think that. I know Libby, and once she gets her head on straight, she's a tenacious little bundle of energy. But people have been kind of skittish around her, and I thought they might not come out to run if they thought she'd be chasing after them with a baseball bat or lurking in the shadows to steal their kids. You know what I mean.

I was all depressed about it, but then, who should show up but Emma Tyler! She's really pretty, just ask any guy in town, and she's been hanging around here a lot. A *lot.* I told Marisol she is totally into me, and Marisol was all, "You are a pig, Leo. You think every woman in a skirt wants you."

Marisol exaggerates. In her defense, she was probably going into labor that very minute, because she kept going on about her contractions, and, sure enough, about ten hours later, she gave birth to a baby girl. Between you and me, I was hoping for a boy, because the last thing Pine River needs is *two* hot-tempered Latinas giving me a sponge bath. Don't think for a minute Marisol is going to leave that little stinker home when she comes back to work. That stinker just better keep her tiny mitts off my new game, *Starbenders.*

So back to Emma. I don't think *every* woman wants me, but come on, I'm not so chairbound that I don't know my own magnetism. And I haven't had *every* muscle atrophy, if you know what I mean, and I know when a chick digs me. Emma Tyler digs me. She's always smiling and touching me. I told Luke and he said that the MND was apparently creeping into my brain and making it seize because there was no way Emma Tyler was hot for me.

I told Luke he should go and get married already and get out of my face, and then he threw me a curve ball and said he *is* getting married. On New Year's Eve. Great, there go all my party plans.

Anyway, Emma is helping Libby pull together the race, and she knows what she's doing because she's like an official Event Planner, and it's obvious that every red-blooded male in town will come out just to see Emma put on some skimpy running shorts and bounce down the street. You should see Jackson Crane practically drool in her presence. Every guy in town is into Emma.

Everyone but Sam Winters, who is still moping over Libby.

Sam dropped by the other day, and I said, "Dude, do yourself a favor and go and talk to Libby. She's doing great on the race."

Sam said, "I don't think that's a good idea," but he was looking the other way when he said it, and I couldn't tell what he was thinking, and I assumed he was being stubborn. Maybe as stubborn as Libby can be, which makes them a perfect match. And that reminded me of Dad's mule.

So I said, "Hey, Dad, do you remember that old mule you used to keep up at the ranch?"

Dad was whittling something, and he looked like he just realized at exactly that moment that Sam and I were on the deck with him and said, "What? Yeah, I remember. Molly was her name."

I said to Sam, "Dad loved that old mule so much," and Dad snorted and said, "I didn't *love* her. But I liked her well enough."

And I said, "He loved her like his first love until she kicked him in the ribs."

"That was that," Dad said, and went back to whittling.

I grinned at Sam, who was looking at me weird, like he couldn't make out the message in the mule story. He was probably thinking he was the mule. He was, but there were two mules in this story, and naturally, I had to spell it out to him.

"He still loves her," I said. "But she kicked him, and it made him mad, so now he acts like he didn't love her so much."

"She was a goddamn mule, Leo," Dad said, like he was insulted I would imply he could love a mule. But he did. Every night at supper he'd chuckle when he told us what old Molly had done that day. Mom once told him to go sleep with Molly if he liked her so much.

"My point is, don't do what Dad did. Get over your mad and go see Libby. You don't want to turn her into glue."

Dad got pissed at the reminder of what happened to Molly and said, "What the hell is the matter with you, Leo?" And I said, "I have MND," and Dad stomped off. But Sam laughed.

Anyway, that's all I said to Sam, because who should come

walking up just then? If you guessed Emma Tyler, you'd be right. She was wearing these killer tight pants and sweater, and I'll just say this, I'm glad Marisol wasn't there, because in the last month of her pregnancy, I think she would have scratched Emma's eyes out. Emma was bringing me some chocolate pudding and Sam was suddenly much less interesting to me. He got up to go and I said, "Hey, don't forget the race! We gotta make this happen, because I am running out of time!"

Sam really looked startled, and I said, "Not *that* time. I mean, yeah, I'm running out of *that* time, but I meant time to get a van before the game."

"We'll make it happen," Emma said, and I wasn't sure she was even talking about the race, so I had to explain to her that Methodists are great, but they aren't that flush in the pockets, and then I had this great idea to call a family meeting to review where we are with the funds, and Emma was hanging on my every word, and when I looked up, Sam was gone.

Just like that old mule, Molly.

# THIRTY-THREE

Sam knew that she ran at the high school track every Monday, Wednesday, and Friday. She generally ran alone, and she ran if it rained or snowed.

Libby Tyler was on a mission.

At first, Sam just drove by, watching her jog around the track. After a couple of times of that, he started to pull over. He knew that she saw him but she wouldn't look at him. She just ran by.

One day, he got out of his truck, hopped over the fence, and ran behind her. He kept his distance, twenty yards behind her. Libby looked back once, and picked up her pace.

So did Sam.

He came Wednesday and did the same thing. She turned around once and shouted, "Whatever it is you're doing? It won't work!"

"Free country!" he shouted back at her.

Sam came back again on Friday. He had no idea what he was doing, really, but he liked running behind her. He liked the way her butt bounced, the way she held her form, her torso upright, her arms tight at her side. He liked just being in the same vicinity as her.

"You're crazy!" she shouted at him. "A stalker! I could call the cops!"

"So call them!" he shouted back at her.

Sam had heard around town that the Turkey Trot was already a success, that a thousand people had signed up to run, double what she'd hoped. After the city personnel and permits were paid, the race would clear more than enough to get Leo the van. Everything else was going to Homecoming Ranch, which was in the process of being converted to a military veteran's rehabilitation ranch.

This, Sam had heard from Tony, who had been invited to serve on the board of directors.

"You must be feeling better," Sam said when Tony told him the news.

Tony had smiled as he lit a cigarette. "I have my moments, I won't lie. But I've got a couple of guys around me now to help. And, you know, Cindy has been coming around."

Sam knew Cindy and figured she'd last about five minutes. But it was a sign of progress, and baby steps were necessary for Tony.

He really admired Libby for what she was doing—taking giant, leaping strides. She'd had a really bad summer, but somehow, she had turned it around and had become the town's little twinkling star with this race and the new plans for the ranch. That was what he called the turn of the page.

But that wasn't what had brought Sam to this track for the last two weeks. He had thought of little else than what she'd said that day in his shed. Libby was right—he *was* a coward. He had turned a blind eye to how he was walling himself off from the world, a little more every day. He had thought that as long as he was dragging other drunks to AA, he was doing what he needed to do. But somewhere along the line, he'd stopped living. The only time in the last two years he'd felt alive, like he was a fully functioning man again, was with Libby. And he'd pushed her out the moment it got a little messy.

He'd felt the void of her in his chest, in his bed, in his life. He didn't know what he was doing, running around behind her on the track, but he wanted her back, and this time, he wasn't going to let fear of falling stop him.

The following Monday, a week before Thanksgiving, he was sitting in the bleachers when she appeared. A front had come through, and it was freezing. He blew on his fingers as she slowly jogged by, warming up. She looked up at him, and from where he sat, he heard her muttering to herself.

Sam watched her do one full turn around the track. When she passed the second time, he walked down on the track and started running after her. Halfway around the track, Libby stopped and whirled around. "Why are you doing this? Why won't you leave me alone?"

"Why do you think?"

"Whatever," she snapped, and turned, started running.

So did Sam.

A quarter around the track, she stopped again and turned around. "You're wasting your time, Sam. Don't you have birdhouses to build? Old ladies to feed?"

He deserved that. "I'm not wasting my time. I love you, Libby. I should have run after you the day you called me a coward."

Libby stood there uncertainly, as if she didn't know what to do with him, as if she didn't believe him. "You *what*?" she shouted.

"I said, *I love you*!" he shouted back at her.

He didn't know what he expected, but he didn't expect her to run. That she did, suddenly sprinting away, across the interior field. She was fleeing.

Sam intercepted her midfield.

But Libby pushed him, and tried to escape. So Sam tackled her, bringing them both to the hard ground, landing on his back with her on top, and then quickly rolling over, trapping her beneath him.

"Get *off* me," she said, kicking at him.

"Not until you listen to me."

She shoved at his chest. "I don't want to hear it!"

"You were right, do you want to hear that? You were *right*, Libby Tyler, I *am* a coward. I was afraid of loving you, afraid of giving all to you and being disappointed. And, by God, I'm still afraid of that, but I'm a helluva lot more afraid of missing out on the happiness I had with you if I don't at least *try*. I've thought a lot about what you said, and you were *right*."

She stopped struggling and glared up at him. "I was right . . . but? There's a but, isn't there? Some rule I have to follow."

"No buts," he said. "I just love you, Libby. And I've missed you so damn much."

"I don't believe you! How do I know you won't decide I'm too impetuous, or too much trouble, or too unpredictable for your carefully crafted life? How do I know that if I get mad at someone, you won't break it off? How can I *trust* you?"

"The same way I'm going to trust you, one day at a time. I'm going to believe that you have learned from the things that happened to you this summer and you've moved on. I'm going to believe that you see a future in us, and you are going to work to make it happen, just like you've made the race happen, just like you've made Homecoming Ranch happen."

"That's too easy, Sam!" she said angrily. "You can't pretend everything is suddenly okay! You can't sweep it all under a rug!"

"I am not pretending everything is okay, baby. But I've thought a lot about what you mean to me. I have thought even more about what happened between us, and I realize, I love you too much to let you go because I have issues. I love you too much to hide behind a birdhouse anymore, okay? I want to move on. I want to be us again."

"Maybe I don't," she said, shoving against him. "Maybe I don't know how I will ever believe that you won't reject me if the going gets tough."

Sam sighed, realizing that his fear of disappointment was matched only by her fear of rejection. He pushed back loose tendrils from her face. "We're a pair, aren't we? So much crap to overcome." He rolled off of her and sat up, looping his arms around his knees. "You're right, Libby. It's a gamble for us both. I guess trust is not something that can be promised, it has to be earned. But I know that I'm willing to do whatever it takes to earn yours."

Libby pushed herself up, too, and sat beside him. A wind swept through the field, and Libby leaned over, rested her head against his shoulder. Sam put his arm around her and pulled her into his side.

"I'm not saying I'm on board with that," she said. "Because I'm not. I'm pretty mad at you."

"I know."

"But if I were to get on board, and I said that I would do whatever it took to earn your trust, too, how exactly would I do that? What would happen?" She looked up at him. "Where do we go from here?"

"We start over," Sam said. "But without the restraining order."

"Or the birdhouses."

He smiled. "Deal."

She nestled closer to him. "I don't really want you to give up making birdhouses. But maybe you could bring one or two up to the ranch?"

He could feel the tide turning, could feel Libby turning back to him. "Sure," he said. "Maybe I'll teach those guys how to make them."

"Perfect. They can squeeze in birdhouse construction between yoga and equine therapy." She laughed. "I'm kidding. Sort of." She looked at him again, her gaze searching his. "Do you really think we could start over? Do you really think we could squash all the little demons that seem to dance around us?"

"I do," he said, and pulled her onto his lap to straddle him. "It won't be easy, and I think we have to be smart about it. But I at least want to try, Libby. More than anything I have ever wanted in my life, I want to try and make it with you. Do you?"

Libby sighed and wrapped her arms around his neck. "Me too. More than anything, Sam. More than you could possibly imagine. But not until I'm through being mad at you."

"I'll make it up to you," he said, and kissed her, his tongue meeting hers, his hands going around her, pressing her warmth to him.

"Show me."

That was it for Sam. He rolled again, putting her once more on her back in the middle of the field. He kissed her deeply, with all the longing that had kept him awake and eaten away at him this last month. His hands moved down the body he'd missed in his bed, slipping under her hoodie and up to her breast.

Libby giggled into his mouth. "We're on the high school track. Won't we get in trouble?"

"Who cares?"

"Well, *I* do," she said. "I've turned over a new leaf and I'm trying very hard to stay out of trouble."

"Impossible," he said against her neck. But he stood up, helped her up, and with his arm around her waist, they ran for his truck.

They made it as far as the backseat, the heavily tinted windows hiding them from the world. And as Sam slid into her, he knew it was right, that his life had never been so right. For the first time in a couple of long, hard years, he wasn't worried. He wasn't afraid. He was filled with happiness and relief.

# THIRTY-FOUR

On Thanksgiving Day, Libby, Sam, and Luke completed the 5k Turkey Trot. Libby's event did indeed raise more than enough to buy Leo's van, as well as provide some starting funds for the Homecoming Ranch Veteran's Rehabilitation Center. It was truly a day of thanks and celebration.

They rushed back to the ranch to prepare for the feast. Bob Kendrick was already there with Leo, who was in the living room, expounding on what his van would look like.

Libby and Madeline had made a turkey and all the Thanksgiving trimmings. They were a long way from the uneasy place where they had started out as newly discovered sisters. There were still a few bumps in the road, but on that day, Libby felt as if she and Madeline could have been doing this all their lives. Madeline felt like a sister.

It was a cold and gloomy day, but Luke and Tony had made sure the heaters were going in the barn, where they intended to dine.

Emma was not impressed with the idea. "So country," she said.

"It's fun," Libby reminded her.

"If you like hoedowns and rodeos, maybe," Emma had said, and had wandered into the living room to sit next to Leo.

When the meal was ready, Libby instructed everyone to grab a dish and head for the barn. Bob Kendrick took Leo down to the barn. They were followed by Jackson Crane, Dani, Libby's mother and her family, Patti and Greg Kendrick, Marisol and Javier and their newborn, Tony and the three vets who were living up at the ranch now, and, of course, Emma, Libby, and Madeline. Only Ernest was missing, having gone to Albuquerque to spend the holiday with his mother.

Libby stood to one side in the barn, watching them all put the food on the table and argue over who sat where.

*This is it*, she thought, happily. This was the thing she had sought all her life. A family, big and extended, all hers. She'd found that place to belong.

She'd had that feeling about Homecoming Ranch from the moment she'd learned of it, that it was hers. Even though she didn't understand all the reasons she'd needed to fight for it, she'd always understood she had to fight. She was fighting for more than a ranch. She was fighting to heal, to grow, to move on with her life, and she'd never felt more content than she did that Thanksgiving Day.

"What are you doing?"

Sam stepped up behind her, put his arms around her middle, and kissed her temple. He was the big reason for Libby's sense of contentment. They'd begun slowly on this second time around, taking things one day at a time, and it was working. "I'm just being thankful," she said, and twisted about in his arms. She went up on her tiptoes to kiss him.

"What's that for?" he asked.

"Because I love you. And to thank you for looking out for me when I wasn't looking out for myself. I don't know where I'd be without you, Sam."

He laughed. "In jail," he said.

They stood together and watched Bob maneuver Leo to the end of the table and set up his liquid food with the silly straw. Everyone was finding their seats, filling wineglasses.

"This is where we belong, Sam," she said. "You and me with all these people. I hope we fill it to the rafters with love."

Sam kissed her, then took her hand in his. "There will be more love here than you'll be able to handle, Crazy Pants. Come on, let's go carve a turkey. And I don't mean Leo."

Libby laughed, and with her hand in Sam's, she went to find her place at the table—right in the middle of all those smiling faces.

# ABOUT THE AUTHOR

CARRIE D'ANNA

Julia London is the *New York Times*, *USA Today*, and *Publishers Weekly* bestselling author of more than twenty romantic fiction novels. Her historical romance titles include the popular Desperate Debutantes series, the Scandalous series, and the Secrets of Hadley Green series. She has also penned several contemporary women's fiction novels with strong romantic elements, including the Homecoming Ranch trilogy, *Summer of Two Wishes*, *One Season of Sunshine*, and *A Light at Winter's End.* She has won the RT Bookclub Award for Best Historical Romance, and has been a four-time finalist for the prestigious RITA Award for excellence in romantic fiction. She lives in Austin, Texas.

## IF YOU ENJOYED THIS BOOK, CONNECT WITH JULIA LONDON ONLINE!

Read all about Julia and her books at: http://julialondon.com/

Like Julia on Facebook: https://www.facebook.com/JuliaLondon

Sign up for the newsletter: https://www.facebook.com/JuliaLondon/app_159324190860499

Follow Julia on Twitter: https://twitter.com/JuliaFLondon

Read about Julia on Goodreads: http://www.goodreads.com/JuliaLondon